Stormy
Cove

ALSO BY BERNADETTE CALONEGO

Under Dark Waters
The Zurich Conspiracy

Stormy Cove

Bernadette Calonego

Translated by
Gerald Chapple

*To Melissa,
Best! from
Jerry Chapple
Oct. 7, 2016*

amazon crossing 🌐

Text copyright © 2015 Bernadette Calonego
Translation copyright © 2016 Gerald Chapple

Previously published in German as *Die Bucht des Schweigens* by Amazon Publishing in Germany in 2015. Translated from German by Gerald Chapple. First published in English by AmazonCrossing in 2016.

Published by AmazonCrossing, Seattle

www.apub.com

Amazon, the Amazon logo, and AmazonCrossing are trademarks of Amazon.com, Inc., or its affiliates.

ISBN-13: 9781503935846
ISBN-10: 1503935841

Cover design by Scott Barrie

Printed in the United States of America

For Hubert

CAST OF CHARACTERS

Lori Finning: photographer from Vancouver

Lisa Finning: Lori's mother (lawyer)

Simon Finning: Lori's father

Clifford Finning: Lori's brother

Andrew Finning: Lori's son

Danielle Page: Lori's friend

Craig: Lori's friend from Vancouver

Volker Pflug: Lori's ex-husband (German)

Franz Ehrsam: Volker's boyhood friend

Rosemarie Ehrsam: his wife

Katja Brosamen: his client

Waltraud: Katja's mother

Erhardt: Katja's father

Mona Blackwood: businesswoman in Calgary

Bobbie Wall: B and B owner

Gordon Wall: her husband

Noah Whalen: fisherman in Stormy Cove

Nate Whalen: his brother

Emma Whalen: Nate's wife

Lance Whalen: Noah's brother

Coburn Whalen: Noah's brother

Ezekiel ("Ezz"): Noah's cousin

Greta Whalen: Noah's sister

Robine Whalen: Noah's sister

Archie Whalen: Noah's uncle

Nita Whalen: his wife

Winnie Whalen: Noah's mother

Abram Whalen: Noah's father

Jack Day: Noah's relative

Ches Mills: Lori's neighbor

Patience Mills: his wife

Molly Mills: their daughter

Selina Gould: Lori's landlady

Cletus Gould: her son

Una Gould: his wife

Mavis Blake: shopkeeper

Aurelia Peyton: school librarian

Lloyd Weston: archaeologist

Beth Ontara: archaeologist

Annie: archaeologist

Will Spence: newspaper editor

Reanna Sholler: reporter

Jacinta Parsons: murder victim

Scott Parsons: her father

Glowena Parsons: her sister

Ginette Hearne: villager

Elsie Smith: villager

Gideon Moore: transport company owner

Rudolf von Kammerstein: German baron

Ruth von Kammerstein: his wife

Tom Quinton: dog owner

Vera Quinton: his wife

Rusty: the Quintons' dog

Hope Hussey: lodge owner

Carl Pelley: detective

John Glaskey: fisherman

Isaac Richards: fisherman

John, Seb, Wayne: fishermen

Joseph Johnston: deceased fisherman

Mitch and Dorice: elderly couple

Richard Smallwood: Anglican minister

NEWFOUNDLAND'S

Great Northern Peninsula

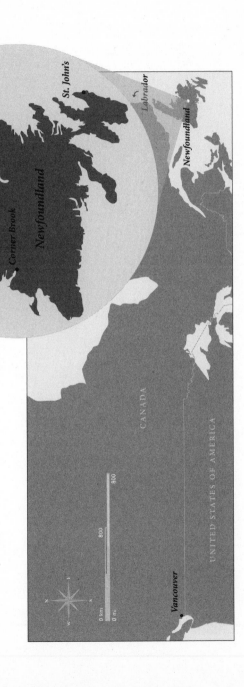

PROLOGUE

He hardly speaks at breakfast. His forehead, eyes, eyebrows, and lips look pinched—like his head is in a vise. He's worried. She knows it.

That night, she'd been jolted out of her sleep again, her heart feeling tight and swollen, like a boxing glove. Her silk pajamas clung to her skin, and a damp chill to her forehead.

She sat bolt upright in bed, gasping for air.

Suddenly his face was right against hers; she'd startled him.

Not for the first time.

He brushed her unruly hair out of her face.

"I heard it again," she said.

The howling. That terrible, incomprehensible, bone-shattering whine that seemed to come from nowhere.

He pressed her to his chest.

"It's gone," he whispered. "Nobody's going to hurt you."

Then he caressed her until she fell asleep in his arms.

She steals a glance at him.

Pretending to be sorting pictures on the computer, she watches him out of the corner of her eye as he sits there, bent over the table, his chin resting in a hand as big as a shovel. He reads the newspaper from cover to cover; it's just the local rag, but he doesn't skip over a thing, not even the classifieds. He's never learned to skim. In his world, there's no place for skimming. Everything must be observed: wind direction, the movement of the tide, wave action, fish movements, what men in the harbor are saying, news and rumors. Especially rumors. If you miss something, or don't care what's going on in the village, then you're soon on the outside looking in. And that can be fatal.

She's only known that since she came into his life.

How did we manage to survive?

Here he is, far from the grave of his boat, the *Mighty Breeze*. Far from the North Atlantic and the steep cliffs, the killer storms and currents. Far from the disaster that pulled him down in its wake.

He's an outsider in Vancouver. A man who doesn't want to be anywhere but on his boat or in his squat little house with green trim. He couldn't even restack the firewood the storm scattered—that's how fast everything happened. He must replay things in his mind over and over, neat and tidy as he is. In the chaos of emotions and threats, he is a man who clings to order.

So all he can do now is read the entire paper. He can't bring himself to skip over even a page. He calls it wasteful, making a face every time he says the word. His shed by the ocean is stacked with pails, old ropes and tools, rusty winches, used nails, lumber from demolished houses, worn-out knives. A man who always expects hard times needs these things.

But he didn't expect the disaster that befell him.

He suddenly looks up, and she feels caught in the act.

"Did you read this?" he asked. "The letters to the editor? People with oceanfront houses are complaining that people walking on the beach keep peeking in their windows."

She smiles, happy that he's found something he finds funny. Nobody in his village has any problem with people constantly looking in their windows. They see everything anyway, never miss a thing. Through trusty binoculars, they spy on the houses on the opposite side of the cove. They know when it's lights-out and when somebody comes home late.

But she'd shut her eyes to what she really ought to have seen.

He stretches across the table to study the classifieds. She never tires of looking at him. A back as round as the leatherback turtle's that washed ashore one day, dead. The morning after they first made love, her fingers felt for his vertebrae and couldn't find them. As if he'd morphed from a sea creature into a human.

If someone saw the way she was watching him now, her fascination would be taken for love.

But it's more like wonder. Silent amazement that they're both here. Together. That he followed her, all this way.

How did we manage to get away?

Did *we get away?*

He's always been so afraid of the city. The cars. The crowds. The pace. Traffic lights everywhere. Eyes that look right past him. Mouths that don't say hello. Losing himself in the sea of people on the sidewalks.

But now, after everything that happened, he feels secure here. Nobody knows him in Vancouver. Nobody knows anything. His name means nothing.

It's been ten months now. He never talks about going back. Not even about the *Mighty Breeze*. Or the kitchen with its loud, ticking clock. Not one word about the cove or the dock with the rotting planks he'd long wanted to replace.

"Don't you want to call?" she asks him occasionally.

He just shakes his head, raises his eyebrows, and looks out the window, checking the sky over the neighboring apartment towers. Then he wants to go for a walk before it rains. His route always leads to the ocean. Not to *his* ocean but to this other, western ocean, the Pacific. Water that never, to his astonishment, freezes over in winter.

She hasn't taken any pictures of him since they came to Vancouver. As if photographing him were cursed. As if her pictures would reveal something she wasn't prepared for. The way he's sitting at the table, turning the pages, his brow furrowed, back arched like a bridge over water, lips pressed together—she doesn't have to capture this moment with her camera. It's already burned into her mind. Exactly like the secret that she must never reveal.

Do visions of what happened haunt him as they do her? She's afraid to ask.

Out of nowhere, the memories appear before *her* eyes, and they're not always the most terrifying ones.

The wall hanging, for instance, in a stranger's living room, of a band of caribou at sunset. Blackish-brown shapes backlit with kitschy neon colors. The caribou stiff, as if blinded by the garish orange and yellow and red.

A wild animal frozen in the headlights' glare, fearfully undecided between safety and doom.

CHAPTER 1

Lori's hands were still so shaky that she repeatedly had to put down her cup. Her hostess had introduced herself as Bobbie, brought her tea, and now pursed her lips in sympathy.

"The truck must have given you a pretty good scare," she said.

Lori nodded and rubbed her hands as if that could stop them from trembling.

"It felt like I was in one of those horror movies where giant trucks loom over little cars and chase them until their victims freak out."

She regretted the words as soon as she said them. She was dramatizing again. As if what happened were a metaphor for her life: Lori with a monster breathing down her neck. But she'd laid those ghosts to rest long ago. What must the elderly woman in the armchair think of her? Was she annoyed at this stranger from Vancouver bad-mouthing Newfoundland? And Bobbie had been so friendly when Lori arrived. The B and B was decidedly a family affair: Lori's hosts lived in the house. Bobbie, whose real name was Roberta Wall—Lori saw that on the Canadian government certification hanging on the wall—must like people a lot. She told Lori she'd been taking care of guests for thirty years.

"Thirty years, and I still think it's fun."

Bobbie had expanded her business two years before. Lori's room was in her in-laws' former house on the other side of a shared garden. All the other rooms were spoken for. Bobbie was expecting participants from a conference "that had something to do with excavations," she said. Lori had taken a quick look at her room. A thin gold polyester bedspread; a little wall mirror framed by imitation seashells. Lori didn't see a bedside lamp, but she always brought a portable reading light when she traveled.

"Oh," she heard Bobbie say, "there's Gordon."

Lori smiled awkwardly, wishing she could just hole up in her room, gold polyester notwithstanding. Why had she chosen a B and B anyway? For this assignment, Mona had given her more than enough to cover a real hotel. But as a freelance photographer, Lori wasn't used to luxuries.

A portly man limped into the living room and plopped down on the sofa.

"Gordon, this is Lori, from Vancouver. We were just talking about how trucks are making our roads so unsafe."

Panting with exertion, the old man nodded at Lori.

"A truck almost ran her off the road," Bobbie continued. "Poor thing feared for her life. People really shouldn't speed with all this snow on the ground."

Gordon Wall coughed and gasped loudly for air. "I can tell you exactly why trucks go so fast. They're paid by the mile and not by the hour, so they drive like hell."

"I couldn't pull over anywhere to let him pass," Lori explained. "There was no place to. I was afraid he couldn't brake fast enough and would ram me."

"They probably warned you about moose crossings but not about trucks," Gordon surmised.

The phone rang and Bobbie took a reservation, giving Lori time to examine the living room. A wall hanging with caribou posed against a background of iridescent neon colors. Assorted plastic flower arrangements. A cuckoo clock and a collection of snow globes. At least a dozen framed family photographs. Lori had already heard how none of Bobbie's six children lived nearby. Lori nearly said something about her own son, Andrew, but bit her tongue. Let sleeping dogs lie.

Bobbie, on the other hand, had probably shared her private life with hundreds of tourists over the years. Lori couldn't fathom why. She would never again allow strangers to meddle in her personal affairs, to gain access to her inner life.

She tried once more to lift her cup without spilling.

A still small voice inside her said, *You always manage to get into other people's houses. Into their kitchens, living rooms, even bedrooms. And what's more, into their souls. It's how you make your living.*

Bobbie hung up and turned to Lori.

"What brings you to Newfoundland?"

A friendly question she probably asked every guest. Nevertheless, it made Lori uncomfortable.

It was the same discomfort she'd felt in Mona Blackwood's office. She'd been late for her appointment because a surprise Vancouver snowstorm had delayed her flight to Calgary.

Lori had assumed the assignment was going to be routine. Yet another portrait of a prominent person. Mona Blackwood was well known in Calgary. Owner of an investment firm that made money in the oil sector. Lots of money. She'd grown up poor in Newfoundland, but moved west to Alberta to seek her fortune. Forty-two, five years older than Lori. Blond, with a chiseled, austere face. Slim, athletic. A woman determined to be taken seriously in a man's world. She wore a black two-piece suit over a white blouse. Lori would have preferred a little color for the photo and considered how to suggest it. She knew the background had to be businesslike and sober, nothing fussy or extravagant. Before staging anything, though, Lori wanted to get to know Mona a bit so she could really capture her in a portrait.

But to her amazement, Mona looked at Lori's photographer's bag and said, "We won't be needing that today."

Lori was taken aback.

"Aren't I here for a photo shoot?"

"I'll explain in a minute. Would you like tea, coffee, some juice, maybe?"

Mona motioned toward some armchairs.

Lori asked for coffee—she'd gotten up early. She'd barely sat down in the black leather chair when she saw the book of photos on the glass table. Her book. The pictures of the apostate Mormon sect in Splendid Valley.

Her name would always be associated with it.

Lorelei Finning. Splendid Valley.

Mona opened the book. Lori noticed her silver fingernail extensions. Interesting detail. A deviation from the perfect businesswoman image. Maybe she was open to having an unconventional portrait taken after all.

"I've read the introduction," Mona began, "but can you tell me some more about how you came to take these pictures?"

Normally, Lori wasn't fazed by the request. It's what everybody wanted to know. How a sect completely shut off from the outside world in a settlement hidden behind high fences, a sect accused of polygamy and trafficking in girls—how a secretive community like that had allowed the photographer Lorelei Finning behind the curtain. Why had they permitted Lori to photograph women, children, and especially men married to dozens of eleven- and twelve-year-old girls?

No one who saw the pictures could accuse Lori of sympathy toward these men. The sect's bishop had examined the photos and authorized them himself. He wanted to create a monument; he wanted to demonstrate to the outside world that everything was proper and correct.

But the bishop didn't understand that images speak their own language, and Lori's photographs were eloquent. She had captured something he was too blind to see.

That was the beginning of the end for the Splendid Valley community. The sect's leaders were hauled into court and sentenced to prison.

The book could have been Lori's big break, but soon after, she'd met Volker and followed him to Germany, a newborn in her arms.

Lori's gaze swung to the large window, over the rooftops, over the glass facades of Calgary's skyscrapers reaching like oil derricks into the overcast sky.

She'd honed her answer to Mona's question long ago. That it took a lot of empathy and patience. That people had to feel safe in order to forget the camera. Lori was almost invisible when she worked, like a fly on the wall. And most important—that you couldn't force anything.

But then to her own surprise, she heard herself say, "The bishop knew he'd be out of office soon. He wanted his regime . . . he wanted his life documented for posterity. He made it easy for me."

Mona scrutinized her, but with good will.

"You revealed everything in your photographs."

"He personally approved the pictures. He and his lousy lawyer."

Mona nodded slowly. "But it really seems like something special happened there. How were you able to reveal so much truth?"

"Those people only saw what they wanted to see. But what they didn't see was the truth behind the pictures."

Lori shook her head. She didn't know what else to say. For her, the best photography was unplanned, intuitive. How could she explain after the fact how she'd managed to capture a particular image?

"Do you ever think back on your experiences there?"

Again Mona's searching look.

Lori thought for a moment.

"Certain things come back to me, mostly little details. Like how the boys threw bottles against the houses out of sheer frustration. There wasn't anything for them to do, no playgrounds or computers or bikes, skateboards. The meadows were covered in broken glass. And nobody bothered to clean it up. They let their horses roam around and step on the broken pieces."

A young woman brought coffee on a silver tray.

Lori wondered where the conversation was going, but she didn't want to push her client.

"I like your eye for detail," Mona said. "I think that you see the camera as an instrument for finding the truth."

That word *truth* again. What was she getting at?

Mona Blackwood laid her silver spoon gently on the saucer.

"I have an assignment for you."

CHAPTER 2

Bobbie Wall's voice interrupted Lori's thoughts.

"So, my dear, are you here on vacation?"

She asked her question slowly, probably thinking that Lori couldn't decipher her Newfoundland accent.

Lori set her cup down.

"I'm a landscape photographer."

"Landscapes? Ah, yes, you'll get your money's worth here. Newfoundland is mainly made of rock." She glanced at her husband. "That's why we call our island 'The Rock.'"

"So I've heard," Lori said, feeling warm from the tea. "Well, I'm hoping my work will give Newfoundland a new name: 'The Rock Star.'"

The elderly couple laughed, and Lori along with them, her anxiety dissipating. She pointed to a photograph of a dark-haired young man in uniform.

"Who's this?"

"That's our son, Ben. He's in the navy. Actually, near where you are; he's stationed on Vancouver Island. But I hope they transfer him to Gander; it's only three hours from here." Bobbie suddenly sounded resigned.

Lori's chest grew tight. If their son wanted to be near his parents, he'd certainly chosen the wrong profession. The military was famous for constantly moving people around. *Mothers suffer when their children choose to live far away,* she thought to herself. Andrew had flown thousands of miles away from her.

A car pulled up in front of the house. Bobbie jumped up with remarkable agility.

"Darn it! The last two weeks, we had hardly anybody, and today every room is filled."

Lori looked out the window and saw a tall wiry man maneuvering a heavy sports bag out of his trunk. Despite the cold, he was wearing a light fleece jacket. A minute later, he joined them in the living room. Clearly, tea was a required first stop for all guests.

"This is Lloyd Weston, a professor of archaeology at the university in St. John's," Bobbie told her. "He always spends the night with us when he's working in the area."

"Hello, I'm Lloyd," the professor said, coming over to Lori. He had an open, tanned face and a square jaw under his trimmed beard.

"Lori's a photographer from Vancouver. A landscape photographer."

The new arrival sat down without taking his eyes off Lori.

"What's your name?"

"Lorelei Finning," Bobbie interjected before disappearing into the kitchen.

"Where have I heard that name before?"

Weston sized her up with some curiosity, but she didn't give him any help.

"You photograph landscapes. Like for calendars?"

Lori thought fast.

"I'm here on commission for a coffee table book," she explained. "A publisher in Calgary is going to bring it out."

That wasn't even a lie, really.

The archaeologist leaned forward. "A coffee table book on Newfoundland?"

"No, on the Northern Peninsula."

"For tourists, that sort of thing?"

Lori folded her arms.

"More of a documentary."

"So what are you documenting?"

"Like I said, landscapes, villages, people who live and work there."

Lori reeled off her answer quickly. Everything was fine, she assured herself. It all sounded completely plausible.

Although she found it quite astonishing that Mona Blackwood was paying her to stay in a fishing village for an entire year. Just to document life and people in an isolated Newfoundland outport.

"Lloyd knows the Great Northern Peninsula like the back of his hand," Gordon Wall added.

"Yes, I guess you could say that." Weston smiled. "So you're heading north?"

Lori nodded, determined not to reveal another thing.

The archaeologist took off his jacket. He was wearing a tight orange T-shirt.

"How long are you going to be there?"

"Oh, several months. I want to capture the different seasons."

"Your publisher must be generous. Your name really does sound familiar."

Lori chewed on the inside of her cheek, something she always did when she was nervous. She had to steer the conversation in another direction.

"So, archaeology. Those digs take a long time, right?"

"Sometimes years."

When Weston took the teacup Bobbie offered, Lori noticed he wasn't wearing a wedding ring.

"I'm flying back to St. John's tomorrow, but I'll be here this summer. Maybe I can show you the burial mound we'll be excavating. We think it's even older than the grave at L'Anse Amour in Labrador, more than seventy-five hundred years old. L'Anse Amour was the oldest known burial mound in North America until now. Our dig is closed to the public, but I'll see if I can make an exception for you."

He took a business card out of his jacket pocket and handed it to her. She glanced at it: "Lloyd Weston, Memorial University, St. John's."

She stood up.

"Thanks. That sounds exciting. Now, if you'll excuse me, I need to rest for a bit after my trip."

She said good-bye and took her cup into the kitchen. Bobbie followed her.

"There'll be some guests staying at the other house, two ladies and their nephew. They're sharing a bathroom, but you've got your own."

Lori nodded and quickly closed the door to the house behind her. As she crossed the lawn, she saw three people getting out of a blue Ford Focus. The women were in their late thirties or early forties, the nephew sixteen at most. A cute kid wearing a leather jacket and a baseball cap.

She collapsed on the gold polyester bedspread in her room and was just nodding off when somebody shoved a large envelope under the door. But she didn't get up until a few minutes later when shouts, rapid footsteps, and slamming doors made it clear that sleep would be impossible.

Despite her exhaustion, Lori retrieved the envelope and scanned the first page, apparently an abstract from a scholarly article about the seventy-five-hundred-year-old tomb of a young teen. She read that the grave was unusually lavish and had probably taken twenty men many weeks to construct. They'd filled it with burial items and layered hundreds of heavy stones over the body. Experts were puzzled by this extraordinary extravagance on behalf of a dead child.

Lori's curiosity was piqued. Maybe Weston would let her photograph the site, despite it being closed to the public. She opened her laptop to look up pictures of other prehistoric burial mounds.

She was a little ashamed of her ignorance about Newfoundland and Labrador. When her mom had heard about Lori's plans, she came down on her like a ton of bricks. Lisa Finning put little stock in discretion and reticence—at least when it came to her personal life.

She used to say, "My parents made everything a secret, so I'm an open book with my kids."

Nobody was safe with her. It was bad enough that she'd named her daughter *Lorelei*. Lori really didn't envision herself as the mythical mermaid up on a rock, enticing sailors into a deadly whirlpool in the Rhine. But Lisa Finning chose it because Lori had come into the world with so much hair.

"I always wanted long, thick hair, but you got it instead, and I like to watch you combing your locks in front of the mirror. Isn't it a pretty name? I can't imagine how you could complain."

Her parents had emigrated from Germany some years earlier, and, one Easter Sunday, her mother announced that they were separating. It was Lori's seventeenth birthday, and her mom's words turned her whole world upside down.

"Your dad's going back to Germany, but I'm staying here. You can decide for yourselves who you want to stay with."

Lori's brother, Clifford, who was just twelve, left the dinner table in tears. Lori simply sat there, stunned. She had known her father was unhappy; he hadn't been able to find a good job as a cardiologist. When an offer came from a German university, he didn't think twice before accepting it—without telling his wife, as her mother told Lori much later. The irony was that her father had actually been born in Canada and only moved to Germany as a child. *Völkerwanderung* at the end of the second millennium.

Her father tried to make Lori's decision easier for her.

"My darling girl, it's better for you to stay here. I can't be a surrogate mother."

He promised she could spend her vacations with him in Germany and that he'd visit them as often as he could.

Which was why it was Clifford who got on the plane to Frankfurt with him. She'd taken her camera—a birthday present from her father—to the airport but couldn't bring herself to take any good-bye pictures.

Lori never saw her father and brother again. An avalanche buried them in their car four months later on a visit to relatives in the Bavarian Alps.

For Lori, the avalanche had been set in motion that Easter Sunday, thanks to her mother's announcement. She swore that from then on she'd always have her camera with her. Just in case.

Her mother had a penchant for delivering dreadful news.

"You're going to Newfoundland?" she'd exclaimed when she heard. "Don't tell them you've got German ancestors."

Aha, here we go again, Lori thought.

"Your grandfather's submarine sank a ship off the Newfoundland coast. A ferry, I think it was. A whole lot of women and children died. He got a medal for it from Hitler himself."

Lori was bowled over. Her mom had never even told her Grandpa was a submarine commander. Why the hell would she share this story now, just before Lori's departure? Whenever Lori remembered it, she got angry all over again.

"What's Grandpa got to do with me?" she'd retorted. "That's all in the past. Let bygones be bygones, farewell and amen. Besides, I was born here, and I'm Canadian. Did you forget? Ca-na-di-an!"

One thing she had to grant her mom: she could take as good as she gave. As a defense attorney, she had to. It was easy to argue with her. A hit, a hit back, like ping-pong, and eventually it was over. Her mom never held it against her.

"It wouldn't hurt to read up on Newfoundland," Lisa Finning had added blithely. "Doesn't that come with the job somehow?"

Of course she was right. But Lori had been slammed with so many rushed, badly paid jobs that, by the end of the day, she was too tired to do anything but take a long bath and watch *The Big Bang Theory*.

◆

She felt hunger pangs but not enough to drive her out in search of a restaurant. She settled for German crispbread and soft cheese and drank what was left of the coffee in her thermos. Good thing Mona Blackwood couldn't see her now! Every dollar saved went into Lori's pocket, and a freelance photographer's pockets were often empty. Sipping her coffee, she entered "girl mysterious death Northern Peninsula grave pictures" in the search engine. Several entries popped up. She clicked on a page and found herself reading not about Weston's seventy-five-hundred-year-old archaeological site, but about a far more recent grave:

No Developments in Parsons Case

Police still do not have a clear suspect in the killing of fourteen-year-old Jacinta Parsons. The girl's bizarre grave was discovered during the construction of a new road between Stormy Cove and Cod Cove, some months after her violent death. Parsons disappeared twenty years ago after leaving her parents' house to pick berries. An autopsy

*revealed she had been suffocated. Although
an intense investigation led to the inter-
views of a large number of people, police
have made no progress in the Parsons case
over the years. Even the numerous objects
found in the grave have provided no con-
crete clues so far. Investigators have been
puzzled about possible motives. "We still
hope that somebody in the local population
will provide a crucial lead," said Detective
Carl Pelley.*

Stormy Cove. Wouldn't you know it. Just where Mona Blackwood was sending her.

Was Mona still living in Newfoundland twenty years ago when Jacinta disappeared?

There was more to this photo assignment than Mona had let on. Lori was well aware of that. The scope of it all was a sure sign. All that money for an entire year. The secrecy around it. But what drove Mona to do this?

Lori had to admit she still knew too little about her client.

And almost nothing about Stormy Cove, other than that it was a remote fishing village with a dry dock. And some fishermen who still went out on the ocean in their little boats.

Was a killer on the loose in Stormy Cove? Lori was pondering whether that should upset her, when her thoughts were interrupted by voices in the hallway.

Lori got undressed and took a shower. She stood under the warm, relaxing water for a long time, moving back and forth. Then she dried her thick chestnut-brown hair, which was cut short at the neck. Lori didn't give a damn about the golden mane of Lorelei, the femme fatale of German legend, who was her namesake. Her mother nagged her now and then to grow her hair long, but it just strengthened her resolve.

She had an elegant profile and perfect ears—the envy of her friends. Volker had told her once that her short hair emphasized her femininity. That was before the nightmare in Germany.

Lori was about to put on a sweatshirt when she heard strange noises coming through the thin wall. It didn't take long to discern the voices of three people having sex. An erotic tryst with the two women and that stripling in the leather jacket they pretended was their nephew!

She felt a stabbing pain in her chest and struggled to breathe.

It was stronger than she was. It was always stronger than anything. She was no longer sitting in a room in Newfoundland.

She is sitting bolt upright in her marriage bed on a huge country estate in Germany. Sounds of intercourse come from the next room. She doesn't go to the trouble of using earplugs anymore. People are every-where. She simply can't avoid them. Why won't they leave her alone? All she wants is peace and quiet. Her fingers clutch the sheets. A man lies beside her. Her husband. She hates him for sleeping so serenely.

She's out of bed in a single bound, grabs her wool jacket, bangs into the bureau, clicks on the lamp.

Her husband sits up.

"What's the matter this time?" he asks.

"If I stay here any longer," she pants, "I'm going to kill someone."

Lori slipped on jeans and her down jacket, put on her red beret, and slammed the door before running out of the B and B. A light was on in the Walls' living room, but she had no desire for human contact. She wandered aimlessly through streets with shabby stores and past houses with ugly vinyl siding. She toyed with the idea of spending the night in an airport motel. But when she returned an hour later, the house was quiet. She heard distant footsteps and murmuring during the night, but was too tired to worry about it.

$$\text{-} \boxtimes \text{-}$$

Over a breakfast of bacon and eggs, Bobbie asked, "Did the people in the next room wake you up? They had to catch a four o'clock flight."

"No, but they were plenty loud before that," Lori replied. She was too grumpy to be diplomatic. "They made quite a threesome, if you take my meaning."

Bobbie lowered a teapot onto the crocheted tablecloth.

"I thought something wasn't quite right," she said. "I saw the nephew's bed all made up like nobody had slept in it!"

She sounded almost cheery, pleased to have found the answer to a riddle.

"The lady said the boy was her nephew, but I didn't swallow that. And I told her I can see through people pretty quick! There you have it again."

She refilled Lori's cup. "You should have called me about the noise. You don't have to put up with that."

Lori picked up her fork. "Is this the first orgy at your place?"

Bobbie smiled. Turned out she was a tough cookie.

"I'd love to know who those people are. You know, Newfoundland is a large island but a small world. It isn't easy to hide something. I'll dig up the truth, believe me."

Only after checking out did Lori realize she should have asked about the murdered girl in Stormy Cove.

CHAPTER 3

Isaac Richards, 46, fisherman, from Stormy Cove

What do you want to know? About the demons? Oh, so that's it. I thought you were talking about the body on the Barrens. Everybody's talking about it now. Absolutely crazy. Who'd have thought that? OK, right, so what do you want to know?

Yes, I was on the boat. Me and my brother John and my pal Seb and Wayne, my nephew. Four of us.

We all heard it. Woke us up in the night.

How long ago? Maybe four years.

Why do you ask, eh? Anything to do with the dead girl on the Barrens?

Well, OK. We'd been working all day. On my boat, yeah. It was the Morning Mist *back then. We took her through the ice. It was May, good weather, no fog. Occasional sun. Don't see that very often in May.*

We caught about a dozen seals that day. Ice was cracking, so we couldn't go out on it. We shot the seals and hooked them on board. After that, we anchored off Great Sacred Island. Yes, the Isle of the Demons.

That's what you mean, eh?

There was a stove on board. It was a bit warm on the boat. A moose roast in the oven. I remember. Wayne'd shot a huge bull moose the fall before, a twenty-four pointer. Giant. We got the roast from him. We had it with potatoes and bread and tea. Like always. No alcohol on my boat, in case you're interested.

We went to bed about ten, after cards.

We talked to them on the other boat. Did I mention the other boat there? Gary's. He had Phil and Ralph with him, all from Fairy Bay.

What we talked about? We radioed Gary about the ice and if it was hard getting through.

Then, like I said, we went for our bunks. I had a sleeping bag.

I probably dropped off right away. At least, I don't remember if John's snoring kept me awake. I was exhausted, been on my feet since five.

I woke up all of a sudden. Heard something. Hard to describe. A hollow moaning . . . or whistling.

It woke everybody up.

We thought at first it was the teakettle. At any rate, we all lay down to go back to sleep. But when it got quiet, we heard the moaning again. Not loud but . . . horrible.

Was it scary? I'll tell you, maid, you don't want to live through that. It goes right through you. Worse than a hurricane. Much worse.

Somebody said, probably Wayne, "It must be the motor cooling off."

It was his little joke. Wasn't the motor, everybody knew it.

We tried to figure out what it was. Wayne went outside to piss, but he couldn't see anything.

Sure we thought of the demons. That's why the name. And believe me, fishermen before us have heard strange sounds out there, sounds you can't explain.

All of us were up on deck the next morning. We saw Gary on his boat. First thing he said was, "Did you hear those weird noises last night?"

They didn't know what they were either. First they thought our boats were scraping together. They got up and scouted around the boat just like we did!

We told everybody about it once we were home.

A lot of people here say they're screams for help from people marooned on the island. Some others think they're people who died in shipwrecks.

Whatever it is, I'm telling you I do not want to hear those sounds ever again. It's like somebody getting his bones sawed through.

And now we've got one more ghost out there. But that's a ghost I specially don't want to meet.

Not after all what's happened.

CHAPTER 4

Lori sensed something strange in the air. First, she'd driven through the mountain range in Gros Morne National Park, where, unsurprisingly, there was still a lot of snow. Friends had warned her she'd be catapulted from the Vancouver spring back into winter. She quickly grasped that it can snow eight out of twelve months a year in Newfoundland. It was March, the sky slate gray, and a strong wind blew in off the North Atlantic. Bobbie Wall had warned her to be cautious, describing loaded trucks getting blown off the road. The highway along the coast was partly bare and relatively dry. The winter tires on Lori's second-hand Corolla—picked up in Corner Brook for six thousand dollars—hummed along with the country music on the car radio.

She rarely met an oncoming vehicle on this lonely stretch, but Bobbie had assured her she needn't be afraid of a breakdown. Nobody was more helpful on the road than a Newfoundlander.

Lori stopped occasionally to consult her map and travel guide about what lay in front of her. But after leaving the Long Range Mountains on the horizon behind her—outliers of the Appalachians—she yielded to the powerful, overawing landscape. She turned off the radio. She felt as though she'd crossed into another era, traveled far back in history.

The mountains seemed like primordial beasts hewn from the rock of the earth.

She didn't know why, but her heart suddenly felt very light.

The houses in the little villages along the way no longer seemed bleak and vulnerable, exposed as they were to the ocean and without the shelter of a forest or hill at their back. Lori now saw steadfastness and defiance in them, qualities she liked to attribute to herself.

It's not nice and cozy here, she thought as her car glided by austere, treeless settlements that sprung up out of nowhere. *Everything's reduced to the bare essentials.* And somehow she liked that.

Just when she decided to snap some pictures—though she wasn't enthralled by the idea of getting out in the icy wind—Lori came upon something that attracted her attention: small groups of people stood along the shore, looking out onto the pack ice. Others were driving snowmobiles back and forth and shouting to one another. Lori pulled over and took out her camera. Her boots sank deep into the snow as she plodded up a little rise, where two men and some teenagers were having a heated discussion. They glanced at Lori, then back at the ice. Lori heard animal cries and a heartrending squeal, mixed with deep, sheeplike bleats. What was going on?

A girl shouted to her, "She's very close to shore, with a baby."

Lori looked out onto the ice, and what she saw took her breath away: seals, as far as the eye could see. Black dots everywhere in an infinite whiteness.

"Oh my God," she blurted out. "This is incredible!"

One of the young men, maybe he was sixteen, smiled at her. He had on a black wool tuque, but his neck was bare despite the cold.

"Really something, ain't it? Never seen anything like it for as long as I've lived."

Ten feet away was a seal on an ice floe, baby beside it, as white as its surroundings. Lori got her camera clicking, her adrenaline pumping. She heard the man beside her talking.

"You're not from here? Well, this is a once-in-a-century event. You don't normally see this."

Lori tried to understand his accent.

"Why not?"

"Because the bay's always frozen over at this time of year. The seals and the pack ice stay way out. Several miles off."

"Yeah, near Labrador," another man added.

"But the bay didn't freeze this winter. Nobody knows why. It was just too warm, so the wind drove the ice and the seals toward shore. We've never seen them this close."

"Not in my lifetime at least," the other man acknowledged.

Through the lens, Lori watched the mother feeding her baby.

"How old are the babies?"

"Maybe two days," the older man answered. "After a week they're not babies anymore. Their pelts turn gray and their mothers abandon them."

"That soon?"

Lori watched as a baby seal slid back and forth on the floe, bleating, while its mother poked her head out of the water every so often to check on it.

The men laughed.

"Yes, by then they've put on a lot of fat and are round as a ball. They can already swim and hunt for themselves."

Lori put her camera down.

"Why's the baby seal over there crying like that?"

The man scratched his head through his tuque.

"I think its mother hasn't come back. She's probably dead."

"What? Is the seal hunt on now?"

"No, it's not open season yet. And the white baby seals haven't been hunted for a long time. Twenty years or so?"

The other man stamped his boots in the snow.

"Since 1987, I think. The mother was probably crushed between some ice floes in yesterday's storm. Often happens."

He looked at her with curiosity.

"Where're you from?"

"Vancouver."

"Visiting?"

"Yes."

"Here, in Rocky Cove?"

"No, Stormy Cove. What's going to happen to the orphan seal?"

"It'll probably die."

"That's awful." Lori's heart contracted.

"Yeah, life and death lie hard together on The Rock."

"Not just here," Lori objected.

"Oh, no, they're extra close here," the man insisted.

"Yep," the other man said, "that's how it is."

Lori was forced to think some more about the proximity of life and death when she began to pass "Moose Crossing" signs. But Bobbie had assured her that the moose would keep to the woods for cover because they can't escape fast enough in the snow. Lori thought "woods" too big a word for the birch and low coniferous trees. Compared to West Coast trees that she couldn't even get her arms around, these thickets by the side of the road seemed puny.

She couldn't see the ocean anymore, just an occasional highway sign indicating that villages were hiding somewhere nearby. The sky clouded over, and a dull feeling filled her stomach.

She thought it best to stay overnight at a hunting lodge two hours away from her destination so she could mentally prepare for her adventure.

Just don't rush things. Approach them slowly. The first impression is critical. She turned off the highway and soon found the driveway of Birch Tree Lodge, a log-cabin-style hotel. The huge logs could only have come from British Columbia. A long way for construction material to travel, more than five thousand miles across the continent. Even the telephone poles in Newfoundland were from British Columbia, Bobbie said.

The lodge's office was a combined reception desk and souvenir shop.

Waiting for the clerk, Lori studied the bottles of iceberg water and the parrots embroidered on the wall hangings. After a while, she followed a sign and found herself in a wide dining room with exposed ceiling beams. Inuit carvings graced the mantel, and a chandelier made from antlers hung from a beam. One of three long tables was set. Lori looked up and saw a polar bear pelt hanging beneath the gable.

"I had it hung extra high so nobody could steal it," said a voice behind her.

Lori turned around to find a short-haired young woman carrying a package of frozen meat. She couldn't have been more than thirty.

"I'll put this in the kitchen and be right back."

She pointed to a large carafe.

"Get yourself some coffee in the meantime. And have a piece of cake. We aren't fussy here. I'm Hope."

Lori introduced herself and did as she was told. She had just started in on her cake when Hope reappeared. Lori now identified her as the owner of the lodge, a very young owner indeed.

"We don't have many guests this time of the year," she said. "How long are you staying?"

"I'm not sure. I'll be in the area for a while, so I'm hoping to rent some rooms or a house somewhere."

"So you're the photographer from Calgary?"

Lori almost choked on her cake.

"How in the world did you know?"

"News gets around fast here, you'll find out. Bobbie called today. We've known each other for years. She thought you'd show up here. It's the only hotel around. Cake good?"

Lori nodded.

"I'm from Vancouver, not Calgary."

"Don't you work for somebody in Calgary?"

Lori hesitated. How would they know that? Then she recalled that she'd mentioned the Calgary publisher to the archaeologist.

"Yes, for a publisher. I'm working on a coffee table book."

"You know many folks in Calgary?"

Lori felt like she was being cross-examined. But Hope might simply be a curious hotel owner who liked to chat with her guests.

"Not many. I know my way around Vancouver better."

"I know some people in Calgary. What's the book about?"

"Oh, rural Newfoundland, fishing villages, the local way of life."

"Who'd ever be interested in such a thing?"

"Me, for example. It's an unknown world for me, and it may not exist much longer if those little outports keep dying out."

"Well, you're right, there."

Hope drummed her fingers on the tablecloth. She seemed to be in perpetual motion.

Outside the window, a boat landing led onto a flat white surface, and Lori realized that it must be a frozen lake. Summer guests must sit on the veranda and watch waterfowl. But to her, the winter countryside seemed forbidding and lifeless.

Turning to Hope, she asked, "Do you think people here will be open to being photographed?"

The answer came without hesitation.

"For sure. Why not? They feel the world has forgotten them. Nobody values small fishermen anymore. The government would rather support huge fleets; the companies make more money and the politicians do, too."

She stood up. "Their first question will definitely be: Why did you come here, of all places?"

Lori didn't say anything, though she'd practiced an answer to that question. Of course, Mona Blackwood's name must never come up under any circumstances. Mona had said the project was to be a surprise for everybody.

"But maybe you could open some doors for me in Newfoundland," Lori had objected.

Mona wouldn't hear a word of it.

"You'll have to open doors by yourself, considering that I've hired you."

✦

Hope went to the counter and then to the front door, where she looked back.

"Just don't take any pictures of our baron from Germany. He's here incognito."

Lori didn't understand until dinner that evening.

From the six people around the table, she picked out the baron by his accent. He was the only one who was wearing a dressy, form-fitting shirt over his bulky body and who hadn't rolled up his sleeves. His bald head shone in the light of the table lamp as brightly as his glasses. Lori guessed he was in his late forties.

"Ah, here's our new guest," he called to Lori jovially, as if he owned the lodge. "Do sit down with us."

Even before Lori had finished her soup, she'd learned from the baron and his wife—she was considerably taller and slimmer than her husband, but not any younger—that their family came from the former

Pomerania and that the baron frequently stayed at the lodge to hunt, and had shot bear, caribou, and moose. Not a word about their title. None of the other diners, all male, introduced themselves. They must not be hunters, Lori thought, as it wasn't yet the season.

The baron dominated the conversation.

"I brought my wife with me this time because we wanted to explore the country by dogsled. Maybe we'll even see a polar bear if they come off the ice into the villages."

Lori looked at him dumbfounded. Nobody had told her there were polar bears.

"Don't be afraid," a man at the end of the table said. "It doesn't happen very often, only when visitors are here from Germany."

Everybody laughed.

"Keep your camera pretty much under wraps," the baron said conspiratorially. "We were having a beer with some people in the Isle View pub and said we were from Germany, and somebody asked if I was a German spy."

He laughed so loudly that Lori almost dropped her spoon.

Hope brought a platter of meat for the whole table. "He was only kidding. People here have a peculiar sense of humor."

"Oh, we know," the baroness said. "We know that already. They see old Second World War films made in Hollywood, of course, and that's their idea of Germans."

"Well, I don't suppose many Newfoundlanders have been to Germany," Lori interjected politely and then wondered if she sounded condescending. She quickly added, "And probably not many Germans have traveled to Newfoundland until now."

"Unfortunately, some Germans were here once and they didn't make a good impression," the baroness said, taking hold of her husband's arm as if to confirm it. "During the War, German submarines did quite a lot of harm, didn't they, Rudolf? You know more about it."

Lori concentrated on her meat, but couldn't avoid hearing the conversation. Furthermore, the baron's eyes were always on her when he wasn't drinking his beer. His gaze was friendly.

"Yes, interestingly enough, Newfoundland was one of the few places in North America attacked by submarines," he said. "They caused a lot of damage on Belle Isle even though they were under artillery fire."

"When did the attacks take place?" asked Hope, who had joined her guests at the far end of the table.

"In 1942," the baron responded. "The Nazis were targeting the iron mines on Belle Isle. They had maps of the island because Germany had imported iron ore from there before the war. They sank two freighters, if I remember correctly."

"Don't forget about the sinking of the SS *Caribou*," someone said.

Now everybody started talking at once. Lori learned that a passenger ferry was fired on by a German sub and over a hundred people, mainly civilians, went down with it.

"That's news to me," a man said who was out of Lori's sight. "I never imagined that the Germans sent submarines to Newfoundland, of all places."

"Why not? After all, Canada had declared war on Germany," another guest said.

The table pounced on the man for forgetting that Newfoundland wasn't actually part of Canada in 1942, but was, in effect, still a British colony. Lori felt sorry for him.

His tablemates bitterly reminded him that Newfoundland hadn't held a referendum on becoming Canada's tenth province until 1948 and became the tenth province the next year. Apparently, it was a decision that some at the table still regretted, and they continued arguing about it until dessert.

"Well, we certainly stirred the pot," the baron said, winking at Lori.

"Yes, you and your historical digressions," his wife joked, though she'd brought up the subject.

The men suddenly got up and left the table, with friendly good-byes. Hope escorted them to the door.

"If anyone around here is a spy, it's them," the baron remarked.

Lori gave him an inquiring look.

"They're here looking for something, and I bet it's oil."

Lori knew there were oil rigs off the south coast of Newfoundland, but was there oil up here in the North?

"They don't tip their hand; everything's top secret. But the oil companies watch one another like hawks, believe you me. The competition for oil is no tea party."

He acted as if Lori knew precisely what he meant.

Hope returned. "Somebody wants to see you, Lori. Can you come right now?"

It sounded like an order.

Lori gave an involuntary shudder, as if there was something to fear.

"Excuse me," she said to the German couple.

On the way out, she whispered to Hope, "Who is it?"

"A cop."

CHAPTER 5

The policeman turned toward her as she came into the hotel office. He was younger than she was, squat, with a little paunch, and his jaw was working some chewing gum. He greeted her with a nod.

"You're traveling through this region?"

Lori said yes.

"This your first time?"

"Yes. Why?"

She couldn't hide her uneasiness.

The officer bobbed up and down on his toes.

"We just want to inform tourists that four polar bears have been sighted along this coast. The game wardens will track 'em down and anesthetize 'em. We'll then take 'em out by helicopter."

"Oh my God," Lori exclaimed. "Somebody at dinner said something about polar bears, but I hoped it was a joke."

The officer grinned.

"No, it's not a joke. A couple of 'em show up here every few years, but right now we just know about these four. It's pretty unusual. Are you planning to go to Stormy Cove?"

"Possibly," said Lori, on her guard once more.

"Two of 'em are over that way. One was nosing around some houses yesterday. Some people put out bait for coyotes, and that attracts the bears. Just be on the lookout. Polar bears aren't afraid of anything."

Lori was tempted to say that the best thing that could happen to her was a polar bear trapped in her lens.

Instead she said, "I appreciate your taking the trouble, but please excuse the question: Did you come here just to tell me that?"

The policeman stopped chewing for a moment.

"Wouldn't our men in Vancouver do the same?" He cleared his throat. "This is rough country here. Last winter a man went for a walk and was never found. Just be sure and use common sense."

Vancouver. So word really had gotten around.

"Of course," she confirmed. "Thank you very much."

All that evening, she couldn't shake the feeling that the policeman wasn't warning her about polar bears. So what was the warning really about?

She couldn't get to Stormy Cove fast enough.

When she'd driven for an hour and a half the next morning and reached the turnoff for the coast, the first rays of sunshine broke through the overcast sky. The heavy, dull snow that had blanketed the landscape the day before now sparkled in the sudden glare. Lori was amazed by the high drifts that the steady, inexorable wind had piled up. Even in all that white, she could sense the hard, rough lay of the land. Trees poking halfway out of the snow looked like scrubby, bony creatures that existed only to struggle. A topography that threatened to swallow you up; nothing but hill after hill and no point on the horizon for Lori to get oriented. She knew a place like this would not forgive mistakes.

After another fifteen minutes on the road, she still hadn't seen a single house. But then she saw something moving out of the corner of her left eye. A snowmobile came up over the hill, pulling a sled filled with wood. The driver turned his head toward her for a second, but she couldn't see his face through the visor. Then the vehicle departed as quickly as it had come. Lori felt like she'd been on the high seas for weeks, and then suddenly birds appeared, indicating land was near.

And indeed, the first building appeared around the next corner. A white cube with slits for windows. The other houses had similar spyholes, and only a few were green or ochre, as if people were forced to use paint sparingly. The firehouse, though, was painted bright yellow, overshadowing the white Anglican church. The signboard out front announced, "Jesus Is Crazy about You." The melody of the pop song "Crazy about You" floated through her mind. Lori had always believed that schmaltzy lyrics reflected human feelings rather accurately, often better than literature.

She was hoping to locate a village store, but the road brought her to a little fishing harbor. Two boats were off to the side, set up on iced-over wooden beams as if they were asleep. Three small boats lay keel up on the shoulder of the road. Lori got out to survey the half-moon of Stormy Cove Bay and a dozen houses on the shore. Another dozen bordered the access road and dotted the hillside protecting the right shore of the harbor from the wind.

The broad North Atlantic beyond the bay was blocked by a small island and could only be viewed from a hill that certainly couldn't be mounted in winter except by snowmobile. Nevertheless, Lori was confident she could get some formidable photographs out of this rough landscape. A mild euphoria came over her, as it always did when a project's creative possibilities took shape before her eyes.

The bitterly cold air snapped her back to reality. She hopped into the Corolla and drove past the church, following the road up the hill, her tires skidding slightly.

She caught a glimpse of a face peering out of a house window, but where were the other villagers? Her watch showed it was noon. The villagers must be gathered for Sunday dinner with their families, unlike solitary Lori. As she was turning the car around, she spotted a man stacking wood, and a snowmobile with a helmet on the seat.

She stopped and rolled down the window.

"Hello! Can you tell me where the village store is?"

The man took his time taking off his gloves, setting them on the snowmobile, and dusting the sawdust off his winter jacket, which had patches of silver tape.

His black wool tuque came down to his eyebrows, but she noted the strikingly dark eyes in his weather-beaten face.

"The village store?" he asked.

"Yes, I heard there's one here, but I can't find it."

She suddenly felt like an idiot. The village was so tiny that she must have seen the store but not recognized it. The guy would certainly get a laugh telling everybody about the dumb tourist.

As he walked over to her car, Lori was struck by his gait. He didn't roll his feet from heel to toe, but planted them flat and firmly with every step, and his body shifted from side to side, like a boat rocking in the water.

He pointed to where she'd just come from.

"Go back to the fork then to the left past the church until you come to the harbor. It's there."

She got out.

"I was just there, but didn't see a store."

The man was so close that she could see stubble on his tanned face. He might have been her age or ten years older, she couldn't say. He was only an inch or two taller than she was, but his broad back made him look taller.

"It's in the old fish plant, right next to the harbor."

Lori couldn't recall seeing a fish plant.

"Could you give me a reference point—a sign or something?"

He seemed to be taken aback for a few seconds, as if she were begging for alms.

"I can take you there," he said at last.

"No, no, you don't have to. It can't be that hard to find a fish plant," Lori said, embarrassed.

"It's right beside the harbor, the only building there," he added.

Lori thanked him and turned to go to her car. The man didn't move. She decided to get one more question off her chest.

"I've heard you have to look out for polar bears around here?"

Once again, he regarded her in silence for a minute. Then he looked at the ocean and said, "Polar bears? Well . . . day before yesterday, one was seen near Ed's workshop, and I heard tell last week that one ran across the road in front of Randy's truck."

He flattened the snow around him with his heavy rubber boots. "Who's it told you about the bears?"

"The police."

He waited for a few seconds. "Who in the police?"

Lori shrugged. "A young man, he said he was cautioning tourists about polar bears."

The man said nothing, as if he had to process the information first. Then he prepared to leave. She heard him say, "Guess they don't have anything better to do."

Lori wished she'd asked him what to do if she did see a bear, but he was already back at his woodpile.

It crossed her mind that, from the way he walked, he must be a fisherman. He was used to rebalancing his body with every movement of the water. On terra firma, it looked like he was staggering.

After all that, she located the store rather quickly. She simply hadn't noticed the little gray building. A lottery sign and an oversized plastic beer bottle signaled the entrance. When she went in, the smell of meat assaulted her nose. A woman was fussing with the hot dog machine beside the cash register.

"These things always drop off the wheel," she complained, wiping the splattered fat off the glass lid with a rag.

When she turned around, the annoyance in her face changed to curiosity.

"Hello," she said, drying her hands on the green apron stretched over her ample bosom. She wore tight jeans under her apron. She might have been forty, with black hair too uniform not to be dyed.

"Nice day out there, eh?"

"Yes, very nice," Lori replied. "Do you often have days like this in winter?"

"No, not very often. Weather's usually bad, blizzards and all. You can't get out of the house for days on end. Ever been caught in a blizzard?"

She dropped the rag into a pink plastic bucket on the floor.

Lori shook her head. "I'm from Vancouver. Our winters are generally pretty mild and rainy."

"From Vancouver. Visiting relatives?"

"No, I—"

At that moment, the door opened and an elderly woman came up to the counter.

"Quick, three lottery tickets, Mavis," she demanded, putting down some coins.

The clerk fanned the tickets out in front of her so that the woman could pick three out.

"Give me three more," she demanded impatiently.

And again she didn't have a winner, and she was out the door.

Mavis threw the torn tickets into a wastebasket.

"This store is well camouflaged," Lori offered. "I had to ask for directions."

Mavis straightened her apron, her bosom heaving. Lori could imagine that men found her attractive.

"Who did you ask?" the clerk inquired, leaning over the counter.

"A man up the hill."

"Where the road beside the church goes up? The last house?"

Lori nodded.

Mavis seemed pleased. "That would be Noah. Dark fellow?"

"Yes, from what I could tell. Somewhat dark."

"They say he's got Eskimo blood in him."

Lori raised her eyebrows. "Eskimo blood?"

"Yes, one of his ancestors probably did it with an Eskimo woman. Noah's the darkest in the family; you don't really see it in his brothers and sisters."

Lori was surprised that Mavis would share such personal information with a stranger. She figured they must have different notions about privacy in this neck of the woods.

"You should be grateful he talked to you," Mavis continued. "He's not really happy if he has to talk to a person. Rather talk to the snowmobiles he's fixing up than to people. Maybe that's why he's so good mechanically."

She laughed.

There was a pause while Mavis sorted out the previous customer's change.

Lori plucked up her courage. "Perhaps you can help me. I'm a photographer hoping to take pictures of this area and the people here. I'd like to stay here for quite a while and move around . . . take my time about it. Do you maybe know of a house I could rent for a while?"

Mavis put her hands on her hips.

"A house?" she repeated, pursing her lips and gazing into the distance. "A house. I don't know. I'd have to ask around."

She thought for a moment. "There are houses empty. Belong to folks gone to work in the Alberta tar sands. But I don't think they rent out. Do you know of a house for rent?" she asked a young man who was just coming in. "The lady here would like to rent one for a bit."

The young man looked Lori over.

"She's a photographer. From Vancouver. She'd like to take pictures of us. And the area."

The young man rubbed his chin. He had on a black jacket marked with yellow and red stripes.

"Selina Gould wants to rent out Cletus's house, so I've heard."

"Really!" Mavis exclaimed, openmouthed.

"Why not?" the young man responded. "That house has been up for sale for two years, and nobody's bought it."

"No wonder they haven't."

Both looked at Lori, then glanced at each other.

"I could talk to the owner," Lori suggested. "Who would that be?"

"The house belonged to Cletus Gould," the young man replied. "Cletus Gould."

"Cletus Gould," Lori repeated, trying to make the name stick.

That got things rolling.

CHAPTER 6

"It's all there, dishes, cutlery, pots and pans, stove in working order, and the microwave's over here."

Selina Gould sped through the house inventory like an auctioneer. Lori practically forgot about the well-equipped kitchen once she saw the living room window. It was big, much larger than the windows in other houses. And no sash windows or smaller panes, which seemed to be the prevailing style in Stormy Cove. Someone—Cletus's wife?—must have ignored tradition in favor of a better view. "Having a view" seemed like a foreign concept to the villagers, whose living rooms faced away from the ocean.

"The fridge is practically new, and we've got well water," Selina said.

Her thick white hair looked like Joan of Arc's helmet in an old movie Lori had seen once. Selina'd told Lori she had nine children, which was pretty common here until recent years. All those babies had obviously taken a toll on the older woman's body. Lori's friend Danielle, who had an esoteric explanation for everything, would surely have concluded that Selina Gould must have swallowed more than her share of bitter pills. But her greatest tragedy had been the loss of her son. Lori couldn't imagine losing Andrew.

"Like to see the bedroom?" Selina asked, but Lori was still admiring the view, where the ocean lay tamed under a frozen blanket and a line of hills embraced the sunny cove like protective arms. It was a picture of absolute peace, a peace Lori sensed was linked to frugality and scarcity.

"Yes, she spent a lot of time at this window," Selina commented, pointing to one of the green-patterned armchairs that Lori knew would take some getting used to. All the furnishings made her flesh creep in protest: the wine-colored polyester lace curtains, the folksy kitchen chairs, the fussy built-in cabinets, the little yellow roses on the kitchen clock, the mother-of-pearl bric-a-brac, and the awful paintings of fruit bowls and water jugs.

But Lori found a silver lining: the more exotic, the better for her photographs.

"He had that window put in specially for her, but it didn't make any difference in the end."

That sounded a bit ominous, but Lori didn't pursue it—it wasn't the right moment. She guessed that "he" was the son who had lived in the house, his wife presumably the "her."

Something was moving in front of a house a little higher than the others on the semicircular slope. Someone was getting on a snowmobile: the man from yesterday. "Noah," the clerk had called him. Lori was surprised his house was so visible from her place. The snowmobile swerved and bounced. Noah's face was turned toward her, his visor open. She quickly retreated from the window.

Selina was already in the back. Both bedrooms were on the north side of the house, a bathroom between them. She pulled back the flowered bedcover in the larger room.

"The mattress is brand-new, the sheets as well. The carpet, too, and the walls have been freshly painted."

Lori nodded and was about to turn away when the woman spoke again.

"He did *not* kill her," she stated and sat down on the bed. "Whatever they tell you, he did *not* kill her."

Lori held on to the doorjamb. She feverishly ransacked her memory for the name—Janis, Jennifer . . . no, Jacinta—the name of the girl murdered twenty years ago. But Selina couldn't have meant her. "Who's supposed to have killed who?"

"My boy Cletus did *not* kill her, I'm saying; she just up and disappeared. She always wanted to leave. Couldn't stand it here. But he didn't do anything to her. She used him and just took off."

Selina wrung her scored hands.

"You mean his wife?"

"He never got over it. She made things hard for him. And I couldn't help any."

"Where's your son now?" Lori asked.

But Selina didn't seem to hear. She smoothed out the bedspread and left the room, Lori following her into the kitchen.

"Do you want to rent the house?" Selina asked abruptly.

Lori tried to play for time. "How much are you asking?"

"Three hundred a month."

Three hundred! You couldn't get a cubbyhole for that in Vancouver.

"I'll let you know by tomorrow."

On the way back to Birch Tree Lodge, Lori mentally replayed the images of her day, like a laptop slide show. One recollection set her a little on edge: the looks exchanged between the clerk and the young customer when they mentioned Selina Gould's house.

Back at the hotel, she went to find Hope, who was at her office computer. She briefly described her house hunting and then asked, "What happened to Selina Gould's son?"

"Suicide," Hope replied drily.

"Ah, so that was it," Lori said. "I mean . . . his mother said something about rumors, that he's supposed to have killed his wife."

"Oh, Selina." Hope shook her head. "Better she shouldn't have told you that. She hasn't been the same since Cletus—since he died." She sighed. "It's true. Nobody knows to this day where Una is. The police searched for her and all, but she probably just up and left Cletus and didn't want anybody to find her. I think she was bored like many of the young women. Not much to do in these villages. No future for them here."

"Where could she have gone?"

"Nobody knows, and that's why the rumors. It bugs people, the fact they don't know. Folks around here are used to knowing everything about everybody."

"Shouldn't her parents know?"

"Una never got along with them. Actually, they weren't her real parents, just her uncle and aunt. She never knew her biological parents."

Hope spun around in her office chair.

"You're going to hear more stories like this one. I mean, about people who disappeared without a trace. Doesn't take much imagination. You can dump a body in the ocean and it'll never be found. No clues. And no witnesses."

She ran her hand through her boyish hair.

"A woman from Port Wilkie disappeared while berry picking and nobody found her. Not for twenty years or more. Until a guy confessed on his deathbed that he'd accidentally shot the woman while hunting. She had a pale kerchief on her head, and he mistook it for a rabbit. And then he panicked and threw the body down an old mineshaft. And in fact, they did find her skeleton down there."

She shook her head from side to side as if she still couldn't comprehend it even today.

Lori seized the opportunity. "Didn't another girl disappear while berry picking? Also about twenty years ago?"

Hope stiffened in her chair.

"Best you don't bring up that old tale in Stormy Cove. It made for a lot of bitter feelings back then. You want to let sleeping dogs lie, believe me. Say, are you afraid of ghosts?"

Lori looked at her, startled. Hope didn't bat an eyelash.

"Cletus killed himself in his bedroom, if that doesn't bother you."

Lori thought for a moment, then smiled.

"Ghosts? But that's . . ." She meant to say "superstition" but avoided the word. "No, doesn't bother me in the slightest," she answered.

Hope turned back to her computer.

"You'll always have a room here if you need it," she said without looking up. "We'll certainly meet again, sooner or later. You've got to get out of that place every now and then, or you'll go bananas."

Lori went to her room. Afraid of ghosts? How silly. A fantasy straight out of the Dark Ages. There was only one thing she was afraid of at the moment: That people in Stormy Cove would want to know everything about Lori Finning. And how fast rumors traveled.

CHAPTER 7

"So you're up at Cletus's place now?"

Mavis's hips swayed as she watched Lori piling the groceries from her cart onto the counter.

"Yes, thanks so much for the tip. I like the house; it has everything I need," Lori said in an emphatically cheerful manner, suspecting the saleslady believed in ghosts too.

"Yeah, Cletus did a nice job on the house, but it didn't bring his wife any luck." That Newfoundland accent again that Lori couldn't decipher.

"Well, it doesn't have to bring me luck, just be convenient. Too bad I can't get any cell phone reception. Is it like that everywhere around here?"

"Pretty much. But I've heard that you can get a signal up there on Stormy Cove Hill."

"How do I get up there? I don't have a snowmobile."

Mavis rang up her groceries. Lori was buying more canned goods and frozen dinners than she did in Vancouver in an entire year. She had to deviate from her principles because of the slim pickings in the fruit and vegetable department. She couldn't bring herself to buy moldy grapes and mushy tomatoes for more than really good ones cost at the pricey Capers Market on Robson Street. The produce had definitely been on a truck for days, seeing as nothing could grow up here except cabbage and potatoes.

"Maybe Noah's got an old Ski-Doo," Mavis offered. "Noah Whalen. You can try talking him into selling you one."

Lori returned her smile, though it seemed a bit malicious.

"Good idea," she said. "I'll do that right away."

She had to crack this nut called Mavis. The clerk in the sole shop in the village was its most important news hub. She remarked as she gave Mavis her credit card, "I like your earrings—they match your eyes."

"Tell that to Noah. They're from him."

"Oh, you're his girlfriend?"

Mavis grinned.

"No, no. Believe me, no woman here wants a fisherman—those guys are married to the ocean. Most of the time they've got no money, and when they do, they plow it into a new boat."

She picked up the white plastic bags on the counter.

"Here, let me help you take your groceries out."

A few minutes later, Lori was driving up the road to the white house with green trim. She didn't see Noah, but she recognized his snowmobile. A black pickup was parked in the freshly shoveled driveway. She knocked on the front door, its paint peeling off.

Nothing stirred. She knocked again, more vigorously.

A car stopped, but nobody got out. Lori dithered, until a voice suddenly interrupted her.

"Just go on in. Nobody knocks around here."

She turned to find a man wearing a baseball cap leaning out the car window. He must have been watching her.

"Walk right in. Best use the door over there."

The man pointed to the left of the house, where some wooden stairs led up to a second entrance. At that moment, the door in front of her opened and Noah Whalen appeared. He looked at her, then stepped outside.

"Stop making such a racket, Brendan, you'll attract the polar bears!"

"You must have something good on your stove," the man shouted back, "if women are lining up on your doorstep!"

Noah made a gesture like shooing away a stray dog.

"Next time I'll sell you guys tickets to the show."

The man laughed and drove on.

Noah looked less sinister without his black tuque. His haircut was old-fashioned, like in pictures of nineteenth-century explorers. He obviously hadn't shaved that morning and looked sleepy. He must have thrown his brown checked flannel shirt on fast because one side of his collar was tucked under.

Instead of saying hello, he asked, "Did you find the store?"

His powerful teeth were uneven, which somehow suited him.

Lori nodded. "They told me you sell snowmobiles."

He glanced at her and then looked away. "Why would anybody tell you that?"

"Because I inquired. I need a snowmobile, a secondhand one. I don't want to spend a lot."

He hesitated. "You ever ridden one?"

"No, but I can ride a motorcycle."

He scratched his head. "Might have something for you but . . . not today, not this minute."

She tightened the scarf around her neck.

"So how long do I have to wait?"

"Depends . . ." He looked at the door and seemed to arrive at a decision.

"Would you like to come in? I just made tea."

Lori blinked away the snowflakes that had started to fall.

"I can drop by later if it's not a good time," she answered.

"Got to go for wood afterward," he said. "Now's good for me."

He opened the door wider.

"Nothing's going to happen to you—there's folks in at least three houses watching."

Lori looked around her. Five houses were visible. What Noah said made sense. There was nothing to do around here but snoop on people.

"As you may've heard, I'm from Vancouver," she explained as she walked into the poorly lit house.

Noah led her up a narrow staircase leading to the kitchen. A cup, sugar bowl, and a can of condensed milk were on a little table. The walls were paneled in honey-colored wood. The furniture looked secondhand, as if it came from a Salvation Army store. Faded pictures of ships were mounted in ornate frames.

Lori marveled at how clean and tidy his place was. No dishes in the sink. Noah offered her a chair covered in a material patterned with birdhouses and watering cans.

"From Vancouver," he said, picking up where she'd left off as he started the water boiling. "Do you live alone?"

He gets right to the point, she thought, folding her scarf and unzipping her down jacket.

"No, I live with at least six hundred thousand other Vancouverites in a rather tight space. And you, do you live alone?"

He smiled, and his serious eyes instantly grew warmer.

"I just thought you might have family there."

Of course. Belonging to any family at all was obviously very important to the people in Stormy Cove. You had to have a clan. She played the ball back into his court.

"What about you? Do you have family?"

He got a second cup out of the cupboard and hung a tea bag on it.

"I've got six brothers and four sisters. But only one sister lives here."

She quickly did the numbers. "*Eleven* children?"

"Nothing out of the ordinary. Didn't they tell you that at the store?"

"No, but I did hear that you give away pretty earrings."

He straightened up with a jerk. "Who told you that?"

"Mavis."

Lori shifted around on her seat. The conversation had taken an unintended turn. Noah filled her cup with boiling water and placed it in front of her.

"Some people talk too much." He pushed the milk toward her.

"Do you have any regular milk?" she inquired.

He shook his head. "Sorry. We grow up here with canned milk."

"And Tetley tea."

She scanned the cans, pitchers, and cups neatly organized by color on the corner shelf—"Tetley" was on all of them. It looked like a promotion.

"Mm-hm, we all have Tetley tea. You're living in Cletus Gould's place?"

"You know already?"

"Word gets around fast here."

"What else do you know about me?"

He drank his tea with his arms propped up on the table. She noticed his huge hands.

"Name's Laura. You're a photographer. You want to take pictures of our outport. And us fishermen. You couldn't find butter in the store because nobody here uses it, and you didn't want margarine. You asked if the school library had Internet and were astounded we have broadband at home."

Lori shook her head in amusement.

"And now all the denizens of Stormy Cove will say I think they've been living under a rock?"

"No, they say you wear a funny hat."

Lori instinctively raised a hand to her head. "It's a beret, that's all."

"Women here don't wear that sort of thing," he announced, as if proclaiming a law of nature. "And certainly not in that color red."

"It's not red, it's orange, but I admit I have a red beret as well, and just about every color—and the name's Lori, not Laura."

He stood up and went to the fridge.

"Would you like some bread and molasses?"

She accepted, though it turned out that the molasses was just cara-melized sugar, and Noah had put margarine and not butter on the toast because it had been like that for generations.

"So what about the snowmobile?" she asked between bites.

He reflected, then said, "I'll probably have one for you next week. But first you've got to learn how to drive one."

He sized up the jacket she'd hung on the chair.

"Got anything warmer?"

"I do. Why?"

"We're going to the Barrens."

Two hours later, after making a stop back in town, Lori was sitting behind Noah Whalen's broad back on his snowmobile. This had surely been registered by several pairs of eyes at the windows.

For a man who couldn't know what he was getting into with a female photographer on the rear seat, Noah showed astonishing patience. Time and again, Lori tapped him on the shoulder because she wanted to capture something with her Nikon. He stopped at once, and she managed to swing her right leg over the snowmobile, which seemed as big as a pony to her. Each time, she took off the helmet Noah had loaned her; it protected her face from the cold airflow that would have otherwise numbed it immediately. She shed her thick mitts and worked the camera out of the bag.

She took pictures of five dead coyotes dangling from a wooden frame like lynched outlaws in a Western, their hind legs lashed together. Noah explained that the provincial government had set a bounty on coyotes—"just a few measly dollars"—because they endangered other animals on the island, especially the caribou herds.

"What happened to their eyes?" she asked.

"Crows or gulls must've pecked them out."

Lori turned away with a shudder.

The snowmobile had a sled for firewood in tow, with a chain saw and a rifle. Lori was relieved to discover that the barrel pointed to the rear. Polar bears crossed her mind, but she didn't want to show any fear.

Probably a lot of people in Stormy Cove had hunting rifles.

Back in the high school library, she had quickly skimmed through her e-mails and casually remarked to the friendly librarian that Noah would be taking her to the Barrens. Just to be safe.

She hastily slipped her numb fingers into her mittens, mounted the machine, and Noah sped away. She held on tightly to the side grips so she wouldn't be thrown off. The machine bounced over bumps and hollows; her back absorbed the thuds. She'd be stiff and sore and exhausted in bed that night.

"Everything OK?" Noah shouted back from time to time. Only the camera bag separated them.

They mounted the crest of a hill, and the houses of Stormy Cove fell out of sight. Noah followed a gently curving, well-traveled trail. The sun disappeared behind some clouds and a pale light fell on the plain before them, casting a unique enchantment over the barren landscape.

So those were the Barrens. Tundra. A swampy, high plateau with sparse vegetation—just as her guidebook had promised. So completely different from the lush rainforest on the West Coast.

Lori raised her visor to get a better look. But her eyes were used to mountains and forests; she couldn't get her bearings on this flat terrain where the endless whiteness was only broken by the dark lines of stone ridges laid bare by the biting wind. Treetops poked out of the snow in several places, as if pleading for release from the snowdrifts threatening to bury them.

A merciless landscape. But Lori felt oddly moved—fascinated by that forbidding terrain she couldn't define. She felt herself struggling to comprehend something important, but it kept eluding her.

The trails in the snow frequently crisscrossed, and Lori was mystified by how Noah knew the way. Twice, a snowmobile rose up out of nowhere with its own sled in tow. The drivers stopped for a moment, raised their helmets, had a brief, friendly chat that Lori couldn't always follow because of the heavy Newfoundland accent. When eyes turned to Lori, names came up in the conversation that she found exotic: Wavey, Flossie, Vonnie, Effie, Nimrod, Alpheus, Eldon, Eliol, Wit.

Lori couldn't resist the temptation to photograph an elderly couple on a snowmobile together, happily united by the chore of laying in wood for the winter. She got enthusiastic permission from both, along with a blend of pride and curiosity.

Before the couple left, the wife shouted to Lori, "Keep the bed nice and warm for him tonight!"

Lori looked at Noah. "Did she really say that?"

He pretended to be working on his helmet. "Probably. People say things like that. Doesn't mean anything."

Lori shook her head. "She looked like such a conservative old lady."

Noah impatiently slapped the rear seat.

"It's the way in these parts. Meant as a joke. We'll certainly hear lots more of it. Come on, up there ahead, you can drive the thing yourself on the pond."

For Newfoundlanders, Lori discovered, a *pond* meant not a small pool, but a lake. Lori crossed the smooth, frozen surface with relative ease, but cautiously, after Noah had explained the machine's levers and switches. Because it was going so well, she made another circle around the pond, going faster and faster.

"Thank God for brakes," she shouted, exhilarated, after coming to a stop.

"No brakes on a boat," Noah said. "All you can do is throw it into reverse."

"Some people do that to other people. Instead of braking, they go into reverse."

She said it without thinking. There was a pause.

Then Noah exclaimed, "What are you waiting for? I've got work to do. Take the right-hand track up there."

The trail circled around rough terrain, and Lori had trouble keeping the snowmobile upright. The sled started to fishtail, and the vehicle threatened to tip over as they came around a curve. Noah took over from her, and half an hour later, they arrived at a slope covered with birch and low, skinny coniferous trees.

Noah grabbed the chain saw and got right to work cutting down and chopping up some trees. Loud screeching broke the silence again and again. When he saw Lori taking pictures, he smiled and kept on working, unperturbed. Now and then, he'd give her a warning shout before a tree groaned and crashed to the ground. She watched him gathering up the heavy pieces of wood. Sweat poured from his brow.

She put her camera aside, wanting to help him load the sled, but he waved her off.

"Your clothes will get covered with resin, and your gloves."

He gestured at the dark spots on his jacket.

"People used to seal up their cuts with resin."

Lori looked down at herself. Her clothes were too impractical, too fashionable for Stormy Cove life.

"Is there a Salvation Army store somewhere? With used clothing?"

"Sally Ann?" Noah shook his head. "We never buy secondhand clothing."

He threw a chunk of wood onto the sled.

"We're not poor."

She felt misunderstood.

"It's no disgrace in Vancouver to buy used clothing. People are happy when they find a unique or particularly inexpensive piece of clothing."

He gave her a look of disapproval. "You don't look like you shop at the Sally Ann, my dear."

"Then how *do* I look? High-end?"

At that moment, they heard the sound of a motor growing louder and louder. A snowmobile came roaring through the trees and stopped at their sled. The driver looked not yet forty and wore a blue-and-white tuque instead of a helmet. He leaned back on his vehicle with arms folded.

"So you're goin' to be famous after all, eh, Noah?" he shouted, eyeing Lori's camera.

Noah's brow clouded over. He turned his face away and bent down.

"You've come at the right time, Ches. This pile's been waiting just for you. Like to tackle it?"

"You got some help already. Isn't that enough?" Ches laughed and looked at Lori. There was something mischievous about him. "We haven't met, but I'm your neighbor. Name's Ches. I'm the house on the left."

Lori pricked up her ears. "With three moose antlers in the gable?"

"Right. You'll have to look in soon. Patience, my wife, would like to meet you. She's a midwife."

"There must be some misunderstanding," Lori responded. "I'm not pregnant."

Ches hesitated for a second, and Noah didn't move.

Lori smirked. "Sorry, my sense of humor takes some getting used to."

Ches laughed again. "Watch out! Newfies make jokes all the time. Mostly about ourselves. Didn't Noah tell you? Or is he still a man of few words?"

Noah thumped a log onto the sled. "You do enough talking for two, Ches. You got your firewood in yet?"

"Lots of time still, my friend. I'm goin' fishin'. Nothin' better than a trout on a plate. Have you ever gone ice fishin'?" he asked Lori.

She shook her head.

"Drop by on your way back. We're on the pond over there." He pointed at the horizon. "Makes a good picture."

He started his motor.

"Bring her over, buddy. She's gotta learn how to fish."

Noah raised his chain saw and pointed it at Ches.

"She's already caught a fish, can't you see?"

Ches laughed and got his snowmobile rolling.

Noah's chain saw began screeching again.

Lori stomped through the snow to a tree stump, its roots reaching up to the sky like a sculpture. A clamorous blue jay flew over, and another. Lori took some pieces of an oatmeal bar out of her pocket and held them out in her hand. The birds landed on it and took off with their booty.

The chain saw fell silent. Noah rubbed his damp forehead.

"Those birds are lucky," he said.

"You are too," she said, holding out a sandwich she'd packed.

They leaned against the snowmobile and ate in silence.

"You don't like Ches?" she inquired.

"Oh, I've got nothing against him," Noah's voice sounded too nonchalant.

"I sort of got the impression he bugs you."

Noah cleared his throat.

"Problem with Ches is he's got too much time on his hands. His wife has a job and he . . . like I said, he's got lots of time. He noses around too much."

"He noses around? What do you mean by that?"

Noah muttered something unintelligible. Lori waited. She was good at it. Photography was 80 percent waiting.

Noah lifted the snowmobile seat up, took out a can of soda, and offered it to Lori. She politely declined.

"Best if you don't tell him much. He doesn't have to know everything."

Noah could have saved his breath. She'd never divulge much about herself to anybody in Stormy Cove, but she couldn't tell him that.

"I'll be friendly with everybody," she said. "I'm a stranger here and want a beautiful book to come out of this."

Noah emptied his can and wiped his mouth with his hand.

"Absolutely right. Can't afford to have enemies in a small place. At some point, you'll need help, and you can't pick and choose your helpers. Everybody's friendly with one another."

But things fester below the surface, she thought to herself.

It was clear that they wouldn't be stopping on the pond to see Ches. She'd have to take pictures of ice fishing later. Lots of time for that.

She definitely didn't want to spoil her rapport with Noah.

CHAPTER 8

She was shivering as she went into her house. She turned up the living room thermostat, just as Selina Gould had shown her. Cletus's house must have been one of the few buildings in Stormy Cove without a traditional wood stove or fireplace. That was fine by Lori. She had ugly memories of a fireplace fire. She made coffee and carried it with her through the small rooms as if she had to announce her presence. She sat down on the bed in the front bedroom. A strange house, but at least she could do anything she wanted with the place. The inhabitants of Stormy Cove probably wondered how she managed to move in without any compunction. Even Aurelia, the nice librarian she called by her first name, had asked her about it yesterday. Lori merely shrugged. Ghosts didn't scare her; it was people that made her fearful. People she couldn't avoid.

Volker hadn't breathed a word about people like them when she'd met him fifteen years ago. He'd come to Vancouver for three weeks to improve his English, but found it more exciting to wander around the city day after day. Lori nearly put an end to that plan when she almost ran him over with her bicycle in Stanley Park. Volker had the presence of mind to save himself by jumping onto the lawn next to the bicycle path. He later confessed that he'd fallen in love with her as she breathlessly explained the difference between bicycle and pedestrian paths.

Volker seldom played by the rules, as she learned on their trips together, which were almost always on assignment for a photo story, and frequently arduous. Nevertheless, they got along famously, and a notion grew in Lori's mind: *if we can travel together so well, we must be meant for each another.* She paid him a visit in Germany, in his attic rooms in Heidelberg; then he went back to Vancouver, and they were secretly married two months later.

Lori's mother felt deceived, particularly after she found out that Lori was supporting them both because Volker, a German physiotherapist, couldn't find work in Canada. Volker grew more and more dissatisfied, and so they decided to move to Germany. Lori threw up on the plane: she was twenty-four years old and pregnant.

Never would she forget the day Volker's best friend, Franz, invited them to the country estate that had been in Franz's family for two hundred years. Franz had offered to let them live there until they found a place of their own. Lori had no inkling that Volker planned on staying put. And another thing she didn't know: Franz, his wife Rosemarie, and their four children shared the huge farmhouse with six drug addicts that they, as practicing Christians and trained therapists, were attempting to bring back to the straight and narrow. Lori didn't find out about any of it until she was sitting in the communal kitchen, a huge room with a long table, fourteen chairs, a grand piano, and a stone fireplace with a fire in it.

Stairs led from the kitchen to the bedrooms. Franz and Rosemarie had a large private room with a TV. Not Volker and Lori. Their bedroom was small and cramped. The people in therapy slept on mattresses in several rooms. They were between sixteen and thirty. Volker criticized Lori for always locking the door to their room. He said you have to trust the patients, that's part of their therapy. From then on, she carried her passport and credit card in a slim tummy belt under her clothes, as if she were traveling in foreign lands.

Lori's role was quickly spelled out. She was to cook every other day for the residential community. The refrigerator and gas stove were much too small by Canadian standards, not to mention for the number living in the house. Lori found it stifling to have so many people around her all the time. She could see an orchard and a chicken coop out her bedroom window—not really places to take refuge. Volker and Franz, on the other hand, would frequently withdraw to a hidden clubroom in the attached barn and smoke hash.

Lori spoke English, French, Spanish, but not a word of German. Plus, she didn't have a work permit, so she occasionally assisted other photographers under the table. Otherwise, she was—and the German word is so felicitous—a hausfrau.

At first, she fought back. She demanded more privacy and space for their baby. Volker promised they'd build another addition on the barn and live there. But in exchange, she'd have to acquiesce to his wish to have their little family stay on the farm. She was in the late stages of pregnancy, exhausted, isolated, and without the strength to refuse. Andrew was born, and he brought some light into her life. But the barn expansion dragged on for months, and Lori's hoped-for nursery was long in coming. Volker opened his own practice in a small town a half hour's drive away. He left early in the morning and came home late at night.

Lori was lonely. She thought maybe if she assimilated more, everything would be easier. She took German lessons from an old teacher in the next village, traveling almost two miles on her bicycle. And she cooked not only for the people in the house, but for the construction workers as well. The constant construction racket really got on her nerves. She missed her mother and friends in Vancouver. And her work. It was difficult to communicate with the people she was living with. Lori felt cut off from community events, but she tried her best. And everybody adored little Andrew. She was relieved to see that her baby was comfortable. Things would turn out all right.

She sometimes looked after the neighbors' children. Once, she staged a powwow for ten children; after all, she knew how much Germans admired Native Canadian and American cultures. Everybody stamped their feet on the floor while Lori played indigenous music she'd brought from Vancouver. The kids thought it was marvelous. Suddenly, shock-faced mothers appeared.

"They thought I had a screw loose," she told Volker that night.

"You don't have to exaggerate" was his reply.

The German mothers didn't entrust their kids to Lori after that episode. To their mind, Lori was more dangerous than the junkies.

Then Lori began to dream in German, which frightened her. Who was she becoming?

One night when Volker was off at a conference, she was sitting in the newly finished recreation room in the barn, and looked up through the big new skylight at the full moon overhead. Andrew was asleep in his cradle. The door to the next room was filled with building materials and had been left open to let in cool air. Then there was a sudden flickering in her eyes. A white apparition in the dark of the next room. She clearly saw it move. And vanish.

Mesmerized, she sat on the edge of the sofa, looked out the window, and meditated. A flash of inspiration made her ask the apparition a question: What purpose does my life in Germany have?

That's when the skylight exploded.

It was expensive, brand-new, recently installed.

It was two in the morning, and Lori, hysterical, ran to the main house with Andrew in her arms. Rosemarie was still awake in the kitchen, doing the accounts. She tried to calm Lori down, rocked her like a child. But for Lori, the message was clear: *I've got to get out of here!*

Nobody could explain the explosion. Lori paid for a new skylight out of her savings.

Then the Katja tragedy.

That was the beginning of the end. Her mother arrived in Germany three weeks later.

A noise. A click at the door. Soft footsteps in the kitchen. Chair legs scraping on linoleum. She could even hear breathing.

She cracked open the door of the little room where she'd chosen to sleep. She'd felt uncomfortable in the larger room, where Cletus had died.

She instinctively reached for her cell phone—you never know—but then realized there was no reception in the house.

She picked up her tripod. She'd used it in Vancouver to ward off a petty thief trying to snatch a camera from her bag.

"Hello?" a high voice called.

A child.

Dropping the tripod onto the bed, Lori opened the door. A little girl was staring at her, bug-eyed, more curious than timid. A pink hairband with purple plastic flowers on it held back her frizzy hair. Pink, too, were the socks she was wearing, her ski jacket, and the stripes on her gray sweatpants. She was perhaps six. Even her cheeks had a pink glow.

Lori put on her cheerful voice. "Hello! And who have we here?"

"I'm Molly." The girl looked past her into the room. "What are you doing in there?"

"That's where I sleep." She shut the door behind her and walked into the kitchen. "My name's Lori. Where do you live?"

The girl pointed to the floor. "Are you living here now?" she asked.

"Yes, for a while. So you're my neighbor, Molly?"

The front door opened again and a noise came from the stairwell. A woman with Molly's round face appeared. She'd removed her shoes, apparently the custom in Stormy Cove.

"Hello, I'm Patience." Ches's wife. The midwife.

"Her name's Lori, Mommy," Molly shouted. "I'm her neighbor."

Lori smiled. "The little tyke's pretty smart."

"I hope she won't keep coming over. You're probably not used to having people bursting in on you."

Patience was plump but well proportioned. Lori estimated her age in the midthirties. She'd colored her hair with green, pink, and blue stripes in strong contrast to her otherwise homely appearance.

Patience led Lori and Molly into the living room as if she were right at home.

"I haven't been in here for a long while. Not much has changed . . . I mean, in the room." She looked around. "The photos are gone, of course. Selina probably took them down."

"Were you and Cletus's wife good friends?" Lori inquired.

Molly had climbed up on a stuffed armchair. Her mother stroked her daughter's hair.

"Sweetie, why don't you run and get your new doll so you can show it to Lori?"

Molly didn't have to be told twice. The door slammed, and Patience took a deep breath.

"Una sometimes took care of Molly when I was called out for a birth. I'm a midwife, you know."

"Right. Your husband told me," Lori said.

Patience seemed puzzled.

"Ches? Where did you meet Ches?"

"I was in the woods with Noah, cutting down trees. He took me on his snowmobile."

"Oh, with Noah . . . you must really have charmed him. He doesn't normally thaw out so fast." A smile flickered over her chubby face.

Lori changed the subject rapidly. She didn't want people to get the wrong impression.

"You must miss having a nice neighbor like Una."

"Oh sure. We often had a cigarette and a rum together when the men couldn't see us." She studied Lori's face for a reaction. "When I was pregnant I stopped smoking, of course. Una worked in the fish plant before they shut it down. After that, she was bored a lot. Poor thing had too much time on her hands."

Lori remembered that Noah had said the same thing about Ches. How ironic that most people in Vancouver complained they had too *little* time.

"So she vanished into thin air, and nobody's heard a thing since?"

Patience looked around the room some more, as if retrieving memories.

"Nobody. They said on TV that this happens more frequently than people think. That people who disappear want to start a new life."

"Did Una tell you about her plans?"

Patience pursed her lips.

"She didn't tell me much of anything. I didn't even know at first that she'd left."

She gestured at the camera on the table.

"So you're here to photograph us? Do you ever do family sessions?"

Family photo shoots? Why not? She could win over the people in Stormy Cove that way.

"Yes, of course, that's all part of it. I . . ."

The front door banged.

"*Mommy*, Granny came over and Uncle Archie!"

Patience straightened her sleeves.

"You'll have to meet Archie soon. He's Noah's uncle, and I'm Noah's second cousin. Archie's like a father to us all. Noah's dad and my dad were killed fishing."

She turned around to look at Lori again before going downstairs.

"It's good if you meet Archie. But not today, he's not in the mood to talk. A polar bear broke into his coop and ate all the chickens."

CHAPTER 9

Two days later, she saw them both: the polar bear and Archie. In that order.

She was leaning against Noah's snowmobile, her cell phone to her ear, and trying to hear her son describe his handball game.

Reception on the hill above the houses in Stormy Cove was better than she'd expected, though it seemed surreal to delve into Andrew's daily life in the middle of this cold white wilderness, out of Noah's earshot but constantly aware of his presence. His bulky snowmobile suit made his silhouette look huge and ponderous; he was like an upright anchor in his monotonous surroundings.

Noah didn't seem to be in any hurry to repair the snowmobile he'd agreed to sell her, despite his reassurances that it wouldn't take long. Clocks in Newfoundland ticked differently than in Vancouver, which wasn't exactly a mecca of hustle and bustle. Lori would never want to trade the leisurely, laid-back West Coast lifestyle for the frenzy of Toronto. But here in Stormy Cove, a slower speed was linked with stubbornness; at any rate, that's how it struck her. If people were already at the mercy of the forces of nature, then at least they didn't want to have the rest of their life dictated to them. This explanation appealed to Lori, even though she suspected Noah didn't trust her to venture out onto the Barrens on a snowmobile all by herself.

"I'm on the right wing now . . ." she heard Andrew say.

His words just poured out of him, which should have made her happy. His year as an exchange student in Germany was off to a good start. And he could stay with his father and his family, which he obviously enjoyed.

Andrew was giving a detailed account of his new position in soccer when an increasingly loud roar drowned him out.

"That's wonderful, Andrew," she shouted. "One sec, something's making a racket here."

She looked at Noah, who pointed skyward.

Above them, a helicopter hovered, an overstuffed net dangling from it.

Noah shouted something that she only heard after three attempts.

"Polar bear!"

"Oh my God! Hang on, Andrew, I'll be right back!"

She thrust her phone into her jacket and fumbled around in her camera bag. The helicopter was flying past. Lori couldn't believe what she saw and clicked the shutter like mad. She zoomed in on a black nose with dirty yellowish fur. Her rapidly beating heart was in her throat.

She didn't snap out of her frenzy until the chopper disappeared over the horizon. Then she fished the cell phone out of her pocket.

"Andrew? Are you still there?"

"What's going on?" His voice sounded amazingly close.

"If you can believe it, I just saw a helicopter with a polar bear in a net!"

"There are polar bears there?"

She knew he'd jump at that.

"Yeah, several of them. They walk across the ice and go into the villages. The game wardens knock them out and take them off somewhere by helicopter."

"Did you get some shots?"

"What do you think? I'll send you some."

"Cool. Germans are nuts about polar bears. They line up to see them at the zoo."

"They're all yours. But you send me pictures of yourself—playing soccer or whatever."

"It's a deal, Mom. Gotta go. Bye!"

She stood there for a while in a daze, phone in hand. She'd wanted to tell him about the snowmobile and that she was going to go ice fishing with Noah's family. That would certainly have impressed Andrew. She felt the cold air on her face.

Let him have his own experiences in Germany, Lori. He's still your son no matter what happens. Hard to let go, that's normal. But he needs his dad as much as he needs you, especially now that he's a teenager.

She felt Noah's eyes on her.

"Everything OK?" he shouted.

She nodded, swallowing a lump in her throat.

The snowmobile glided up to her, and she put on her helmet as she climbed on. Noah tore off, and Lori ducked behind his shoulders to escape the cold wind. As they bounced over stones and roots hidden by the snow, she held on with all her might. The trip seemed to take forever. They crossed a level surface that she recognized as a frozen lake, then she saw some black and colored points moving back and forth on it. Noah finally slowed down, and the snowmobile came to rest. Lori slid off her seat, feeling like she'd been through the wringer, and pulled off her helmet.

Her mood improved when she saw people all around her, holding rods over holes in the ice and waiting intently for a bite. A young man squatted down to show his young son how to move his rod back and forth to lure fish. A group of young women in pink, turquoise, and bright blue ski jackets eyed her, but were distracted when a man with an ice drill almost slipped and fell on the slick ice.

"Nate," Noah shouted, "maybe you should've brought a cane!"

The man came over to them.

"At least I've got the proper equipment to drill with; you might need some yourself very soon."

The bystanders all laughed, while Lori pretended not to understand.

"My brother Nate," Noah said. "Always has to have the latest gadget. An iron bar is good enough for the likes of us."

Nate looked at Lori. "Have you ever gone ice fishing?"

She shook her head.

"Well, then, it's about time. Everybody has to donate a fish today. Here's a good spot."

He revved the drill, and water gushed up through the hole in no time.

Noah put a rod in her hand.

"I need to take pictures," she protested.

"Lots of time for that. Hold the rod at this angle, then wiggle the line back and forth in rhythm."

She gave in, mainly not to make Noah look silly in front of the two dozen people watching keenly.

She met their gazes and smiled.

"If I freeze, then somebody's got to light a fire under my bum," she shouted playfully.

Now she had the crowd on her side. Until then, she'd thought ice fishing was a solitary endeavor in a little wooden shack. But this event was very obviously a family affair. Lori supposed they were all Noah's kinfolk. The young women, most of them under twenty, were obviously whispering about her; she could tell by their furtive glances in her direction.

Noah was talking with an elderly man who held his rod barehanded. But she felt the cold penetrating her feet and hands even through all her layers of clothing. How long was she going to have to stand still and move a little rod back and forth?

A sudden tug on the line. She jerked up her rod—and indeed, a little fish dangled there! When several people applauded, she could hardly hide her delight.

"Beginner's luck," Noah said, taking the fish off the hook.

"What kind of fish is it?" she wanted to know.

"Trout."

The four-year-old came running to grab at the flailing fish.

Lori seemed to be in just the right spot because she pulled out two more good-sized trout in a short span of time.

The plastic bags people had brought began to fill up with fish. Lori wandered around with her camera, introduced herself, and asked if she could take pictures. Nobody had any objection, but nobody asked questions or struck up a conversation.

People gradually started to drift away and gather around a fire on the shore. Old iron pans were unpacked and the trout fried.

The elderly man Noah had been talking to came over to Lori just as she was pointing her camera at the happily babbling teenagers who'd taken off their boots and were warming their feet by the fire. That the photographer from Vancouver showed interest made the kids all the more boisterous.

The man offered her a can.

"Here," he said, "this'll warm you up."

Lori saw it was beer.

"How nice of you, but I'd rather not. I'd love some hot tea."

"No tea here," the man informed her. "This'll warm you up faster."

His round head rested on a massive neck, and his head was as bare as his hands.

Lori laughed and shook her head. "I don't drink when I'm working."

The man wouldn't let it go.

"Maybe that's what they do where you come from, but we do things differently out here."

While Lori was wondering how to react, Noah stepped in.

"Archie, she's got to get used to things. You watch, in a few weeks she'll be more Newfie than we are."

He took the beer, opened it, and handed it to her.

"Here, one swig to get used to it."

Lori saw she couldn't refuse a third time and took a sip. Archie watched her with evident pleasure.

"There's a good girl," he muttered, a smile deepening the folds in his furrowed face.

Noah took the can out of her hand and took another drink before saying, "You haven't tried the trout yet. Fried in lard, you don't want to miss it. Come on."

He escorted her over to a cluster of stunted fir trees a little ways off from the crowd and handed her a paper plate. Lori sat down beside him on the snow and cut her fish with a plastic fork. The trout tasted so good that she almost forgot about her cold rear end.

"So that's your Uncle Archie?" she asked with her mouth full.

"Mm-hm." Noah picked a bone out of the corner of his mouth. "He's not my real uncle. His father died in a fishing accident and his mother couldn't handle fourteen children. When that happened back then, you simply scattered them around to other families. Archie was taken in as one of our own—made no difference to Granny. He's the last surviving brother of seven because he was the youngest."

"Their mother isn't alive?"

"No."

"And these people are all family?" Lori asked, gesturing toward the gathering.

"Pretty much. Family's everything here. You don't survive without family."

"Sometimes you don't have any choice." Lori's words slipped out unexpectedly.

"Why?" he asked with a sideways glance.

"My dad and brother lost their lives in an accident. Their car was buried by an avalanche."

Noah didn't reply. Lori realized that he processed difficult information in silence, whereas she shielded herself by talking. Maybe she was more like her mother than she thought.

"I was fifteen and all alone."

"What about the rest of your family?"

Lori understood that he meant uncles, aunts, cousins, grandparents, and so on, but she said, "It's just me and my mom."

She couldn't take sitting in the snow any longer and walked closer to the fire. A gust of wind blew the flames in her direction. She stepped back and bumped against Noah, who was walking behind her.

You either freeze to death here or you burn, she thought.

Two of the girls approached her, their faces aglow with the heat of the fire. They didn't look at Lori when they asked Noah, "Is she coming tomorrow night to darts to take pictures?"

Noah shrugged. "Ask her yourselves. You're not usually so shy."

"Darts?" Lori asked. "Where do you play?"

The girls told Lori there'd be a dart contest in a pub in the next village. Lori was intrigued, sensing a perfect opportunity to get shots of more inhabitants of Stormy Cove. She promised to come.

On the way back, Noah stopped by Uncle Archie's well-heated cabin in the woods, where Lori was offered a rum and Coke. She accepted with a smile. Best to get on the right side of the clan chieftain. In exchange, she was allowed to take pictures of the inside of the cabin and of the men with their drinks; of the typical nylon lace curtains; of the divan with at least five layers of patchwork quilts in wild color combinations; of a girlie calendar pinned near the front door—a freebie advertising the Northern Lights Garage in Crockett Harbour. She tried to strike up a conversation with Archie's wife, Nita, a wiry little woman, but she scurried about the whole time, washing glasses, shoving wood into the stove, and making sandwiches. Lori sat down on the divan, as every other seat was taken. The men clustered around a little table, talking about hunting, new pickups, the roaming polar bears, and the urgent need for repairs to the wharf.

It was very warm in the cabin, and Lori fought off a sudden exhaustion that threatened to overtake her. Her eyelids kept closing. All of a sudden, she heard Noah say, "I've got to get going before she falls asleep."

His brother Lance, who was sitting at the table, shouted, "She's probably bored stiff!"

"She worked too hard today," Archie added, "and drank too little beer."

Lori protested, but Lance slapped Noah on the shoulder. "You should take her for a good, big snowmobile ride, say, to the Isle of Demons."

"Lots of time for that," Noah replied, putting on his jacket.

"Haven't got all that much time; ice'll be breaking up 'fore you know it."

Nita wiped the table with a damp cloth.

"Don't listen to him," she said in an unexpectedly resolute voice. "Nobody's ever lost anything on the Isle of Demons."

Lance laughed. "Everybody's afraid of the demons. Maybe somebody should go see if there are any demons there at all."

Nita raised her voice. "Of course they're there. Not a fisherman around who hasn't heard them voices."

"Right," Archie spoke up. "There've been demons on the island ever since they marooned the French princess on it."

"French princess?" Lori was puzzled.

"Marguerite was her name," Nita said. "She was an orphan and came to The Rock on her uncle's ship. Her uncle left her on Great Sacred Island with her lover and her maid as punishment."

"Oh, come on. Don't lay that old story on her," Lance said.

But Nita shut him up. "Because her uncle . . . because he didn't want Marguerite to marry against his will. Everybody died but her, even the child she'd given birth to on the island. Marguerite was rescued, eventually."

Archie nodded. "It's a true story. Happened five hundred years ago."

"The island's cursed," Nita said.

Lori turned to Noah, who was already at the door. "Have you ever heard the voices?"

"Now look who's awake." Lance laughed.

"I'll tell you about it," Noah said as he opened the door.

But not that day.

When they arrived at Lori's place, a car was parked in the driveway.

She slipped off the snowmobile and removed her helmet. A gangly young man got out of an old Ford Explorer and walked straight up to her.

"Hello, I'm Will Spence from the *Cape Lone Courier*. Are you Lorelei Finning?"

Before Lori could reply, the snowmobile's motor started up. When she turned around, Noah gave her a little wave and quickly disappeared over the hilltop. She found her photo bag lying in the snow.

The young man grinned. "Man, is he in a hurry. That's what you get for working for a local paper."

Lori picked up her bag. "Hi. How may I help you?"

The journalist tossed his keys back and forth from one hand to the other. His greased hair stuck up in an unkempt circle above his forehead, the way stylish men in Vancouver had been wearing theirs five years earlier.

"Do you think we could talk?"

Lori had no choice but to invite him in. She put on the electric kettle in the kitchen.

"I need hot tea. Would you like some, too?"

"Prefer coffee. Isn't that what they drink in Vancouver?"

"So you know about Vancouver. Where'd you hear that from?"

Lori tried not to let her irritation show.

"Where from? Just about everybody here knows that. A famous photographer doesn't show up in this godforsaken place every day."

"Sounds like you're not from here either. Am I right?"

He grinned again. Lori figured he was no more than twenty-five.

"Dead-on. I'm from St. John's. But I couldn't find a decent job there so I'm out here in the sticks. Now I'm editor-in-chief, reporter, and photographer all rolled into one. Of course my pictures aren't as good as yours."

She ignored the remark. "I hope instant coffee will do. That's all the local store has."

Will Spence laid his business card on the table and came straight to the point. "I'd like to write a short piece on you, what you're doing, and why in the world you came *here*."

Lori couldn't see a way to extricate herself from this trap. Maybe it wasn't so bad, though. An interview could help control any information about her that was being bandied about, though she probably wouldn't be telling Spence anything that was news to him.

"I'm working on a coffee table book about life in a Newfoundland fishing village because it's a world that may soon no longer exist."

The journalist scribbled in a notebook he'd taken out of his pocket.

"Was this your idea?"

"No, I'm on assignment from a publisher."

"In Vancouver?"

"Calgary."

Spence's ballpoint stopped for a minute.

"Why would people in Calgary be interested in what goes on in a Newfoundland outport?"

She wanted to say, *Ask the publisher*. But she couldn't open that can of worms.

"Oh, I don't know. They've brought out books about cowboys and trappers and now it's the fishermen's turn."

"And why does it have to be Stormy Cove?"

She blew on her steaming tea.

"I saw an article in the *Globe and Mail* that mentioned Stormy Cove . . . and Crockett Harbour and Saleau Cove."

She paused to give Spence time to write it down. He probably didn't think much of recording devices.

"But basically I chose a place at random. That's often worked out well."

She opened a box of ginger snaps and arranged them on a plate. Spence snatched one up without being asked.

"How do you like the folks here? What's different from Vancouver?"

She served up some polite civilities: how friendly and helpful people were, how hard their life must be in such a tough landscape, and yet how content they seemed to be. That she'd been invited to go ice fishing, and the fried trout was fantastic. That all she missed about Vancouver were the cakes in the Belgian bakery on Watson Street.

The interview burbled along until Spence snapped his notebook shut. He ran his eyes around the room.

"I was in this house two years ago, before the accident."

"What accident?"

"Cletus's accident."

"Oh, his suicide."

"Suicide? Is that the line they fed you?" A smile played around his lips. "Believe me, Cletus did not want to die. He choked to death on a pen."

She wrinkled her forehead. Was he messing with her?

Spence was visibly amused by her bewilderment.

"Bet you'd never thought of that, eh? But hundreds of people suffocate because they suck on a pen and accidentally swallow a piece of it. It's mainly former smokers who need something in their mouths. That was the story with poor Cletus."

Now she recalled something she'd read on the Internet about how, statistically, pens are more dangerous than shark attacks.

Spence's gaze drifted over to Cletus's bedroom door.

"Of course nobody told you what really happened. Makes sense. You know why? Because it happened while he was watching hard-core porn on his computer."

Lori gasped.

Spence wallowed in the effect of his revelation.

"His wife probably didn't share his . . . preferences. Maybe that's why she took off."

Lori broke a piece off one of the hard cookies. "Any sign of her?"

"Nah. Many folks just want to vanish and begin a new life. I can empathize with them. Away from the crazy scrutiny of a tiny outport. Who can blame them?"

He pushed back his chair.

"By the way, she was Jacinta Parsons's friend. You heard about that case?"

Lori played dumb, and Spence relished staging another scene.

"Jacinta was fourteen years old and disappeared while berry picking near her home. She went missing for half a year . . . maybe eight months. Then they found her body in a grave with all kinds of burial objects, like in ancient graves. So then they suspected people working around the local excavations—archaeologists and the volunteer helpers. The police interrogated them all several times. But her killer hasn't been found to this very day."

He got to his feet.

"Can I take your picture outside? My camera's in the car."

Lori nodded. She put on her jacket and beret and followed him out. The role reversal felt funny to her, but she smiled at the camera, glad his visit was over. Now she just wanted to get in bed and close her eyes.

Then the reporter turned around one more time.

"Was that Noah Whalen on the snowmobile? Best not to tell him we talked about Jacinta Parsons. They were close back then—it was an awful time for him."

CHAPTER 10

Aurelia Peyton, 45, librarian

I knew who she was right away. Besides, no strangers ever come to the school library. Vera told me about her—Vera filled in for me for a month when I went to visit my daughter in Alberta, in Fort McMurray. Her husband's a truck mechanic in the tar sands. Anyway, I found out from Vera she was a photographer. She's renting Selina Gould's house, where they found Cletus. 'Course, none of us would want to live there after all that's happened in the place. But maybe it doesn't bother her. I mean, not everyone's so sensitive to things like that.

No strangers come here in winter. But even if Vera hadn't told me anything—I mean, she doesn't look like one of us. She wore this flat cap pulled down at an angle over her forehead. Yellow, not like the tuques we wear here. And there were rhinestones sewn on the front. And she wore a scarf around her neck that looked like fur, but when I saw it up close, it was wool that shone like fur. And she had silver rings hanging from her ears—hard to describe.

I know this might not interest you: she came here the first two times because of our computer. She told me who she was and why she was here. She noticed I was working on a rug—we call it rug hooking—something

I always do in the library. There's never much going on. She was amazed I didn't knot the wool but simply pulled it through. She took pictures of me too. That's really a hoot: me, a photographer's model! I had to laugh when I told my husband about it. I should have put on something more stylish. But she really is very nice.

The third time she came, she made a beeline for me without taking her shoes off at the door—a sign says to do it but strangers never seem to see it. So I didn't say anything. She asked about the Isle of Demons, so I went to find her a book on it. I said something like, "Crazy story, eh? Just abandoning people on an island. How are they supposed to survive?"

"You mean it's really true?" she asked me.

Now, somebody wrote that the Isle of Demons was near Port Wilkie, but that can't be, because the island there is much too near the coast—you can get to Port Wilkie by raft. The Isle of Demons has got to be farther out to sea or the story doesn't make sense. It's gotta be Great Sacred Island, and I told her that straightaway.

Then we did find a book, wait . . . where'd I leave it? Ah, here's the one. It's the history of Marguerite de la Rocque de Roberval. I know I'm not saying it right. French is not my strong suit. Whatever. Actually, she wasn't a real princess, just from the nobility. An orphan. Her uncle and guardian was Jean-François de la Rocque de Roberval.

It says in the back that the Robervals were probably Huguenots. Now, I know a thing or two about French Huguenots because I'm descended from them, believe it or not. The king of France back then wanted to make Newfoundland and Canada his colonies, you see.

Did you know that the French settled this part of the coast in the sixteenth century? Not many folks do. We still have a lot of French names around here, Saint Lunaire, for instance. And Quirpon. L'Anse aux Meadows—you're right.

Look, it's in here: In 1541 King François of France appointed Roberval as his representative in Canada so he could colonize New France. I'll read it to you:

Roberval's three ships were late in leaving La Rochelle in France, on April 16, 1542. Marguerite was on a ship with Roberval and two hundred convicts the French king had specially pardoned so they could work on this expedition. The ships arrived in St. John's on June 8, 1542, and stayed for several weeks.

Things somehow went wrong after that. At any rate, Roberval headed north through the Strait of Belle Isle into the Gulf of St. Lawrence. It says here that, somewhere en route, Roberval marooned his ward Marguerite, her lover, and her maidservant on an island.

The photographer seemed desperate to know why. But nobody knows, exactly. All it says here is:

Roberval was known to be a spendthrift and a cruel man, but there is no known explanation for his marooning Marguerite and two other persons on an inhospitable island in an unforgiving climate.

Marguerite lived on the island for at least twenty-seven months—more than two years—before being rescued by a Breton fishing ship in the fall of 1544. After returning to France, she tutored young girls. Roberval came back to France and was appointed minister of mines by the king. He was allegedly murdered in Paris in 1560.

Excuse me, but sometimes I go on and on about these things. It's not every day that somebody's interested in this sort of local history. In any case, there's one more detail I should mention. Marguerite's lover is supposed to have been a soldier from the ship. It's said she was carrying his child and that the soldier, the maid, and the baby died on the island. But nothing is for certain; there are no historical documents.

Lori—the photographer, that is—seemed amazed that at least part of the story was true. And she said, "I must have a look at this island someday." Her very words.

I didn't tell her the Isle of Demons is haunted. She'd probably have laughed me out of court if I did. I expect she wouldn't have rented Cletus's place if she believed in things like that!

Did I loan her the book? Yes, I did. And I gave her a good piece of advice along with it.

"Never go out to sea with just one other person," I said. "Always have three or four in the boat. That's safer."

I don't have any idea why I told her that. It was just a spur-of-the-moment thing. Surprised her, I could tell.

But you see today how right I was, eh?

CHAPTER 11

The Corolla's headlights sliced through the pitch-black night. Lori could only make out blurry shapes in the dark. No street lamps, no lights in the houses, no posts with reflectors. Just a dreadful blackness; the snow banks on the shoulder were all that the headlights picked up. It was never this dark in Vancouver. Lori thought back on one night in the wilderness when she'd gone out to photograph a canoe by moonlight for an ad—a friend had talked her into it—and how she'd been astounded at how bright the moon could be.

She'd have given her right arm for that moonlight now, when she couldn't even see the sky through the windshield. The road had been plowed, and a high wall of snow lined both sides, making Lori feel she was in a tunnel. She should have gone to the pub with someone else instead of just getting directions. She'd asked Patience twice, just to be sure, but the place was obviously harder to find than her neighbor imagined.

In Vancouver, she often drove alone at night. But this inhospitable winter darkness grew scarier and scarier. According to Patience, she ought to have reached the pub long ago. She'd only come across one oncoming car on her way out of Stormy Cove. Tonight was the big darts tournament between Stormy Cove and Crockett Harbour, a major winter event, Patience had said, so there should have been plenty of vehicles on the road.

She braked carefully to a stop and turned on the interior light. Patience's sketch showed two forks on the way out of town. Had she somehow taken the wrong road?

She decided to turn around and go back the way she'd come. The lane was narrow, but she didn't have much choice. The maneuver went well at first, but then the rear tires didn't catch. She tried again. Nothing. She was stuck. The wheels spun, sunk into the snow, and she couldn't go backward or forward. An icy fear seized her. She needed help.

She automatically reached for her cell phone. No reception.

Feverishly, she weighed her options. Walking back was out of the question. All she could do was wait in the car until another car appeared, hopefully before the gas ran out—and the heater stopped. She didn't even have an emergency kit—no candles, toilet paper, matches, no warm blanket or food. And her car was dangerously blocking the road as well.

She felt more ashamed than panicky. Panic might have come later, but after a few minutes, headlights appeared in the distance. Lori almost burst into tears. A truck. It stopped and two people emerged. She first saw Patience's worried face, then Ches coming up close behind her.

Lori rolled down the window.

"My wheels—" she started to say, but Patience interrupted her.

"You're stuck in the snow!"

Ches surveyed the situation without a word. Lori got out.

"I was trying to turn around because . . ."

"You see," Ches said to Patience, "that's what happens when you let somebody who doesn't know the place simply take off alone."

Patience gave Lori an apologetic smile.

"He bawled me out for not going with you. Wasn't until afterward I realized how easy it'd be to take the wrong road." She wore a look of deep contrition.

"I'll get you out," Ches assured her, running to his truck for some pieces of carpet. He shoved them under the wheels and got into Lori's car. The wheels found traction, moving the car a few inches. Ches adjusted the pieces and repeated the procedure. Five minutes later, Lori's car was free and pointed in the right direction. She started to thank him profusely, but Ches waved her off.

"My fool wife should have put her mind to it."

Patience shook her head. "He's right. I should have known better. We'll show you the way to the Hardy Sailor."

Ches backed up until he found a spot to turn his truck around safely. Lori followed in the Corolla, but her relief gave way to a new worry: Would Patience still want to be her friend after her husband had raked her over the coals in front of a strange woman? They were neighbors, and Lori had hoped Patience would introduce her to other women in Stormy Cove. She had to find a way to smooth things over.

Ches made an unexpected right turn and another one five minutes later. It really was a very different direction from the one in Patience's map. She'd best not mention that to Ches, or he'd chew his wife out some more.

Lori saw a brightly lit building in the distance. A few minutes later, Ches parked the truck in front of a blue, white, and yellow sign: "The Hardy Sailor Lounge." Even before she opened the car door, Lori heard loud, hammering music. She grabbed her photo bag and stuffed the map inside. Patience and Ches were waiting for her at the entrance. She followed them into a large hall, and a tsunami of laughter, shouts, screams, amplified music, stamping, and clapping surged toward her. As she froze for a moment, blinded, the path that Ches and Patience had cleared for her through the melee closed up, and she lost them. She could scarcely believe her eyes. Where had all these people come from? The coastal villages were so tiny. Patience reappeared and pulled her through the crowd to the bar. Ches already had some bills out.

"What're you drinking?" he shouted.

Lori reacted fast.

"This round's on me," she said to the woman behind the bar. "I'll have a light beer."

The barmaid stopped in her tracks.

"Huh?"

"The lightest beer you have."

"What does she want?" the barmaid asked Ches.

"Give her a Moosehead Light," a voice behind her piped up.

Lori turned around with surprise. Mavis, the saleslady from the store, raised her own bottle up high, looking like the Statue of Liberty.

The barmaid took Ches's money and plunked down a skinny bottle with a moose head on it. Apparently, Lori's words were ineffective here. She toasted Patience and Ches and discovered that she liked the brew. Mavis had been swallowed up by the scrum.

"Where do you think I can find the owner?" she asked Patience. "I have to get his permission." She pointed to her photography equipment.

"Vince, can she take pictures in here?" Ches shouted to a squat, jug-eared man standing at an old-fashioned cash register. The man came closer and gave her a friendly look.

"So, you're the photographer from Vancouver. We thought you'd changed your mind. The girls have all made themselves extra pretty for your pictures. Girls young and old!" He laughed and others joined in.

"Now we'll all be famous!" somebody yelled.

"Only the pretty ones, not an ugly sack of potatoes like you," another man hollered.

Everybody screamed with glee.

Somebody tugged at Lori's sleeve. She recognized the two girls from ice fishing. She was scarcely able to wave at Patience and Ches before the young ladies corralled her toward a roped-off area, where the dart game was starting. The teams were ready, and the music got turned down for the announcer to explain the rules. Lori had played darts a couple of times in her life and hadn't done too badly. Tonight, however, she wanted to capture the tension and concentration on the players' faces, and the wild cheering at a bull's-eye.

She couldn't see Noah anywhere, even though Patience had said he was one of the best players around. Why wouldn't he come on a night like this? Did he not want his picture taken? Or did he have more important things to do?

She focused her camera on a woman who looked at least seventy. She leaned slightly forward, arm bent, her dart hand pointed like a bird's beak, completely absorbed in the task at hand. Lori pressed the shutter release repeatedly. She soared with euphoria whenever she knew she'd caught the right moment.

"What's that lady's name?" she asked the girls.

"That's Elsie Smith. She's seventy-six and a great-grandmother, isn't that incredible?" The girl's voice rang with pride.

Lori watched Elsie and her teammates exchange high fives. The interaction between the generations was touching.

As the evening wore on, both alcohol consumption and the noise level increased. Lori had finished her beer long ago but didn't want another. As always, when she was out with people in the evening, she quickly reached a point where she couldn't imagine anything nicer than climbing into bed with a good book. And as always, she felt a little bit guilty about not being a night owl. She couldn't shake the idea that nighttime was more exciting than the rest of the day and that she was missing out.

She made a deal with herself to step outside for no more than five minutes for a breath of fresh air. Smokers lolled around in small groups in front of the entrance. She zipped up her jacket and put some space between herself and the clouds of nicotine. Back when she had resettled in Canada after leaving Germany, she'd surprised herself by taking up smoking, and again a year later by quitting cold turkey.

A shape emerged from the parked cars. She didn't recognize Mavis until the illuminated signs shone on her face.

"Where's our guardian angel?" the saleslady shouted at her. Mavis must have drunk more in the past few hours than one bottle of Moosehead Light. Her tongue had trouble getting around the words.

It suddenly crossed Lori's mind that she hadn't seen Patience or Ches for a while. But she figured Mavis wasn't referring to them.

Against her better judgment, she said, "I hope I've got more than one guardian angel!"

"He comes and plays every time," Mavis went on. "He must have gotten held up."

Her jacket was open despite the cold, and her plunging neckline was eye-catching. Lori resisted the temptation to cover the woman's bare skin with any warm material she could find.

"So Mr. Cape Lone Courier came to harass you?"

Lori shouldn't have been surprised, but nevertheless she was unprepared to hear that her meeting had been advertised all over Stormy Cove.

"Yes, somebody must have tipped him off about me."

Mavis didn't take the bait. "Will Spence is sure to have told you a few things, eh?"

Lori's reply was cautious. "It obviously wasn't the first time he'd been in Cletus's house."

"Well, he certainly isn't about to go into any of the Whalens' houses."

Mavis pulled her jacket over her chest. Her breath was as white as the cigarette smoke at the entrance.

"Why's that?"

"Because Noah dumped Will's sister Blanche for Glowena Parsons. Blanche never got over it."

"Parsons?" Lori dropped her reserve. "Like Jacinta Parsons?"

"Sister."

Lori took a moment to absorb this new information. Her head began to hurt, but it might have been the cold.

"Will Spence told me Noah was a close friend of Jacinta's."

"He told you that? What a jerk. He should've kept his trap shut."

Lori suspected that alcohol was making Mavis say things she'd regret later. She decided to unashamedly exploit the situation.

"So you were Noah's girlfriend after Glowena Parsons?"

"No, there was a woman from Port Wilkie in between, but I never met her."

Lori thought for a moment before asking, "And how many have there been after you?"

"All I know is Una was crazy about Noah. Una and Jacinta had been best buddies. But Glowena got preg—"

She stopped short as a man came toward them. Lori recognized the pub owner.

"I caught you," he shouted. "Ches asked me to drive ahead of you so you don't take the wrong turn again. He had to go home, couldn't wait any longer."

It struck Lori that he made no mention of Patience, as if she didn't exist. But Ches's thoughtfulness impressed her.

"She can follow me," Mavis said, butting in. "I've got to drive home while I still can."

Lori wavered, but Mavis grabbed her sleeve.

"Come on, I won't lead you astray."

Lori was going to need some convincing.

CHAPTER 12

A drowsy Lori was having breakfast in her bathrobe the next morning when the side door was yanked open. These sudden intrusions always made her wince.

"Paper!" a voice rang out, which explained the disruption of her privacy but didn't restore it. She quickly combed her hair with her fingers and peeked around the corner. The paperboy, a freckled kid in oversized running shoes, brandished the *Cape Lone Courier*.

"You're in it," he exclaimed. "Page four."

She made a face. "Will it ruin my day?"

The boy seemed baffled but then laughed.

"No, no, it says you took pictures of Justin Timberlake when he was in Vancouver. I'm a huge fan."

Aha, Will Spence had sniffed around her website.

"A fan in Stormy Cove! I would love to have told Justin. He's interested in things like that."

The kid beamed. She pressed two dollars into his hand and threw the paper on the table. Best to get this over with quick.

First the picture. Well done, she found. She didn't look like a ghost or ten years older. That was something. But the caption! "Lorelei Finning Wants to Succumb to the Fascination of the North."

Not off to a good start.

Sorry, St. John's! The well-known Vancouver photographer Lorelei Finning has snubbed Newfoundland's capital and intends to spend several months in our neck of the woods. The result will be a coffee table book portraying the faces of our families, the boats of our fishermen, and the traditions of our everyday life.

She skimmed over the rest of the article—Justin Timberlake was actually mentioned—until she landed on a passage.

Incidentally, the name Lorelei *is part of a legend where a beautiful mermaid would sit on a rock above the Rhine River in Germany, combing her golden hair and bewitching the fishermen in their boats. They were so besotted that they didn't watch out for dangerous whirlpools and were pulled under to their doom. Their ships were wrecked on the rocks. So fishermen, you'd better watch out!*

Lori stared at the words. She could see they were meant to be funny, but that was cold comfort. This wretched name would hound her all her life. She pushed the paper away. She was furious at Spence, furious at herself for not changing her name by now, and furious—yet again—at her mother for foisting it upon her.

Lisa Finning didn't have to listen to constant allusions to *her* name. For these dumb jokes to follow her all the way to Stormy Cove, the end of the Earth! But her anger also led to feelings of guilt. Her mother was all the family she had.

She recalled how her mother had rescued her in Germany. She'd shown up out of the blue on the estate. She could still picture her shocked face and hear her saying, "My dear child, I don't recognize you"—words that Lori could have said to herself every day in front of the mirror. Skinny, hollow cheeked, dark rings under her eyes, the corners of her mouth turned down. This was another person, not her. As soon as she got her alone, her mother said, "You're coming home with me to Canada and the boy's coming too." Lori knew she was right. She was afraid that Volker would try to get in the way, but amazingly, he didn't. She only found out after the fact that he'd already uncoupled himself from her in heart and mind. And he wasn't the type who'd fight her for their child—she had to grant him that.

"Do what you think is right," he'd said. His going-away present.

Why in the world was all this resurfacing now? The morning had begun so peacefully. The sun's rays made the ice crystals sparkle out on the cove. The sky dissolved into a rich cobalt blue. Great weather for pictures. She'd wanted to e-mail Mona Blackwood her first update today, but that would have to wait. A quick shower and out the door.

A snowmobile pulling up at the house spiked her plans. The driver hadn't even put on a helmet.

Noah.

He didn't come to the door, just stayed put.

Did he expect her to come out?

That's just what she did, of course, putting on her winter jacket and beret. She stuck her head out the door.

"Do you want to see me?"

He came nearer.

"Going to Great Sacred Island on the Ski-Doo today."

"The Isle of Demons?"

"Yes. Today's your big chance. Ice is solid, but for how long is anyone's guess."

"Right away?"

"In an hour."

He'd already turned around, apparently in a hurry. But then he came back with a Ski-Doo suit.

"Put this on. It'll be cold."

She caught the bundle and went back inside.

Her skin tingled after the shower. Maybe it was the body lotion, maybe her anticipation. The Isle of Demons. Marguerite de la Rocque de Roberval.

Banished to an isolated island for disobeying. Love, disaster, death, rescue. Maybe Lori would be the first woman after Marguerite to ever set foot on the Isle of Demons.

She checked the time. Twenty minutes left. She absolutely had to drop in on Patience. She trudged to her neighbor's house and knocked before entering. She still couldn't bring herself to just barge in.

Patience was doing the dishes. Lori hadn't seen a dishwasher in any of the homes. Patience must have seen her coming—her kitchen window provided a perfect view of Lori's comings and goings.

"Up so early?" Patience said to welcome her. "Did it get too late last night?"

Lori assumed her neighbor knew exactly when she'd come home, but eagerly picked up on it.

"Oh, I'm not a night person at all," she allowed, "and I got a few good photos in the can. I'd like to thank you again for helping me."

"Helping? I made it harder for you, I—"

"No, no way do I want you to think that. I'm so glad to have you as a neighbor, I feel so much . . ." She wanted to say "safer," but Patience might take that as a criticism of Stormy Cove.

". . . more at home here," she said.

Patience smiled, her bright face blushing. "Sketches were never my strong point."

"But you make those wonderful bags and wall hangings!"

"Who told you about that?"

"One of the girls in the pub."

Patience changed the subject. "Did Vince show you the way home?"

"No, Mavis did. She was about to leave anyway and persuaded Vince I was in safe hands with her. Luckily, she drove pretty slow, if you take my meaning."

Their eyes met, and Lori thought she could read a conspiratorial understanding in Patience's eyes. Then she remembered Noah.

"I've got to go, unfortunately. Noah wants to take me to Great Sacred Island today."

Patience looked alarmed. "To the Isle of Demons? That's much too dangerous. The ice out there is really cracking up."

"Noah says it's still stable enough."

"What does he know? Nobody takes a snowmobile out to the Isle of Demons this time of year. Twenty years ago, a whole family fell through the ice."

Her face got even redder, not out of embarrassment this time but anger. When Lori didn't say anything, she redoubled her efforts.

"You know the island's cursed, eh? Everybody knows that. Nobody would go over there!"

If she hadn't spoken those last words, Lori would have been inclined to take her concern about the ice seriously. But she was wary of superstition's firm grip on the people of Stormy Cove.

"I'll discuss it with Noah," she said to placate her. "And I certainly won't take any unnecessary risks. My mom wouldn't like it one bit. I promised to call her this evening."

Her words were meant as a conciliatory ploy; she'd never have played the mom card otherwise. But she saw they hadn't been enough to assuage Patience.

Time was running out. Lori felt that tingling sensation again.

"I really must go, sorry, but thanks for the warning. Really, I truly appreciate your concern. Bye."

Patience was polite enough to respond.

Lori felt uneasy as she left the house. But the moment she sat at Noah's back on the snowmobile, her qualms evaporated.

"Most years the ice isn't strong enough for a snowmobile," he explained. "The pack ice is loose, there are channels all through it. But sometimes the ice gets firm right up to the land so you can cross. Believe me, I wouldn't do it if it was dangerous."

She believed him. People who had to survive on the ocean knew it inside out and respected it too much for any foolishness.

They came round some hills on soft snow and sloped down onto the well-frozen pack ice. Lori felt the change at once. They were constantly thrown from one side to the other. The snowmobile bounced over sharp edges raised by ice blocks grinding together, creating a surface like sandpaper. Bumps ambushed them from beneath a deceptive layer of fine snow. Noah had to constantly evade the larger drifts, and Lori felt like a polo player on a horse. Start. Stop. Start. She concentrated on not losing her balance. When she took a quick peek at the dark seams in the ice, Patience's warning crossed her mind. What if the ice suddenly opened up below them, if the snowmobile hit a thin spot? Now that the houses of Stormy Cove had disappeared behind the hills, her surroundings appeared much more menacing and the dangers significantly more real.

To quell her rising fear, she called on a childhood trick. When she used to swim in the Pacific, she had the irritating habit of imagining a shark coming at her through the dark water. It was all in her mind because there was really no threat of sharks in the waters around Vancouver. As a child, she'd make herself take five more strokes before she could run to shore. Once she'd swum five strokes, she gave herself five more. This was how she could swim farther and farther out, enjoying every stroke she'd wrested from the make-believe shark.

Now, on the ice, she started to count. She had to get through sixty seconds so she could tell Noah to turn around and head back to shore as fast as possible. After sixty seconds, she gave herself sixty more. Eventually, the shore was far away and the Isle of Demons much closer. Its rugged cliffs pierced the blue sky. She could make out the outlines of a wrecked ship on the rocky shore. Noah hadn't mentioned that. She rapped him on the shoulder, and he stopped the snowmobile.

"What's that?" she asked breathlessly after they'd removed their helmets. She took out her camera.

"British freighter, the *Langleecrag*. Ran aground and broke up in a snowstorm—1947, I think."

"The ship was sailing in winter—wasn't the water frozen?"

"No, no, it was November. I think it was supposed to pick up wheat in Quebec."

"Any fatalities?"

"Two men drowned. Crew had to hold out on the island for four days."

"It took that long to find them?"

"They sent out an SOS, but the guys from Newfoundland couldn't tell exactly where they were stranded. And the weather was much too bad. You should be here for a winter storm sometime—nobody wants to go outside."

"Then what happened?"

"A whaler from St. Anthony went to look for the men. Finally found them and shot a harpoon onto the island. The men wrapped it around a rock. Then they pulled a lifeboat along the rope and the men were shuttled off."

"How many?"

"About forty, I think."

"They could easily have frozen to death," said Lori, who'd gotten cold in the meantime.

Noah nodded. "Yeah, they only had a bit of sailcloth for shelter. Let's get going, isn't far now."

Lori looked at her watch. The crossing had taken a whole hour. But they made landfall faster than she'd expected. They found a place to gently transition onto land, and the snowmobile was once again on soft snow. Noah didn't stop by the shipwreck but accelerated for the steep climb to the crest of a hill. Lori clutched the grips with both hands so she wouldn't fall backward. They'd almost reached the top when the snowmobile threaded a narrow pathway between some low fir trees.

At that moment, everything happened very fast. The skis got stuck, the motor stopped abruptly, and the snowmobile tipped over. Lori was thrown off and skidded down the slope. She felt her helmet bang on the ground several times. Then her boots hit something under the snow to break her fall. She lay on her back, but didn't dare move so she wouldn't slide down any farther.

She slowly raised her head.

Through her smudged visor, she could vaguely make out the snowmobile up on the slope. She felt a sudden terror. What if the snowmobile slid down after her? Lori tried to crawl to the side, but she couldn't control her feet. With the courage born of desperation, she quickly rolled over onto her stomach, which caused her to slide some more, but she was able to use her boots to come to a stop.

Her helmet blocked her view, and she was busily wiping it off when she dropped a glove. She tried to pick it up, but now her helmet slipped out of her hand and rolled down the hill. Good—at least she could see clearly. And what she saw was that the snowmobile wouldn't fall on her—something was holding it up. A body lay beneath it. Noah. She saw his head and helmet, an arm, a shoulder.

She heard him shout.

"I'm coming!" she yelled as loud as she could.

She dug the toes of her boots into the slope until she gained purchase, a technique she knew from skiing. What luck that she was wearing hiking boots and not her felt-lined rubber ones. But she was missing a glove.

She was breathing hard, her heart hammering. The slope seemed endless, but the higher she climbed, the more it flattened out. Finally standing beside the snowmobile, she was relieved to see that it was on the edge of a flat hilltop.

Otherwise, the situation was terrible. Noah was pinned on his back, the weight of the snowmobile pushing him down into the snow.

She carefully opened his visor.

"Are you hurt?" She tried to sound strong.

He blinked at the sun.

"I don't know."

"Are you in pain?"

"No, I don't think so. There's just a lot of weight on my legs. Can you lift it up some?"

"Lift it? How?"

"Just half an inch. Maybe I can get out."

She knew she couldn't. She would have had to stand on the slope, and the snowmobile easily weighed five hundred pounds. What's more, she ran the risk of it tipping toward her, and they both would be hurtled down into the deep valley.

"Impossible," she said, shaking her head.

"Try the ax. Skis are caught in branches under the snow."

Lori couldn't recall whether she'd ever had an ax in her hand before. But she didn't want to sound discouraging.

"Where is it?"

"Under the seat. Got to be there."

She gently opened the storage compartment. There really was an ax in the tool collection.

"Should be a rope in there too."

She pulled out a rope with a bright object hanging from it. She plucked it off and put it back inside. It looked like a carving of a fish or a bird.

Noah's plan was to tie the rope around a fir and try to raise the snowmobile, but there wasn't a tree around that fit the bill.

Next, Lori gave it an honest try with the ax but didn't have the arm strength to cut through the knotty branches. She stood up, covered in sweat.

"Got a chain saw hidden under the seat?"

Noah forced a smile. "It's OK, takes a lot of muscle."

"I'll go for help," Lori offered. "How far is it to Stormy Cove?"

Contrary to all reason, she fished her cell phone out of her inside pocket and held it up in the air. No reception on the island, of course.

"Walking? Forget it. Much too far. And too dangerous. Just got to wait."

"Wait? For what?"

"Until we're missed. If I'm not back by nightfall, they'll come looking for me."

"Did you tell your brothers where you were going?"

"Don't have to, they've seen me out on the ice."

Patience knows where we are, Lori thought.

She looked at the time. At least four hours until dark. Plus, it would probably take several more hours for anybody to reach them. Assuming anyone would volunteer to go to the Isle of Demons—in the dark.

The best Noah could hope for still meant staying buried in snow under the vehicle for six or seven hours. She knelt down beside him.

"Are you cold? Do you need anything?"

"Not too cold yet. But thirsty. There's a bottle of Mountain Dew under the seat."

She found the green plastic bottle under a rag and took off the cap; Noah took it with his free hand. She helped him put the bottle to his mouth.

"Better already," he said, handing her the bottle. "The bad news is I can't take a piss."

She had to laugh in spite of herself.

"I made sandwiches. Are you hungry?"

"A little. But maybe wait an hour to stretch our provisions."

He spoke calmly, as if he'd already accepted his fate. What choice did people here have? Mortal danger lurked everywhere. You could get lost in a snowstorm, capsize on the ocean, be stranded on an ice floe, drive into a moose, meet up with a polar bear, die of injuries before you could get to a distant hospital.

They don't rebel against their conditions, Lori thought, *they submit to them.*

By contrast, she found that hard. She stomped impatiently back and forth like a tiger in a cage. What rotten luck! She was finally on the Isle of Demons and she couldn't explore it.

She squatted down next to Noah.

"Are there any traces of Marguerite on the island?"

"Who?"

"Marguerite, the French countess or whatever she was."

"Not that I know of. There are a few deserted houses and sheds on the other side. Folks used to fish here in summer."

"I guess they weren't afraid of demons."

"Maybe they were, but they had to keep their families alive."

A lull in the conversation.

She was aware they'd have to talk for hours to pass the time. It was difficult enough to chat with Noah, let alone when he was trapped under a snowmobile.

Or maybe not. Here, he was at her mercy. The idea terrified and invigorated her at the same time.

A question slipped past her lips before she'd really decided to ask it.

"Were you and Jacinta Parsons friends?"

He moved his head, and his helmet shifted.

"What?"

"Were you friends with Jacinta Parsons?"

"Why do you ask?"

There was no going back now.

"Somebody told me."

It took him a while to answer.

"I knew her sister."

"Her sister was your girlfriend?"

"Why do you want to know?"

Yes, why? What was Jacinta Parsons to her? Why was she interested in Noah's relationship to her? What business did she have rooting around in old sorrows that people here didn't want to remember, upsetting these folks who had welcomed her without pretense?

Because things like that didn't simply go away. Because they left traces. Traces in people's faces, in their eyes, in their body language. Eyes that looked the other way when Lori's camera emerged, smiles that turned sad, backs bent as if under an invisible burden.

That's what she couldn't say to Noah. She'd have bared too much of herself. But what justification could she offer?

Noah saved her from her dilemma.

"I hear something," he shouted.

"What?"

"A motor . . . can't you hear it?"

She strained to listen into the stillness that a slight wind barely disturbed. Yes, there was something! A low drone.

"A snowmobile!" she shouted, her eyes scanning the surroundings. Noah raised his free hand.

"Yes, got to be a snowmobile."

"We need to make some noise!"

"Don't have to. They'll just follow our tracks."

They stopped talking and concentrated on the approaching sound. All of a sudden, a snowmobile materialized at the foot of the slope and stopped.

"We need help!" Lori bellowed, waving her hands.

But the driver had already spotted them. He made a wide circle, gunned his machine, sped up the shoulder of the hill with a roar, and came to a halt on the flat part of the ridge. Then he dismounted and took off his helmet.

Archie.

He quickly sized up the situation.

"I'm so glad you're here; it's much too heavy for me," Lori explained, but Archie ignored her.

"How'd this happen?" he asked Noah.

"Skis caught in some branches under the snow."

"Anything broken?"

"Don't think so."

Archie turned to Lori.

"Come over to this side and hold on tight right here." He pointed to the steering handle. "I'll lift up the machine."

Lori followed instructions. Archie took off his gloves, grabbed hold of the snowmobile with both hands, heaved, and stood it upright. Lori could hardly believe how strong he must be.

Noah moved his limbs, his face calm. Archie picked him up under the arms and helped him to his feet.

Noah put his full weight on his feet, took a few steps, and stretched his upper body. He took his helmet off and rolled his head in a circle. Archie watched him without uttering a word.

"Well?" Lori asked.

Noah shrugged.

"Everything's OK, far as I can tell."

Archie picked up the ax and started chopping the branches.

"Move it forward a little," he said.

Noah got on the machine and started it. It made the curve without any trouble.

Archie's face beamed with satisfaction. Without looking at Lori, he told him, "You go on ahead. Best she comes with me."

It seemed like a power play to Lori, but she didn't dare protest. Noah made no objection either.

Archie put on his gloves. "Now do you believe the island's cursed? You should never come back."

Lori just thanked him profusely for his speedy help.

As she got on the snowmobile behind Archie, she wondered how he'd gotten there so quickly. Had he seen them on the ice? Was he so convinced that something awful would happen on the Isle of Demons? Whatever the reason, Archie must have had a single thought: to go after them as swiftly as he could.

CHAPTER 13

Needless to say, news of the incident spread through Stormy Cove like wildfire. Lori avoided inquiring eyes by holing up inside, editing photos on her laptop. She especially didn't want to see Patience because she suspected her neighbor might be miffed that she'd ignored her warning.

Even so, Patience popped in the next morning with freshly baked muffins.

"You must have gotten a proper scare," she said with a look of concern. "So lucky that Archie found you."

Lori made coffee and asked, "How did he know we needed help?"

Patience, in her element, proclaimed, "Archie knows everything."

She eyed the can of condensed milk Lori was putting on the table.

"Do you have any milk powder? That's what I take in my coffee. Most folks here do."

"Really? No, sorry, I'll get some right away."

"So many new things to get used to, eh? By the way, did you know Noah broke three ribs? He was in the hospital yesterday because every breath hurts."

Lori looked at her in surprise. "Is he still in there?"

"No. You can't do anything for broken ribs; they've got to heal by themselves."

She cast an inscrutable glance at Lori and then attended to her coffee.

"It's not your fault—anything can happen on a snowmobile. Ches and me were out on the Barrens once when the motor conked out. We had to walk six miles in the snow to get home. It was almost dark when we got back."

Lori studied the pale, round face before her and was awash in gratitude. No blame. No schadenfreude. No "I told you so."

Instead, her neighbor said, "You should go visit him."

"Is that how it's done here?" Lori teased, but Patience was serious.

"He probably feels . . . He might have the idea you think badly of him."

"Why should he? You said yourself it could happen to anybody."

"Maybe men here are different from men in Vancouver," Patience said, finishing her coffee. Then she stood up.

"People have to see that you stand by him."

Now Lori understood. This was about Noah's reputation in Stormy Cove. Other men might look on him as a failure.

She connected the dots. Noah wanted to show everybody that the Isle of Demons was a place like any other and that only cowards would be afraid to go there. And then he of all people had to be rescued there. So now it was up to Lori to restore Noah's manly honor. It was, in a manner of speaking, required of her.

Patience had demonstrated great empathy in educating her about this.

She took her neighbor's arm in a spontaneous gesture.

"Thank you for the muffins . . . and everything."

Patience turned red and sped down the stairs.

Lori saw how her story had swept through the village when she went to buy wine. Mavis glanced up quickly and brushed her hair back on both sides with a lascivious motion, then tossed her head so that her hair framed her face again. Her lips were red and moist.

"Just so's you know: he prefers white."

Lori wanted to storm out of the store. She went back to the wine shelf to stall for time and take some deep breaths.

Lori, swallow your pride. You've got to live with these people for months. You have to rely on them. Chalk it up to an exotic experience, a grand adventure.

Mavis popped up beside her.

"I recommend Footloose; it's not expensive and won a prize."

Lori took her up on it.

Driving along the bay, she reflected that her day had been like a black-and-white photograph. The leaden gray of the sky gobbled up the few colors visible in the village. She recalled a vacation she'd taken in Mexico, the sparkling green and blue and orange and red. It's funny how people in Mexico or Newfoundland don't fight their environment; they mirror it.

She remembered reading that the houses used to be painted in red ochre made from soil mixed with cod oil. But Selina Gould had told her the vinyl facades in Stormy Cove were now white, because it was the cheapest color.

As white as the church, whose sign proclaimed a new piece of wisdom today: "If you can't sleep, don't count sheep—talk to the shepherd."

Noah's house was white too, and she noticed a silver-colored car parked in front. Just as she was considering coming back later, a slim woman came out the side door of the house and walked past Lori's car, not without giving her a quick, curious look.

So I'm not the only lady caller, Lori thought.

She went in without knocking, wiped off her muddy boots, and found Noah at the sink, dish towel in hand.

"I thought you were in too much pain for things like that," she remarked by way of a greeting, setting the wine bottle on the table. "Well, then, I'll just take my present right back."

Noah hesitated before flashing her a grin.

"Sure, the bottle, not the contents. I need it for a disinfectant."

"I hear you've got three broken ribs?"

"Just one. It's not so bad. Can't do any heavy lifting. Have a seat. Glass of wine?"

"Why not. But be warned: when I drink wine, I can't stop talking."

Noah was about to open the bottle, but Lori took it away from him.

"You're not supposed to work, and don't you forget it."

She filled two water cups—no wine glasses at Noah's. Mavis was right: the wine wasn't bad at all. And in Stormy Cove, no less, where they all drank beer or rum. Noah very calmly went back to the dishes. She was fascinated by the way he dried a perforated spoon. He pushed the towel into every little hole and over the spaces in between, then checked the spoon in the light from the window before going over the handle once again. Then he hung it on the wall where it would have dried just as well without the towel.

Lori took off her down jacket, then her thick sweater; her blouse was warm enough. Newfoundlanders heated their homes to beat hell. Noah had on a T-shirt with a frayed collar, she noted. She pointed to his glass.

"Don't let the wine get warm; it's pretty good."

He sat down and took a swallow. His fingers rubbed at the Formica tabletop as if trying to remove a spot. Dark stubble graced his cheeks, chin, and neck. His voice sounded rough.

"Is this what they drink in your world? Movie stars, politicians, rich people?"

The newspaper article. Justin Timberlake.

"What else in the *Cape Lone Courier* caught your eye?"

"It said you had some pictures in *Playboy*."

"Did you also see that they weren't nudes but portraits of a young woman writer who'd published a short story in that issue?"

"Yeah, I know they weren't nudes. Though nobody here would be upset by that. We don't live on the moon."

Lori had no illusions on that score, certainly not since that energetic threesome in Bobbie Wall's B and B.

Lori thought she detected a mischievous tone in his voice, a change of mood she hadn't counted on.

"To answer your question: white wine is supposed to be more to *your* taste, if I've been correctly informed."

"Who informed you about what, exactly?"

"That you like white wine. One of your old girlfriends told me."

He frowned. Then his face relaxed.

"Mavis, eh?"

Lori cocked an eyebrow, and his mouth expanded into a gentle smile.

"She was messing with you."

"What? You don't like white wine?"

"Not particularly. I'll take beer."

"Why would Mavis do a thing like that? I—"

"Newfie humor . . . playing a joke on somebody. Me and white wine. She's going to get a lot of laughs with that story."

Lori felt duped. "Sounds like I'm going to have to play my own pranks on a few people. We'll soon see about that special sense of humor."

He tapped his fingernails on the tabletop. Lori looked at his muscular lower arms with their bulging veins. She felt a sudden longing to be taken into those arms.

She was pleased when he took another drink and said, "Ah, it's nothing. They're sure to gossip about me anyway."

"What do they say about you?"

He smiled again, but his lips trembled slightly.

"Aha, the wine's taking effect! You're starting to talk."

"Certainly," Lori replied, "somebody has to drink it since you'd rather have a beer." She had revenge in mind. "Mavis told me that Una Gould had a soft spot for you and that you went out with Will Spence's sister and then had two other girlfriends before you started flirting with Mavis. Oh, yes, and while we're at it, Jacinta Parsons's sister was in there too, or have I been misinformed?"

Noah rubbed his stubbled chin and stared at the table in silence. Then he got up and began to scour a dirty pan with a dishrag—to Lori's mind, a completely inappropriate cleaning method. She'd have liked to shove a scrubbing brush into his hand. But it suited him, somehow, she reflected. He pitted gentle against tough.

Noah said nothing for some time. Her impulse was to get up and walk away.

But then the photographer in her took over. Sitting tight was half the battle. Patience. Ride out the suspense. Let pauses sink in. No eye contact. Don't push. Just wait quietly.

"When you're fishing on a big boat," Noah began, "you're five, six weeks at sea. Two, three days at home, and then it starts all over again. Aren't many women who . . . go along with that. Particularly young women. They want to go out, to a dance, the pub—not mope around the house."

He held the rag under the tap, wrung it out, rinsed the pan, and resumed his scrubbing.

"They meet another guy or move on—to the city, looking for work or they go to school, or train for something . . . And when you get back off the ship, your girl's up and left. So you look for a new one." He cleared his throat. "Ever since fisheries here have been having a rough time of it, girls don't want to marry a fisherman anymore. They've got other options."

He paused to inspect the pan. And to buy time.

"Sure there are girls who want me. But *I* don't want just anybody. My brothers bug me and say I need somebody to do laundry and clean house and cook. But I don't need a woman for that; I do it myself. I want somebody interesting."

Lori poured herself another glass. It dawned on her that this guy was revealing things about himself that he'd kept carefully buried.

"Una . . ." He snorted. "Una chased everybody. Really. All the people around here can confirm that. Just the way she was."

Lori moved her glass in little circles on the table. She bit back the opinion that Una's behavior might have been seen differently if she'd been a man.

"You knew Jacinta's sister."

"Yes, Glowena."

"How old were you two?" Lori softened her voice, not wanting him to feel interrogated, but aware this might be her best chance to learn about that time.

"Glowena was seventeen, I was a year older." He turned around and leaned back against the kitchen counter, his hands grasping the edge. "I really liked Glowena. We . . . we spent a lot of time together. She was always in a good mood, not like me."

He glanced over at Lori, who listened, impassive.

"When Jacinta disappeared, then . . . then everything changed. Glowena pulled away. Worried about her family. Hardly ever saw her. Even when we were together, we weren't very happy, as you can imagine. Glowena blamed herself for Jacinta."

"Why should she?"

"Jacinta had helped with the dig that summer. You know, that ancient Indian grave with the skeleton. A summer job to earn some money. It was Glowena's idea. She didn't want Jacinta hanging around with Una. Wanted her to make new friends. But it was no use."

"Do you think . . ."

Noah was silent, so Lori finished her thought.

"Do you think that Jacinta and her killer met at the dig?"

"Glowena thought so."

"But do you?"

He wiped his forehead with the palm of his hand.

"I don't know—I really don't know."

"What happened to Glowena?"

"She moved away—the whole family moved away. After they found Jacinta's body. I couldn't stop her."

Glowena broke his heart, Lori deduced.

"Did you ever see her or speak to her again?"

"She came back once for her great-aunt's funeral—died of cancer. Six years ago." He looked out the window. "Hardly recognized her. She . . . she'd changed an awful lot. Felt sorry for her."

"Did you talk about the past?"

He shook his head.

"We're not very good at talking around here. She just told me she was married, had three kids. We were like strangers."

For a while, only the ticking clock could be heard.

She wondered what Una Gould's role in this tragedy was. Had Jacinta met her killer through her wild friend? And years later, Una had disappeared as well. Was this what Mona Blackwood was aiming for by sending Lori out here on a supposed book project? There had to be a way to ferret out Mona's intentions without putting her name in play. Who *was* this woman who'd hired her, really?

She'd had enough wine. And Noah unquestionably regretted being so candid. It was time to go.

She stood up briskly, almost knocking over her glass as she put on her sweater and jacket. She felt Noah's eyes on her. When she looked up, he turned away and screwed up his face. He must have been in pain.

She instinctively laid a hand on his arm, but took it away quickly.

"Thank you for taking me to the island. I really value your support. If you need any help . . ."

He escorted her to the door.

"I'll manage. Thanks for the visit." He hesitated. "One thing you mustn't forget: don't get mad if somebody plays a trick on you. Folks don't mean it like that. It's like . . . passing the time, you see?"

She nodded and left the house. The cold wind immediately blew away the doughy feeling in her head from the wine. As she descended the hill, a silver car passed her. The dark-haired woman she'd seen leaving Noah's house was behind the wheel.

Was she on her way back to him?

Noah's words reverberated in her brain.

It's like passing the time.

CHAPTER 14

From: Lori.Finning8w5@belwaycarrier.com

To: M_Blackwood@FVDglobal.com

Sent: May 2, 2013

Hello Mona,

This is my first report from Stormy Cove, as promised. As I told you two weeks ago on the phone, I found a rental quickly and have made some initial contacts. I haven't bought a snowmobile yet because the man fixing one up for me is still looking for parts. But he gives me a ride on his if I have to take pictures somewhere. People here really take their time doing things, which I have to get

*used to. Everyone has been welcoming,
though they're observing me as much as I
am them. I expected more mistrust, especially with my camera, but it didn't happen.
The people are proud that Stormy Cove and
its residents are going to be documented in
a book.*

*I'm very busy processing my photographs
and notes. A few days ago, I visited an
elderly dart champion named Elsie Smith. I
wanted to get her permission to publish my
pictures of her. She told me how she'd met
her husband, Garfield. There were no streets
here (forty or fifty years ago), and young
men would go from village to village, where
girls would gather and chat with them.
Garfield only had eyes for her, she said, smil-
ing like it was only yesterday.*

*She invited me to Sunday lunch, which they
call* dinner *here. It was Elsie's birthday. Half
her family was there (five out of eleven
grown-up children and their children, plus
a great-grandchild, because a seventeen-
year-old had already had a baby [!]), and
I was allowed to take pictures, which was
fascinating. You know all about this, but
I found it interesting that Sunday dinner
always looks the same (potatoes, cabbage,
seabirds, chicken, salted pork, peas pudding,*

carrots/beets/turnips), but NO FISH!
There's no fresh fish right now, I know that,
but the sheds are stacked with dried cod.
Apparently, fish is considered too ordinary
for a Sunday. And to think I pay a fortune in
Vancouver for fish even if I buy it right off
the boat on Granville Island.

When the food was ready, the men—and
only the men—sat down at the table (there
wasn't enough room for the women, too few
chairs) to eat first. The women ate on the
sofa or the carpet or standing in the kitchen.
Even Elsie wasn't given a place at the table! I
asked why, and she explained that, in the old
days, the men came home from fishing and
had to eat fast and then hurry back to their
boats. Women ate later. I said, "But the men
aren't fishing now." Elsie's daughter and the
girls laughed at me.

"We don't know any other way," they said.

Of course, I got some terrific shots.

Nevertheless, I found the family atmosphere
very pleasant, with gossip and hugs. It struck
me that relatives here hug, but not couples,
because any visible evidence of romantic affection by a man is seen as a sign of

weakness. (Uncles do hug their nieces a lot, which I regard as completely hypocritical!)

One of the topics of conversation was a fisherman's huge dog that runs around free, scaring kids and mothers and killing chickens, but nobody dares say anything to its owner. The people here avoid conflict at all costs. Because it could be that someday you'll need that dog owner's help. I've seen the dog, actually, and he really is intimidating. Of course, I'd rather run into him than one of the polar bears (I've seen only one, and it was in a net, so I still don't have that longed-for polar-bear shot).

And this might interest you: Stormy Cove apparently has a skeleton in the closet. Twenty years ago, a fourteen-year-old girl named Jacinta Parsons was murdered. It must have traumatized the people here—nobody wants to talk about it. The killer was never caught. It's all hush-hush, but one of the locals suspected a member of the team excavating a prehistoric Indian gravesite. Jacinta's grave is said to be similar to the prehistoric one.

At Elsie Smith's party, we talked about how far back her family goes and about her Irish ancestors who settled the coast at Stormy Cove. I foolishly pointed out that the settlement surely began more than eight thousand years ago—the nearby grave of the Indian teenager proves it. One of Elsie's male relatives said, "Better they'd never found that grave." When I naïvely asked why, he said, "Because it's only brought us terrible luck." And somebody else said, "Only a mainlander would stick a body in a grave like that." It was obviously an allusion to Jacinta. Then a young kid piped up, "Yes, because we fellows would dump the body in the ocean and nobody would find it." The boy had evidently crossed a line because his dad said, "Shut your mouth!" and the subject was changed immediately.

Something else about the pictures: I'd like to shoot some in black-and-white, because I visualize them better that way. It creates more drama, more emotions in the observer, the effect is—how can I say—more sublime, dignified (I can't think of a better word right now), but it's also more revealing. Black-and-white photos are like windows into the soul. What do you think?

The ice in the bay should break up soon, and then fishing will start up. I pray I won't get seasick.

I'll send you some photographs soon. The Internet speed in the library leaves much to be desired, but my home phone should be in next week and a proper Internet connection too. That will make things easier. I'll let you know my number.

All the best,

Lori

The librarian looked transformed. No longer the gray bookworm. It took a while for Lori to figure out what it was. Her hairdo. Gone was the flat, helmetlike haircut that so many Stormy Cove women had, and a bold creation with feathered ends strutted in its place.

"I like your new hairstyle," Lori said. "It looks good on you."

Aurelia beamed.

"I was visiting my sister in Corner Brook, and she talked me into it. It's the first time I've been to a different hairdresser."

"Where do you normally go?" Lori inquired, secretly happy she'd been able to snap Aurelia in her earlier, unchanged state. She'd looked frumpy but somehow more authentic.

"To Patty's Haircuts. Everybody gets their hair cut by Meaney."

"You can tell," Lori blurted out.

Aurelia didn't take offense.

"What can you do? She's the only show in town. I can't drive six hours to the hairdresser's all the time."

Aurelia felt free to talk since Lori was the only other person in the library, which resembled a gymnasium. The only other people Lori had seen so far were a couple of schoolboys surfing the Internet. When she came during school hours, it was just Aurelia. Many of the books she leafed through had never been taken out.

Lori put her hand on the back of her neck, where her hair was longer. She'd probably have no alternative but to drive down to Corner Brook. Or . . . or let her hair grow like the mermaid's. The idea was less upsetting than usual.

Aurelia looked at the books she was sorting. "Any new leads on Marguerite?"

Lori smiled. "You've no doubt heard about our bad luck on the Isle of Demons?"

Aurelia nodded, her eyes still lowered.

"Things like that happened a lot to Noah. He was a daredevil as a young man. Archie always had to get him out of a jam."

"Looks like nothing's changed. Archie really did save us."

Lori looked out the window. Although a snowstorm was predicted for that afternoon, there was no sign of it yet.

"What's there to see on the Isle of Demons?"

"I think some ruined houses. They must have collapsed completely by now."

"Is there any fresh water?"

"Yes, otherwise Marguerite wouldn't have survived."

"Have they ever found anything on the island that might be connected to her?"

"Not that I know of . . . and there was nothing in the book I gave you, eh?"

Aurelia sat down and resumed work on her rug. She was obviously setting in for a long chat, but Lori was anxious to get home before the storm hit. She had one final question.

"If it's true that her lover and maid died there, and maybe a child, then there must be graves somewhere."

"Graves? I can't imagine you could find something like that after all this time. I've never heard a word about them."

It flashed through Lori's mind that the word "grave" was far from an innocuous word in Stormy Cove. It would always evoke Jacinta Parsons's violent death.

She put on her beret.

"I guess I won't be catching another ride out to the Isle of Demons anytime soon."

"Perhaps you should try someone else next time," Aurelia offered as she pulled a green thread through the canvas mesh.

The librarian's voice was friendly, as always. But as Lori got to her car in the first flutter of snowflakes, she felt uneasy.

Was Aurelia trying to warn her about Noah? He didn't come across as a daredevil. Weren't a lot of men risk takers when they were young? She had been too—selling her little house, giving up her job, moving to Germany with Volker. That time it was her mother who got her out of a jam.

Nevertheless, the thought gnawed at her: *What kind of jams had Archie gotten Noah out of?*

The storm did not materialize that day or the next. She waited anxiously to see water replace the sheet of ice on the bay.

Lori decided to go back to Birch Tree Lodge for the weekend in order to get some distance on Stormy Cove and its residents. One in particular. She also wanted to drive to Corner Brook to stock up on olive oil, garlic, butter, German crispbread, and Gouda cheese—things she couldn't find in Stormy Cove.

The day before she planned to leave, a telephone company workman put in the phone line and Internet connection. Lori felt like a desert nomad who'd just gotten running water. She called her mother out of pure joy.

Lisa Finning was not in her office. Her secretary informed Lori that she was tied up with a trial for the whole week. Lori left her new number and said it was nothing urgent.

She held on to the receiver, deciding whether to call her friend Danielle, who was at her parents' in France and hard to reach, or Andrew—but she'd need to wait until it was evening in Germany.

Then, a sudden inspiration. She took a business card out of her desk drawer and dialed the number. A man's voice answered at once.

"Hello?"

"Is this Lloyd Weston, the archaeologist?"

"Yes, this is Lloyd. How can I help you?"

"Hi, Lloyd, this is Lori Finning, the photographer from Vancouver. We met at a B and B in Deer Lake. You gave me your card."

His voice perked up.

"Lori. Yes, of course I remember! How's it going up in the northern wilds?"

"I'm settling in slowly. Folks here are very friendly."

"Yes, aren't they? It's a completely different world up there."

"You can say that again. But it's exactly what I'm looking for."

"Are you calling to find out when I can take you to our new excavation site? I'm drawing up a work schedule right now. I've got to organize and supervise thirty people. A logistical challenge, I can tell you. But you and I could go up there ahead of the others."

"I'm *very* interested. I read your report on the first grave and found it really amazing."

"You've piqued my curiosity. What in particular did you think was amazing?"

Lori didn't have to think twice.

"That the Indians made such a lavish grave for a boy or girl more than seventy-five hundred years ago . . . and that nobody actually knows why even today. And that there seem to be so few of these burial mounds around here, that it's so very exceptional for the Indians in the region."

"Maybe there *are* more, but my common sense tells me that if there were, we'd have discovered some by now."

Lori sensed that Weston was eager to talk about his work, so she was encouraged to keep picking his brain.

"What do you think . . . I mean, how do you see the reason for this unusual burial—was it a hunting accident, and the Indians were trying to appease the gods? Or was it a human sacrifice? Did the tribe kill the teenager all together, in some sort of ritual?"

A sigh at the other end.

"If we only knew. As an archaeologist, I try to avoid speculation. What we do know is that it would have taken a number of families to build such a grave, considering their primitive means. Just imagine: They probably dug that trench in the sand with caribou antlers. Then they hauled up twenty-five-pound stones from a stream bed, three hundred pieces of rock, that's an enormous job—just a sec, there's a call on the other line."

She heard a beep and he was gone. Suddenly she remembered the whistle carved from bird bone that was found in the grave. The article said it could still produce sounds even after seven thousand years! Some things in this world truly were virtually imperishable.

Weston's voice interrupted her train of thought. "Sorry, things are crazy around here. Where was I?"

"I asked if it could have been a human sacrifice."

"Maybe, maybe not. But it's irrelevant. What I mean to say is, those people led an incredibly hard life: hunting caribou in early winter, then fish and birds and seals and walrus in the summer. It was a constant struggle for survival—and they nevertheless put valuable time and energy into an elaborate burial ritual. That's the crucial point."

He's not answering my question, Lori thought, so she pushed it.

"I was just thinking it would be interesting to know because of that murder case, Jacinta Parsons. I'm sure you've heard of it."

There was a slight pause before Weston replied.

"Heard of it? God, the whole business was a nightmare, for the girl's family, sure, but for our team too, because the cops suspected practically every one of us."

"I've been told that Jacinta's grave was similar to the Indian one."

"Look, the cops never disclosed how they formed that hypothesis. And they never said what exactly was found in the victim's grave—the so-called grave attributes. Officially, they said that since only the killer could know those details, they wouldn't be made public. Though there's one case we know—" He stopped. "Why are you interested in all this?"

Lori chose her words with care.

"Because people here are still bothered by the murder, even if most of them don't want to talk about it. It's shaped the village psyche."

"And you know why? Because the murderer could be one of their own, a neighbor, a father, some friend. But it's easier for them to suspect us."

"What were you about to say before?"

"Well . . . I can tell you, because it's already in the record. An amulet turned up in Jacinta's grave that had a tiny hole in the top. The police asked me if it was an artifact from the Indian grave. Maybe one that was stolen. But I saw at once that it couldn't possibly be from that period. The police consulted an independent expert, Professor Howard Byers at Dalhousie University in Nova Scotia, and he confirmed that the ornament was of recent origin, maybe ten years old, or not even that."

"Jacinta had a summer job at the dig, didn't she?"

"Yes, and she wasn't the only one. We hired some fishermen, for example, because they're strong and never get tired and aren't afraid of hard work."

"Didn't they fish in summer?"

"Some days, if the wind was up, they couldn't even leave shore. So they came and shoveled dirt for us."

"Do you suspect it might have been one of them?"

"I'm not ruling anything out . . . because the cops never did. I remember they really grilled this one young fisherman because he used to drive Jacinta home a lot. But they couldn't pin the murder on him. To say nothing of our guys."

Lori felt her stomach cramping.

"Do you remember his name?"

"No, I'm afraid not. But he was one of those silent types—and boy, could he shovel."

"You mean to say, he could have dug the grave?"

"No, no, for heaven's sake. I just mean he was a good worker." Weston paused. "You sound like a detective. Intending to crack this case after twenty years, Ms. Finning?"

Now it was her turn to protest.

"Oh, no! I'm just curious, that's all. A photographer has to be interested in people. Comes with the job."

"Yeah, I get it. I do that too—root around in the mud and maybe uncover something now and then."

The remark was supposed to be funny, but Lori picked up on a bitter undertone in Weston's voice. Before she could reply, he said, "I only hope our dig doesn't run into any complications this time. Those villages will become a tourist attraction in a few years, and the locals can only profit from it."

Lori instinctively understood what he was saying: Eyes on the future and don't look back. Don't dig up old tales or open old wounds. Don't get the locals riled up; archaeologists depend on their good will.

She thought it ironic coming from a man whose job was bringing the past up to the surface.

An image came to mind: a sketch on the abstract that Weston had left her in Deer Lake.

"One more question," she said. "The skeleton in the Indian grave was buried face down, wasn't it?"

"Yes," he affirmed, "and it's very uncommon. Bodies are normally put in a grave facing up. Or in the fetal position. Then the head's turned to the side, as a rule."

"And the Indians placed a heavy stone slab on top of the corpse. And the mound contained three hundred heavy rocks, as you said."

"Yes. Why?"

"I'm asking *you*."

"You mean what was the motive for these actions? Again, it's dangerous to speculate. It might be they didn't want the dead child's furious spirit to escape."

"And haunt them." The words escaped her mouth.

Weston's laugh was barely audible.

"I can see it'll be fascinating to work with you. I'll let you know when I'm coming up north. I have your number now."

Lori said good-bye and hung up. She paced aimlessly between the kitchen and the study, back and forth. The conversation had triggered mixed feelings in her. Was Noah the fisherman who had driven Jacinta home? If so, then it should put her mind at ease, since the police had apparently raked him over the coals and come up with nothing. Anyway, it was only natural for him to take his girlfriend's sister home. That way he had an excuse—if he needed one—to see Glowena.

Stormy Cove must have known about Noah's interrogation. How did the villagers react? It couldn't have been easy for Noah and his family.

She stopped in the kitchen and shook her head. *It's all speculation, Lloyd Weston would say, pure speculation.* Maybe they'd never know the truth. She went to her study to pick out some pictures for Mona Blackwood.

Her joy over the phone line was short-lived. Lori was packing her suitcase just before noon, when the storm broke with alarming fury. Raging gusts of wind whirled the snow into the air, and gigantic drifts formed in no time. Within a couple hours, they buried her car, and she couldn't make out any distant shapes outside. Just a white, milky, scary wall.

The wind howled and whined at a volume that drowned out all other sounds. She couldn't believe how fast it happened. She didn't dare risk a trip to Birch Tree Lodge now. And when she picked up the receiver, she was met with an icy silence. The line was dead.

The lights went out shortly thereafter.

She collected the candles she'd left in the living room and bathroom. Of the five, three were just little scented votives. There were emergency candles in the car, but they were now beyond reach. She started to shiver. Of course—the oil heating system ran on electricity! Why the hell hadn't Cletus and Una installed a wood stove? Every home in Stormy Cove had one. Una probably thought wood was too old-fashioned.

Just as Lori realized how unpleasant her situation was, the door creaked open and then slammed shut.

"Lori! Are you there?"

She ran through the kitchen and found Noah standing on the landing in full snowmobile gear.

"Noah!" was all she could get out.

"You can't stay here with no power. Pack what you need most and come stay at my place until it blows over."

Caution outweighed her relief for a few seconds.

"Oh, I'm sure I can just go to Patience's. Don't trouble yourself on my account."

"Patience isn't home. Family's all in Crockett Harbour at her mom's. She couldn't get back, road's blocked. Kids have to stay the night in the school. Come on."

She realized she had no choice. Her bag was already packed, so she quickly added some food.

"What's that?" Noah asked.

"Food, just in case."

"Leave it here, I've got enough. No room on the snowmobile."

He handed her a helmet.

"Put this on in here."

It dawned on her that she didn't have a clue how long a Newfoundland storm might last or how dangerous it might be.

"Did I miss a storm warning?" she said, slipping her ski pants over her jeans.

"Weather here is fickle. Always has been. Don't often see snowstorms like this in May anymore, but sometimes the weather just goes crazy." He picked up her bag. "Gold bars in here?"

"No, just my laptop and photo bag."

She didn't want to leave them in an unlocked house.

"Just kidding," he said as he opened the door. A gust of wind almost ripped it from his hand.

The snowmobile was already buried. Noah swept it off with his hands. On the ride over, Lori had to literally trust him blindly, because she couldn't see a thing. It was like being in a centrifuge. She'd never before felt so at the mercy of raging nature. But she didn't doubt for a minute that Noah would get through.

A few minutes later, as Lori stood on the first floor of his house, shaking too hard to push her helmet off her head, she felt a wave of gratitude wash over her.

It had only been a short ride, just a little taste of what could happen to anybody caught out in a storm here. Did she ever lead a sheltered life in Vancouver!

She fumbled clumsily at her helmet until Noah carefully lifted it off. She heard a loud drone and looked around to locate the source.

"The generator," Noah explained. "I've always got power."

Lori knew she'd have to get used to the noise, but for the moment, all she felt was relief that she lived in a village where nobody was denied help in an emergency.

Noah took her through the kitchen, where there was an indefinable spicy smell, and opened the door to an adjacent room.

"Here's where you can sleep."

Two massive old-fashioned dressing tables with mirrors occupied either side of the small space, their corners splintered. Green-and-red-flowered Turkish towels were stacked on the shelves. A tiny window didn't let in much light. The metal frame bed reminded Lori of a hospital, as did the walls that were painted the same green as the ruffled comforter. Faded pictures of boats, icebergs, and lighthouses hung on the walls, just like in the living room, and a metal stovepipe in the corner punched through the ceiling.

She was grateful for the room's cozy warmth; everything else was secondary.

Noah disconnected a laptop lying on a rough-hewn desk and took it into the kitchen. Lori dropped her bag beside the narrow bed and followed him, closing the bedroom door behind her to keep the kitchen smell out.

"Hungry? Like some moose meat? Got a roast in the oven."

Lori wasn't exactly keen on eating moose, but she was famished.

"I'll give it a whirl," she said hesitantly, not wanting to get his hopes up. She'd eaten blubber and muskrat on a photography trip in the Arctic. Moose couldn't be any worse.

Noah put a big piece of meat and a roast potato on her plate and passed the margarine.

"For the potato."

"Oh, right, everybody here uses margarine," Lori said. "I couldn't find butter in the store. How can you live without butter?"

"We grew up with margarine, never saw butter. Tea?"

She nodded. She watched, amazed, as he dumped four teaspoons of sugar into his tea. But she couldn't detect an ounce of fat anywhere on his body.

"Just one for me, please," she hastened to say.

He stopped in midair.

"You sure?"

She smiled.

"Yes, I'm for moderation in all things."

"Then you've come to the wrong place," he said as he sat down. "Nothing moderate here."

He spread margarine and molasses on some white bread before dipping it into his tea.

"Why aren't you eating? Need something?"

She looked down at her plate.

"Just vegetables. And a knife."

Noah shook his head—his mouth was full—and took a knife out of a drawer. She cut into the chunk of meat and started to eat. The meat had a tangy flavor, as her mother would say, but it wasn't unpalatable. *Very lean,* she thought.

Noah watched her, looking pleased. He cut the tender meat with his fork.

"Pardon me, but I don't eat vegetables. Turnips, carrots . . . and onions, if anything."

"No broccoli? Cauliflower? Zucchini? Beans?"

"Just canned white beans. And cabbage, of course. Hate cucumber, and tomatoes and watermelon make me puke."

Lori couldn't help shuddering a little. "No salad?"

"Rabbit food."

"Where's the variety in your meals, then?"

"Variety? Who needs it? In summer, I eat fish, fish, and fish. Cod, mackerel, salmon. Mainly cod. Could have it every day of the week. And shellfish: crabs, lobster, snails, squid, mussels. Isn't that varied enough?"

She nodded.

"It's definitely healthy."

"Omega-3 oil."

She laughed. The storm raged outside, its whistling and rattling blending with the generator's drone. She felt she was in good hands.

Dessert was a bowl of cloudberry jam and condensed milk. The berries smelled like baked apples, and Newfoundlanders indeed called them bakeapples.

"Picked them myself last summer. About eight quarts."

The lines in his tanned face were relaxed, and he occasionally hummed a bit as he ate. Lori wondered how long Noah had lived alone. Then she remembered the woman she saw coming out of his house a week ago.

She offered to do the dishes because she couldn't resist the temptation to watch him surreptitiously as he dried them. He was just as meticulous as the first time. He, in turn, regarded her with amusement as she briefly rinsed every cup and every fork under the tap.

"Is there a sewage treatment plant here?"

He shook his head.

"Then where does the sewage go? Surely not . . . ?" She pointed to the bay.

"Yup. Where else? Same in all the places around here. Can't have a treatment plant for eighty people."

She scrubbed the plates until they shone. Maybe it was unfair to judge. After all, she swam at the beaches in Vancouver, within sight of huge oil tankers anchored out in the Pacific waiting to be unloaded in the port. God knows what all they dumped in the ocean. People the world over used the ocean as a garbage dump, but here she could envisage more graphically how dirty dishwater went directly into Stormy Cove Bay.

She was warming up. Noah wore a loose shirt that was better suited for the heat level in the house than her sweater. On the spur of the moment, she took it off and smoothed out her T-shirt. She felt his eyes run over her body before he lowered his gaze.

"It's warmer than a summer's day in Vancouver," she quipped.

Noah nodded. "You can't regulate a wood stove like electric heating. But I'd never ditch my wood stove. Lots of folks did, like Cletus, when we didn't have all these power outages. And look what's happened."

Lori felt a growing but pleasant fatigue and couldn't suppress a yawn.

"I think I'll take a nap if you don't mind. I love my beauty sleep."

He checked to see if she was serious before saying, "Go ahead, I just hope it won't make you even more beautiful."

As she was lying down, she heard the front door open and close and a man's voice shout for Noah. She couldn't catch every word, but she heard the visitor say, "I just wanted to make sure she found a good place to stay. People from Vancouver haven't the foggiest about blizzards."

Now the voices came from the kitchen.

"Where is she? You got her hidden away?"

"Lying down, she's tired."

"Oho! Already got her into the bedroom. Well, there's another reason a snowstorm can be a good thing."

"Riiight. Maybe you should be home with your woman. She can't run away tonight if you want her to give you something."

During the ensuing laughter, Lori got out her earplugs from her bag to block out the din of the generator and the storm.

She managed to doze off for a while and felt refreshed when she sat up in bed. She heard the noisy generator—power must still be out—and the rampaging storm. Sitting on the edge of the bed, she mused that it must be possible somehow to record this force of nature. She unpacked her camera and opened the door. Noah was sitting at the table reading a fisheries magazine, a young woman pulling crabs out of a crate on the cover.

He looked at the camera in her hand.

"Never take a holiday from your job, eh?"

"You don't either," she retorted, pointing to the magazine. "I'd like to see if I can get some good shots through the window. Maybe from this angle over here."

Storm outside, safety inside—she was trying to get them both in one shot. She settled into her work and, once she was confident she'd got something, transferred the pictures to her computer right away.

Noah stood in the doorway.

"May I see the results?"

She waved him in and took him through it picture by picture. He stood so close behind her chair that she could smell his aftershave and feel his body heat. She tried to concentrate and not notice the hand he was leaning on the desk beside her laptop.

Her heart skipped a beat when she saw what she'd been aiming for. The window with the old-fashioned curtains, the picture of a shipwreck on the wall, family photos below it, with happy faces and a painted duck decoy; outside were plumes of snow whirling up from snowdrifts, like white ghosts in an infernal dance. A blast of wind was just blowing a pile of snow off the neighbor's buried car, revealing a headlight and a part of the windshield. An almost unreal moment—captured for all time. She quickly copied the image into a folder and turned to Noah, to see if he was impressed. His brow was furrowed.

"May I see them again?"

"Yeah, sure. Something wrong?"

He didn't say a word, looked at picture after picture.

"I have to ask you to delete them all," he announced.

She looked up at him in surprise.

"Why?"

"Because the photographs on the table are personal. I don't want them published."

"But you can barely make out the faces, they're—"

"Can you delete them?"

"Yes, of course, but tell me—"

"Then please do it right now."

Reluctantly, she deleted one image after another, and he stood behind her until she finished. Then he went out and she heard him fussing around in the living room.

She sat there, perplexed. *He's within his rights,* she thought. *He has a right to his privacy, just like I do. As a photographer, I've always respected that.*

But she couldn't bring herself to delete the picture in that folder. *Later,* she told herself, *later.*

Noah reappeared.

"You can try it again now."

She collected herself and nodded.

It was worth the effort. Her second set of shots was almost identical to the first. There were still photos on the little table. Men fishing, women berry picking. But two were missing.

CHAPTER 15

Winnie Whalen, 72, Noah's mother

Am I what? Surprised? No, not one whit. But I'll tell you what: he doesn't have a damn thing to do with that girl.

People can say whatever they want.

As for that photographer—don't trust her far as I can throw her.

People just talk because Noah's different. Always was.

Different from the rest, who the hell knows why. Gave me trouble even when he was born. Came out feetfirst, and I was a week in bed. Hard for a woman to even imagine, a week in bed. With eight brats. Noah's third youngest.

Another kid came almost every year. More and more people in a house with no power. We got water from the well, did it 'til the youngest was ten. Hated doing laundry. Crap from thirteen people. No washer, just a washboard. Lord, how my hands hurt. And keeping an eye on the stove so's it didn't go out. Things never stopped in our house. And then away to the wharf to salt and dry fish.

We had cows too.

Cows were Abram's idea 'cause he wanted fresh milk. But then one walked in front of the fish inspector's car. Bloody idiot. There was hell to pay. Had to tether them after that. And milk them every day. Also did the hay. And the garden—planted turnips and cabbage and rhubarb. Picked berries in summer, bakeapples and blueberries and partridgeberries and wild strawberries. And baked my own bread—twice a day. No end to the cooking. Damn food always burned, hadn't time to stay at the stove.

You want more about Noah?

He takes after me, in looks. Dark hair and dark skin, not blond like Abram and no blue eyes. Eskimo blood? Who fed you that bullshit? No Eskimos in my family. Anyways, there are dark-skinned people all over the world. You think every Mexican's got Eskimo blood? Cut the bullshit.

Gimme some more questions, or I'll turn on the TV.

Yes, Noah was always up to something. Didn't come home when dinner was ready. Hung around on the cliffs at Devil's Claws, where Barton Wicks's boy fell off and drowned. Spanked him. With a leather belt so he'd damn well feel it. Abram couldn't stomach it, left it to me.

I'm telling you, women here gotta wear the goddamn pants or they're finished. Life's hard. I didn't want this life. Often damn near killed me. I could only have a good cry at Aunt Vernetta's—mother was long dead. Aunt Vernetta said if other women can stick it out, so can you. That it wouldn't be fair to Abram if he lived by himself. He worked hard and loved the kids.

Life here ain't for wimps.

Or crybabies from the city.

I saw her go into Noah's house. I can see it all out my window.

If you ask me, it was that photographer. She wanted to be rid of the other woman. It bugged her that a girl was hanging around the wharf. She got in her way.

Mavis told Cassie how Lori behaved at the store. If she didn't find something, she'd bitch. Looked for butter and didn't find any. "How can anybody live without butter?" she said.

We've lived without butter for generations, and if we think marge is better, then it'll do for her, too. Mavis didn't tell her that, of course. We're friendly folks.

Why doesn't he want a woman from Stormy Cove or Crockett Harbour or Isle View? Hardly any girls left here. Not good enough for them here. It's Corner Brook or St. John's they want. Or farther away. Hardly anybody but old widows around here now, like me and my sister Cassie. I put it to him: What's wrong with Jessie? She can cook and do the laundry and help you in the woods. She'd be good for you. Jessie works in the fish plant during the summer, not lazy. Got divorced two years ago, but you can't be choosy in these parts.

"Mother," Noah told me, "I don't need a woman to wash and cook, I need somebody to talk to."

Since when does a body need someone to talk to? Abram's dead, and after they dragged him out of the water, Archie took over the tiller.

I told Archie my mind: "Abram's shoes are much too big for you, Archie." Didn't like to hear that, naturally. Could tell by the look on his gob. Snapped his jaw shut and curled his lips in tight to his teeth.

His mother gave him away to Abram's parents to raise him, and now he acts like the family boss.

But nobody forgets Abram. Noah called his first boat Abram's Pride.

Yes, of course, women fish here too. What a stupid question! I often went out with Abram. Agnes, our youngest, was ten. Up out of bed at four in the morning, in all weather, nothing could stop me. The old people in the house had to pitch in. Felt good on the boat. Felt free. Always used to working hard.

I helped Abram with the nets, picked fish out of the mesh. We caught cod, herring, mackerel. And crabs. Hauled up the crab pots and tossed them into plastic tubs. Wind, water, rain, cold, sun—couldn't slow me down!

Folks said I looked pretty much content. The kids sensed it too. Never got out the leather belt ever again. We had a bit more money for Christmas presents, two for everybody instead of one. And I got a nice blouse, sometimes.

But never a dress. Just wore pants all my life.

Many folks take me for a man at a distance. Real convenient sometimes. What do I mean?

None of your goddamn business! Told you too much already.

CHAPTER 16

They weren't alone for long. Noah's brother Nate burst in as they were in the middle of playing Scrabble. Nate and his wife Emma lived next door. Lori was surprised that Noah just dropped the game as if that was a completely natural thing to do. He and Nate went down to the basement without explanation, where they began spreading out a net and mending it in the dim light. Lori followed them with her camera.

She watched them mending the torn mesh with a needle and colored twine. While they joked around, Lori took close-ups of the concentration on their faces and of their bearlike hands—she'd never have guessed they were so nimble fingered. They chatted about the storm and the kids holed up in the schoolhouse that the obliging people in Crockett Harbour had fed and comforted. The children would be spending the night on cots in the gym because the road was still impassable. Then talk turned to a neighbor's father who was in the hospital and probably not long for this world. But they kept coming back to the weather and ice conditions, and how long it would be until the ice broke up and they could finally get back on the water.

To Lori's ears, it sounded like an urgent incantation: Nate would repeat Noah's words in a friendly mutter. She started to feel uncomfortable about eavesdropping and went upstairs. Her laptop screen displayed the last of her storm pictures from earlier.

She copied the photo to the folder dated May 7, where she came across the picture she'd filed earlier and not deleted. She zoomed in to see the framed pictures on the little table more clearly. Two of them were in the foreground. One was of a group of young people standing in front of a dockyard; she could make out fishing vessels behind them. She didn't recognize any faces; the picture was probably fifteen or twenty years old, so the people would have changed. The second photo looked like a posed family portrait, the kind that used to be taken at weddings, though she couldn't spot a bridal couple. Some family members were sitting in the foreground, others at the back, all dressed in their finest. All except a dark-haired man near the right edge; his arms were folded and his legs spread wide apart, like a cowboy's. He wore a partly unbuttoned shirt and jeans, and glared at the camera half challenging, half bored, as if he'd been forced to come to the party. She then recognized Noah but with some difficulty, because the young man before her had a smooth, open face. Subsequent years had etched it deeply.

She was also struck by the face of a pretty young woman, almost a girl, whose expression Lori knew from young actresses certain they were on the verge of their big break. Hungry for recognition, but at the same time a little truculent because the success they felt entitled to wasn't coming fast enough. This young beauty didn't fit in with the unassuming fishing family in an isolated village in the extreme north of Newfoundland. She didn't look like the other women, who Lori presumed were Noah's sisters.

But then she had to admit that her own brother Clifford hadn't looked like her either; sometimes siblings just didn't.

She went back to the first photo, the one at the dockyard, and now noticed that the group was made up of young men clustered around a woman in a striped blouse. Lori couldn't tell if this woman was also in the family portrait; her face was blurred.

"Like some fish?"

Lori jumped. Noah stood in the doorway. The howling storm and noisy generator had drowned out his footsteps.

"Still no power?" she asked as she furtively whisked the picture off the screen.

"Even if there was, I'd keep it secret so you'd stay for dinner." He grinned.

Nate appeared to have gone home.

"I had no idea you liked to cook."

"Don't expect too much. I can make two meals: fish and moose."

It had grown dark, but the screaming wind was no quieter. Lori understood why early man had made ritual sacrifices to the forces of nature in order to placate them.

When they sat down to the meal Noah had prepared, Lori couldn't find any fish in it.

"It's fish 'n' brewis, fish and hard bread," he explained while she jotted notes in her red book. "Soak hard bread in water, then mix it with dried cod softened in water as well."

"Peasant food," she said without thinking.

"Yes, anybody could afford fish and bread. Poor people in Newfoundland used to live on lobster in the old days; it was cheap, lots of it. Rich folks used to give it to their servants."

"Fish and shellfish are getting scarce now, eh? And awfully expensive, even in Vancouver, where people live right on the Pacific."

"Expensive in the stores, maybe, but the money sure isn't going to us fishermen. We're making less and less with what we catch."

Lori served herself some applesauce that stood in for the vegetables Noah didn't think important.

"So somebody must be getting rich," she said. "Middlemen."

"Yeah. Some people make a fortune at it, while we struggle. Pretty frustrating these last few years."

Lori thought about the men she'd gone out with in Vancouver, who were quick to drop hints about all the money they were intending to make. Noah seemed to be saying the opposite.

After they'd washed and dried the dishes, Noah suggested they finish their game of Scrabble. As he stood beside the table, his long, heavy arms seemed to pull him downward.

"Hope this isn't boring you," he said.

She felt an impulse to embrace him, but her caution overpowered her desire. She didn't want to make things complicated in Stormy Cove.

"No, no, not at all. When . . . when I was married I'd have loved to play games like this with my husband in the evening, but . . ."

She fell silent, afraid of revealing too much.

Noah sat down and pushed the board between them.

"He didn't like games?"

"We lived in a big house with another family and some patients, so we were rarely by ourselves."

"I don't get it, patients? Was it a hospital?"

Lori shook her head, already sorry she'd brought up her marriage. It was so difficult to explain.

"The house owner was a therapist helping drug addicts, and he cared for a bunch of young people in recovery. They'd live in his house for a while until they could find a place of their own. And we lived in the same, really huge house because . . . my husband and the therapist were childhood friends and—he just didn't want to live anywhere else. But it was very hard on me—I mean, with so many people around. I'd rather have lived alone with him and our child."

Noah rubbed his chin and stared at the Formica tabletop. Had he been thrown off guard by her disclosure?

"Always were a lot of people in our house too: eleven kids and two adults, not counting visitors," he remarked, "but living with strangers—that's another story."

She nodded in assent. "You can feel very much alone even with a lot of people around you."

"Did *you* feel alone, even with your husband and child?"

"Yes, my husband worked in town and would come home late at night. And then somebody else commandeered him."

She visualized Katja standing before her, a girl who'd had to walk the streets as a twelve-year-old. She was nineteen when she came to the Lindenhold estate and was still pretty despite her past, but—as Lori could see today—she was an immensely needy child. She wanted to discuss her writing with Volker for hours, pieces she hoped to publish, even though Volker was no creative writing expert.

One night, Lori's patience was exhausted, and she aired her frustration in their bedroom.

"You're not jealous, by any chance?" he'd responded.

Lori felt like her head was going to explode.

"Maybe, but the point is I'm practically still a newlywed and I'd like to spend a little time with my husband—alone! Is that so hard to understand?"

Volker responded with a lecture on marriage as a union of two individuals that stays vibrant by means of external relationships. He informed Lori that she was arguably attempting to compensate for her father and brother's deaths by demanding undue attention from him.

After that, Lori felt more inadequate than ever. Especially compared to Rosemarie, Franz's wife, who supported her husband in everything, unquestioningly. Rosemarie was magnanimous, never jealous, and had no doubts about her husband's love. She understood a therapist's work. Why couldn't Lori be like Rosemarie?

Suddenly, she felt a warm hand on hers. Noah's worried face and dark eyes were before her.

"What is it? Did I say something wrong? You look so sad."

She tried to smile.

"Oh, I shouldn't bring up old times—they're over and done with."

She was not the helpless, browbeaten stranger anymore, always trying too hard to be a good wife and always failing. Nowadays she was careful never to be too dependent on other people.

That was the reason she had to be on her guard with this ruggedly handsome fisherman who offered her food and shelter, who was now leaning over the table toward her. It would be the height of imprudence to get attached to a strange man in a remote village at the end of the earth. And yet her skin burned beneath his touch.

Noah squeezed her hand before getting back to the Scrabble board. "Whose turn?"

He was far ahead on points, to her chagrin, since she prided herself on her talent for Scrabble. But he used uncommon words for all things fish she didn't know, or tools, or machine parts—vocabulary she was powerless against.

He beat her, and it turned out he was a poor winner.

"I win!" He wrote above his name on the score sheet. "Never thought I'd be better than you," he said teasingly. "After all, you speak proper English and we only talk Newfinese."

"Oh, come off it! In a moment of triumph, you should treat your opponent with grace."

"Not if I'm up against a mighty opponent like you."

"Aren't you the loudmouth! Why do people say you're shy, again?"

"All strategy, my dear. If you don't say much, you can't say anything wrong."

"OK, then you'd best say nothing at all, or else—"

"Or else I'll annoy you even more?"

He was right, of course; the defeat irked her. But she was also irritable because it was her bedtime, and she had to forgo being near him.

"I'm really tired," she said abruptly. "If you don't mind, I'll go to my room. Thank you so much for everything you've done for me."

They stood up at the same time, and for a second, she had the feeling he was going to hug her. But the moment passed, and he said instead,

"I'll build up the fire some more; it'll keep you warm all night." He paused. "Mind if I watch TV for a bit? I'll shut the generator off after."

She assured him it was fine. Washing her face in the bathroom, she heard him adding wood to the stove. She scurried into her room and locked the door carefully so he wouldn't hear.

Then she got into pajamas, took out her notebook, and sat on the bed; the metal springs protested loudly. She made herself pick up the pen and watched as words appeared on the paper.

I don't want any amorous complications, I must maintain a neutral position, I can't screw up this assignment. I've had it with passing affairs, I don't want to get burned again or risk any more heartache. My career's back on track, I've got grand plans. How could I put them at risk for a bit of warmth next to a physical body? I can get a cat for that.

She giggled softly at that last sentence. The touch of levity felt good, better than old murders and conspiracy theories and a small town's deep dark secrets.

Even so, she plunged into a mystery novel. She heard Noah turn on the weather channel—what else?—but the report was repeatedly interrupted, probably by the storm pounding on the satellite dish. Eventually, he turned the generator off and her reading light blinked out. She wrapped herself in a multicolored patterned quilt as the bed squeaked.

She woke up with a start in the middle of the night. It took a while to figure out where she was. There were muffled voices in the house.

A man's and a woman's. She recognized Noah's mellow sing-song. But who was the woman? She sounded insistent, pleading. A door slammed and footsteps came nearer. Should she venture out of her room and play Little Miss Naïve and ask what was up? She decided she wasn't comfortable with the thought of Noah seeing her in her pajamas. So she stayed in bed, her heart racing, not daring to move and make the springs squeak. Not until the house was quiet again did she gently roll onto her side, but the angry storm whistled in her wakeful ears for a long time.

In the morning, she came into the kitchen freshly showered to find Noah at the stove. The aroma of fried bacon reached her nose.

"I don't hear the generator," she yawned.

He turned and gave her a scrutinizing look, as if trying to read her face.

"Yes, power's back, phone, too. Want some bacon and eggs?"

"I'm so famished I could eat my boots."

Her eyes focused on the kitchen clock. Twenty to ten.

"Am I wrong, or has the storm let up?"

"It has, but doesn't mean anything. Could get really bad again this afternoon. Road's still closed, and the kids will stay at the schoolhouse no matter what."

"Then I should eat my breakfast fast and get back home before it starts up again."

Noah handed her a full plate.

"You can stay here as long as you want."

"That's nice of you, but I have to call my mom and my son." She assumed a mischievous tone. "I'm not here on holiday, if that's what you mean."

Noah didn't return her smile. He scraped the last bacon scrap out of the pan and dropped it onto his plate. Two pieces of toast popped up in the toaster; he spread margarine on them with great care.

"Hope we didn't wake you up last night?" he asked.

She wiped some bacon drippings off her chin.

"I did hear something once. Voices. Was that you?"

"Emma came in and kicked up a fuss. Nate's wife. My sister-in-law. She wanted me to take Mother in. Nate went and got her because of the storm. But Emma and Mother can't stand each other." He sipped his tea, loudly and a little sloppily. "Mother isn't an easy woman. Used to calling the shots. And she cusses. I think you'd be kinda shocked."

Lori's breakfast tasted better now.

"Look, I should go home. Then you could have your mom here."

"She doesn't want to come. My kitchen's not good enough for her. Emma always wanted a new kitchen. So she has to put up with Mother." He sounded amused.

"My mom hardly cooks at all," said Lori. "She eats out or gets delivery. She just works too much."

"What's she do?"

"She's a defense attorney."

"A lawyer?"

Lori nodded. He kept eating in silence.

"Why, is that a bad thing?"

He took his time answering.

"The less you've got to do with lawyers, the better."

"Well, I've got no choice, she's my mom."

"Yep," he said and fell silent.

She thought it best to drop it.

But he suddenly announced, "You can ask me anything you want. Just ask, I'll answer."

"Oh," she responded, "what do you want me to ask?"

"Dunno . . . it's up to you." He cleared his throat.

Did he expect her to do the same for him? But she couldn't. There were things she had to keep to herself.

Lori had learned that Noah didn't ask many questions anyway. People in Stormy Cove generally weren't forthcoming with questions for her. She had the impression they were curious but at a loss as to what to ask this outsider whose life was so different from their own. They had no frame of reference for Lori's world, no connection to it.

Noah broke the silence.

"Next week there's a mummers' competition at the Hardy Sailor Lounge you shouldn't miss."

"What are mummers?" she asked, grateful for a new subject.

"It's an old custom, from our Irish ancestors, I think. At Christmastime, people dress up in old bed sheets and masks and go from house to house and dance a jig in the kitchen and are given something to drink. Booze, of course." He winked at her. "Went a lot when I was younger. But I can't dance. And I always threw up because they gave you all kinds of booze: rum and whisky and vodka and homebrew—awful."

"But it's not Christmas! Why the competition?"

"Oh, Vince's idea, to lure more customers into his pub, I suppose."

"Will you go in costume?"

"Me? No. And you won't get me to dance either."

She folded her arms and leaned back.

"So who says I want to dance with you?"

"Every woman wants to go dancing. I just look stupid. I'm sure you're a lot better than me. They'll ask you to dance, look out."

She laughed.

"I'll be too busy taking pictures." She put down her knife and fork. "Really, Noah, many, many thanks for your hospitality."

He wiped his mouth with the back of his hand.

"I'll take you home so you can have some peace and quiet."

When they were putting on their snowmobile suits downstairs, she noticed a picture of a ship on the wall.

"Is that your boat?"

He glanced at it.

"*Was* my boat."

"Is it the one that caught on fire?"

"Yes. Who told you that?"

"Can't remember. Somebody in the pub? Is it true that it was arson?"

"You've been talking to the wrong people."

He put on his helmet and opened the door.

So much for all those questions he said he'd answer, she thought to herself.

She slipped out the door, and the icy wind hit her like a punch in the face.

CHAPTER 17

The first thing she did when she got home was to follow Noah's advice and turn on the tap. After some initial splutters, water squirted out— the pipes weren't frozen. The fridge hummed, and a buzzing sound told her the phone was working. Lori took a deep breath. She turned up the heat and set all the flashing clocks to the correct time. She yearned for a state of normalcy. Outside, the storm was still blowing.

She went down to the basement and took the laundry out of the dryer. As she was wiping down the outside of the washing machine, the rag fell between the two appliances. When she picked it up, she felt something hard between her fingers. It was a thumb-sized object shaped like a primitive bird. Somehow it looked familiar. Where had she seen something like that before? It was a bone carving in a rather spare style. A talisman or key-chain fob? She stuck it in her pocket and hung up the rag.

Back in the kitchen, she made some strong coffee and opened her e-mail.

Mona Blackwood had written back, about a dozen words. *Great pictures. My compliments. Can you get me the names of the people ice fishing?*

Lori puffed out her cheeks. What an odd request. Why was her employer interested in that particular picture?

At least Mona was happy with the photos. So she was on the right track.

Her mother had written too. *There was a report on TV about a blizzard in Newfoundland. I tried to call you, couldn't get through. Is everything OK?*

Lori looked at her watch. It was seven in the morning in Vancouver. She went to the phone.

"I'm so happy to hear your voice, my dear girl. I tried calling all night but nobody answered."

Lisa Finning's voice sounded a little rougher than usual. Her mother didn't often show that she worried about her; she'd once told Lori, "I don't want you to feel you're not free to go wherever you want." Maybe her mother was afraid of clinging to the only child she had left after Clifford's death.

Lori's friend Danielle talked with *her* mother on the phone almost every day. She thought it odd, as if Danielle hadn't cut the umbilical cord. Lori knew her mother didn't expect daily phone calls or even want them. She'd tried to raise her daughter as an independent, self-sufficient woman like herself. When Lori fell into an unhealthy dependency on her German husband, her mother had blamed herself and felt she had to rescue Lori to atone for her supposed failure.

Lori reasoned later that it was probably inevitable for her to look for a man to be dependent on—fallout from the trauma of losing her father and brother. But she'd never discussed it with her mother for fear it'd make her feel guilty. After divorcing Volker, Lori had a few casual relationships, but she never again moved in with a man. She often wondered if she was trying to prove to her mother that she could, in fact, be an independent, self-sufficient woman.

"Lori?" a voice at the other end asked.

Lori hurried to tell her about the events of the past twenty-four hours. Seemed more like a week.

"A man took you to his place?" asked her mother, seizing the bull by the horns, as always. "Why would he want to help you?"

"Everybody helps everybody else here. It's just that he was the first person to come check on me since he knew my neighbors were away."

"You do realize that people will take it that you belong to him now?"

"A single woman probably can't avoid that in a small village," Lori replied as nonchalantly as she could. "How's the trial going?"

Her mother's client was a female teacher accused of seducing a thirteen-year-old student.

"I'm confident I can keep her out of prison. Luckily, she hadn't written him any e-mails or love letters."

"If the accused were a man, would you lose?"

"No, those days are over, my darling. Women aren't assumed to be innocent little lambs anymore, and that's good. How's your work going?"

"Surprisingly well. Just imagine: people here *want* their picture taken. I don't get any resistance. And there are subjects everywhere I turn. People here live like it was fifty years ago . . . except they have electricity now, and paved streets, and the Internet."

"An idyllic world, huh?" she asked, her voice dripping with irony. Lisa Finning had seen more than her professional share of ugliness.

Lori couldn't resist mentioning Cletus Gould's death by suffocation and his predilection for hard-core porn.

"Did his wife know?" her mother wondered.

"No idea, but she apparently left him. Why?"

"In every case I've seen, women are totally shocked when they find out. And they usually don't want to believe it."

"Mom, have you ever heard anything about the Jacinta Parsons murder?"

"Jacinta Parsons . . . yes, sounds familiar. The girl in that strange grave, right? Do you mean that murder took place up where you are?"

"Yes. What do you know about it?"

"Let me think for a moment . . . What I mostly remember is how secretive the Newfoundland police were. They somehow . . . didn't seem aboveboard. I remember we discussed it at the office. We thought the way they were going about the investigation meant that nothing would come of it. I think they were trying to put the finger on the people working on the excavations. But nobody was going to swallow that. The poor girl. They still haven't caught the killer."

"I know. And I've got a feeling that people here know it wasn't an outsider—even if they don't come right out and say it. That's my impression anyway."

"Remind me when it happened?"

"Almost exactly twenty years ago. If you've got time to find out more, I'd be very interested."

"Pretty name, Jacinta. Maybe I should think about paying you a visit up at the North Pole."

"Not sure that's a good idea, Mom. They don't treat dogs particularly well around here."

Her mother had a soft spot for abused animals and was on the board of the province's SPCA.

"Oh, no! What do they do to them?"

"They chain them up and never walk them. Chained outside even in the coldest weather."

"But that's awful. You've got to light a fire under them, dear one. You've got to tell them that dogs are social creatures and need to move around."

"They'd just see it as meddling . . . criticism from an outsider. They grew up like this—used to have sled dogs that were working dogs and not pets, and they were tied up all summer . . ."

"Sled dogs ought to be treated decently as well," her mother cut in.

Lori was sorry she'd brought it up, afraid her mom would try to turn her into the standard-bearer for animal rights in Stormy Cove.

But her mother just said, "At least take one of the dogs for an occasional walk. But not in a blizzard."

Lori promised to, even if she didn't know how she'd manage something like that.

"It's a tough balancing act, Mom. I don't want to suck up to them, but I also can't be judgmental. I want to be myself. I want to portray the people the way they are, with all their strengths and weaknesses."

She heard her mother heave a sigh.

"My dear girl, you're so different from me; you take after your father. I'm convinced that people *like* you. Remember: nobody needs to know anything about our German grandfather and submarines."

Lori chewed on the inside of her mouth. Her mother seemed really stuck on that.

"You won't believe this, but when I was at a lodge for the night on the way here, some kind of German baron was there. And what did he go on about? German subs off Newfoundland. Of all things!"

"A baron? What was his name?"

"Who knows? I've got his card somewhere."

Her mother was suddenly in a hurry.

"I've got to get to court, sweetie. I'll let you know about Jacinta. It'll take a little time, got a lot on my plate. And don't let that nice man from the village wrap you around his little finger. Take care."

"I can look out for myself," she said, but her mother had already hung up.

That's Mom. Doesn't pull any punches, Lori thought.

Outside her window, the wind blew large snowflakes around like fluttering rags. Lori watched the spectacle, lost in thought. Conversations with her mother often ended with a question mark. She didn't know why. Probably because she was a lawyer and used to keeping her cards close to the vest? No point in worrying about it.

She felt a slight jab in her thigh. The talisman. She fumbled for the birdlike object in her pocket and put it on the kitchen table. Maybe she would make a key-chain fob out of it. Mona Blackwood's question crossed her mind. She found the ice-fishing photograph on her laptop and opened it. There were at least a dozen faces, and she could only name a few of them. She didn't want to ask Noah just then, but Patience could certainly help her. She squinted out the kitchen window and could actually make out the outline of her neighbors' blue pickup. She printed out the photo and put on something warm. But even the short walk showed her that this storm was still merciless. She could barely keep her eyes open, and she wouldn't have been surprised if she'd strayed off in the wrong direction.

She struggled to open the front door with her thick gloves on, but it opened all of a sudden as if by a phantom hand that then pulled her inside.

"You shouldn't go out in this weather, my love," Ches said. "I thought you were at Noah's."

She pulled her hood back and gasped for air.

"Yes, I was there yesterday, but he brought me back today."

"Why? It's dangerous to be all alone. He should've kept you at his place. Come on in."

Lori took off her boots and parka and followed him up to the main floor.

"Patience isn't here?"

"No, she's at her mom's in Crockett Harbour. She has to stay there until the road's open."

"Then how did you get back?"

"I took her there and came back before the storm. Come sit down."

Lori stayed on her feet. She couldn't remember seeing his truck in front of the house yesterday.

"I just wanted to ask Patience something, about people's names in some pictures, people I don't know."

"Maybe I can help you."

She paused. Her instincts urged her not to be alone in the house with Ches.

"Oh, it's nothing urgent. Really just an excuse to have tea with Patience."

"Ah, good idea. Not many people drop in for a chat."

"But Una must have."

Ches folded his arms and cleared his throat.

"Una had other women friends . . . Patience would go on and on about births, and Una—I mean, maybe she didn't want to hear about them. If you get my meaning."

"I don't," Lori replied.

Ches rubbed his back against the edge of the kitchen counter and gave an embarrassed laugh.

"Una and Cletus didn't have children."

"Oh, I see."

Lori wondered if Patience, as a midwife, wasn't bound by doctor-patient confidentiality. Or whether such rules even applied in Stormy Cove. She turned to leave.

"I'll come by when Patience is back. She wanted to show me how to make a wall hanging."

"Well, I certainly can't show you that. But I'll walk you home."

Lori protested to be polite but was actually relieved to have help getting home safely.

The power was still on. She was working on her photos and notes when the phone rang.

"Lori?" a woman asked.

She didn't recognize Patience's voice right away because of the static on the line.

Where had she gotten Lori's number? From Noah? She'd never given it to anyone else in Stormy Cove.

"I just talked to Ches, and he said you wanted something from me—some people's names or something?"

"Oh, it's nothing. I just thought you could help me identify people in my pictures."

"Couldn't Ches help you?"

Patience sounded tense, maybe in reaction to the nerve-racking howling of the storm.

"He offered to, but I was actually looking forward to seeing you—and it really isn't pressing."

"He could at least have offered you a cup of tea."

"Oh, no, I'm fine. I've got a lot to do here. I was at Noah's yesterday and had to drop everything here."

"Noah takes good care of you, doesn't he? He's a good man."

"Yes, everybody's very kind to me," Lori agreed diplomatically.

"People are worried about you for sure. Selina Gould saw you leaving the house. She was very concerned. You can't go wandering in a storm like that."

Selina Gould. Of course. Patience had gotten Lori's phone number from *her*. The landlord had to contact the phone company to get a line put in. Every step she took was monitored.

"I hope you can come home soon," Lori said. "Molly is sure to be homesick."

Patience giggled.

"No way. Molly loves it at Granny's. But I've had my fill of storms. A couple of babies are due soon. And I don't want to miss the party at the Hardy Sailor. You're coming, of course."

"A party? Noah said it was a mummers competition."

"Oh, that was postponed. No, it's a talent show. But don't expect much. Sometimes it's awfully embarrassing." Patience sounded downright jolly.

"I wouldn't miss it," Lori promised.

"See you then," Patience said.

Late that afternoon, when it was already dark, Lori was seized by a craving for vegetable soup. She was peeling carrots in the kitchen, when a lightbulb suddenly went on in her head.

The bird carving. She remembered where she'd seen something like it before: in the storage compartment under the seat of Noah's snowmobile.

CHAPTER 18

Three days later, the blizzard let up as abruptly as it had begun. Silence had never seemed so loud to Lori. Driving to the Hardy Sailor, she felt a sort of pleasurable expectation at seeing people again and plunging into some hustle and bustle. She was not disappointed: The Hardy Sailor was already bustling by ten, and it was almost impossible to move around by eleven. By twelve, you had to bellow to be heard above the din.

On a stage in the middle of the room, the talent show Patience had mentioned was already underway, and Lori quickly realized that "talent," for some more inebriated participants, was merely an excuse to draw attention to themselves. Four men had to drag a fifty-year-old guy off the stage who couldn't play the guitar or sing, but did both. The same thing did *not* happen to a young woman in a black camisole and pink stockings, though she couldn't sing either. The singer who followed had some talent, at least, and earned a lot of laughs. Her song was about being a "Newfie spy"—always at the window with her binoculars, watching everything and everybody in the village.

People joined in on the chorus, even Aurelia from the library, who surfaced beside Lori and explained that the song was a parody of an old popular Newfoundland tune. Lori caught a glimpse of Patience and Ches in the crowd, but she'd found a good corner for taking pictures and didn't want to give it up. Some customers waved at her, others simply gawked out of curiosity. More people surely knew her than the other way round. Then she heard her name being called and turned to see Mavis approaching with a cold bottle of beer and the deepest plunging neckline in the place, while shrieking, "A ladies' beer for the lady; no calories."

Knowing better than to refuse, Lori couldn't take offense at that and accepted the Moosehead Light gracefully.

Mavis waved her arms.

"Where's your Romeo?"

"No idea," Lori replied, ignoring the insinuation. Didn't she tell Noah she'd come? In Vancouver that would have been a firm invitation, a date.

Mavis pulled a face.

"He's probably at the bar like always. He waits for women to find him so he doesn't have to make any effort himself."

"He's sure to be having white wine." Lori grinned, then stuck out her tongue at Mavis, who gave her the finger and smirked back.

A band was setting up on stage. Ten minutes after midnight—dancing was to begin any minute now. Lori was in no mood to dance with strangers smelling of alcohol, but mostly she wanted to keep an eye on her equipment.

She scanned the crowd again and caught sight of Noah. He was wearing a shiny black shirt, unbuttoned at the top. He wasn't looking at her but at a dark-haired woman who was shouting something to him. It was the woman who'd come out of his house before. He shook his head, but the woman came closer and said something that made him laugh. He put his hand, in which he held a bottle of beer, on her shoulder for a second. Her hand reached farther down and grabbed him by the genitals. He laughed again and pushed her away gently.

Lori felt her face freeze. She turned her head sideways to avoid Noah's eyes, but realized Patience had caught her looking. Lori wanted desperately to get out of there. She barreled through the crowd without looking right or left. Two people said something, but she pretended not to hear and pushed on ahead.

When she tore open the door, she noticed she was carrying her ski jacket over her arm. The shock of the cold made her retreat inside and hastily put the jacket on. She zipped up and bent down to pick up her camera bag.

"Leaving so soon?" someone behind her asked.

Nate, Noah's brother.

She nodded.

"You've got to stay. We all want to see Noah finally dance."

Nate was visibly tipsy. Until then, he'd hardly dared make eye contact with her. She turned toward the door.

"He's already found somebody he can dance with. Have fun watching."

She was in such a hurry to get to her car that she almost slipped on the snow. A truck had parked right behind her, so she couldn't leave.

"What goddamn little shit did this?" she shouted.

A young man stood nearby, smoking a cigarette.

"Is this your pickup?" she shouted.

He shook his head but came over.

"It's Brent's. Why?"

"Why? He's blocking my car!"

"Oh," the man said, his face hidden under his baseball cap. "You can just repark it."

"I can?"

"The door's unlocked and the key's inside. Everybody does that around here."

The man hopped into the truck and turned on the motor. Now Lori realized she'd seen him once in the village store. He backed up several feet and blinked the lights.

Lori pulled out and turned onto the road. She was still in a rage but plenty sober enough to drive carefully through the pitch-black night.

When she got home, she looked at the clock: still early enough to call Vancouver and vent.

She paced up and down like a tiger. Then she called her friend Danielle, who'd had twins three months ago, but got the answering machine.

Maybe she should call again in a while once the babies were in bed. Besides, what was she going to say to Danielle anyway? That she was furious because some man was having fun at a party, somebody she wasn't even involved with? And that women in Stormy Cove could apparently be pretty bold?

She'd make a fool of herself. Now she'd have questions to answer. Are you falling for the guy? Is he falling for you? What's the deal between you two? Is there even one at all?

That's how women in Vancouver thought. Customs were different here in Stormy Cove, and she really hadn't learned them yet.

She'd try her friend Craig. He was sure to listen patiently to her story without dramatizing it. Sometimes it seemed like Craig knew her better than she did herself. He knew how to make a mouse out of an elephant and put things in perspective.

She picked up the receiver, and a busy signal indicated she had a message.

"This is Lloyd Weston. I'm at the Birch Tree Lodge. Maybe we could get together so I can tell you more about our dig. It would be nice if you could find the time."

Screw your dig! she thought, slamming the receiver down. She knew perfectly well she was taking out her frustration on the wrong person, but she had to unload it somehow.

She grabbed a quart of milk from the fridge, impatiently and awkwardly, and it hit the floor, making a white mess. Swearing loudly, she got a dish towel. At that moment, the side door opened and somebody called hello.

Patience.

"I'm up here," Lori shouted back, mopping the floor. "Don't bother taking off your boots, I'm cleaning the floor anyway."

She was still on her knees when Patience came into the kitchen and sized up the situation.

"You've spilled some milk," she said in a matter-of-fact voice. "Who drinks milk on a Saturday night?"

Lori looked up at her, and they both laughed.

Patience gave her a hand up. Lori flung the dish towel into the sink.

"What are you doing here? Is the party over already?"

"No, but I saw you take off." Patience's fingers kneaded her gloves. "Don't be mad at Noah because of . . . Ginette's always like that when she's had one too many. A lot of women do that—it's a long tradition. In the old days . . . they all would grab a guy by the balls."

She took the towel out of the sink and wiped a white splash off the refrigerator.

"People in Vancouver don't behave like that, I'm sure, but here . . . nobody gives it a second thought."

So Patience had seen it all and drawn her own conclusions. Lori had underestimated her neighbor yet again.

"Noah and I are not an item, even if a lot of people think we are," Lori said primly. "He can do whatever he pleases."

"Well, Noah and Ginette aren't an item either," Patience said. "I think she did it on purpose, to annoy you."

"What? Why?"

"She's always been like that. She flirts with men, and when she's drunk, she throws herself at them. We all hate her."

Lori was so surprised at the candidness that she didn't ask who Patience meant by "we."

"Have you ever told Ginette that to her face?"

Patience looked at her in astonishment.

"Told her what?"

"That you find her behavior completely out of line?"

"No, no. People . . . people would hold that against me. Then I'm the bad girl."

A momentary silence. Patience cocked her head and looked at Lori. "Are you going back to the Hardy Sailor? Noah's sure to be missing you."

Lori shook her head. "You know, at first he wanted me to go there so badly, then he didn't show up until midnight and . . . he's probably embarrassed if people think that he and I . . . and there's nothing going on, I swear."

"It's all Ginette's fault. Noah's a good man, you'll see." She turned to leave. "I've got to go. Ches is waiting in the truck."

It crossed Lori's mind that she hadn't heard the truck come back. What would Ches think about all this?

"I feel terrible that you two went out of your way twice because of me."

"Oh, it's nothing. But you shouldn't hold it against Ginette; she's not worth it."

With that, she rattled down the stairs and slammed the door.

This was exactly what Lori didn't want to have happen. To take sides with some villagers or get caught up with their lives so that she couldn't be a neutral observer anymore. But how could she stay aloof from this closely knit community that fate had thrown together? As long as she was living here, she had to depend on their help and on being one of them, or else she'd never get the book done. She had to live in peace and harmony with them and set her emotions aside, hiding them behind a smile even when she didn't feel like it.

She needed some space—even if only for a few days. And maybe she needed a nice archaeologist.

CHAPTER 19

Mavis gave Lori an amused look as she paid for gas at the store.

"You left much too early. The party didn't really get started until late."

Lori feigned absorption in entering her pin number. She hoped Mavis would shut up and not tell her what had happened after she'd left the bar. In vain.

"Even Noah danced! Imagine that. He practically never dances."

"How nice for him," Lori commented, keeping herself composed.

If they can do it, so can I. Harmony and steadiness no matter what.

Maybe it was the saleslady's cheerful expression that prompted her to keep talking.

"I'd have liked to stay longer, but I needed to get up early this morning. I'm meeting an archaeologist at the Birch Tree Lodge who's going to take me to see his dig. Next time I'll certainly stay for the dancing. I owe you a beer!"

Mavis handed her the receipt.

"Maybe it's good you left so early. Ginette had lousy luck. Somebody slashed her tires."

Lori was about to leave, but spun around.

"What? Are you sure?"

Mavis was obviously pleased at the effect her words had.

"Of course I'm sure. Saw it with my own eyes."

"That's awful. Who'd do such a thing?"

"Somebody who can't stand her, maybe."

Lori shook her head.

"In Vancouver, I wouldn't be at all surprised, but here?"

She went to the door.

"I hope the police catch whoever did it soon."

Mavis banged the cash register drawer shut.

"The cops? They're too slow. Scores get settled differently around here. There's sure to be payback."

Lori's heart was pounding as she drove out of the village. She kept seeing Mavis's smile of schadenfreude. Did the villagers of Stormy Cove believe *she* had slashed Ginette's tires? Probably Patience wasn't the only one who saw the episode in the pub. And Lori had attracted even more attention with her sudden departure. She could have slashed Ginette's tires and taken off while everybody was partying inside.

Now Mavis would tell everybody that Lori was skipping town: *How suspicious is* that! *Just so happens she has to go to Birch Tree Lodge right away.*

When the car began to fishtail, she snapped out of it.

Keep calm, Lori, keep calm. You're not the center of the universe here. Nobody would suspect a photographer from Vancouver would do a rotten thing like that. Ginette isn't popular in Stormy Cove. Maybe she led some guy on and then dumped him, and he got even. Mavis's schadenfreude was probably directed at Ginette, not her.

After a while, she'd settled down enough to take in the landscape. Walls of snow soared up everywhere. It seemed like a white Monument Valley, with mighty rock towers and bizarre shapes. But the road was well plowed. Some plows must have cleared it early that morning, restoring order immediately after chaos.

The farther she got from Stormy Cove, the more she relaxed. The stillness of the frozen landscape and the soft hum of the motor tended to lull her. She greeted the mountains on the horizon like old friends and waved to a lone oncoming trucker. As she came round a curve, she saw two moose disappear into the bush before she could whip out her camera.

She reached the lodge in two hours. There wasn't a single car in the parking lot. Had Weston left? She hadn't told him she was coming.

Someone came outside from the office and waved when Lori opened the car door. It was Hope Hussey, the owner. Lori was struck again by how young she looked in her light purple fleece jacket—but very self-assured.

"Come into the dining room," she shouted. "I need coffee, and you look like you could use some too."

"Am I the only one here?" Lori inquired.

"No, no, we've got a bunch of Canadian archaeologists, but they're over in Port aux Choix today, looking at the finds in the museum."

Hope went around the lodge building and opened the door from the patio. The soothing warmth of the fireplace streamed toward them at once. Hope made for the counter and started the coffee machine.

"Have you ever been to Port au Choix?"

Lori shook her head.

"Interesting place. They've dug up Inuit and Indian settlements. Forty-five hundred years ago, there were Indians living on the coast there, but the climate was warmer then. Where did I put those muffins?"

She found them in a plastic container behind the counter.

"Gooseberries. Picked them myself."

She put the muffins on a plate and continued as she got out two mugs.

"Yes, and when it got cold again, the Eskimos came, about twenty-eight hundred years ago, I think it was. They built homes with whale ribs covered with sealskins. And after the Eskimos, the Indians returned, about two thousand years ago. That's my history lesson for today. I tell it to all the guests so they don't think Newfoundland history began with European immigrants."

They sat down in the brightly lit lounge, with large windows on three sides. After the confined spaces of the buildings in Stormy Cove, Lori felt like a fish released from an aquarium into the sea.

The aroma of good coffee reminded her of the cafés in Vancouver.

"But there are none of the original Indians in Newfoundland today, are there?"

Hope stirred her coffee vigorously.

"No. First of all, the Europeans drove them away from the coast and into the interior, so they couldn't fish anymore and almost starved to death. Next, we infected them with our diseases and exterminated most of them that way. And some were butchered by European settlers."

She leaned back against the sofa.

"So what are you escaping from that brings you here?"

The question came so unexpectedly that Lori had to laugh in spite of herself. She stalled by sipping her coffee.

"I simply had to . . . I had to make sure that another world was still out there. More than the cosmos of Stormy Cove."

"Wow! For a Vancouver gal, Stormy Cove must have been a tremendous culture shock. How did you get through the storm?"

Lori had to smile at the expression "Vancouver gal" coming from a woman younger than herself.

"A friend took me in when the power went off. My place just has electric heating."

"Yes, nothing beats a good wood stove and human warmth."

Something in Hope's voice made Lori prick up her ears. It sounded as if she knew more than she was saying.

"What have people been telling you?"

"That one of the fishermen's after you."

Lori was speechless.

"Watch out for sweet talk," Hope admonished. "Men around here are super attentive until they've tied the knot, and then they do more or less what *they* like."

Lori stiffened her back, ramrod straight.

"Oh, I see lots of public affection—like at the Hardy Sailor last night, it sometimes gets *very* physical."

"Sure, kissing and grabbing between friends and relatives, but not between spouses."

"So is it in good taste when guys and gals who aren't married grab each other between the legs in front of the whole world?" Lori asked angrily.

Hope looked quizzical.

"Not anymore . . . why? Did you see something like that? People really ought to know that nowadays that's called sexual harassment, even here. But years ago—well, it used to be perfectly normal. And I must say that nobody interpreted that behavior as sexual. It was more . . . an everyday gesture. I know . . ."—Hope noticed Lori's raised eyebrow—"I know it sounds odd to an emancipated woman from Vancouver, but I'd be the first to tell you the truth if that wasn't so. People were just cruder then, even when they were being affectionate."

Lori said nothing. There was no point in arguing with Hope about personal boundaries or transgressions. She didn't want to open up a second front in the Birch Tree Lodge. But Hope evidently felt the need to talk.

"Women here are strong, believe me, they're not submissive crickets on the hearth, but in the end, it's always a man's world. When I took over this lodge after my father's death, everybody expected the business to go belly up. They simply didn't think I could do it. Hunting and fishing—that's a man's business, and if a woman tries to make money from hunting and fishing, they'll undermine you."

"But by now they must admit how successful you are, right?" Lori objected.

"Yes, nobody utters a peep about it. Money talks."

Hope's laugh had a hard edge to it. They sipped their coffee in silence until Hope reopened the subject.

"I want to be straight with you. I heard that one of the Whalens took you to his place during the storm."

"I imagine you even know what we had for dinner," Lori said drily.

"Noah Whalen. Does it bother you that people know that?"

The muffin crumbled between Lori's fingers.

"I find it disturbing that these matters are broadcast far and wide. It's—"

"You need to understand it's not just gossip. It's important to be informed and to know the person next to you and what he's doing."

"But where's the privacy in all this?"

"Security takes precedence. People here don't die anonymously in their homes like they do in big cities, where somebody only discovers them weeks later."

"No, here they're killed, and the body's found months later in a peculiar grave."

Hope said nothing at first but started rubbing her right arm rhythmically.

"There was a rumor making the rounds that it was one of the Whalens, but I don't know for sure who or from which family. Lots of Whalens around."

This was supposed to be a pleasant chat, Lori thought to herself. If only she hadn't brought up the subject of Jacinta. But now there was no going back.

"Are you trying to warn me about something, Hope?"

"I talked to Lloyd Weston about all that business. His team is coming back this summer because they discovered another prehistoric grave. 'Lloyd,' I said, 'it will open up old wounds if you start digging up there.'"

"And what did he say?"

"Maybe that's a good thing, because then they'll talk about Jacinta again, and maybe somebody will come clean."

"How well do you know him?"

"He and his team were staying at my father's lodge when it happened."

She looked at her watch and jumped up.

"I've got to see to dinner. Making butternut squash soup and chicken fricassee with orange sauce."

She charged off, her steps echoing on the wooden floor.

Lori looked out on the frozen lake and noticed dark cracks in the ice. Was that because of the storm or was spring finally on the way?

She mulled over Hope's words. What was that all about, the rumors about it being one of the Whalens? The name *Whalen* was as common around here as *Smith* and *Lee* in Vancouver. If she meant Noah, why didn't she just come out with it? Lori couldn't fathom Hope's motives. This capable and resolute woman didn't seem inclined to gossip. Lori decided to bring it up with her again.

But for the moment, she felt like getting some fresh air after those long, stormy days trapped inside. A little while later, as she was tramping along a snowmobile trail through the woods, the silence and motion-lessness of the surroundings covered her like a blanket. She noticed how calm she felt—even her coffee palpitations faded away—and there was nothing beyond pushing her body harder, the crunch of her steps in the snow, and her dripping nose. She marched ahead as if in a trance. No living creature, no movement disrupted her concentration.

She had to confess that it was sometimes good just to give yourself over to the elements. To something so powerful that was impervious to you. Lori understood intuitively, for the first time, that serenity and equilibrium could be achieved in this way. She suddenly experienced a lightness of being, as if her soul were vibrating like a shimmering dragonfly.

The path snaking its way through the bush was navigable only because snow-covered treetops marked it. The underbrush was buried in snow. Lori kept sinking into it, and exhausted, she decided to turn back.

But the way back seemed much longer—had she really gone that far? Her blood sugar sank, and she scolded herself for not putting a chocolate bar in her backpack. Soon she was thirsty but resisted the temptation to eat snow. Hadn't she read somewhere that thirst was one of the biggest problems for those first white Arctic explorers when their fuel was exhausted and they couldn't melt snow? If they'd swallowed snow and ice, their body temperature would have dropped dangerously low, and they could have rapidly frozen to death.

She came to a fork in the trail she didn't remember. Which way had she turned? She looked around for some clue, but everything appeared uniform and nondescript. The trail, she said to herself, must end in a loop back to the lodge where guests would go for snowmobile rides. She took the path that led straight ahead, but a deep feeling of insecurity set in.

After twenty minutes, tired and numb, Lori heard the roar of a snowmobile. When it came through the trees, she didn't recognize Hope at first. But she'd happily have hitched a ride with a complete stranger; that's how desperate she was.

"You should have let somebody know where you were going," Hope said through her open helmet. "You can get lost fast in this place."

Lori clambered up on the rear seat. Back at the lodge, she learned that one of the kitchen staff had happened to see Lori leave and told her boss. When she wasn't back after two hours, Hope went looking.

"My dear girl, girl, girl," Hope said in the warm lounge, but she didn't sound unfriendly. Lori felt like a naughty child nonetheless.

She had two cups of bakeapple tea and half a chocolate bar, then retired to her room to lie down. She woke up to a knock at the door and somebody calling, "Dinner's ready!"

She was so sweaty that she showered and put on a fluffy wool sweater. Entering the empty dining room, she heard a loud medley of voices coming from the lounge. The table had one place setting. Hope brought her a heaping plate of food.

"Take your time," she said. "The others are already having coffee and carrot cake, but I'll save a piece for you."

Lori smiled in gratitude and dove into the chicken à l'orange. She was still a bit dopey from her nap.

"Would you like some wine with that?" a voice behind her asked.

Lloyd Weston put a bottle and briefcase on the table and took a seat across from her.

"But of course." Lori held up a glass to him.

"Wonderful to see you here. How are you getting along in the northern wilds?"

"Famously. Some things need getting used to, but I suppose people have to get used to me as well. Nobody's chased me away yet."

She tried to strike a comic note, and Weston played along.

"Why should they? A photographer from Vancouver has enormous conversational value. How is the photography going?"

"Really well. I've already got many great pictures, and it can only get better when they start fishing."

"I don't doubt it. I love this area."

She asked a cautious question.

"After all that's happened? You weren't exactly treated very well last time."

"Yes, I love to come back here, though many people don't see why. But look, I'm an archaeologist and I know that people sometimes do strange things to assuage their demons and their fears. Now just as in earlier eras—makes no difference. This innocent girl's murder triggered a fear they had to keep in check by making accusations of guilt."

He picked up his glass.

"As you see, I'm drawn back to this place again and again. We're having the annual meeting of the Archaeological Society here, and I can't think of a better place than this lodge. Let's drink to the projects that have landed us in this wild part of the world."

Their glasses clinked.

As Lori swished the wine back and forth in her mouth, she eyed him discreetly. He looked different somehow than she remembered. Of course: the beard! He was clean shaven and looked younger as a result, less professorial.

"Hope told me," she said, to revive the conversation, "that you stayed at this lodge during the first dig. This must feel a bit like home to you."

Weston laughed.

"Better than home, because they cook for me, and I don't have to take out the garbage."

"Hope's father really saved us back then," the archaeologist continued. "We were at another lodge at first, closer to the dig. But then it burned down."

"Oh, how awful! Was anybody in the building?"

"No, thank goodness. It was just before we quit work. Most important of all, the artifacts we'd found and all our documents were in an office trailer. That was an enormous piece of luck."

Lori patted her mouth with her napkin before asking: "Was that after . . . I mean . . ."

"After Jacinta disappeared? No, that happened about a week later. I know what you're driving at. You're thinking it might have been revenge."

He shook his head. "No, on that day the world was still in order, if you will, and everybody was sympathetic and glad nobody had been hurt."

"But some things were lost—clothes, personal ID, and items like that?"

"Of course. Many people lost some personal belongings, but you have to realize—archaeologists would much rather lose their own things than have their research destroyed. It would have been a loss for all of Canada."

"And the lodge owner?"

"He was lucky as well because he was insured and started up a new business with the money. But I actually wanted to give you this."

He set his glass down and opened his briefcase.

"These are pictures of our earlier digs, so that you can see how things work. This is the boulder layer after we took away the vegetation on top. Here's the layer with the walrus tusk and the quartz knives. And here you can see how the skeleton was positioned in the grave."

He pushed one picture after another across the table.

"Here's the harpoon point and the whistle made from animal bone. And this is a pendant made of bone or antler, you see the hole at the top—"

"What's that?" she interrupted him. One of the objects looked familiar.

"That's a projectile tip, made of bone, but we don't know from what animal. The prehistoric Indians hunted walrus and seals using this projectile."

"A bird!" Lori exclaimed.

"It could be a bird bone, but we don't know."

"No, it looks like a bird, don't you see? The wings on both sides, the pointed skull, the beak!"

Weston took a closer look at the photograph and said, cautiously, "Yes, you could look at it that way, a stylized bird. Very stylized. But it most probably is an arrowhead."

"I found an arrowhead like that at my place in Stormy Cove. Same size, same shape."

Weston studied her.

"Where did you find it?"

"Between the washer and the dryer. It looks exactly the same. Could be a copy."

Weston's face suggested skepticism.

"This arrowhead is the oldest of its kind that we know."

He put his hands flat on the table and stretched out his arms as if he were holding the table down.

"It vanished the night of the fire. I can't describe the exact circumstances because the police don't want them made public—and to be honest, we don't either because it's too embarrassing. But I can tell you one thing: it reappeared eight months later."

Lori looked at his slim fingers, now raised like claws. Weston did not continue. She pieced the puzzle together.

"Was the arrowhead found in Jacinta's grave?"

Weston continued to look at her without a word.

"Maybe I was wrong," she stuttered. "I . . . um . . . a lot of objects could look alike. I thought it was more like an amulet really, a pendant. Or a fish with fins above and below. Certainly not . . . not a spear tip or an arrowhead . . . not a projectile."

To her surprise, Weston seemed satisfied with this explanation. His eyes stared past her. The voices from the lounge grew louder, and some footsteps approaching the dining room distracted him. He muttered, "I agree—there must be some mistake, but you can send me the arrowhead when you get home. You've got my address."

He smiled.

"Have you tried the carrot cake yet? Divine, I tell you."

Lori stood up when he did and was glad that he turned to two men and a woman standing in the dining room.

She thought of the arrowhead under the seat of Noah's snowmobile, just like the one from her laundry room, and her temperature rose. She might be mistaken about one, but not two.

CHAPTER 20

Lori managed to shake off her dark thoughts. All evening she played poker with Weston and two of his female colleagues, who would occasionally share hair-raising stories about their digs in exotic countries. Lori soon realized that she was sitting across from experts who forgave her not only for knowing next to nothing about archaeology but also for being a mediocre poker player.

"We refined our poker skills sitting out in the Pampas, miles from anywhere. We had to kill time for hours on end," the women explained graciously.

The next day, they took Lori on a snowmobile tour—she was given her own machine—that started on the trail she'd hiked the previous day. She saw now how she had taken the wrong path back. What in the world would have happened if Hope hadn't come looking for her? The sun was shining now, and the snowscape looked almost colorful beneath the deep blue sky. Lori found the snowmobile easier to steer than she'd expected. She accelerated on flat stretches and savored the weightless feeling. She learned how to shift her weight around a curve and to avoid tree branches and boulders. When their party glided from the woods onto a broad plain, a vast, stunning horizon opened out around them. The expanse and boundlessness made Lori feel she was swimming over huge white waves. All of a sudden, she wished Noah were with her. But she suppressed the desire at once and concentrated on the snowmobiles ahead.

Weston didn't bring up the subject of the dig planned for that summer, though he sat next to her and chatted all through dinner. She was grateful that he wasn't pushy in any way. An archaeologist probably learned to be patient, like a wildlife photographer. Or a female photographer in a Newfoundland village.

When the other guests left the next day, melancholy settled in. The rooms felt empty and the sudden quiet disconcerting. Lori no longer felt the need for quiet contemplation or withdrawal. It was time for her to leave too.

She found Hope in her office with the cook, shopping list in hand.

Before Lori could open her mouth, she exclaimed, "You're leaving us again so soon?"

Lori laughed.

"How'd you guess?"

"Oh, that look in your eye says homesick, eh, Sally? Doesn't it, eh?"

The cook shrugged, smiled, and left the room.

Lori made a face. "Do you mean homesick for Vancouver?"

"No, no, I don't mean that. No fishermen waiting for you there."

"Noah Whalen and I are not an item, if that's what you mean. He's just a very nice man."

"Yeah, of course he is, my dear."

Hope scribbled something on the list while Lori kept talking.

"Hope, it seemed like you were suggesting that one of the Whalens was suspected of murdering Jacinta. Why did you tell me that rumor? It doesn't really seem like you."

Hope looked up. In the harsh office light, Lori could see dark rings under her eyes.

"You've got to learn to live with rumors like that if you want to be with Noah. It's not about to go away."

"But I told you! Noah and I—"

"I had to learn to live with rumors myself. When Gideon's lodge burned down, people whispered that my father set it on fire so *he* would get more customers."

"But the police ruled that out, right?"

"People trim their truth the way they want it, my love. Word is, you slashed Ginette's tires out of jealousy."

Lori froze.

"What? You heard *that*?"

Hope put her hand on her shoulder.

"Don't get upset. People don't really believe it. It's just a good story, fun to pass on, spices up your daily routine. Truth be told, nobody trusts you to handle a knife properly."

"So why would they say that?"

"It gets their mind off things, that's all. Simple as that."

She opened the door to the adjoining room.

"I'll make up your bill. When are you heading out?"

"After lunch, if that works for you."

Hope nodded and went back to studying her list.

She brought the bill when Lori was having soup and a sandwich in the dining room by herself.

"Do you remember that German baron from last time you were here? He asked for your name and e-mail address."

Lori lowered her spoon.

"Why?"

"He wanted to send you something about submarines. In any case, I passed them on. Maybe you'll hear from him."

Lori was confused. What made the baron think that she of all people was interested in submarines? She hadn't said a word about them.

But Hope snapped her out of her ruminations; she was going shopping in Corner Brook.

"I'm sure I'll see you back here soon enough," she called in a cheery voice before dashing out of the lodge.

Lori looked out on the snow and noticed that the cracks in the ice had grown wider. Drops of water fell from the fir branches even though it wasn't raining. As she carried her suitcase to the car, she tried to put her finger on a change in the air. Her cell phone rang.

The voice she heard made her heart skip a beat.

"Lori, where are you? Why don't you ever call me?"

"Danielle! I can't believe it's you! Give me just a second and I'll be all yours."

She threw her bag into the car and got in.

"Lorelei Finning, I haven't heard a word from you! I was beginning to worry."

Lori felt warmth spreading through her abdomen.

"I figured you were up to your ears in baby stuff and didn't want to bother you."

The last two times Lori was in Danielle's apartment, it was chaos: screaming children, diaper changes, and relatives scurrying around and constantly interrupting them with questions and advice. Danielle had looked so exhausted that Lori would have loved to whisk her away to a beach in the South Seas—she looked worse than she ever had when she was running a busy photography agency. But at the moment, she sounded more feisty, a bit pugnacious even. This was the old Danielle Lori knew from the days when the two of them fought side by side to get better contracts for freelance photographers.

"OK, so I've got twins, but that doesn't make me a leper! I sometimes feel like I've fallen off the face of the earth. People look at me kind of funny."

Lori heaved a sigh.

"Oh, I know exactly how you feel, Danielle."

Her answer released mutual heartfelt gushing that lasted until they were all caught up on each other's life and could find space for some critical feedback beyond the much-needed declarations of empathy.

"Keeping your distance? Now listen up!" Danielle exclaimed. "You can't fence yourself off from village life, Lori. That's just not possible if you're going to spend a whole year there. You're a human being, not a traffic light that only turns red or green."

"But I want to be a neutral observer. That's always been my strong suit."

"Sounds good in theory, but in reality—bottom drawer, no, the left one, yes, that's it—sorry, my sister's looking for some onesies—as I was saying, in the real world you've got to get in there with people. We've talked about this a lot."

"Yes, but—"

"I know what you're going to say, but you know what? I think you're still schlepping Germany around behind you. Somehow, you're still convinced that . . . that, if you just get a teensy-weensy bit assimilated, the world will come crashing down on your head."

I've never told her about Katja, Lori mused. If Danielle knew about her, and how she died, she wouldn't talk that way. But it had been so long now. And Lori didn't want to dredge up that nightmare again.

She gave Danielle a brief version of the situation with Noah, but it was somewhat censored because she hadn't gotten everything straightened out in her own mind. Then she got going on the scene in the Hardy Sailor.

"Now they think *I* slashed her tires out of jealousy!"

Danielle laughed.

"What a coup! Think about your future memoirs! There are intrigues in every village—I mean, those people live on top of each other. They're no saints any more than we are in the big city."

"I never expected *saints*; I'm not that naïve."

"I think you want to be an observer without being observed yourself—no, without being affected—inwardly, I mean. Does that sound about right?"

Lori was getting uncomfortable in the cold car. Her friend could read her like a book. But why did she always have to express everything in psychobabble?

"Oh, come on. Could you please just cheer me up a little?"

"OK. I'm terrific at that! Lori, you can sleep at night, you're free as a bird, you have no money worries, you go on many adventures and you'll probably have some thrilling sex soon—while, in my case, passion has hit rock bottom. The kids are all-consuming for the moment. Ralph must really feel abandoned."

At that instant, something flashed through Lori's mind: What if Cletus had something to do with Una's disappearance? What did that insolent kid say at Elsie Smith's house? With an ocean next door it's easy to make bodies disappear. They'll never find them if the current's right.

She shivered.

"Don't worry yourself about that, Danielle, it'll come back. It's nature's way. I read that when men become dads, their testosterone level plummets and—"

"How are you getting along without Andrew?"

"I feel really crappy sometimes, but I have to learn to let him go."

That sounded like more psychobabble, but at the same time, she knew she was right.

"Enjoy your time with the kids, sweetheart. It's really special to be the center of their universe for a while."

She heard Danielle sigh.

"Why do we always want precisely the thing we don't have?"

Lori pondered this question on her leisurely drive back to Stormy Cove, having decided against stopping by Corner Brook after all.

Did she yearn for Noah because it was preposterous for a photographer from Vancouver to take up with a fisherman in the remotest corner of a remote region?

Snap out of it, Lori! The last thing you need is to get even more involved.

It was no accident that she hadn't told her friend about Jacinta's death and Una's disappearance. Danielle would just have said that murders can happen anywhere, so why not in a fishing village? Just because there are fewer inhabitants? She'd probably have accused Lori of stirring things up out of sheer boredom.

The road in front of her car shone. No ice, just moisture. Gulls floated on easy wing beats through air that seemed more transparent than a few days ago. Rivulets emerged from the snow banks beside the road. Lori came to a sudden stop at the turnoff to Stormy Cove. She had to make a firm resolution that she could keep during the coming days. It materialized suddenly in her mind: she would stand up to them.

But then she realized that she didn't know who "them" was supposed to be.

A truck was coming out of the turnoff. *They're probably wondering what I'm doing, stopped here like this,* Lori thought. She recognized Archie Whalen behind the wheel; beside him was—could it be? . . . Patience. What was she doing in Archie's truck? Maybe her car got stuck, and Archie had come to her rescue.

But when she made it home and pulled into her driveway, she saw Patience's car but not Ches's truck. She went for her bag in the trunk. The sound of a motor came nearer and stopped. Patience climbed down from Archie's truck and waved to her.

Archie got out too, and they both came over.

"We were worried about you," Patience exclaimed. "We wondered if something had happened."

Lori immediately felt guilty. Of course people here would be worried—what did she expect?

"I was at the Birch Tree Lodge for a few days," she replied. "Snowmobiling."

"Oh, *that's* where you went," Patience said, looking at Archie, who was frowning. "We asked all over but never thought of that."

She seemed a little miffed that Lori had failed to inform them.

"I'll be sure to let you know next time," Lori promised, but something held her back from saying she was sorry. Maybe the disapproval in Archie's eyes. Besides, she *had* told Mavis, and the village store usually functioned like a radio station anyway.

Archie cleared his throat.

"Tomorrow is Sunday dinner at Nate's, for the whole family. We're expecting you too. With your camera."

It sounded like an order; the message was crystal clear. The invitation said he was on her side, the outsider's, the "tire-slasher lady's" side. She was almost touched as she thanked him.

"Don't bother to have breakfast; there'll be lots to eat," Patience chimed in. "And before I forget: You need the names of those people in the ice-fishing picture. I can drop by this evening."

"What do you need names for?" Archie wanted to know.

"To archive them," Lori replied. "Later generations will surely want to know who's in the photo. It's like a historical document."

She remembered that she'd given Ches a different reason a couple of days ago. Archie and Patience exchanged looks.

"I'm getting the impression spring's here," she said, walking to the front door with her bag. "Am I wrong?"

"You're right! The ice is breaking up," Patience shouted back.

Lori heard Archie's truck leave as she entered the house. She turned up the heat, filled the kettle, and took a look around her mini-empire. She felt like she'd been gone for an eternity.

The contact with the outside world had done her good. She felt on the same wavelength as people like Lloyd Weston. He too was a visitor from the outside world; he'd had some unpleasant experiences up here but nevertheless wasn't intimidated.

As she sat at the table with her hot coffee, she replayed the conversations of the past few days.

Then put down her cup with a loud rattle.

Her eyes looked all over the table. Then under the table. Nothing.

The arrowhead was gone.

CHAPTER 21

The item that Lloyd Weston had identified as a projectile tip was nowhere to be found, even after a thorough search. And Lori was absolutely certain she'd left it on the table.

The doors to the house had been unlocked during her trip—nobody locked their doors in Stormy Cove. Selina Gould hadn't even given Lori a key. She'd taken her computer, photography equipment, and all her valuables with her to the lodge and so hadn't given burglars a thought.

But who would go into her house while she was away? Selina, checking up on her tenant? Patience or Ches, who might have been worried? The paperboy, who regularly went into people's homes? Or little Molly, who was curious enough to sneak into a house that had been empty for so long and now had an interesting outsider living in it?

But when Patience came over that evening, Lori couldn't bring herself to ask about it directly, afraid Patience would interpret the question as a sign of distrust. She was leaning over the ice-fishing photo and busily writing down the names of the people in it in capital letters on some notepaper. She'd already written down seventeen names, but couldn't make out a man in the background.

Two vertical creases appeared between her eyebrows.

"I'm not sure, it could be . . . Fred, Fred Bartlett. Or . . ." she said, bringing the picture closer. "No, I'm not sure. Better ask one of the Whalens tomorrow. They were there, after all."

She pushed the picture away from her with an apologetic smile.

"By the way, Emma told me the party tomorrow is a potluck."

A potluck; she'd have to bring something like everyone else. She offered Patience a glass of sherry and drank to their friendship. Maybe the drink would loosen her neighbor's tongue enough for her to tell Lori more about Noah.

"So who's going to be there?"

Patience shrugged.

"The whole family, I suppose. It's Greta's fortieth."

"Who's Greta?"

"Noah's oldest sister. You've never met her?"

"No, only Nate. And Lance. There should be lots of people there tomorrow."

"Yes, six brothers and three sisters, not to mention the little kids. The teenagers won't be coming. They don't like family gatherings."

Lori did the math.

"Does that make ten siblings?"

"No, eleven." Patience stopped. "One sister isn't coming. Robine never comes."

"Why not?"

Patience blushed.

"Don't tell anybody you got it from me, but Robine . . . she went off when she was twenty-one and never came back. She . . . um . . . she had a girlfriend."

Lori was startled.

"A girlfriend? What's so bad about that? A young woman has to have friends."

Then she saw the red glow on Patience's face and suddenly got it.

"Oh, she loved women . . ."

Well, now, wasn't that an interesting revelation!

"So what did the family think about that?"

"They were mortified, I think. Nothing like that had happened in Stormy Cove before." She burst out laughing. "And Robine was very pretty, and all the boys chased her. And then"—she held out her hands—"well, it shows how you can fool yourself."

"Where'd she go?"

"Somebody saw her in Montreal, but that was—let me think—maybe ten, twelve years ago. I heard she sends postcards regularly, from Barbados and Hawaii. And once from Paris."

"So is it certain that she's still alive?"

Patience gave her a look of surprise.

"Yeah, of course she's alive. Her lawyer sent a letter once—about some legal matters."

Lori offered Patience another sherry, but she turned it down.

"Thanks, but I'd better go get supper started."

She stood up and an almost roguish smile flitted over her face.

"You're in demand at all the events because of that camera, you know. Ever since those pictures you took of Elsie Smith's family, everybody wants to be in your book."

"Well, lots of them will be! But about Robine? What do you think about lesbians?" Lori asked as Patience was putting on her jacket and boots by the door. She couldn't help sounding her neighbor out, but she didn't expect the answer she received.

"Oh, every woman can be a lesbian, for all I care. Then they wouldn't have to fight about men so much."

She opened the door and disappeared.

Lori put the glasses in the sink. She was sure the pretty, beaming young woman in the pictures that Noah wanted her to delete must be Robine. Was he so ashamed to have a lesbian sister? She couldn't imagine that. It didn't add up somehow. Anyone who puts up a strange photographer from Vancouver overnight isn't afraid of associating with women who don't fit the norm. Her intuition told her that he wanted to protect Robine from something. But what? Why did he want to do everything in his power to stop her picture from appearing in a published book?

He couldn't avoid her tomorrow at the Whalens' party; the mere thought made her tingle. But she dismissed it immediately because she had to think of what to bring the next day. She should have asked Patience for advice.

And she'd forgotten to ask one other thing.

Who had been Robine's girlfriend?

CHAPTER 22

Ice floes were rocking on the waves by the next morning. For the first time, Lori saw open water in the cove. Her eyes strayed over to the trees beside the house that now poked up higher out of the snow cover. The layer of melting ice on the cliffs sparkled in the pale light. When she opened her bedroom window for a minute, she heard a few muffled gunshots.

Men in the harbor were fiddling around on their boats or just hanging around together.

Lori drove down to the harbor, passing a chained-up husky squatting miserably in front of its doghouse. She strolled along the wharf and listened to several fishermen discussing the weather. No trace of Noah. Nor of Nate and Archie.

"Do you mind if I take some pictures?" she called to the fishermen.

"Sure," came the reply.

"I'd have shaved this morning if I'd known," someone shouted. The others laughed.

An elderly man turned to her.

"We were lucky this year. It's the right wind to keep the ice away from shore until it melts."

"When does fishing start up?" she inquired.

"Next week, twentieth of May, for lumpfish. Do you know what lumpfish are?"

Lori didn't.

"We fish for them because of the roe. It's a little cheaper than sturgeon caviar."

She snapped a shot of a young man just as he hopped off his boat onto the jetty. He came over.

"You should come out with us tomorrow and take pictures. But you'll have to get up early. We head out at five."

A voice behind her replied, "You'll have to install a new motor first, Hart, so she doesn't conk out every ten miles."

She recognized the speaker without turning around. To hide her embarrassment, she picked up her camera and panned until it was aiming at Noah's face. Then she pushed the release.

"Who says I conk out every ten miles?" she quipped.

"I meant the boat. A boat's a 'she,' my dear," he said with the faintest of smiles. "Everything that causes problems is feminine."

Hart laughed. "Yeah, every machine's a 'she.' The truck, the computer . . . and the TV too, when it doesn't work."

He seemed to take no offense at Noah's barging in. Lori had a retort on the tip of her tongue, but she restrained herself. She was there to take photographs.

"Which boat is yours?" she asked instead.

"Over there—the *Mighty Breeze*."

There was pride in Noah's voice, though he tried to sound cool. Lori felt his gaze on her back as she turned toward the boat. Suddenly, Archie stepped on deck.

"Does he go out fishing with you?" Lori asked.

"No, he just helps with repairs. He's got his own boat, the *Bella Vista*. So you're coming to the potluck?"

She nodded. Now that they'd seen each other at the wharf, she could feel more at ease about going.

"Your uncle said I can take pictures. Is that really true?"

He glanced over at Archie, who was out of earshot, and said, "If that's what he wants . . . best I ask Mother as well. Don't see any problem with it. She knows what you do and she'd like to meet you."

He stood with his hands in the pockets of a jacket he'd thrown on over his blue overalls. He looked left and right to cover the lull in the conversation. Lori pretended she was watching the other fishermen. Then Archie shouted something from the boat, and Noah trotted off.

Lori parked near Nate's house two hours later. She hoisted out the large bowl of potato salad she'd made following her mother's recipe, which had come down from *her* German mother. She'd never yet met a person who didn't rave about it.

She saw a man going through the door and decided to follow him in. A sharp, sweet smell hit her. At first, she could only make out shadowy outlines in the dim light. On the floor in front of her was a row of big black-and-white birds. Many had red bullet holes in their white belly feathers. When her eyes had adjusted to the light, she could see several men sitting on upturned pails; one of them held up a bird as a greeting.

"Don't get your hopes up," he shouted. "It's not going to get eaten today."

Laughter accompanied his words.

Lori swiftly recovered from her surprise.

"Doesn't matter, still makes for a good picture."

"Go ahead," another man shouted.

She put the salad bowl on a box.

"Are all of you Noah's brothers?"

"Brothers, nephews, cousins—take your pick!"

"And uncles."

"A big family," Lori said as she snapped away.

"You bet!"

There were wet feathers lying everywhere, and water was bubbling in a huge pot. Obviously, plucking was a man's job.

"And what kind of ducks are they?"

"Eider."

"Did somebody shoot them this morning? I heard shots."

"That'd be Jack over there."

A figure stepped forward out of the dark, a boy Lori figured was seventeen at most. He still had his shotgun on his back.

Interesting. A young teenager who'd shot two dozen ducks for grown men to pluck. He stood there with his legs wide apart, one hand on his hip, the other against a wooden post: every inch the proud hunter. She lay down on the floor to shoot from below, ignoring the dirt on her jacket. Then she entered his name in her notebook: Jack Day.

"I'm Noah's cousin's son," he said as she put away her camera. She had him point out the way to go upstairs.

She took off her shoes before entering a brightly lit kitchen filled with loud voices and laughter, and with women and children, for the most part. Curious eyes turned in her direction, but nobody came over to welcome her. She put the salad on a large table loaded with brimming bowls and plates, and looked around the open living and dining room. Noah wasn't there to help her navigate this difficult moment.

She approached a woman putting a plate of Nanaimo bars on the table.

"Hi, I'm Lori. Where can I find Greta?"

"Greta?" She scanned the crowd. "Over there," she said, making a not very helpful nod toward the left corner of the living room.

Fortunately, she added, "I don't know how she does it, but I always see her with a baby that isn't hers."

Lori spotted a woman with strong arms rocking an infant while carrying on a lively conversation with the people ringed around her. She was blond and animated, with cheerful facial features that didn't look at all like her brother's. While not pretty as Robine had been in the picture, she radiated a freshness and health that even the most expensive cosmetics couldn't fake. Lori worked her way over to Greta, who suddenly noticed an unfamiliar face. She called out, "Are you that photographer from Vancouver?"

All of a sudden, it was noticeably quieter, and Lori felt the onus of being the focus of everyone's attention.

"Thank you for inviting me to your birthday party," Lori said, "and happy birthday!"

She handed Greta a small box containing a pretty key chain with a killer whale carved from gray-blue argillite by the Haida First Nations.

"Oh, I knew if I invited you then everyone would come by to have a look at you!"

Greta laughed at her own joke, and that set the whole group laughing. She said to an elderly lady on the sofa behind her, "Mother, this is Lori from Vancouver. She takes photographs and we're all going to be in her book."

Noah's mother. Short, gray hair, astonishingly thin for a woman who'd had eleven children, with dark, almost angry eyes beneath thick eyebrows. A bit masculine, which didn't surprise Lori. Anybody around here who was too soft didn't survive. Particularly during the grim old times when this woman had raised her passel of kids.

Noah's mother threw her a disparaging glance and said, "You won't like the weather here. You won't be able to stand it for very long."

Lori hadn't counted on this kind of welcome, but her voice struck a jaunty note as she said, "I'm not here for the weather, Mrs. Whalen, I'm here for the fat fish. Fish are so expensive in Vancouver, I can't afford them anymore."

That elicited a general murmur and some heckling.

"Yes, we've got fat fish here, alright," a woman hollered, "and yummy fishermen!"

"Maybe they're not fat enough for her!"

"She's already got one on her hook. Don't get your hopes up, Blake."

Another woman: "Are you a hangashore, Blake?"

A loud outburst of laughter.

Greta turned to Lori. "Hangashores are guys who don't actually fish—they just hang around on the shore and flirt with the women left behind."

"And stick them with kids," a woman muttered.

"Stop that whispering," Noah's mother shouted.

"Oh, you always act like you're hard of hearing but your ears are sharp as tacks!"

Greta bent down to her mother and put a loving arm around her shoulders. They obviously understood each other well. But that same mother had kicked one of her daughters out of town because she loved women.

Suddenly, the energy in the room changed. Archie Whalen had arrived with a crew of men in his wake, Noah among them. He scoured the room until he saw her, but didn't come over. *Peer pressure,* Lori thought to herself.

The men charged the buffet. Lori caught the attack with her camera. Then she got shots of a gaggle of half-grown girls in skintight stretch pants and T-shirts. They must have ordered their provocative clothing from the Sears catalog; Lori had picked one up in the village store too, and browsed through it at home. Girls always found ways to keep up with fashion, even in Stormy Cove. Lori was so busy with her camera that she didn't get to eat until the buffet had almost been swept clean. There was only one dish nobody had eaten from: her potato salad was untouched. The paltry remains of another potato salad, gleaming with mayonnaise, lay on a platter. It probably wasn't even real mayonnaise, Lori guessed, but the substitute they called "Miracle Whip" in these parts.

Nursing her injured pride, Lori served herself some of her salad, combined it with a chicken leg, and ignored the rest of the remains. Since every seat was taken, she ate standing up, while prying eyes fastened on her off and on. She sipped at her beer. Noah still hadn't talked to her. He was engaged in an obviously marvelous conversation with the young mother of the baby. Was he trying to show his family that the rumors about him and that Vancouverite were completely unfounded? Just as Lori was starting to feel thoroughly uncomfortable, somebody invited Greta to cut her birthday cake. The cake was flat as a box of chocolates and covered with white icing and mint-green garland-like decorations. Lori reached for her camera.

Greta divided the cake into pieces and began to distribute the plates. Then one of Noah's brothers—it was Lance—smashed a piece of cake all over Greta's face and hair—hard. Lori automatically put down her camera and yelped, "Hey!"

Every head turned toward her.

Greta just shook her head, laughing, and gave her brother a playful slap. Some cake seemed to have gotten into her right eye, and she tried to rub it out with her finger. Someone gave her a paper napkin and she hurried off to clean up.

Noah was suddenly at Lori's side.

"Is everything OK?" he asked.

"Why'd he do that?"

"Oh, it's a ritual here, but it's not as common as it used to be." He looked a little embarrassed. "You didn't take a picture, did you?"

Lori shook her head. Was that all he was interested in? That his family might be seen in a bad light?

He served her a piece of cake.

"Best cake around."

This time he stayed at her side while she stuffed herself in silence.

Greta came back into the kitchen, her damp hair hanging down on one side. She took Lori's arm.

"Come with me, I'm opening my birthday cards."

Lori followed her into the living room, where Greta opened her envelopes and took out some bills. Lori was astonished to see her hand the money over to another woman, who counted it carefully and wrote the amounts on a sheet of paper. So that's what people were looking for: money, not for a pretty, but maybe unwelcome, key chain.

"Three hundred and twenty dollars," the woman announced, and all the bystanders acknowledged their satisfaction with the haul.

Now Greta opened Lori's little package and held up the key chain. Lori was embarrassed, but what could she do?

"What's that?" a little girl shouted.

"A key chain," somebody said. "A whale."

Fortunately, Greta saved the situation by giving Lori a hug and thanking her.

Lori needed a glass of water and some fresh air. The men had congregated in the kitchen, each with a can of beer in hand. Noah gave her an inquiring look. She pushed past him to the faucet, but Archie intercepted her.

"You don't want water; only animals drink water around here."

Archie's tone of voice told her that he now regarded her as a friend of the family. She dodged yet another debate about drinking by showing Archie the ice-fishing photograph.

"Who's this man? I haven't been able to get his name."

Nate Whalen leaned over the picture before Archie could respond.

"That's Gideon. Gideon Moore."

"Is he related to you?"

"Gideon is Archie's buddy. They used to fish together."

"And then the boat burned down," a man shouted, who was a little tipsy. "Then Gideon bought a lodge and it burned down, too!"

"And Gideon got a lot of money from the insurance, and bought a helicopter and now he's—" shouted a young blond red-faced man who Lori hadn't seen before.

Archie cut him off.

"None of your bullshit, Taylor! Gideon works hard and doesn't spout off all the time like some guys here."

But the young red-faced man was full of Dutch courage.

"Archie, you've got to admit that some guys made a nice pot of money from boats that burned. You can't even get insurance in Saleau Cove anymore because so many boats were torched all of a sudden."

"Not for houses either," another man broke in vehemently. "And how do you explain the pictures hanging in the new houses that were hanging in the ones that burned down?"

The men laughed, but not Archie.

"You're a bunch of blabbermouths," he thundered. "Stupid gossip, nothing but stupid gossip."

He left the crowd, and the rest of them stood around, looking a bit chagrined.

Lori and her questions had once again brought discord into a family party.

Two couples with children got up to leave. Maybe it was time for her to go too. She looked around at the guests and was startled to see one of the very young, provocatively dressed girls sitting in a man's lap. *Her uncle or her father?* The man crossed his arms over the girl's chest and jiggled her breasts up and down. Lori was shocked, but none of the bystanders seemed to find anything wrong. She tried to locate Noah, but he wasn't around.

He didn't show up until she'd said good-bye to Greta and her mother and a few others and was putting her salad bowl in her Toyota.

"Do I get some of that?"

She straightened up beside the car.

"Nobody touched it, not even you. Does it look *that* unappetizing?"

"No, no, not at all. It's just that people here only eat what they know."

"It's just a damn potato salad, anybody can see that!"

"Maybe it looks different, dunno . . . I'd like to try it."

"But not in front of all the guests, oh no!" she said. "You'd never do that."

He said nothing but looked out on the bay. Then he said, "I can bring some sausage and moose meat."

She couldn't be angry with him. He'd grown up in this world, and he obeyed its rules. He had to keep on living here long after she moved on.

"OK," she said. "The salad will taste even better tomorrow."

His clouded face brightened.

"Yes, a lot of things improve if you let them sit for a while."

I must remember that, she thought as she started the motor.

CHAPTER 23

It was five in the morning when she slogged down to the harbor with leaden feet. She waddled like a duck in the heavy rubber boots Noah had lent her, and her life jacket felt like a suit of armor over the winter jacket that was bulky enough already. It was drizzling, and her hood didn't keep the dampness off her face.

Get over yourself, Lori. It's not a beauty contest, just a job.

Her only consolation was that Noah, who, together with Nate, was shoveling crushed ice into brightly colored containers, looked just as ungainly in his rubber jacket and pants.

Lori was shivering. She didn't know if it was the aftermath of the flu that had chained her to her bed for the past week or the chill of the gray dawn. How could it still be so cold at the end of May! Snow still clung to the hilltops. In Vancouver, the cherry trees began to bloom as early as March.

Maybe it was also the anticipation of her first adventure on Noah's fishing boat that sent shivers down her spine. She hadn't seen him for ten days, and wasn't thrilled for him to see her with her nose rubbed all red, her swollen eyes, and a lingering air of the sick bed on her. Patience had insisted on coming over daily, making tea and bringing food Lori was too feverish to eat. The nearest doctor was a three-hour drive away. What did these people do if they had heart attacks and other emergencies?

Nate interrupted her thoughts.

"Do you get seasick?"

She shrugged.

"Never happened before. Will it be rough today?"

"Nah, sea's pretty calm. Sometimes it gets to me."

"What? A fisherman who gets seasick?"

"For sure, and I'm not the only one. If it's really blowing out there, it's no fun, no fun at all."

But he smiled all the same.

The brothers heaved a box of ice on board. Then Noah held out his hand.

"Welcome aboard, milady."

He helped her climb onto the rocking boat and find her footing among the buckets and white plastic bags. Then he slacked off the ropes from the bollards. Nate started the engine, and the boat chugged out of the cove. Lori kept a hand on the jamb of the wheelhouse door and watched the village of Stormy Cove vanish into the thin morning fog. The boat hugged the coastline, and its tall black vertical rocks.

Lori felt the boat rolling, breathed in the salty, fishy air. She was filled with a dizzying sense of lightness and freedom, and she felt deeply insignificant but uplifted by the sublime power of the sea.

Noah sat on the railing, his rain hood pulled up over his baseball cap. Lori sat down beside him.

"How many times have you set out from this cove?" She had to yell to be heard over the engine.

"Thousands of times. I know every rock and every shoal."

He pointed a finger at the cliffs.

"Over there are the Devil's Footprints. Do you see the claw marks in the stone? There's the White Dog, the bright-colored rock that looks like a dog from this side. And over there's the Oven, a cave."

He looked at her.

"Rain doesn't hurt your camera?"

"No, not this little drizzle. But I wouldn't take it into the water."

"Can you swim?"

"Of course. You?"

He shook his head.

"I don't know any fisherman who can swim."

"Why aren't you wearing a life jacket?"

"It's pointless. You'd freeze to death just like that in this cold water."

"Not if somebody can pull you out of the water fast. Surely you don't freeze in a minute."

He shook his head again and said nothing. Lori knew him well enough to know she had to drop it. But then there was a new sound.

"The hydraulic hauler," Noah shouted when he saw the puzzled look on her face. "Hauls in the nets."

Lori photographed the nets coming up over the bow, the wriggling fish caught in the mesh, and Noah pulling at the stern. He grabbed the fish with his orange rubber gloves, freed them from the mesh, and threw them on the deck, where they still twitched a little, their mouths snapping in the air.

Filled with curiosity, she studied their plump, slimy bodies: gray blue, greenish, sometimes nearly black. The upper fin was almost as big as a rooster's comb. So that's the lumpfish. Or lumpsucker—she'd looked it up on the Internet. Genus *Cyclopterus* in the family Cyclopteridae, a description she found delightful.

"They don't have scales," she yelled.

Noah laughed.

"Fat bellies make up for it!"

She knew he meant the roe in the females; it's what he was after. Her camera caught Noah throwing the nets over the rail and gradually sliding them back into the ocean. The boat started up again.

Noah took a big, sharp knife and opened a lumpfish's belly. Caviar gushed out, thousands of tiny pink fish eggs that he dripped into a white bucket. He shoved a hand into the open belly and cleaned out what was left. She grimaced.

"Are the fish dead? Do they suffer?"

Noah looked up briefly as he kept working. She repeated the question.

"No, they don't suffer. Do you hear a loud scream when I slit them open? They don't have any feeling, these fish."

His argument was unconvincing. But what right did she have to question thousands of years of fishing tradition? She enjoyed eating fish, not to mention lobsters and crabs and mussels and snails. She'd tried going vegetarian when she was very young, and had failed miserably because of her love of meat and her inability to concoct enough tasty meals.

It was a long day. The boat went from net to net—eighty in all—and Noah and Nate worked without a break for ten hours. All Noah wolfed down was a chocolate bar and an apple, Nate a sandwich washed down with Mountain Dew, which he offered to Lori. After one swallow of the sugary soft drink, she opted for tea from her thermos, but that put her in a bind. There was no toilet on the boat. Men simply peed over the rail. Noah handed her a big pail and closed the wheelhouse door so she'd be undisturbed.

She didn't get seasick; however, she was frozen stiff after several hours and longed for solid ground underfoot. She'd taken enough pictures of roe and nets and the ocean and fishermen in green rubber clothes. But the brothers worked tirelessly. She didn't dare ask if they could maybe put her ashore in the early afternoon.

Finally, when Noah was eating his apple, she asked with feigned indifference, "So, when is quitting time?"

"We're not paid by the hour," he replied. "We try to get in as much as possible."

When at last they neared Stormy Cove harbor, surrounded by fluttering, screaming gulls, Lori heaved a sigh of relief that didn't escape the men's notice. They laughed.

"Next time we won't drag you out for such a long day," Nate said. "But you've got to experience for once what it really means to fish."

"And that wasn't a tough one," Noah chimed in. "In summer we sometimes don't get back until eleven."

"Can you still see in the dark?"

"Oh, sure. We've got searchlights."

Her questions obviously amused the fishermen, whose spirits were already high due to a good haul. They estimated the day's catch at around eight hundred pounds.

When they moored, the buyer's truck was ready to go and the driver was impatiently waiting for his load.

"You want to sell her too?" he shouted, an eye on Lori as she climbed out of the boat onto the wooden planks.

"You don't have enough to buy *me*," Lori shot back. "Where do you send the caviar anyway?"

"To Europe. Mostly Germany."

"That far? Don't Canadians like their native caviar?"

The driver laughed.

"Germans pay more, I guess. There's a reason why lumpfish roe is called German caviar." He grabbed a bucket and pushed it onto the back of the truck. "The guy who has the import company, he comes to Newfoundland now and then. Supposed to be a baron, or so I've heard. Posh people probably eat the stuff for breakfast." He laughed again.

A baron. Lori hesitated.

"Does he stay at Birch Tree Lodge?"

"No idea. Possible. It's the only hotel for miles around."

Noah and Nate began to clean up the boat.

Lori couldn't get warm fast enough.

She shouted them a good-bye and got into her car.

Her most urgent need had a name: hot chocolate.

When she got home, she didn't even bother to check her messages on the computer or the telephone before going straight to bed. A wise decision.

In her exhausted state, she wouldn't have known how to deal with the surprise that awaited her.

CHAPTER 24

The next day, Lori cursed the fact that there were six time zones in Canada and that Vancouver was four and a half hours behind Newfoundland. She absolutely had to talk to her mother, but had to wait until noon before she could call, even though her mother wasn't one to sleep in on the weekend.

"I thought you'd call yesterday," her mother said without standing on ceremony. "I didn't even go to the movies."

Lisa Finning was a film buff, and Friday night was her sacrosanct film date that she only canceled in extreme emergencies. She usually went to the last show, around ten. But it wasn't like her to lay a guilt trip on her daughter, even for missing this ritual pleasure; she hadn't even complained that she wouldn't be seeing Lori for almost a year. Her mother was of the opinion that every woman was responsible for her own happiness. She must have had some other reason for giving up her movie date—Lori knew that right away.

"What? Are you feeling okay?"

"No, no, there are riots in the inner city, and I am quite upset about it."

"Riots? Why? Not another hockey game?"

"No, not this time. The provincial government cut the minimum wage down to eight dollars. It's a real scandal; nobody can live on that. And at a time when the big corporations are paying less and less taxes."

"Since when do you have social justice in your soul, Mom? I hardly recognize you."

"Social justice—you don't have to be dramatic, dear heart. It's simply not right for so few to have a lot of money and so many to have so little. It's not good for the economy because who's going to buy the goods we produce? It isn't good for society because the middle class is declining. And it isn't good for democracy because it undermines stability."

Normally, her mother only got this exercised about mistreated dogs and cats. Usually, Lori got the impression she preferred not to talk about social ills at home because she had to deal with plenty of them at the office.

Under normal circumstances, Lori would have sounded her mother out and tried to figure out what was going on with her, but today she let it be. She had something more urgent to discuss, having heard this message on the answering machine that morning: "My dear, I've found out something about the case we talked about, something to do with a person you know. Call me at home, sweetheart."

A person you know. Lori's stomach shrank at once, like a wool sweater in hot water.

"Mom, forgive me for changing the subject, but please tell me what you found out."

"Ah, yes. I might have known you'd be more interested in that than riots in Vancouver. I was able to have a brief conversation with the investigator in charge of Jacinta Parsons's file. He rather covered his ass, I must say."

"Why did you say you were interested in the case?"

"I told him my daughter was in the area where the murder occurred and I wanted to know if I should be concerned for her safety."

"What? You said *that*?"

"No, my dear, I'm joking. I told him that I was writing a book about extraordinary murder cases, which is true, and asked whether he could give me any information on the Parsons case."

"But Mom, you're writing a book about murders in *British Columbia*."

"He doesn't have to know that! Do you want the info or don't you?"

"Of course. So?"

"As I said, the guy wasn't very cooperative. But he told me that the file was still open, that is, the case is still being investigated, though I had the impression not very actively."

"What about the person I know? Who is it?"

"I'll get to that, my dear. Let me finish. I told him the things found in the grave made the case especially interesting because they were supposed to have been copies of those found in an ancient Indian grave. Up to now, I'd only heard of one case like that, in France, since I researched the topic."

"You did?"

"I needed to do some spadework, Lori; the little bit you told me wasn't enough. In any case, he thawed out a touch when I gave him some details concerning the French case—I won't bother you with them now—and we started to chat. But listen to this: The killer in France was arrested because of an item in the grave. She made a fatal mistake: she threw in a ring that could be identified."

"Was she copying a prehistoric grave as well?"

"No, a medieval grave, and the ring looked exactly like a piece of medieval jewelry. You know young people's tastes, and rings haven't changed much in the course of modern history."

"I still don't understand how the murderer was caught."

"The murderer was actually a woman, remember. She killed her romantic rival and then put her own ring into the grave. She thought investigators would conclude that somebody wanted to frame her and that it was impossible for her to be the perp because it wasn't logical that she'd give herself away like that. It worked for three years. But she was wrong."

"Mom, this is too confusing. I haven't the slightest idea where this is going."

"My point is, it's the same thing with Jacinta. The investigator told me there was an object in Jacinta's grave belonging to the lead archaeologist. But they assumed it had been stolen and planted in order to shift suspicion onto him."

"A personal object? A prehistoric item?"

"No, his hunting license."

"What kind of license?"

"A government gun permit, for hunting."

Lori was silent for a moment so she could process her mother's report. Then she said, "And what about the person I know?"

"I was talking about the archaeologist, naturally."

"Lloyd Weston . . . How do you know I know him?"

"You told me you met him at the lodge, my dear."

Lori now recalled she'd e-mailed her mother about meeting him. She thought she'd be pleased that her daughter was meeting people who weren't fishermen.

Lori's body relaxed. She felt hugely relieved. Her mother hadn't turned up anything about Noah. Of course, the investigator might have held back information about him. And there was still that matter of the arrowhead under the snowmobile seat. On the other hand, wouldn't somebody guilty of murder make such an important piece of evidence disappear? Burn it in a stove or toss it into the ocean?

It seemed strange to her now that Weston hadn't quizzed her more about the artifact. He'd been so quickly satisfied with the idea that she must have been mistaken. And now it had vanished from her house.

"What else did you discover?"

"Not much, because I would have had to officially request access to the files to get it. And then things get complicated."

"I'm amazed the investigator revealed the business about the hunting license in the grave. That's really something only the killer could have known. Why disclose something like that?"

"Oh, my dear, now you're thinking like a detective! I imagine they hoped that after twenty futile years of searching that they'd make more progress by leaking information than by keeping it secret. And I assume they have more arrows in their quiver that only the perp can know."

That made sense to Lori. After all, the police had told Weston about the carving in Jacinta's grave.

Her head was swimming in a dense cloud.

"So what was your take-away from this whole thing?"

Her mother didn't answer, but Lori stayed with it.

"Mom, did it seem like the investigator maybe isn't so sure anymore that the archaeologist is guilty now that you told him about the French case?"

"No, I rather think . . . that they fear for his safety. A hunting license sends a different signal than a ring does."

"But Jacinta wasn't shot. So what's the signal?"

"That the killer thinks Weston knows something and he'll be shot if he squeals."

Lori thought about that. She recalled her conversations with Weston. He'd never given the slightest impression of being in danger. On the contrary, he'd come back to the same place for a dig on a second grave.

Lisa Finning's thoughts turned in a different direction.

"How are things with that fisherman? Have you got something going with him?"

"Mo-*ther*! Do you always have to be so direct?"

"Yes, I do, can't help myself, you know that. Why beat around the bush?"

"I went out fishing with him yesterday, on the ocean . . . and—no, we're not in a relationship."

"But you like him a lot, don't you?"

"Let's say . . . I don't fully understand what I feel. It's a tight little world here, and I'm kind of lonely."

"But that's something we're familiar with, no?"

She knew exactly what her mother was referring to.

"No, it's not like in Germany. My photo assignment is interesting and, believe it or not, the people here speak English just like we do."

Her words came out more sarcastic than she intended. But her mother didn't take the bait.

"Just be careful, my dear. A year is a very long time."

"I know, Mom. And thanks for the info on the case," Lori said, striking a more conciliatory tone of voice. "I really appreciate it. Talk to you soon."

"And if you feel lonely, then go take some poor dog for a walk. It'll do both of you some good," her mother said.

Lori stared out the window onto the bay. The sun's rays pushed tentatively through patches of gray fog. The hills looked like shaggy animals, gradually molting their white coats and showing some dark spots. Springtime in Vancouver had something soft, optimistic about it. But out here, in the north of Newfoundland, nature seemed to be saying to people: we're only giving you a short breather, don't get too happy. There was a pride, an untouchability in it that appealed to her. The rocky landscape was uncompromising, untamable. It remained what it was, unwavering.

Her gaze wandered over to the boats. Noah's wasn't there. He and Nate must have gone out early that morning.

She pictured him in her mind's eye, freeing the fish from the net, one after the other, radiating the calm of a person who was doing what he believed he was fated to do.

She often felt he was watching her when she was busy with her camera, scanning her surroundings for the best subject, the best angle, the most compelling composition.

Maybe they weren't so different after all; maybe they had more in common than she supposed.

A warm, hopeful feeling flooded over her.

But that exposed a weakness that she had to cover up swiftly.

Be careful, a year is a very long time.

CHAPTER 25

Beth Ontara, 45, archaeologist

*You're asking me questions you already know the answers to, aren't you?
I mean, you know damn well I first met Lori Finning at the Birch Tree
Lodge. My impression of her? You know what first struck me? When Lloyd
introduced her to our group, she remembered everybody's name, that's a
dozen names—even though they were all talking. I didn't even remember Lori's name at the beginning. Is that what they call a photographic
memory?*

*Naturally, we were curious to find out how Lloyd knew this pretty
photographer from Vancouver. We wormed it out of him right away—he
can't keep anything to himself. But when we asked Lori why she was here, I
thought she seemed a little . . . let's say . . . uptight. My gut feeling was that
she wasn't telling us the whole story. Annie and me talked about it afterward
before going to sleep. Annie thought it was funny that a photographer like
Lori would be living in a desolate village, an outport—just to make a book
of photographs. I mean, who's going to buy a book like that? Maybe a few
homesick Newfies living somewhere else in Canada. And why's a woman
like Lori interested, anyway? She didn't look like a person who knows how
to be away from a city like Vancouver for very long. Archaeologists like us*

are used to living in the field. We can eat cold beans out of a can if we have to and wear the same underwear for three days.

Not that she was all dolled up or anything—I don't mean that. Her nails weren't even polished. I look at my nails a lot, and they're almost always dirty. Comes with the job.

Certainly doesn't come with hers. Although . . . she liked bright colors, I remember that, but maybe that's typical for Vancouver. They're all semihippies in that city—either that or they imitate the movie stars who make films there. No, never been there. Not interested either. There are enough Newfies in Western Canada already who really don't want to be there.

What did I want to say? Oh, right, she had something . . . sophisticated about her. You know, like somebody who can tell you right away who a quote came from and . . . or what material an expensive evening dress is made of. And she read the book reviews in the Saturday Globe and Mail. *And somebody like her winds up in a godforsaken hick town on The Rock? You've got to wonder.*

Yes, we went for a snowmobile ride, and she came with us. And she played poker afterward. With Annie, me, and Lloyd. No, we didn't talk about Stormy Cove. Don't recall it ever came up. We talked more about our crazy experiences on our digs. She was very interested, and it made her laugh.

Lori hardly ever said anything about herself. I got the impression—assuming you want to hear my impressions—I got the impression she's a good listener, and that gets people to talk. And maybe we yakked so much because Lloyd sprung for a good red wine.

Jacinta Parsons? Name never came up, and Lori didn't ask about her either.

But we weren't surprised Lloyd wanted to hire her to take pictures. Lloyd's ambitious. Don't get me wrong—I'm OK with that. We archaeologists need more recognition. More recognition brings more money—I have a good head for business there. Lloyd convinced himself that her photographs would get him into the international media. That was a smart move.

Of course, he couldn't predict what would happen next. But it probably wouldn't have stopped him.

The business with Jacinta Parsons didn't stop him either. It was a terrible situation for all of us. Worst-case scenario. Sure, we look for bodies, but hey, they're at least a thousand years old. You know what I can't figure? Why the locals spread those rumors about Lloyd. A seven-thousand-year-old grave—I mean, what more do those folks want? It's such a win for the area. It brings the tourists and . . . it rescued the place from being nothing. And how do they thank us? By making us look bad.

We've got nothing to do with the nut that killed Jacinta.

Did I know her? It's on file. Did you read the files? I didn't have anything to do directly with the village folks who worked for us. But when Annie got sick, I took over her job drawing up the work schedule. Jacinta came to see me because she only wanted to work on days when somebody could drive her home, either her older sister or her sister's boyfriend, a fisherman from Stormy Cove. Jacinta said it's what her mother wanted. Until then, she'd only come to work on days when her friend Una did.

The second time I talked to her was on Lloyd's birthday. We celebrated in the Hardy Sailor. Yes, exactly, the night Gideon's lodge burned down. She was standing around after work so I asked if she was being picked up. She said yes, and she had a birthday present for Lloyd. I told her he was already at the Hardy Sailor. She should get there fast to join us for supper. She wanted to know if our whole team was at the bar, and I said it was. I was in a hurry because I'd organized the meal and everybody was waiting for me. That's the last time I saw Jacinta.

What present? Jacinta's birthday present for Lloyd? No idea what happened to it. Probably a quilt or something local like that. Lloyd would certainly have been delighted. Women work on one for three months and then sell it for fifty dollars because they don't have a clue how much their work is worth.

We learned about the fire just after dessert. It was bad, awful. And we didn't know at the time that it was only the beginning. It's a miracle we managed to keep on working under those circumstances. And you know, the locals stayed on working for us on the dig. It wasn't as if they boycotted us. Even the younger women showed up at work; their parents evidently had no objections. We paid well. I ask you: Would they have done that if they'd really believed we were connected with Jacinta's disappearance?

Just Jacinta's sister didn't come anymore, and her friend the fisherman didn't either. I heard later he was a suspect. Apparently nothing came of it. But the past always catches up with you.

It just occurred to me. Poker—I mentioned our game at the lodge. Well, Lori said she didn't have the foggiest idea about poker. She made typical beginner's mistakes at first. Joked about it. Later we played for money, not much, just twenty bucks a stake. She lost her money, of course. We raised it to fifty and then a hundred. But Lori won the last hand. Four hundred bucks. We were flabbergasted. Annie and me tried to analyze the game afterward. Lori must have been watching us like a hawk the whole time. She must have filed it all away in her brain. Like our names. But she still played the innocent. We completely underestimated her!

If you ask me, Lori's a woman who keeps her cards close to her vest. Pun intended. Though I don't really feel like joking around.

CHAPTER 26

The miserable husky belonged to a man called Tom Quinton, as Lori learned from Patience, and his house had the only double garage in Stormy Cove. Patience also said the Quintons were the only ones in town with a dishwasher. Tom drove the snowplow and the fire truck and sometimes the school bus when the regular driver couldn't. Besides, he owned three pickups. Lori imagined a man with so many vehicles would have little empathy for members of the human species that sometimes chose to go on foot.

Fortunately, she got some help from Tom's wife, Vera, who offered her a cup of tea in the kitchen. Lori spotted the fabled dishwasher.

"Folks in Vancouver walk a lot," Vera Quinton said. "It was on TV. There are walking trails everywhere with a white line down the middle so cyclists don't run into the walkers. Is that really true?"

Lori nodded. "I go jogging every day in Vancouver, but I prefer just to walk here, and . . ."

She wanted to say that she felt safer with a dog, but changed her mind.

"And it's more fun with a dog."

Tom Quinton wasn't so easily persuaded.

"This dog will drive you nuts. It takes off and doesn't listen when you call it."

"I'll just keep him on a leash," Lori countered.

"A leash? We don't have a leash." Tom laughed at the absurd idea. His wife butted in.

"Tom, you can tie a rope to his collar. That works too, y'know!"

Quinton growled a kind of acknowledgment and stood up. "This dog is—we took him in. He ran up to us because—"

"He belonged to Gideon Moore before," Vera interrupted him again. "The dog always ran away from Gideon, though he denies it. We brought him back a few times, but then it got to be too much, so we just kept him."

Vera tapped her fingers on the table.

"Gideon was unhappy with his wife, you see. He's got a young one now, and he built a house for her. The dog probably wasn't good enough for him either. Now they've got some kind of little lap dog. I heard they paid six thousand for it."

"I could buy an outboard motor and a speedboat for that," Tom grumbled.

"Or two weeks' holiday in Hawaii," Vera shot back.

Her husband snorted. "That would be throwing money away. I don't need a sunburn."

Vera's mouth morphed into a thin line.

"It would be nice if you could introduce me to your dog," Lori said, getting to her feet. "That way he could learn not to be afraid of me."

"Rusty's a good dog, doesn't bite," Tom assured her on their way outside.

As they approached the husky, he pulled at his chain furiously. But Lori quickly realized that this welcome break from his desolate life just excited him and that he wasn't vicious. She waited until Tom had calmed Rusty down and then let him sniff her hands and clothing thoroughly while avoiding any eye contact.

"Does he obey commands?"

"Only sit and stop," Tom replied as he tied a rope onto Rusty's collar. "Go ahead and try."

"Sit!" Lori shouted.

With his glacier-blue eyes, Rusty first looked at his owner and then at her. He seemed confused.

"Sit!" Lori commanded again.

This time, the husky obeyed. She rewarded him with a dog biscuit she'd bought at the village store. Nothing beats the power of a treat.

She let the dog sniff her hands again then stroked his neck. The dog was docile. He'd evidently never been beaten, just neglected, left all by himself. A dog that needed to run but was never allowed to. What a sorry life.

Tom walked them out to the street, where she went off with the dog alone. Rusty trotted along in front of her, stopping frequently to investigate scents and peeing to leave his mark. She didn't attempt to train him, just let him run around as free as possible.

A strong, offshore west wind was gusting over the cove, rather aggressively, angrily. She had to keep adjusting her hat and sticking strands of hair back under it.

That's what you get when you grow a mane.

Whitecaps sparkled on the bay. Ribbed waves hurried toward the ocean, like a carpet made of the backs of shimmering insects. The snow on the hilltops had melted.

She made her way briskly past the last houses. Faces appeared and disappeared in the windows. She was creating a stir. Walking a dog in Stormy Cove just wasn't done, as Vera had informed her. Life was hard for the villagers, so why not for their dogs as well? If you didn't survive, it was your own fault. If there were any cats in the village, Lori hadn't seen them, either outdoors or in a home. On the other hand, there *were* dogs—all of them tied up, some with doghouses, some without.

Nobody seemed to give it a second thought. That's the way their parents had done it, and it's all the villagers knew.

Lori had photographed some boys and girls a few days before, shooting at wild ducks. The oldest girl was maybe ten. The next day, Lori went with an eleven-year-old schoolgirl to a hill behind the village, and her camera recorded the girl taking dead snowshoe hares out of traps where the animals had died in terrible pain. Lori's brain told her that these kids were simply learning to survive in a brutal and threatening environment. But her mother had brought her up to protect weak and helpless beings, especially animals.

She hardly saw Noah over the next several days. He was out hauling his nets on the ocean every day, from five in the morning until dark. Catching fish sucked up all his energy. Nothing seemed to matter for him but life on his boat. She'd gone out twice with him and Nate, but the magic of the first trip wasn't there, just the grinding slog and the cold, so that after a few hours, she was bored. Lumpfish just weren't photogenic. She'd go back out once the authorities announced the opening of the cod season. She'd read that no fish better embodied the essence of Newfoundland life. When she listened to fishermen talking on the wharf, they would of course discuss shrimp and mackerel and lumpfish and herring; but at some point, they'd always come back to cod, and then in almost reverent tones, as if referring to a mystical being. They just called it "the fish," as if it didn't need any other appellation.

She'd read that cod was so abundant five centuries ago that it fed half of Europe and kept its economy running. But in the last fifty years, it had been overfished almost to the point of extinction. Draggers from Spain, Portugal, France, and Great Britain used to haul millions of tons from Newfoundland waters. As cod stocks kept shrinking, the Canadian government declared a two-hundred-mile protective zone around the Newfoundland coast; it had been off-limits to foreign fleets since 1977. But the zone had little effect because Canadian deep-sea trawlers—floating factories with gigantic fish capacity—continued doing the foreigners' job. Not until cod had almost disappeared did the Canadian government, in 1992, ban cod fishing on the Grand Banks, in the greater part of the Gulf of St. Lawrence, and in the coastal waters off Newfoundland. The politicians in the capital, Ottawa, didn't stop the overfishing until even the big trawlers with sonar couldn't find enough cod in the Atlantic and moved to other fishing grounds. Noah told her that the small coastal fishermen had warned about overfishing for ages, but everyone turned a deaf ear.

"And yet we're the ones who suffer the consequences," he pointed out.

Today they had to keep strictly to very small catch quotas that were being lowered little by little every year.

It seemed to Lori that the cod's near extinction was like a crime novel, and she could have listened to Noah talk about it for hours. But for a few days now she'd sensed that he might be evading her.

Rusty pulled her along a grassy edge, eager to run as much as he could on his longed-for excursion. She slipped twice, whereupon the dog would impatiently turn around and look at her. Up on the crest of the hill, she had to brace herself against some squalls with all her might. Lori pulled her hood over her beret, then tied the leash around her waist. She squinted over the entire horizon. The Isle of Demons looked like a bulwark amid the waves breaking on its cliffs. The abandoned Marguerite must have seen the mainland in the distance on some days, but it was too far away to reach, and nobody knew she was battling for survival out on the island. She would certainly have carried out a thorough and constant search for some sign of life in the surrounding waters. Like Lori was doing now.

There was ocean as far as the eye could see. But no boats. Impossible for Noah to have gone out in a wind like this. Was he at home, recovering from all the exhausting work?

Maybe she should have him over for dinner, as she'd long promised. Until now, it was only the subtle fear of too much closeness that had been holding her back. And Noah surely had more important things to think about right then, she told herself.

Rusty tugged on the leash.

"I'm sure you think there are more important things in life," she yelled at him as they moved on. Finally, there was no more snow and no more ice underfoot, just grass and low bushes and stones and soil. The dog's energy was transferred to Lori, and she walked much farther than she'd planned to. The final stage saw her staggering down the street, and it wasn't long before a pickup pulled up.

"Want a ride?" Nate shouted.

She shook her head. "It's OK. The dog needs some exercise."

"Well, you'd better get to the beach. Capelin's in. You've got to take pictures!"

"Which beach?"

"Right around the corner from the wharf. You can't miss this!"

Capelin! Now Lori wanted to climb onto the back of the truck, but Nate had already driven off.

She'd heard about those little fish: cod food in large schools that are a sure sign of the cod's arrival. She upped her pace, and Rusty was thrilled. She got to the Quintons' place a half hour later, a white bungalow with a gable still bedecked with Christmas tree lights.

She tied up the husky and took off his makeshift leash. She tried to avoid his sad eyes while slipping him a dog biscuit.

Vera Quinton stuck her head out the door.

"Weren't you gone a long time! Like a cup of tea?"

"No, I've got to get to the beach. Capelin's in. But I think Rusty's thirsty. Would you give him some water?"

Vera nodded, and Lori could only hope she'd do it.

She sped to her car and down to the bay. From some distance away, she spotted the beach. People with buckets and nets on wooden poles were running around excitedly in the water. It looked like half the population of Stormy Cove was there. Lori jumped out of the car, grabbed her bag from the truck, and mingled with the crowd. Nothing was more important than the pictures she was about to shoot. The waves bringing in the capelin sparkled like chains of jewels when the sunlight hit the fishes' white underbellies. Schools of them rolled up onto the beach like dancing lights, covering the sand with their small, flipping bodies, where rubber boots tromped them into the sand if they weren't dead already. Lori trained her lens on a young man stomping around in the water and scooping fish out of the waves with a net. He'd already filled two plastic buckets and had three more at the ready. Little kids gleefully ran up and down the beach with different colored sieves. Their cries mingled with the calls of the gulls circling overhead. Lori got swept up in the people's exuberance and delight at the ocean harvest. She recognized Molly, proudly holding up a capelin, but didn't see Patience anywhere. Molly was wading out into the waves in her boots until they came over her knees.

Lori looked around for Patience or Ches to see if they were keeping an eye on their daughter. Then she saw Noah leaning on his truck; his head was pointed in her direction.

"Can you watch Molly and make sure she doesn't go out too far?" she asked a woman in rubber boots who was watching the goings-on with folded arms.

The woman gave a friendly laugh. "Not to worry! We won't let anybody sink! Too many people here for that to happen!"

Lori took her point. In the village, it wasn't just parents who felt responsible for the children—every last relative and neighbor did too.

She looked back at Noah, who hadn't moved. He had his hands in his vest pockets and his baseball cap pulled down partly over his face.

He knew exactly what would happen, she thought: it wouldn't be long before somebody would come by and strike up a conversation. But she couldn't resist going over to him.

He spoke first, without moving a muscle.

"You should catch a few capelin, for lunch. Taste good."

"Why don't you show me how—you're not even lifting your little finger." She leaned against the truck beside him, mimicking his posture.

"Naw, I do enough fishing. Today's for relaxing."

She looked at him from the side.

"I haven't seen your boat for a long while."

"Went to Saleau Cove for five days, going for halibut. And turbot."

"Oh, so that was it."

He'd gone off without saying a thing. Didn't he think she'd be interested? Would want to record it with her camera?

Disappointment rose up inside her like bitter stomach acid. She saw some men with full buckets shaking the contents into larger containers that were then loaded onto trucks.

"Wouldn't that have been good for my book?"

He cleared his throat. "I thought about that, but . . . we were out for five days and six nights. We only landed to unload. It . . . well, six men on the boat—there wasn't a bunk for you. And nobody had time to wash up. Or change their underwear."

She listened to him, to his words and hesitant tone of voice. *There's something he's not telling me.*

"I hiked in the Rockies for a week without washing once," she said.

"You don't know what it's like out there. Storms can pop up anytime." He was talking faster than usual. "Lucky the catch was a good one, but the sea was up, and we all got seasick."

"You too?"

"Oh, happens all the time. It's wicked. Wicked."

She waited a beat, then decided to go for it.

"So it's not because you basically didn't want me along?"

His eyes fastened on her for a split second, then on his boots. "What do you mean?"

"Maybe you feel . . . maybe it bothers you if I'm on the boat."

"Bothers me? No, not at all. What makes you think that?"

"Maybe I'll be in your way and ask dumb questions and watch everything you do."

"No, doesn't bother me. I kind of thought . . . maybe you'd find it boring on board." Pause. "Maybe . . . you don't always like being around fishermen."

Now you've got to tell him, Lori. Now you've got to say: I like being around you. But I'm also afraid to be.

But instead, she said, "I don't always know how to act, what's right and what isn't. I'm a cautious person. But that doesn't mean that . . . that I'm not interested in what you do."

When he stayed silent, she added, "And I really like talking to you."

He scuffed up some dirt with his boots. Then he suddenly said, "My father died fishing for scallops in Saleau Cove."

She turned to him with a shocked look on her face.

"How did it happen?"

"He was hit by a scallop rake and thrown overboard."

"Oh my God! That must have been terrible. How old were you?"

"Seventeen."

"Were you . . . there on the boat when it happened?"

"No, not me, but Coburn was—my oldest brother. And Scott Parsons."

Seventeen. Glowena Parsons must have already been his girlfriend by then. Jacinta was murdered a year later. When suspicion fell on Noah . . . *if* suspicion fell on him—she mentally corrected herself— he'd lost the father who could have defended him. Archie must have assumed that role.

"You still miss him, don't you? Twenty years can take away the pain but not the loss."

"Taught me everything about fishing. He was a good man."

Lori realized that his words amounted to an expression of love for his deceased father. She wished she could say the same thing about her father. But she didn't know how. What had *her* father ever taught her? He'd left her behind in Canada to advance his cardiology career. But if he'd have lived, he could have helped a lot of people with heart disease. And he probably would have taken her with him if her mother hadn't fought for her. But that's not how a seventeen-year-old girl thinks. She thinks: *Daddy abandoned me.*

Noah's voice snapped her out of her thoughts.

"Do you see Mitch and Dorice?"

"Who are Mitch and Dorice?"

"Over there, that elderly couple. They're way over eighty but take part in everything."

Lori saw an old woman in rubber boots wading in the water while her husband dipped his net into the waves. Their faces radiated enthusiasm and delight.

"I've got to get them," Lori exclaimed. But before she reached the old couple, somebody beat her to it. A young woman, also with a camera. Her blond hair fell over her shoulders in two loosely tied braids; her bright blue form-fitting jacket just came down to her waist. Below it, her black stretch pants noticeably outlined her derriere.

Lori waited impatiently while the young woman constantly changed her angle. Lori could tell from her frantic movements that she wasn't dealing with a pro, but not a novice either. The woman made it impossible for her to photograph the old couple because she was always in the shot.

The blond finally lowered her lens and looked around, but Lori couldn't tell if it was for new material or to attract the bystanders' attention. Her braids swung around her attractive, made-up face, reminding Lori of Britney Spears in her early days. What the hell was this pop cutie doing in Stormy Cove?

The answer wasn't long in coming. The blond caught sight of Lori's camera, and a winning smile lit up her face.

"Oh—am I in your way?"

Lori's response was a polite smile.

"We can take turns," she said, hoping it didn't sound too patronizing. She felt like a grandmother next to this peppy young thing.

She took a few pictures, skillfully and with concentration, then checked the camera display. The woman was hanging around, watching her with interest.

"Are you a reporter too?"

Reporter. Lori tried to mask her surprise.

"No, a photographer. Who are you working for?"

"The *Cape Lone Courier*. I'm doing an internship with them."

"You from around here?"

The young woman laughed, making her braids bounce. Hair a little thin, Lori observed, but means nothing with a face like that.

"No, I'm from Ontario, from Trifton. About an hour from Toronto."

"You came all the way to Newfoundland for an internship?"

"Yes, I got lucky. It's not easy to get an internship with a newspaper! I've just *got* to get a foot in the door, then hopefully things'll get better." Her teeth glinted between lips covered with pale lipstick. "Who are your pictures for?"

"For a book." Lori had no desire to explain further.

"Oh, cool! You have to tell me more about that. I really want to take lots of photos. But I've gotta get back, gotta get this story into print. Are you staying here? We're sure to run into each other. I'm Reanna, Reanna Sholler. And you?"

Lori now noticed the tattoo on her neck. A little lizard.

"Lori Finning."

Reanna turned around with a playful wave of her hand and catwalk-stepped toward the parked cars. Her ass wiggled.

Lori looked over at Noah. He was at the pickup's tailgate, his hand on the side wall. He wasn't looking in Lori's direction this time. His eyes followed Reanna Sholler until she drove off in her Ford Mustang.

Lori was attacked by a stabbing pain.

She pretended to be busy taking pictures, snapping furiously, but her thoughts were racing.

Well, what did she expect? A woman like Reanna provided exciting relief from the monotonous, humdrum routine of life in Stormy Cove. Reanna would turn heads even in Toronto, especially in those pants. Men *do* look, after all. Women too, like Lori; after all, she was professionally prejudiced, having taken many portraits of beautiful women. She knew how they could become even more beautiful in front of a camera.

With time, people here had become accustomed to having the photographer from Vancouver among them. She'd lost her novelty value. Reanna was the new sensation.

Lori bit her lip. She'd been prepared for anything. That she'd get an unfriendly reception. That people wouldn't want their picture taken. That she'd get sick and have to go home. That she'd never find a place to rent. That the pictures wouldn't turn out so great. But she wasn't prepared for a cute young woman, an outsider like herself, who also wanted to publish photographs of the area.

Suddenly, Noah was beside her.

"I can take you out tomorrow to the icebergs if you'd like."

He seemed almost timid as he looked at her.

Her heart leapt to her throat.

"Icebergs are here already?"

"Yes, out by Seaflower Bay. Supposed to be very little wind tomorrow."

"Yes, that would be fabulous, I'd love it." She paused for a moment. "Don't you have to fish tomorrow?"

"Hardly any lumpfish now. Pay more for the gas than I make for the fish. Cod season opens in three days."

She caught the glint in his eye. That gave her wings, the lift she needed.

"Would you like to come over for dinner this evening?"

He shifted his weight from one leg to the other.

"I'd like to but . . . I gotta go to Saleau Cove for some equipment for the boat. A guy's selling something I really need."

He almost stammered. "I . . . I'd like to take you but Nate's coming and the truck will be full up with stuff."

Lori could tell that he was genuinely sorry to miss the opportunity.

"No problem," she assured him.

"Will you ask me another time, or have I screwed up?"

They both laughed.

"Have no fear. I can't wait to dazzle you with my culinary artistry. Tomorrow at nine?"

"I'll be there."

Feeling exhilarated, like she'd downed two glasses of white wine, she drove down the winding main street of Stormy Cove. She'd barely set foot in her house when the phone rang. She quickly took off her hiking boots and ran through the kitchen to the living room.

"Lori?"

She didn't recognize the voice.

"It's Bobbie, Bobbie Wall. From the B and B in Deer Lake."

Deer Lake. It seemed so long ago.

"What a pleasant surprise," Lori said, wondering how Bobbie got her number.

"Remember that funny business when you were here? Those people in the next room?"

"You mean . . . the orgy?"

Bobbie giggled.

"Yes, exactly. I know who it was and thought you'd be interested!"

Lori wanted to say it's probably more interesting to you than me.

"The people are from your area," the old lady got there first.

"You mean Vancouver?"

"No, from Stormy Cove. That's where you are, eh?"

"Yes," Lori said, with some hesitation. *What in the world?*

"The kid's name is Jack Day."

Jack. The really young hunter. Seventeen. Noah's cousin's son.

"And the woman who said she was his aunt is Ginette Hearne."

Lori's breath caught in her throat. She could see Ginette before her, in the bar, grabbing Noah's crotch.

"And the other woman?"

"Don't know yet. But she's probably not from Stormy Cove, or I'd have found out."

Lori didn't have any questions. What she had now was enough food for thought.

"Funny, eh?" Bobbie said. "What are you going to do?"

"Me? Why me?"

"Well, I thought that since you're already there . . . maybe you should appeal to this Ginette's conscience. What she's doing is wrong in God's eyes."

Lori knew instinctively what was behind it. Bobbie didn't want to get involved—and couldn't anyway because of her B and B—but she'd like to see somebody put an end to what she considered sinful behavior. She apparently wasn't aware that having sex with a minor was also a criminal act in Newfoundland.

"You're absolutely right," Lori assured her as calmly as she could, "but that's something the locals should settle among themselves, don't you think?"

Bobbie Wall was not about to give up.

"Maybe you can warn Jack's mother."

"I don't know his mother. Besides, it was . . . I just *heard* it; I didn't see anything."

"Just wanted to let you know. Because two of them are from Stormy Cove and you—"

"That's very kind of you, thanks, Bobbie. How's your husband keeping?"

"He was in the hospital for two weeks, because of his legs. But he's coming along. By the way, Lloyd Weston's beginning a dig next week. He was here and mentioned you."

"Well, then, I'm sure I'll be hearing from him. Take care, Bobbie."

"You too. And if I find out the name of that second woman, I'll call again."

Lori hung up. Jack and Ginette. She could hardly believe it.

Other people in a village as small as Stormy Cove must know about it too, right?

Maybe she should sound out Noah about it.

But she'd have time for that tomorrow.

Best if nobody else was around.

CHAPTER 27

That her hopes were misguided became apparent when Lori went down to the wharf the next morning. A slim silhouette beside Noah's familiar figure set off warning bells. Her suspicion was confirmed as she came nearer: Reanna Sholler.

Lori resisted the impulse to turn on her heel and head for the car. What did her mother always say when she was in a tight spot in the courtroom? *Don't leave the trench when you're under fire.*

Lori gave Reanna a brief once-over when they said hello and saw that the pretty intern had brought some heavy artillery with her. A red imitation leather jacket, skintight stretch jeans, and thigh-high leather boots. Reanna's blond hair was brushed back over her forehead and tied with a scarf.

That very morning Lori had stared in the mirror and noted that the Stormy Cove climate had really done her good. Her dark eyes shone, her skin had a fresh glow, and her thick, grown-out hair fell in gentle curls around her face. She looked more attractive than she had ten years ago.

But now her mood darkened when a merry Reanna reported that she'd landed a new assignment.

"I've wanted to see icebergs for a long time, and today's my lucky day because Will's planning to do a feature and sent me out. Isn't that mind-blowing?"

Reanna had the same habit maybe young people in Vancouver did, piling on sentence after sentence without a break, so that Lori instinctively had to catch her breath. And Reanna wasn't done yet.

"He said somebody in Stormy Cove would take me with them, and so I came here, and it so happens I find this nice man here, and I hope you don't mind if I come along?"

Lori exchanged quick looks with Noah. His face reflected the pleasure of a person certain he's in for an interesting experience. The irony of the situation didn't escape her. Noah would never have told Will Spence he'd take someone out on his boat, so Spence sent a Trojan horse. Lori hadn't the slightest desire to grin and bear it. She was royally pissed off.

But the old pro in her took over. She'd learned over her eighteen years on the job to suppress her personal feelings in favor of the client's. Bitchy models, celebs with their outlandish demands, magazines that changed their assignment at the last minute, waiting for people for hours, amateur know-it-alls who told her how to take pictures, editors who said her photos were inadequate so they could beat her down on her fee—she'd been through it all and come out alive.

She looked at Noah.

"Anybody else going out? It would be good to have another boat in the picture. To give some idea of an iceberg's size."

"Rick Kline just left ten minutes ago with relatives of his." He rubbed the back of his neck. "It's a good day—sunny and almost dead calm. Doesn't happen much."

"That's wonderful!" Reanna exclaimed. "I can't wait. I'm ready to go!"

Lori had to admit that her enthusiasm was a bit contagious.

"OK. Let's do this," she said and watched Noah take the young woman's hand and help her from the higher dock into the motorboat.

Reanna plopped herself down in the bow. Lori realized the consequences at once: she'd have an obstructed view forward. *Damn it!*

She didn't deign to look at Noah as he helped her into the boat. But she couldn't ignore the touch of his hand. Her self-denial didn't go that far.

The boat quickly left the cove behind and skirted the prominent rocky point near the fishing village of Isle View. The weather was perfect for photography, a soft, golden morning light that made for excellent contrast without creating a diffuse effect. The circumstances couldn't have been any better in that regard.

She'd rather have turned her back on the other circumstances, but Reanna looked back and asked Lori to duck. Then she took several shots of Noah and served him up an enchanting smile.

"Icebergs probably aren't anything special for you," she shouted at him. "You see them every year."

"Oh, they're nice to see," Noah replied with some excitement. "But they often cover our nets and wreck them. We can free up the small ones, but can't do anything about the big ones."

Lori looked at Noah. "How do you free them?"

"With ropes. Sling a rope around them and the boat can pull them away."

She was about to ask him if there was a chance of a photo op when Reanna butted in.

"I've absolutely *got* to see that!"

Then she suddenly uttered a sharp cry: icebergs loomed on the horizon, swerving around the rocky point of land. Lori counted three colossi. Her pulse raced. What a constellation! *An Ice Triptych*—that's what she could call it in her book; that would sound properly grand. White pyramids, sharply defined against the steel-blue sky. Noah throttled down, and Lori held her zoom lens as tightly as she could in the rocking boat. At that moment, Reanna changed position, and Lori almost fell off the wooden bench.

"Watch it!" Noah shouted, and Reanna apologized profusely.

Lori forced a smile and decided from then on to announce when she was about to shoot. In the meantime, she had to wait patiently until Reanna was finished.

"Don't lean out on the same side," Noah warned them. "This boat's tippy."

Oh, wonderful, Lori thought to herself. Sometimes she just let the camera motor run, in the hopes that at least one picture wouldn't have any blond windblown hair or glaring red jacket in it.

Noah circled the icebergs at a safe distance.

"Noah, can you get a bit closer?" Reanna shouted.

He shook his head.

"These things can break up anytime or tip over and pull the boat under."

"That would give me a good story!" Reanna winked at him.

Lori had no desire to observe Noah's reaction. She concentrated on the marvel of nature unfolding before her.

The icebergs resembled tremendous sculptures that changed constantly as the camera angle varied with the boat's movements. One minute she saw a dragon with a serrated back; the next, a mountain landscape with a peak jutting upward, and then a gigantic ocean liner with a steep bow. The ice had a bluish sparkle in the warm light. Some dark lines reminded her of colored veins in white marble. Seen from behind, a network of diagonal grooves ran down them as if carved by a hammer and chisel.

The icebergs rocked on the ocean, water dripping from their flanks. Then Lori sighted another boat. She waited until it appeared in an elegant archway through the ice, shouted "Don't move!", pressed the release, and heaved a sigh. At least this was one picture Reanna hadn't ruined. She noticed some birds on the top of one of the icebergs. Were they murres or gulls? If circumstances had been different, she'd have asked Noah, but she opted to keep words to a minimum. Their attitude toward one another was almost businesslike. Lori had no desire to compete with Reanna the flatterer.

Still, Noah made a great effort to steer the boat over to some places at Lori's request. That put her in a conciliatory mood. On the return trip, she even managed to smile when she couldn't prevent Reanna from taking her picture. She knew from experience that anyone who stares at the camera with a pinched and angry look will wind up doubly punished.

"That was awesome, really cool!" Reanna enthused when they were back on land. "So nice of you to take me with you. A day I'll never forget!"

"It's OK, it's OK," Noah said, and Reanna hugged him like they were old friends. Noah produced an embarrassed laugh and then swiftly stuck his hands in his pockets.

"Cod fishing starts Thursday. Hope the weather plays along."

"Oh, maybe Will can send me back here. That would be terrific! Much better than sitting in the office!"

She looked at Lori.

"And I definitely want to see your pictures. I'm so interested. You'll see mine in the paper, of course. And I'll put a few on Facebook."

"But please, not the picture of me," Lori said quickly. "I wouldn't want that."

Reanna took her arm.

"No, not a problem. After all, you're here incognito, I do know that much."

She laughed and ran off with a brief wave.

Lori put away her cameras and ran her fingers through her hair as if it were still short.

"Many thanks for the trip," she grinned, stepping a little closer. "I'm gonna give you something for the gas."

If Reanna treated Noah like a friend, so could she.

"Oh no, no way. Today was fun."

His eyes wandered from her to the direction of Reanna's departure, then back to her.

"You want pictures of us cod fishing? Come along anytime, leaving at five in the morning. Really, Lori. Anytime."

She shouldered her camera bag.

"Yes, I'd love to come, but it's no good for me if somebody else is taking pictures too. People get in the way, as you no doubt saw today."

"I know—wasn't the plan. She just turned up this morning and . . . I couldn't say no. Rick's boat was already gone. I can take you out again if you want, but I don't know exactly when. The cod . . ."

His eyes wandered over to the parked cars. Lori's throat tightened. She heard a motor start up. Reanna's Mustang.

She folded her arms across her chest.

"I'll go have a look at the pictures I shot today. It's not your responsibility to keep taking me out there. I don't want to be a pain in the neck."

She could hardly believe that they were talking like this. It seemed to her as if the bond between them that she'd sensed until yesterday was broken.

"Oh, not at all. Not at all. Been more exciting since you've come." He almost sounded befuddled.

Sure. Pretty girls from far away are exciting.

And two are more exciting than one.

Particularly when nothing much happens in Stormy Cove. You don't want to miss any of the action.

"Thanks again," she said and went to her car.

Was he watching her leave the way he'd watched Reanna? She fought off the temptation to look back.

She stopped at the store to pick up milk and bread. Nosy Mavis eyed her expectantly as she came in the door.

"So, did you get a lot of iceberg photographs?"

"Who told you about that?" She still couldn't fathom how news got around Stormy Cove so fast.

"Easy. Rick's sister was just here. Rick went out with some of the family. She drove them to the wharf."

Mavis stretched and her bosom heaved. Two rhinestone broaches glittered on her green turtleneck sweater. Lizards again.

Lori felt like reading the weekend *Globe and Mail* or the *Vancouver Sun* or a glossy like *Vanity Fair* or a chic interior decorating magazine like *Elle Decor*. And having a real Italian espresso with it and a butter croissant fresh from the oven.

But only tabloids made it to Stormy Cove.

She picked one of them up and skimmed the headline: "Ellen DeGeneres and Portia de Rossi Finally Want a Baby."

Mavis planted both hands on the counter.

"There's nothing about Hollywood stars to get excited over anymore. Women can marry women and adopt kids and it's on the front page."

"Not only Hollywood stars," Lori added. "I'm good friends with a lesbian couple, and they adopted two children. They go to school, and nobody gives a damn that they've got two mothers."

"Yeah? Well, that would be a first in these parts. Wouldn't go down well with some people." She smoothed her sweater. "When Jacinta noised it around that she'd seen Robine Whalen necking with a woman, there was hell to pay."

Lori dropped the tabloid.

"Jacinta saw *what*?"

"Didn't you know? Jacinta told her parents . . . and maybe a few others that she'd seen Robine kissing another woman."

"Who was she?"

"A woman from St. John's, one of the archaeology gals. Only a rumor back then. You never know what to believe. Well, we've found out in the meantime what's with Robine."

"How old was she then?"

"Let me think . . . fifteen or sixteen. She started early . . . But girls here do that with boys too."

"So how did . . . what did her family say to that?"

"Didn't believe it, naturally. I mean, the Whalens and the Parsons—I shouldn't gossip like this, but they aren't exactly the best of friends. Ever since Noah's dad drowned they—"

She cut herself off when the door opened. Greta Whalen called out.

"Hello. Can I join the coffee klatch?"

She was wearing a sweatshirt with "Newfies Rock" on the front and gray sweatpants. Her blue eyes sparkled.

"Coffee's over there." Mavis flapped her right elbow at a thermos on the shelf. "We were just talking about icebergs. Lori went out with Noah and a new reporter from the *Cape Lone Courier*."

Greta poured coffee into a paper cup.

"What do they need new reporters for? Nothing ever happens here."

"She's a trainee, still learning," Lori explained. And then to Mavis, "Any fresh bread today?"

But Mavis wasn't finished with the subject.

"What's a kid from Ontario doing here, I'd like to know. There are more papers there than here. And she sure don't look like a reporter, more like a model."

Greta sipped her coffee. "Where's she from in Ontario?"

"Trifton," Lori responded.

"Trifton? Is there a place anywhere that's really called that?" Mavis frowned.

"Trifton," Greta repeated, musing. "She told some people she's from Timmins. Like Shania Twain. How old is she?"

"I'd say early twenties. What about that fresh bread?"

Mavis reached into a bin behind her and pulled out a rectangular loaf wrapped in plastic.

"It costs thirty cents more now—can you believe it? Because wheat's gone up. A farmer keeps making more money, and it's the fisherman who gets less and less."

"But fish in the stores are more and more expensive," Lori said. "Something's not right. Somebody's raking it in very nicely."

She paid for the bread and milk and said good-bye.

When she got to her car, she heard her name called. Greta caught up with her.

"That reporter. Did she really say Trifton?"

Lori ran her fingers over the notches in her car key.

"Yes."

She didn't want to hear another word about Reanna Sholler.

"If you see her again, could you ask . . . could you find out a bit more about her? Her parents, what they do, what school she went to?"

Lori looked at Greta in surprise.

"I don't actually know the woman. We only met by chance."

"Oh, I thought you'd taken her under your wing, sort of."

"Why should I? Will Spence is her boss, not me."

She opened the car door and dropped the groceries on the passenger seat. Greta hadn't moved. Lori had the feeling she wanted to ask her something, but she evidently changed her mind.

"OK, then . . . I'm curious to see what's in the Monday paper." And with that, she left.

Lori's head was buzzing. She could hardly focus on anything as she drove through Stormy Cove. Robine with a woman archaeologist. And now Greta with her peculiar request. How could anyone make any sense of all the little intrigues?

Did the police hear about the rumors surrounding Robine? And could they know that Jacinta's spying was the apparent source? Did Lloyd Weston know about it? How did Robine take the gossip? And the Whalen family?

And why the animosity between the Parsons and the Whalens? She couldn't understand what Mavis was trying to get at.

When she thought back on her conversations, Greta's behavior seemed odder and odder. The locals always found things out in no time flat. Why was she asking for Lori's help? Had Noah . . . maybe roped his sister into finding out more about Reanna? But she rejected that out of hand. It wasn't Noah's way of doing things. She doubted that Noah confided anything about his personal affairs to his family at all. She couldn't imagine him talking to anybody about his feelings.

Something was bugging Greta. Something she didn't want to disclose.

She sighed. *Oh, why did that reporter have to show up right now!* As if things weren't already complicated enough.

When she returned home, she saw a flashing light. The answering machine. She pushed the button.

"Hello, this is Lloyd Weston. We're flying up to the site in a few days. I want you to come. In fact, I'd like to hire you to photograph the site! Please call me back."

Lori filled the kettle and made a sandwich with wet packaged ham and mushy tomatoes—there wasn't anything better at the store.

Then she e-mailed Mona Blackwood to tell her about Weston's offer and get her opinion. Maybe there was a conflict of interest, and it was best to get these things out in the open. She didn't want to blow it with Mona, but the dig might be valuable for the book. Next, she downloaded the iceberg pictures onto her laptop and went through them slowly. She knew that at least a few shots must have come out well, but what she found exceeded her expectations. What a haul! Of course there were some crappy ones, courtesy of Reanna, but also several that took her breath away. She was good in the studio—that, she knew—but her real love was outdoor photography. And she could explore that passion to its fullest extent in this powerful, wild, inspiring landscape.

She beavered away on cataloging and editing the photos, not stopping until it had gotten dark outside. Then her eagerness flagged, and the events of the day caught up with her. She suddenly felt tired and dejected. She stretched out on the sofa and closed her heavy eyelids. But the images wouldn't leave her in peace. She was immediately back on the boat, cruising by icebergs. A face bulled its way into view—blond hair streaming in the wind. Lori pushed away the image, brought back the icebergs and their massive, sparkling sides, the peaks and the arches, the seabirds on their crest, like dark sprinkles atop frosting.

But then a face returned, framed in blond hair. It was not Reanna. Katja.

In the kitchen on the Lindenhold estate.

Lori rolled over onto her side, but the memories couldn't be kept at bay—they fought their way through with too much force.

The icebergs vanished. She found herself in the kitchen at Lindenhold, a pile of snap beans on the table in front of her for trimming. It was dark in the kitchen, but the autumn sun was shining outside. It had attracted everyone else to the garden; she had to make supper all by herself.

A door opens. Katja, asking, "You know where Volker is?"

She's wearing a miniskirt over her shiny leggings, a low-cut blouse, and her blond, unkempt hair falls over her shoulders. The dark rings in her pale face are not as pronounced as during the first few weeks after she arrived. A young woman, from one of the finest families, who had drifted into drug addiction and was looking for a cure and stability in Lindenhold.

Drifted. Volker's word. As if somebody had forced cocaine on Katja. So where does an addict's responsibility kick in, Lori had argued. The word "responsibility" hadn't sat well with him. He'd lectured her that Katja was to be treated as somebody who is recuperating, like from a long illness. Lori tears off the thin threads from the bean pods with her knife. She doesn't look up as she says in her halting German, "He doesn't have any time right now. What's the matter?"

"I've got to talk to him. Where is he?"

Now Lori looks up.

"He's with Andrew."

"Can he come down for a moment? I've got to talk to him."

Lori shakes her head.

"He's playing with Andrew. He has a family. He has a child. Do you understand? Andrew wants to be with his daddy too."

"He can still do that," Katja shouts impatiently, flinging back her unruly hair. "I just have to have a quick word with him."

She moves toward the door to the attic steps, to where she thinks Volker and Andrew are. But Lori is quicker. She stands in front of the door, knife in hand.

Now only English comes out of her mouth. She knows Katja learned English in school.

"Leave Volker alone! You've monopolized him enough. He's not your therapist. He has a little child who needs him. Andrew needs his dad, and you're not going up there. You have no business being in our room. I've had enough of you taking advantage of his good nature. He can't just be there for you whenever you want. Enough is enough. You only think about yourself. How about you trim these beans and contribute something to the community. Make yourself useful for once."

She stands her ground, clutching the paring knife.

Katja stares at her, flabbergasted. Then she looks wildly around the kitchen. Until her eyes settle on something. She moves toward it in slow motion. She opens the drawer and takes out a knife.

Lori thinks, *She's going to attack me!*

She breaks out in a cold sweat.

But Katja runs out of the kitchen, the knife still in her hand.

Lori's first thought is of Andrew. She races up the attic stairs and almost breaks down the door. Nothing. Volker and Andrew are nowhere to be seen. She yells their names and charges downstairs, through the empty kitchen and the corridor and outside.

"Volker! Andrew!" she screams in desperation. She sees Rosemarie standing by the rabbit shed.

"Where's Volker?"

Rosemarie comes over.

"What's the matter, Lori? What's happened?"

Lori's almost out of her mind.

"Where's Volker?"

"Down at the pond. Lori, what's up?" Rosemarie's face is tense with worry.

"She's got a knife! She's got a knife!"

Lori runs down to the pond. She sees Volker and Andrew feeding ducks and screams their names again.

Volker turns around and stays rooted to the spot. Then he takes Andrew's hand. The boy looks at her in confusion.

When she reaches them, she can hardly speak.

"She's got a knife," is all she can manage.

Volker grabs her by the shoulder.

"Who's got a knife?"

"Katja. She . . . she took a knife out of the kitchen drawer and . . . and ran out of the kitchen!"

Volker frowns.

"You've got a knife, too, Lori. What happened?"

She is panting.

"I . . . I thought she wanted to help me with the beans, but . . . she got a knife out of the drawer and just . . . took off."

"But that's no reason to scare us like this, we—"

"Volker, we must find Katja immediately," a voice behind them says. Rosemarie's determined tone brooks no contradiction. "I'll go get Franz. You stay with Lori."

Lori had never heard Rosemarie speak so decisively.

Katja couldn't be found that night. The police arrived the following morning. They discovered Katja at a friend's place in town. She'd overdosed. The kitchen knife was discovered later in the shed at Lindenhold, where Katja had stolen a motorbike to go into town. But the investigators never found out about it.

Volker, Franz, and Rosemarie kept Lori out of the police investigation as much as they could. It was in their own interest as well. They wanted the community for recovering addicts to keep operating. Lori was surprised that the "incident," as she called it, didn't make bigger waves. Katja's parents seemed to adjust quickly. It was also possible that Lori wasn't being told everything. Just the way she never told Volker the whole truth. He never really pursued it. She had the impression that this was the first time he'd questioned whether it was good to raise Andrew in this unusual community. It occurred to her later that this was the reason he didn't object to Andrew's going to Canada with her. For years afterward, Lori used her child's safety to justify her stubborn refusal to admit her share of the blame for Katja's death. But it cost her a lot of energy to relegate this ghost to the cellar of her unconscious.

Somebody ought to warn Reanna, she thought, as she made a nightcap in the kitchen.

Somebody ought to warn her about me.

CHAPTER 28

The wind blew so hard the next day the fishermen didn't even think about going out on the turbulent sea.

Lori decided to take a walk around the bay with Rusty and her camera. She had an exposed spot in her sights, a spot where the wind was so powerful that all the few gnarled firs there could do was to bend with it and grow almost horizontally to the ground. The symbolic value of the image was obvious. A life pulled between submission, resistance, and adaptation—a fine balance between mistakes and triumphs. Except that mistakes here could rapidly be fatal.

That was a nice way to put it. She made a mental note to add it to her travel diary later.

She kept to the lee side at first, but after reaching the high plateau, she had to brace herself against gusts of wind with all her strength. She was amazed at how the little frame houses were able to brave constant onslaughts year after year. Rusty kept pulling his rope vigorously; he was clearly irritated by her leisurely pace and frequent stops and would have gone a hundred times farther by now without her. But when she squatted down near the cliffs in order not to be whisked off by the wind, he sat patiently beside her, picking up scents from every direction. While she was taking pictures, she had to tie the leash around her waist, which the dog liked even less. She'd read somewhere that huskies can run for eight hours nonstop. But here in the Canadian North, most of them spent their lives on a short leash. Lori found the mere thought unbearable and untied the rope around her waist. She could show him places that he'd never see otherwise—and vice versa. She ventured farther afield with Rusty than if she'd been walking alone.

They returned to the village at noon, and with a heavy heart, she chained Rusty in front of his doghouse. She decided to have lunch and then go read up on cod fishing in the library. She'd had it with Internet research and longed to run her fingertips over printed paper.

Aurelia was busy shelving books when Lori came in. Her face lit up.

"So nice to see you, Lori! I often think of you when I see a book you might be interested in. Have you discovered anything more about poor Marguerite?"

Lori shook her head.

"She'll probably remain a mystery, but I haven't given up hope of getting back to the Isle of Demons someday."

"You certainly will! Somebody will take you there, I'm sure. And then you absolutely must tell me what it's like."

"You can count on it. But today I want to read up on cod."

"Cod, sure, that's easy. Take a look at this big book here; came out recently."

Aurelia pulled a tome off the shelf and laid it on a table in front of a window.

"Isn't it beautiful?"

Lori didn't know whether to be happy or intimidated by the book's size.

"This whole thing is about cod?"

"Why, yes, there's a lot to say. Cod dominated Newfoundland history for a long time. And European history."

"You're using the past tense," Lori remarked.

Aurelia blushed, as if caught out.

"I'm afraid the good times are past—but don't tell the fishermen that. They're still hoping the cod will come back."

Did Noah hope that as well? There was so much she wanted to ask him. All of a sudden, she was dying to be on the boat, watching him fish. The legendary cod. She imagined taking photos that might almost seem biblical. She felt Aurelia's eyes on her.

"I've heard that the official catch quotas set by the Ministry of Fisheries in Ottawa are very low. How low, actually? I wonder how much cod they're still permitted to catch at all."

"Will you be going out cod fishing?"

"Yes, tomorrow, I hope, if the wind dies down."

"Who with?"

"Noah, or anybody who'll take me along."

"It must make Noah proud that you show so much interest in his work."

Lori avoided Aurelia's curious gaze and opened the book.

"Do you think so?" she asked offhandedly.

"Well . . . a lot of women think those guys always stink of fish and don't make much . . ."

Lori was at a loss as to how to take that. People always wanted to know the exact nature of others' relationships. And if they couldn't, they speculated. Even when the parties in question weren't sure about it themselves. Lori repeatedly asked herself if she was being fair to Noah. Was she really any different from the women for whom a fisherman wasn't good enough? She'd never really thought it through. Maybe Noah was only an exotic eyeful for her. A diversion for as long as she was there on her book project. Did she respect him enough for his hard work, his humaneness, his tenacity, his . . . ?

"It must be entertaining for the men when you're on board," Aurelia continued.

"Yes, I'd like to think so, even if I mostly just get in their way," Lori replied airily, to change the subject. "Is your husband a fisherman?"

"He used to be, but he gave it up and sold his license. He drives the second school bus now. And I work in Gideon Moore's office off and on when he needs secretarial help."

"Are you glad he doesn't fish anymore?"

Aurelia toyed with her pencil.

"Yes, I am. It made me anxious when he was out on the ocean. We have three kids. I didn't want to be a widow." She paused and raised a hand as if fending something off. "Joseph Johnston's funeral is this Friday. Did you hear about his terrible accident? No? He slipped on the deck of his boat and fell into the fish hole. Head first. They couldn't do anything for him. Like I said, Friday's the funeral. Another new widow in the village."

"Like Noah's mother." The words escaped Lori before she could stop them.

"Yes, Winnie never recovered from that tragedy. Sure, Archie looks after the family, but . . . when Noah's dad was alive, he and Archie . . . oh, what am I saying? I mustn't gossip."

"It's not gossip," Lori assured her, eager to learn more about Noah's family. "Nothing secret about it. I'm sure the whole village knows."

"Everybody knows, that's for sure. But . . . anybody else will probably tell you the same thing: the two of them didn't always fish in the same waters."

Lori looked at her without saying anything. That encouraged the librarian to continue.

"Archie will never be another Abram Whalen, no matter how hard he tries. He simply isn't made of the right stuff. He'd really like to, but . . ." She shrugged. "I don't want to keep you from your book. You can borrow it. You'd be the first, though it's been here a while."

"The first? Isn't anybody here interested in a big book about cod?"

Aurelia put on the cardigan she'd thrown over her chair and watched the children coming in from the corridor linking the library to the school.

"Somehow the interest in fisheries has dwindled. I think most folks secretly think that fishermen are losers."

She said it with a tinge of regret, as if she felt guilty of treason—she, the wife of a man who'd given up his fishing boat for a school bus.

Lori started to leaf through the book, and in a few minutes, she was buried deep in the descriptions, the numerous illustrations, tables, statistics, and particularly the old engravings and photos from a lost age.

It was quickly clear that this book wasn't only about a fish that once fed half the world but about a part of history she didn't know anywhere near enough about.

She felt a sudden cold draft from the door and halfheartedly turned her head. The woman who'd come in paid as little attention to her as was possible under the circumstances.

Lori was startled to see Ginette in the library, but she found out why when the woman made a beeline for the computer.

"Your computer still isn't working?" she heard Aurelia say.

"Dunno what's wrong with the damn thing. I've already lugged it to Corner Brook for repairs, but it's going crazy again. Piece of shit!"

Ginette sat down noisily, and Lori was glad she had her back to her. But the atmosphere in the room had changed. Though she kept on reading, Lori's concentration waned.

Fifteen minutes later, she went to Aurelia to check out the book. Then she put her running shoes on and shut the door behind her. A moment later, she saw Ginette coming out of the library behind her.

On an impulse, Lori began to run, catching up to Ginette before she could get in her car.

"Can I ask you something?" Lori began.

Ginette didn't answer, just stared with outright suspicion all over her face. The wind blew her cropped curly hair in all directions. Lori had on a beret, as always. She decided not to pussyfoot around.

"Do you remember Bobbie Wall's B and B in Deer Lake? You were there last March with a young man and a woman. Was that woman Una Gould?"

Ginette was dumbfounded.

"Who . . . what . . . you stalking me or something?"

"I happened to be staying in the next room. I couldn't help hearing, even if I didn't want to."

Ginette tried to keep her composure. She put her hands in her jacket pocket.

"Then you know if Una was there or not."

"Well, I wasn't being nosy. I didn't even stick my head out the door."

"Then it's none of your damn business." Ginette pulled out her keys.

Lori braced herself against the wind.

"Maybe not mine, but other people might be interested."

Ginette gave her head a shake as if irritated by a child's petulant behavior.

"You're crazy. Una? Una, of all people?" More vigorous headshaking. But her resistance was losing steam. "If you ask me, something happened to Una. Something bad. I can't prove it, but she didn't just cut and run. You didn't know her, but I did. If she took off, then it certainly wasn't by herself."

"Then with who? With you?"

"With me? Why the hell with me? No way was Una interested in women! She'd have gone off with a man! Is that so hard to figure out? But he obviously gave her the runaround."

Lori noticed the white-and-black stripes on Ginette's press-on nails.

"Who was the man?"

Ginette swayed her body back and forth like an elephant would his trunk and didn't move her feet one inch. Her whole demeanor radiated anger and impatience.

"If you can't find *that* out, then I can't help you. I'll tell you, though, she certainly wouldn't have run off with a guy who can't pay his bills. She already had one of those at home."

With that, she opened the car door and got in.

"And stop sticking your damn nose in my business!" She slammed the door.

"What's that mean, gave her the runaround?" Lori shouted, but Ginette revved her motor in response.

Lori was frustrated as she watched the orange Pontiac Sunfire disappear. Then she remembered she'd left her scarf behind. Aurelia was waiting with it in hand.

"Lucky again," Lori acknowledged.

The librarian looked concerned.

"You shouldn't listen to Ginette. She's always spreading rumors about people. Women like her are a disgrace to our community. They come on to our guys, but they're only after their money. Never lift a finger except to try and worm some dough out of a man. We don't need women like that in Stormy Cove. They should stay the hell out."

Lori hadn't expected such rough language from Aurelia. The residents of Stormy Cove hardly ever criticized anybody in public, and she found Aurelia's emotional outburst so intriguing that she dared to ask a delicate question.

"Ginette mentioned a man Una tried to run away with, but he left her in the lurch. Do you have any idea who it was?"

A mistake. Aurelia's face immediately shut down.

"Now you see the harm women like Ginette can do. I don't want to hear another word of it."

"Sorry. I didn't mean to air dirty linen in public. Thanks for my scarf."
She turned to leave, but Aurelia stopped her.

"You should get to know a better class of women. Would you like to come to a potluck supper tonight? We have it once a month, me and some women who are fun to be with."

Lori waited a few seconds. What could she bring this time that wouldn't be rejected like her potato salad? Aurelia misinterpreted her hesitation.

"None of Noah's close relatives; you probably see the Whalens often enough," she said quickly. "In case that's what you were thinking."

"Thanks, I'd really like to come. I just can't stay too long because of getting up to fish tomorrow morning."

"Sure, I understand perfectly. Six, then?"

Lori nodded and Aurelia described the way to her house.

On the drive back, the crosswind was so strong that she had to steer hard against it. The ocean was like a roiling gray metallic broth. The whitecaps were thick on the waves. Anybody in a boat out there was a dead man. Raging spray splashed against the bare cliffs and the houses near the shore. Lori drove up the hill and noticed the light was on in her living room. Hadn't she turned it off this morning? Then she saw the yellow Mustang. And Reanna in it.

What's she doing here? And how did she find out where Lori lived? Of course, from Will Spence, who'd ambushed her at home many weeks ago.

Reanna had on a baseball cap, her blond hair in a ponytail. She looked like an American college girl. A very pretty college girl in a bright green windbreaker. She flashed her even teeth in a broad smile as she got out. She squeezed her arms against the sides of her slender body, her hands in her jeans pockets to keep the wind off her as much as she could.

"Hi, Lori! I've been waiting for you."

Lori didn't feel like inviting her in in spite of the weather. She was friendly, but businesslike.

"Unfortunately, I only have a minute. What can I do for you?"

"I heard there are some archaeological finds around here and that you were going to some dig. Can you give me a tip, colleague to colleague, where it is and how to get there?"

"Who told you that?"

"Will found out about it from somebody, don't know who. So it's true?"

Lori calculated before answering. No point in denying it, so just give a tiny fingernail of information.

"I've heard about it too, but I have no idea where it is. I'm not really interested in archaeology for the moment, got other plans. Sorry I can't help you."

She picked up the cod book.

"Can't Will Spence tell you more about it? He knows everybody here."

Reanna rolled a stone back and forth with the toe of a boot.

"He's too busy, that's why he wants me to take care of it. You don't know the archaeologists?"

What did Reanna already know? She must have discovered that Lloyd Weston was leading the dig. So why had she come to pester Lori?

"My book has to do with fishing life, Reanna." She lifted up the book. "Cod is taking up all my time."

She laughed like this was a funny joke. Fortunately, Patience appeared, carrying a plastic bag.

"Can you pop in," her neighbor called, "if you've got a minute?"

Lori went toward her.

"Sure can, I'm coming right now."

She waved good-bye to Reanna, who was still standing beside her car, went upstairs with Patience, and took off her shoes. Patience pulled a bowl out of the bag and set it down on the table.

"This is a mousse I made with crabs from the freezer. Not as good as when I make it fresh, but the gals like it a lot, and Aurelia told me you're going to the potluck tonight, and I'm disappointed I can't because I've got to help get the fire hall ready for a birthday party. You can take the mousse, if you like, so you don't have to cook anything."

The bush telegraph was working fast today. Lori was delighted all the same.

"That's so sweet of you, Patience! I was really at a loss about what to bring. Who'll be there tonight?"

"All the really nice gals. Nobody you know, but that's OK. We always have a great time together. What did that blond want?"

"Oh, she's an intern with the *Cape Lone Courier*. She was with us yesterday when we went out to the icebergs. She's trying to sniff out a story, like reporters always do."

"She wants to be like you, Lori. She's telling everybody she wants to make a book of photographs."

"Oh, she does, does she? Then she'd better learn photography first." Lori tried to sound casual, but Patience's remark touched a sore point.

"Why did Ginette go after you today?"

The question came out of the blue, and Lori almost dropped her cod book.

"Oh, she just made some noises about how I shouldn't stick my nose in her business. She probably was referring to Noah."

The words popped out so fast that it took a second for her to realize that it was a bit of a lie.

"What kind of noises?" Patience's otherwise round face looked almost pointy with curiosity.

"She said Una would never have run off by herself because she had something going with a man and wouldn't have left without him. And I asked who it was and Ginette said: You can't even see what's staring you in the face. And so I wondered if she meant Noah. Though I really can't imagine she did. Maybe she's only trying to spite me."

Not a peep from Patience. Had she put her foot in her mouth? Was all this too candid for Stormy Cove? She looked at her friend, whose face was now drained of all color. Lori felt a pain in her chest.

"Was it Noah, Patience?"

Please don't let it be Noah!

Patience, startled by Lori's imploring tone, laid a hand on her arm.

"No, no, it was certainly not Noah, absolutely not. Ginette lies like a rug—you can't believe anything she says. She knows—"

At that moment, the phone rang.

Patience picked it up.

"Go ahead," Lori said, "I've got to get back anyway. See you tomorrow."

She was afraid Reanna was still staking out the house. But there wasn't a trace of her.

The phone rang in Lori's place too.

She wasn't surprised to hear Lloyd Weston's voice.

"We're flying in with the chopper on Friday. Are you good to go?"

"Yes, where should I be?"

"I'll pick you up at your place. We want to keep the site as hush-hush as possible."

Lori almost laughed out loud. Keeping something secret in Stormy Cove—that was a sheer impossibility, especially if Weston was coming to her house. Surely the archaeologist couldn't be that naïve. But something was on the tip of her tongue.

"A reporter from the *Cape Lone Courier* came over to my place a while ago. She'd heard you were bringing me along to take pictures and wanted to know exactly where the dig was."

"What? Who did she hear that from?" She could hear the concern in his voice.

"Somebody or other told Will Spence, the editor, about it. She claims she doesn't know who it was. The strange thing is . . ."

"Yes."

"I just think it's strange that Will isn't taking over such an important story himself. The reporter's just an intern."

"What's her name?"

"Reanna Sholler. She's from Ontario."

"Sholler? S-h-o-l-l-e-r?" There was a pause while Weston noted the name.

"Well, we don't want that paper up there yet. And no lady from Ontario either. We have an arrangement with Will Spence—that much I can tell you. When we're ready, he'll get his story, but not yet. You're still with us, though?"

"I think I should get my publisher's permission, pro forma; they're paying for the book, after all. But it shouldn't be a problem. I've already told the person responsible, so I'm sure that it'll be all right."

"I'm counting on you, Lori, I think our cooperation is an opportunity for us both."

CHAPTER 29

Lori swung her backpack over her shoulder. It was filled with leftovers from the potluck—they'd been pleased to watch Lori stuff herself all evening. How could she have resisted the crusty rolls, the pasta salad with coconut and exotic spices, the chicken casserole with creamy cheese sauce, the incredibly fine lasagna, the sweet berry soufflé, and the innumerable tempting desserts?

"Where do all these delicious things come from?" she asked time and again. "Did you pull them out of a hat?"

That evening, she had to throw all her prejudices regarding Stormy Cove cuisine overboard. And her prejudgment of the women who had very carefully studied their recipes and ordered ingredients on the Internet that weren't available locally. Lori was ashamed she'd never thought of doing that herself. She'd mourned for her delis and exotic restaurants in Vancouver instead of using her imagination. These women might be living in a remote place, but they weren't lacking in imagination. In that merry circle, she'd learned how much she'd missed until now. For instance, the name of the dealer in St. John's who paid the most for handmade wall hangings (still far too little in Lori's opinion, but she kept mum). Or in whose homes there was drug dealing. She also learned which couples weren't so keen on fidelity and that it was common in the Hardy Sailor to get your butt pinched or your breasts groped.

No mention of her run-in with Ginette, though Lori was sure they all knew about it. She pitched in with stories about Vancouver, about citizens fighting to raise chickens in their urban yards, about residents protesting against the light in their bedrooms from neon signs, and about the Celebration of Light—the international fireworks competition at English Bay.

The women laughed and gossiped right along with her, and Lori wondered why she'd never met any of them on the street before. She concluded that social life here mainly took place behind closed doors, and you had to be invited inside. She realized on the way home that, to her great relief, none of them had so much as hinted at Noah. As if obeying a code of honor.

Lori was just putting a camera around her neck when she caught sight of Noah pacing around on the wharf. It was patently obvious that he was afflicted with cod fever. Elated, she walked down to the boats, her heart beating with expectation. Nate was bustling around the *Mighty Breeze*. Before she could reach him, though, Archie blocked her path.

"You'll have to come with us today," he said.

Lori couldn't tell if he was serious. She tried humor.

"Oh, what a nice feeling; everybody wants me. Fortunately, the season is long."

"But you're coming with us for the first day—sure to bring us luck."

Right then, a female figure walked past her, headed for Noah's boat. Lori watched while Nate helped Reanna on board. It happened so fast that she'd stayed nailed to the spot beside Archie, unable to utter a syllable.

She looked over at Noah. He met her gaze, paused indecisively for a second, and then came over to Archie's boat.

Archie shouted, "She's coming out with us today. You can have her afterward for as long as you want."

He grinned, but the expression on Noah's face was serious. He took off his chunky gloves and looked at Lori.

"Are you OK with that?"

"Do I have a choice?" she shot back.

Archie laughed.

"I'll find you a life jacket. And you'll need rubber boots."

Noah put his gloves back on. He frowned as he shot her another quick look and turned around briskly.

Lori followed Archie into the shed, where he handed her an orange life jacket, but he couldn't scare up any rubber boots.

"Just stay out of anything messy," he advised.

If only I could, she thought.

Archie's boat was bigger than the *Mighty Breeze*, and she discovered a portable toilet on her tour of the deck. No worry on that score at least. She saw two rifles on the wall outside the wheelhouse. She bumped into Coburn, Noah's oldest brother, along with two other men: Bill and Ezekiel, "Ezz" for short. Coburn identified them as "my second and third cousins."

"Why do you need the guns?" Lori wondered.

"To scare off the gulls," Coburn explained. "We don't want them to shit on the boat."

She was in a surprisingly good mood by the time they reached the open sea, the coastline behind them still clearly visible. She couldn't escape the pull of the unending mass of water and what it concealed. What did these men feel, she was curious to know, since they never swam or dove in the ocean? Noah told her he'd wanted to go on the boats even as a little kid, but his father didn't take him out until he was twelve. Since then, all he wanted to do was fish. One of the first times they really talked, she'd asked him what happiness meant to him. He said, first, fishing, second, living in Stormy Cove, and third, a wife to share his table and bed. At the time, she thought it advisable to play it cool in order not to arouse false expectations.

Noah's boat followed them at first, and Lori managed to snap some pictures without Reanna in them. She was probably talking to Nate in the wheelhouse.

The thought that Reanna would be spending a whole day around Noah irritated her. But the *Mighty Breeze* disappeared from view, and the thought that Noah knew Lori was in the company of four men filled her with spiteful satisfaction.

The day got better and better. A loud, hard smack made everyone on board jump.

"Over there!" yelled Ezz, a young man with whiskers and steely arms.

"A humpback!"

They all waited in suspense for the whale to reappear. And indeed, a gray colossus breached a mere sixty feet from the boat. Lori was so stunned that she almost forgot to click the shutter. Then she let the camera run automatically to capture a series of pictures. Archie stopped the boat. Lori knew that the men couldn't wait to make it to their nets, and she was grateful for his patience.

The humpback breached again, right beside the boat this time. It must have gone underneath. Through her lens, she could see white lines on its dark skin, as if somebody had mindlessly drawn a tangle of loops with chalk. Some of the lines must have been open wounds, because pockets of water hung from them. The black-and-white spotted edges of its tail fins brought to mind one of her mother's fashionable silk scarves. Masses of yellow barnacles were stuck around its mouth. Lori was bowled over by the whale's fishy odor.

But then she lost her eye for details because the whale's breaching held her completely in thrall. The mighty animal shot out of the water like a torpedo, executed a half turn in the air, and fell like an enormous sack of lead back into the water. Maybe there was more than one, because the time between breachings grew shorter. The beasts made an astounding amount of noise when their tails slapped the water; it sounded like the slamming of a hundred car doors. Lori thought about shooting some video, but right then, photographs were more pressing.

"Why are they doing that?" she shouted as a whale leapt once more into the air with incredible agility.

"Probably having lunch," Archie roared.

Afterward, Lori couldn't say how long the spectacle had lasted, but she knew she'd gotten some fantastic pictures of it. She'd also captured the concentration on the fishermen's faces, men who'd probably seen this many times before but were still impressed by the gigantic creatures sharing their fishing grounds.

Archie started up the engine again. They reached the first nets two hours later. Lori couldn't make out the brightly colored buoys until they were practically on top of them.

"Look out! It's gonna be wet and slippery!" one of the men shouted. She couldn't distinguish one from another in their heavy, green rubber clothing, brilliant blue gloves, and black baseball caps. The boat rocked fiercely as the wheel of the hydraulic winch in the bow began to haul the heavy nets on board. Lori had her camera at the ready and fought fiercely to keep her balance. She saw only water at first, then something white glittered below the dark surface. Fish bellies. Many, many fish bellies. The men grabbed the nets and plucked the fish out one at a time. They were almost three feet long and thicker than a man's thigh. So *that* was cod.

Lori zoomed in on a fish flopping around on the deck. Its back was covered with small dark spots broken along its length by a striking white line. The brown coloration was stronger on the head, in marked contrast with its bright lips. Lori spotted the sharp teeth in one of them. A very photogenic fish.

Ezz and Coburn swiftly cut the cod's throat, slit open its belly, and pulled out the guts. Screaming gulls appeared all around the boat and swooped down at the slimy waste arcing toward the water. Many birds caught their meal in midair. Lori was relieved that nobody actually fired warning shots to shoo away the gulls; they performed fantastically for the camera.

The boat filled up with cod. Lori had to be careful not to step on the twitching, gasping fish. Some had already died in the nets, the thin green nylon cords cutting into their soft flesh. She snapped them in front of a scuffed-up wall, hoping to recreate the effect of a Dutch Renaissance painting she'd seen in Amsterdam—a somber still life in shades of brown.

Lori was struck by the contrast between the colors of nature and the fishermen's shiny cobalt-blue rubber gloves. They disentangled sculpins from the nets and tossed them back into the sea because they were out of season; the same for mackerel, herring, and a lone sturgeon. Coburn took pains to teach Lori the different species.

The gutted fish landed in plastic boxes, and Ezz shoveled ice on top of them. Archie grabbed a huge cod in each hand and posed with his trophies for Lori's lens. Even with his powerful arms, he could only hold up the heavy fish with great effort. The muscles in his red neck bulged, and his jaw trembled. Lori quickly clicked the shutter to help him out, and that got him talking. He said he'd set out his nets at different spots.

"I used to have a hundred nets, but those times are long gone. These days the Ministry of Fisheries only allows us six nets."

She'd be with them until day's end; there was no escape. The distant coastline was just a narrow strip.

A surprise awaited the crew at the third station.

A massive steel-gray body was thrashing back and forth in the net and splashing water into the air.

"A shark!"

The words shot through Lori like a jolt of electricity. She bent over the rail to see what was going on. Her enthusiasm instantly morphed into anxiety. The shark's tail fin was tangled up in the net, and no matter how it twisted and flailed about, it couldn't get free.

"A porbeagle, a mackerel shark," Coburn shouted.

Lori watched the shark go under and resurface.

"Are they dangerous?"

As if to answer, the struggling shark turned on its back and opened its jaws wide.

She instinctively stepped backward.

The men laughed.

"They're pretty aggressive, yeah, and they might attack people." Ezz held her by the arm for a moment, as if to lend his words more emphasis.

"But you're not going to kill it."

"No, that's illegal. But we've got to calm it down, or we'll never get the ropes free."

Lori had no time to think about what that might entail. She snapped away as Ezz and Bill drove hooks on wooden poles into the shark's rough skin; it put up a fight, but to no avail. They pulled the shark up the side of the boat, and Archie grabbed its tail. Coburn sawed through the nylon cords with a sharp knife, one at a time. With two hooks in its body, the shark was at the mercy of the men. The instant Coburn cut the final cord, the fishermen yanked their hooks out of the shark's blood-covered body. It bolted and disappeared in the ocean.

Lori lowered her camera; only now did she process what she'd just observed.

Archie read the shock on her face.

"It'll survive," he said. "He was lucky."

Lori looked intently over the water as if she might still spot the shark out there. *He was lucky.*

Maybe that's what life ultimately boils down to, she thought. *Some people are lucky, and a whole lot aren't.*

Maybe she was like that shark and had got entangled and been wounded—and now she was free. But Jacinta didn't make it. And maybe Una didn't either.

Toward two o'clock, their boat neared an island where she spotted hollows and niches and fissures in the cliffs. Though none of the men identified it, Lori recognized the silhouette. The Isle of Demons. The engine cut out.

Archie joined her.

"We usually don't break for lunch, but with a lady on board, we'll make an exception."

He smiled when he saw how delighted she was. Lori was so hungry she could have snacked on one of the cod.

She sat down on an overturned bucket, like the fishermen, and shared the ample provisions in her backpack. The men were happy to accept and covered up their surprise with jokes.

"We'll take a woman out anytime if she'll run a restaurant on the boat."

"Then you'd have to tip, mister."

"For the meal or her pretty smile?"

"Take care she doesn't feed you to the sharks!"

"Who's afraid of sharks? It's women you've got to be afraid of, man!"

"Sharks only eat mainlanders, not Newfies. Newfies are too tough, eh?"

"Where did you get that from, boy, that's—"

"Quiet! You guys hear that?"

They sat motionless, listening. They didn't have to wait long. An extraordinary sound arose, soft at first, then more and more penetrating. The scream hit them like a thunderbolt. A mournful, ear-piercing howl and whine. Like a terrified animal that can only emit distorted sounds. The wailing receded, then blared like a siren until it became unbearable.

Nobody on the boat said a word. No funny remarks broke the spell the unearthly whining cast. Now it sounded like a begging, heartrending moan that crescendoed into an alarming howl.

Then a sudden quiet.

There they sat, glued to their buckets. Lori was aghast as she looked into the men's now haggard faces. Before she could open her mouth, Archie stood up.

"That's enough. We've still got nets to pull in."

He went to the wheelhouse and started up the engine.

Ezz, who was staring at the island in a trance, said to Lori, "He wants to move on because he thinks this will bring us bad luck."

"What will?" she gasped. "What *was* that?"

"The demons," Coburn told her.

"What demons?"

"Who knows?"

Now they all talked loudly and all at once.

"It's the dead baby of that French princess they marooned out here."

"The island's bewitched."

"They say she had a baby, and it died, and its ghost haunts the island."

"And her lover's ghost, and her maid's."

Lori's hands trembled. She was choked with fear.

"Has anybody seen a ghost out there? Has anybody ever looked? Maybe it's a wounded animal."

Ezz's laugh sounded forced.

"You can try. Maybe you'll find something. But nobody's going to go with you, eh, Cob?"

Coburn shook his head.

"Folks have been hearing that howl for a good long time. Father heard it a lot and Grandfather, too."

"Practically every fisherman has. I heard it once a few years ago at night, when it's even creepier. We couldn't sleep, remember, Bill?"

"Mmm. Wouldn't have thought I'd ever hear it again. And in the middle of the day too. Wouldn't be surprised if . . ."

Bill didn't finish his sentence because Archie returned, glowering. She very much wanted to ask Bill what he wouldn't have been surprised by, but her instincts told her he wouldn't give her an answer as long as Archie was around.

After that, the taciturn men pulled in net after net, but didn't bring up the subject again, making it all the more sinister.

When the familiar houses of Stormy Cove appeared, Lori's stomach was still tense. She saw the *Mighty Breeze* some distance away, bobbing up and down. But she was still under the spell of the howling demons, the blood-curdling wailing and howls ringing in her ears. Even when she spied Reanna strolling around the wharf, she hardly felt a twinge. She couldn't see Noah anywhere; maybe he was busy with his boat.

Coburn helped her off the boat, and she took pictures of Archie and his crew unloading the fish. But it didn't take long for Reanna to find her target. Lori first tried looking away and ignoring her. But that blond shock of hair was ever present no matter where she pointed her camera.

Don't get worked up. Summer's just beginning. She'd have lots of opportunities later to get shots of fishermen unloading their boats.

Suddenly Noah appeared, walking heavily in his rubber clothing and boots on his way to Archie's boat, where Bill was piling up crates.

"Well, how was it?" Lori asked him. "Big catch?"

"Not bad," Noah answered. "Two thousand pounds. But the engine gave us problems at first. We had to come back and fix it."

He gave Lori a searching look, his baseball cap shading his eyes.

"How'd it go with Archie?"

"Amazing, actually," she replied. "We saw humpbacks that jumped really high. And a shark in the net. A mackerel shark. We cut him free and he swam away."

She refrained from mentioning the Isle of Demons because Archie joined them, satisfaction written all over his face.

"We'll take her out again. She brought us luck."

Not a word about the ghosts.

She gave him a slight, joshing shove.

"Other people want me to bring them luck, too."

"You owe me a case of beer," Noah said, "because I gave her to you."

"The shark didn't eat her," Bill joked. "She must be a Newfie."

Without any warning, Reanna was at her side. Her nasal voice interrupted them.

"Actually, Lori is half foreigner, right, Lori?"

Before Lori could compose herself, Bill said, "Well, everything's foreign for people like us—Ottawa, Halifax, Calgary, Vancouver . . ."

"For sure Quebec," Noah chimed in.

The men laughed.

But Reanna didn't leave it alone.

"I've heard your mom's German. Do you go to Germany very often?"

Lori felt her anger mounting, but she controlled herself.

"My mother's Canadian, Reanna, but she has relatives in Germany," she replied as calmly as possible, given the situation.

"Is it true she's a defense lawyer? Who has she defended?"

Lori counterattacked.

"What about you, are you from Ottawa? Or Trifton? Or Timmins? Or neither? We've heard all sorts of different things."

Reanna merely shrugged and trained her lens on Bill and Archie. Noah was watching her intently, as Lori noticed out of the corner of her eye. Reanna prattled on without paying any attention to him.

"You don't look like guys who are afraid of sharks, am I right?"

Bill gave an embarrassed laugh, but Archie didn't sound at all amused when he said, "Only an idiot isn't afraid of anything."

To Lori's surprise, he winked at her before leaving.

Bill and Noah went back to work, leaving the two women by themselves on the jetty.

Lori weighed the idea of asking Reanna why in the world she knew so much about her mother. But she desperately didn't want to get sucked into another conversation, and so she shot some more pictures while the fishermen unloaded the boat and containers of fish disappeared into the buyer's truck. What she wanted most of all was for Reanna to vanish with the fish and the truck, but the reporter was still hanging out on the wharf when Lori said good-bye to the fishermen.

Lori could see Reanna in the car's rearview mirror, loitering around the boats. What game was this kid playing?

I should have pushed her into the water, camera and all. The men would have had a tough time saving her since they can't swim.

The thought amused her for a moment until resentment gained the upper hand once more. She drove up the hill far too fast.

The sky above the hills was so bright that it almost blinded her. It crossed her mind that tomorrow was the longest day of the year, and then the nights would grow imperceptibly longer.

Little Molly came running over as Lori was getting out of the car. A pink blur on the bright green grass.

"You got a big package," she shouted breathlessly. "Can I watch you open it up?"

"Where is it?"

Molly took her hand.

"Come on, I'll show you. Mommy put it inside."

She went in with Lori. And, sure enough, a large carton was sitting on the chest freezer in the basement. Lori looked at the sender's name: her mother.

"OK, let me take my jacket off first, then we'll open it."

Molly scrunched up her nose.

"You stink like fish—eeew!"

"What? Oh, you squeamish little mouse! You're in a fishing village, Molly! Everything smells like fish here."

"But you usually smell different—a lot better. I want the perfume you got."

Molly ran ahead of her as she lugged the heavy package upstairs and pushed it onto the kitchen table.

She cut through the layers of tape with a kitchen knife and had just opened the box when the phone rang.

"You can start unpacking," she said to Molly and ran into the living room.

"I'm in luck—got you on the first try," Mona Blackwood said by way of a greeting.

"You can say that again. I'm just back from fishing."

"What are they going after now?"

"Cod. But we saw whales, too—and a live shark caught in the nets."

She peeked at Molly, who was setting two small paper bags down on the table—Lori's favorite coffee.

"Sounds exciting. I'm convinced it'll be a terrific book. I don't want to keep you long—I imagine you're dying for a hot shower. When are you going to the dig?"

"The archaeologist wants to take me this week, but I told him only if you agree."

"Go right ahead, no problem. Can we use the pictures in our book?"

"Yes, but if I understood him correctly, he's hoping to offer them to international magazines first."

The line went silent for several seconds, and Lori thought she might have overtaxed her employer's good will. But then Mona said, "As long as we have some pictures that are exclusive and not published anywhere else beforehand—I can live with that."

"I'm sure that's possible. I'll pass it on to Lloyd Weston first thing."

Molly was checking out a package of German baked goods with great curiosity.

"Lloyd Weston's leading the dig?"

"Yes, do you know him?"

"No, not personally, that is . . . just by name. Is that reporter from the *Cape Lone Courier* still causing you problems?" Her question came out of the blue.

"Well, today . . . she was on another boat, luckily. But she kept getting in the way while they were unloading it." Lori laughed to disguise her frustration. "It's really mind-boggling that, of all the fishing villages up here, she just *had* to pick Stormy Cove." She shook her head, though Mona couldn't see her. "And now lo and behold! She wants to make a book out of it. That's—bizarre."

"What's her name anyway, and where's she from?"

"Reanna Sholler. I don't know exactly where she's from because she tells some people Trifton, Ontario, and others Timmins, like Shania Twain, and some that she's from Ottawa. Maybe she doesn't want anybody to find out much about her."

"Really odd, as you said. I understand why you're not happy about it. I'd feel the same way if I were in your shoes . . ."

"Plus, she's obviously been sniffing around behind my back. She learned that my mother's a defense lawyer and has relatives in Germany. And she wanted to find out at all costs where the dig is so she could come with us."

Molly held something up triumphantly in her little hands. *Armani* soap! Lori's mother had dug deep in her wallet.

"That's very annoying." Mona's voice turned steely. "You don't have to put up with that. I'll think about it. Maybe I'll come up with something."

Lori was surprised that Mona had taken such an interest in her situation. After all, it wasn't her problem; Lori was old enough to take care of herself. But it helped to talk it over. And she was also pleased with the compliment that followed.

"Keep doing what you're doing, Lori. I think your photographs are outstanding. I'm eager to see what you'll come across next."

What I'll come across next.

Of course, she was on a mysterious mission. Mona was subtly reminding her.

But Molly distracted her by pressing the Armani soap to her nose. "Mmm, that smells so good!"

After hanging up with Mona, Lori's focus was on the treasure trove scattered over the table, which reminded her of the care packages her mother used to send her at summer camp: Italian salami, various sauces in bags, goat cheese, sheep cheese, spices from India, a lemon press, two wooden ladles (Lori had told her she couldn't find any in Stormy Cove), American magazines, including *Newsweek* and *The New Yorker*, the mascara Lori swore by, cookies—and the Armani soap Molly didn't want to give back. Lori had to think fast.

"You know what? That's a present from my mom, but I'll let you have some so we can both wash with it. Isn't that a great idea?"

Molly looked at her.

"But you only got one."

"Let's cut it in half," Lori replied, picking up the knife she'd used on the package.

She cut off a big slice of soap, making a mess all over the table. *Giorgio Armani's hair would have stood on end,* she thought, handing the piece of soap to a beaming Molly.

"I'll wrap it up so you can show it to your mom," Lori said. "I have to make a phone call."

Molly took the hint and stood up. She pulled out a candy from her pants pocket.

"That's a present from me," she announced magnanimously. "The lady gave it to me."

"She was delivering the mail?"

"No, the lady who came here today."

"Who was that? I wasn't here all day."

"Don't know. She left."

Somebody coming to visit? She would ask Patience; she'd know for sure.

Molly slammed the door in her rush to get home and show off her prize.

A hot cup of tea—at last! And a salami sandwich with sheep cheese.

She went to the computer after her meal and sent Andrew a long e-mail, regaling him with tales of the whales and the shark and the spooky Isle of Demons. He was very much into ghost stories and would love it.

Then a short note to let her mother know her marvelous package had arrived and that she'd call soon.

She was browsing through her in-box when an e-mail from her mother came in, sent from her BlackBerry.

"Did you see the article I put in there?"

What article?

Lori checked the shipping box again and discovered a crumpled envelope at the bottom.

She opened it and thought at first it was something from her mother's library of legal journals. But then she realized it was written by an archaeologist, a woman. Lisa Finning had highlighted a passage with a Magic Marker.

The day before the fire, Lloyd Weston had us take all our finds out of the lodge and store them in a container near the dig. Lloyd must have had a premonition. To us, it was a minor miracle.

Lori looked up the byline. The name sounded familiar. Beth Ontara.

The archaeologist she'd met at the Birch Tree Lodge.

Lori guessed immediately what her mother was getting at. It was a most peculiar coincidence that valuable objects were moved to safety one day before the archaeologists' lodgings burned down. She doubtless suspected there was more to it than premonition.

The phone rang. It was sure to be her mother.

Wrong.

"Lori?" Noah's voice. He sounded hoarse.

"Yes?" was all she could get out.

"I . . . I just wanted to say that you . . . that we'd like to take you out with us tomorrow. I talked to Nate and . . . we're not taking anybody else . . . just you."

"Oh, that's very nice, but—"

"Only if you want to. Weather looks good for tomorrow, hardly any wind."

"I'd love to go out again, Noah, but tomorrow—tomorrow I'm going to have a look at an archaeological dig."

No sound at the other end. She added hastily, "I was invited to take some pictures, and naturally, I can't pass up this opportunity. It's a onetime chance, you see."

"Yes, yes, no problem. I just didn't want . . . didn't want you to think you weren't welcome on board."

His halting speech betrayed the amount of courage it had taken for him to make this call. Lori grasped for words too.

"I know, I know, Noah. It's just something . . . that gets in the way, somebody running around with a camera. It's not . . . ideal."

"I get it. But I don't see . . . I mean, the *Cape Lone Courier* won't send us somebody every day."

"There's more going on here than the book that she apparently wants to write. My publisher doesn't like that. There are hundreds of fishing villages. Why did she head straight for Stormy Cove?"

There, she'd come out with it. The elephant in the room had a name.

"I . . . I don't know either."

These fishermen must certainly be pleased by so much attention from two women, Lori thought.

"How are you getting to the dig?" he asked.

"By helicopter."

"Who with?"

"Lloyd Weston."

"Ah."

A pause ensued, grew larger and larger.

"Well, then, like I said . . ." Noah seemed anxious to end the awkward conversation.

She'd have loved to talk to him some more, to say something that might have restored some closeness between them. But she was tongue-tied.

Then a lightbulb went on in her head.

"We heard the demons, today. It was terrifying. It was . . . I've never heard anything so scary."

He seemed surprised.

"Archie was at the Isle of Demons?"

"Yes, we stopped for lunch. Then it suddenly started up. What is it exactly? What makes a noise like that?"

"Dunno. Nobody knows. It's a mystery."

"Why doesn't somebody just go there and find out?"

"Nobody's ever seen anything. Some people from an oil company landed a chopper there once, but they didn't see anything either. Maybe it's the wind blowing through holes in the cliffs."

Lori didn't buy it.

"It was so frightening," she repeated.

"Yeah, I know. I hope you sleep OK tonight."

"You too, and thanks for the phone call."

". . . so, have a good day tomorrow," Noah said.

She sat there for several minutes as if turned to stone. What kind of a mess had she gotten herself into? Her feelings were all jumbled up like wet nets in a wharf shed.

She got into the shower but shivered, even under the hot water.

Vera Quinton, 43, housewife, part-time worker in the fish plant

I think she really went for Noah Whalen. I mean that gal Reanna. Word got around fast. Not Lori. She's—how can I put it—a little . . . she doesn't let every Tom, Dick, and Harry get near her. I bet she gets along better with dogs than people. No, just a joke, wasn't serious. My Newfie sense of humor.

She's been trotting around with Rusty lately; she softened us up right proper, but I don't mind, really. If that's the way she wants it—be my guest. I mean, she can't talk to the dog, of course. Must be real boring. Would be for me, at least. But she sometimes chats with us people.

Lori didn't have to do much; people came right up to her because they all want to be in the book. She took a picture of me too. Quilting. My quilts are in demand, but honestly, I'm sick of it, because I'm always supposed to give them away for free—to the church fund, the fire department, the school bazaar, the old people's home. You know what? I put in a hundred and twenty hours of work on a quilt like that.

And Gideon's wife tried to give me just fifty bucks. A good piece of needlework isn't worth a damn around here, not a tinker's damn. So I said, that's it for quilting.

Reanna really buttered everybody up. That's how young people are these days, not only the CFAs, as we call mainlanders because they Come from Away. Same with the kids here. They want everything, and right this minute. No, don't have kids myself. Not sure why, whether me or Tom's the problem. We've never been looked at. Tom doesn't want that. There's a lot he doesn't want.

I'll probably be dead before I get to Las Vegas. Or Puerto Vallarta or Maui. Tom won't shell out one red cent for that type of thing. Only for trucks and boats. I only got a dishwasher secondhand because Gideon got a new one. This one wasn't good enough for his wife. Tom always tells me:

"Life here isn't good enough for you." Always the same damn thing. Oh, sure, sometimes I'd like to just take off. What's here anyway? Nothing. No Walmart, no Costco, not even a Tim Hortons. No movie theater, no spa, no jewelry store. Gotta go to Corner Brook for all that, six hours one way by car. Tom says it's three hundred bucks for gas. He only drives down there when he wants a new chain saw. And when a bit of a storm's up, then the TV conks out. And then it's just dead here.

Nothing's really working well anyway. I can't live off garage sales or fire department raffles. And I haven't played darts at the Hardy Sailor for years. Besides, it's the friends of the house that always win the prizes, if you take my meaning. We play poker at Rosie's sometimes, but the ante's a measly two dollars. It's a joke. All I ever do is yawn.

Lori's been places, that's for sure. You can tell by looking at her. She gets to travel. I'd like Las Vegas best of all. They've got real terrific hotels, and restaurants and amusement parks, and the Céline Dion show. And casinos of course. I used to play the slots in the Hardy Sailor. Nearly every day. Until Tom noticed how much cash I was putting into it. He made me stop.

I sneak off now and then, when he's away. But with the peanuts I make at the fish plant in the summer, you can't get anywhere. Or I'd have hit the jackpot long ago.

On the Internet? Who told you that? Sure, I know some people who gamble on the Internet. Tom would put a stop to that right away, believe you me. Does he know anything? Aw, c'mon, men don't have to know everything. Tom should be happy I don't drink. I sometimes think, if I did, at least I'd have a little bit of fun in my life. But I go to church and don't drink.

If you ask me, Lori—she knows more than all of us put together. She takes her camera into all the homes and chitchats with people. Mavis? Yes, Mavis knows a lot too, because people come to her store to gossip. But a lot of us don't tell Mavis anything. But when Lori said in the store that if everybody told the truth, then no innocent person in the village would be a suspect—that says to me that she knows a lot. So she should damn well say what she knows. If innocent people are under suspicion, eh?

CHAPTER 30

The weather the next day was exactly as Noah had predicted: a breeze as soft as cat fur tickled her cheeks as she left the house. She'd pulled her hair back, a few wisps held with rainbow-colored kids' clips she'd found in the store, but she hadn't gone so far as to call it a ponytail yet. She thought the hairdo looked perky, complementing the thrill of adventure flowing through her veins. Noah's phone call had kept her awake for a long while. She still shuddered a little just thinking about it.

By contrast, the water in the bay radiated a lazy calm. Young coniferous trees and carpets of moss on the hills sparkled green in the morning dew. Two moose grazed in a clearing, a female and a bull with massive antlers.

Lori's gaze scanned the sharp outlines of the coastal rocks that rounded off the cove like defiant palisades, with an occasional gap where the open sea poked through. She couldn't spy any boats on the horizon, not even through her telephoto lens. The Isle of Demons appeared to be very far away—a thin dark streak melting into a grayish-white blur.

Perfect weather for Rusty's daily walk along the beach and to the other side of the hill to look for icebergs. But just then, a beige SUV rolled into her driveway with Lloyd Weston at the wheel. He pulled up and waved at her through the window.

She climbed into the SUV and laid her tripod and backpack on the back seat. Weston was beaming.

"Everything's perfect. It's real chopper weather."

Lori couldn't deny that he looked good. With his hair cut very short and his beard gone, he looked younger than his fifty-some years. The less hair, the more attractive he was. And you can't say that about most men. But she kept it to herself.

"Good photography weather too," she responded. "I hope it stays this clear."

Weston put the car in gear.

"We're in luck: there's no rain forecast for the next several days. So we're in no rush to set up camp."

"Where will it be?"

"About a mile and a half away from the dig itself. An easy walk. We don't want to disturb the immediate surroundings."

"Yes, and it's better for pictures too—nothing messing up the shot."

"We're just now taking equipment and supplies up there by chopper. We'll bring the rest by ATV."

The SUV passed the last houses in the village, and Lori wondered how many eyes were watching them.

"That must cost a heck of a lot, the helicopter and all," she remarked.

"NORPUNT's shelling out for the chopper. It's good PR. An oil company that also cares about the country's history."

"Will you put up a sign with the company's logo at the dig?"

Weston grinned.

"Not to worry. It's all untouched up there at the moment. Your first pictures should record everything the way we first found it."

"Who actually discovered the burial mound?"

"There are lots of old, old stories about hunters who first noticed it. They used it as an orientation point. They called it the Rabbit's Back. It really does stand out on the plain, you'll see."

"And when did you see the grave for the first time?"

"From the chopper."

"The oil company's?"

"No, with Gideon Moore. He's flying us there today."

"So NORPUNT hired Moore?"

"Right. We don't want too many people to know. Gideon can keep his mouth shut; I've known him for years."

Lori could see in the rearview mirror that they weren't being followed. So Reanna had been foiled. She looked back at Weston.

"What about me—can I keep my mouth shut too?"

Weston looked her in the eye before turning onto a gravel road that Lori hadn't noticed before.

"Of course. It's in your own interest, after all. If people get wind of this, you can kiss your exclusive photos good-bye. I know how the media can be."

A little presumptuous, but Lori understood why: Weston was standing before the second great discovery of his life. He was man in victory mode. Her mother's article crossed her mind.

"If it's a camp with tents, where are you going to store the finds this time?"

He looked at her in surprise. "Why do you ask?"

"I read an article by one of your colleagues—"

"Beth Ontara," he shot back.

"Yes. She said it was a miracle that the artifacts had been transferred to a trailer one day before the lodge fire."

"Well, now . . . so that article is making the rounds in Vancouver, is it?"

When Lori didn't respond, Weston continued.

"Beth is very modest. She was the one who kept urging me to find a better place to store them. She said too many people were going in and out of the lodge, and we couldn't keep tabs on everybody. It's her I have to thank for the miracle."

Lori thought she heard a slightly sarcastic undertone in his words. Seen in a critical light, Beth had drawn attention to her superior's inexcusable carelessness. Had she shouted in triumph when she'd been proven right? Everyone would have seen how smart she was. And how the chief archaeologist had put everything in jeopardy. And then Beth went and published an article about the oversight. That couldn't have been unproblematic for the ambitious Weston.

"What a coincidence—that the fire broke out just one day later." Lori was talking mostly to herself, but Weston observed drily, "You're not the only one who's wondered about that."

The smile was gone from his face. "The writer will be flying with us today."

"Who?" Lori turned toward him. *Not Reanna!*

"Beth. She's on the dig too."

Lori had assumed as much; after all, Beth had been at the Birch Tree Lodge. Lori remembered her as a tomboyish woman inclined to ribald humor.

She breathed a sigh of relief.

"I can't wait. Please help me keep people from walking into my shots."

"No problem." Weston was now rather aloof.

They arrived at a paved area next to an old barrack. An orange helicopter sparkled like a giant fat bakeapple on the gray landing area, next to some crates that had been unloaded off a pickup.

"This is an old airstrip from when the zinc mine was still working," Weston explained.

She noticed a paved road on the opposite side of the pavement; Weston had apparently taken a less-traveled shortcut. He parked the SUV beside the pickup.

One of the men in overalls came over and greeted her like an old friend, although they'd only met when ice fishing, and Lori hadn't even known at the time who Gideon Moore was.

"We're gonna have to make two trips, with all this here matériel," Moore said to Weston, flicking his head in the direction of the crates.

Weston looked at the men unloading more boxes. "Is that a problem?"

"No, I talked to the people at NORPUNT and it's OK."

He was looking at Lori but directing his words to Weston.

"We'll take the lady first, eh?"

"Yes, then she can get right to work."

"And who else? Beth or you."

"Me," Weston replied. "Where is Beth anyway?"

"Over there, checking the lists. She crosses off whatever's coming with us."

Weston thought for a moment then turned to Lori. "We'll take out your stuff so I can park the car."

Lori took her backpack off the back seat. Moore was Johnny-on-the-spot and snatched up her tripod.

"Is that all you have?"

She nodded. "Did Lloyd tell you I'll be needing a safety net?"

"Yes, I've taken photographers up in the chopper before. One of them wanted pictures of icebergs from above."

"And where do *I* sit?" someone behind them asked.

Lori turned and found herself face-to-face with Beth Ontara.

"Hello," Lori said. "Nice to see you a—"

"I *must* be on the first flight. I know where everything has to go. Otherwise it will be chaos, and I'll waste time getting everything back in order."

Lori noticed Weston's body tensing up. "It's better if you fly with the second shipment, Beth. Somebody has to oversee everything here and make sure nothing's left behind."

Beth furrowed her brow. "Can't you do that?"

She was dressed for a serious hike, in black and khaki and with her short hair hidden by an orange baseball cap with the words "Gideon

Air" on it. She looked tan and fit, like a high-performance athlete. She reminded Lori that archaeology meant more than office work—it involved rooting around in the dirt. And probably pushing around huge heavy rocks, like those at the first grave.

Weston was the boss.

"I'm flying with Lori so she can get to work while the light's still good."

Beth grimaced. "Worst-case scenario, we can always use my pictures," she said tartly.

Gideon put an arm around her hips.

"You already had an extra ride in my eggbeater. You've got nothing to complain about."

Beth raised her eyebrows but left his arm on her hip until he took it away.

Lori was amazed at the familiarity between the two. What had Vera Quinton told her when she'd come to walk the husky? Rusty had been Gideon's dog, and Gideon had replaced his first wife with a younger one and built her a new house in Saleau Cove. Beth was perhaps in her midforties, Gideon in his midfifties.

Weston started the SUV.

Gideon handed her a yellow object. "You've got to put this on."

"A life jacket?"

Beth beat him to it. "Yes, we're flying over water. You've obviously never been in a copter."

Lori didn't like the sneer on her face. She had pleasant memories of their evening playing poker, but she was probably caught in the middle of something between them.

"Never with a life jacket," she replied, laughing to break the tension.

Gideon grinned, but Beth took a rather critical view of Lori's attempts to put the life jacket on properly. She finally helped her out.

"Pull this tab if you land in the water."

"We're not going into the drink," Gideon shouted. "Not if I'm the pilot."

"I should hope not. This thing's brand-new, after all."

Beth talked as if she owned the helicopter. Lori's eyes followed her as she walked back to the pickup with a brisk stride. The life jacket felt like a straitjacket. Would she be able to move well enough to take pictures?

Gideon seemed to read her thoughts.

"Everybody's got to wear a life jacket—even German barons," he said, stowing her tripod and backpack in the helicopter's belly. "He didn't grumble, and his wife didn't either. You know them, by the way."

Lori was silent.

"The German baron and his wife."

"Uh-huh."

"Yeah, you met them at the Birch Tree Lodge, right?"

"Hmm." Lori feigned preoccupation with her camera.

"He knows everything about German submarines in Newfoundland."

The turn in the conversation made Lori uncomfortable. But Gideon seemed to take that as encouragement.

"My mother was in one of those subs when she was a kid—1939. She was ten. Told me about it some years back."

Oh, not this again, Lori thought. Why were German submarines dogging her? She wanted to see a seven-thousand-year-old burial mound, not listen to tales about the war.

"The sub surfaced at Saleau Cove, by Port Saunders, at dusk. Mom's from there. Only about two hundred residents. No streets and no electricity and just outhouses."

Lori looked around. Weston had wandered over to a group of workers beside an old shed on the edge of the runway. He couldn't save her.

"Water's very deep at Saleau Cove," Gideon continued, having found a way to kill time until the crates were ready. "Subs could be protected from attack down there. If people there saw Allied ships on the ocean, they knew German subs might be in the vicinity."

He fished a handkerchief out of his overalls and blew his nose.

"So they'd put blackout curtains over the windows so there were no lights. I don't mean electric lights; they only had kerosene lamps. Same here, even in 1939."

Lori nodded and was immediately sorry she had. But Gideon would have gone on talking anyway.

"Kids weren't allowed on the beach, but you know how kids are. Wouldn't have thought, though, that mother was such a little rascal. She went down to the harbor with a gang of kids. They saw a sub, and all of a sudden, the tower hatch opened. Some men climbed out, and mother said they were very friendly and invited them to look inside the sub."

Now Lori couldn't control herself anymore.

"This sounds like one of those yarns about extraterrestrials who abduct children in their spaceships."

Gideon gave a good-natured laugh.

"Exactly. I cracked jokes about it at first, just like you. But mother got mad. She thought we didn't believe her. But she remembers the swastikas on the walls. At least, that's what she told me. The crew took the kids into the galley and gave them oranges and chocolate. Mother had never seen an orange in her life!"

Lori saw Weston walking over the runway. What would he say to this bizarre story?

"Mother was really impressed by the engine room. A man put her on his lap and stroked her hair. Mother was a blond, you see. And the German was, too, and she said he kissed her on her forehead and said, 'What a sweet little girl!'"

"Did your mother understand German?" was Lori's malicious question.

The pilot didn't bat an eyelash.

"No, the crew apparently spoke a little English. They brought the kids back to shore after and waved them good-bye."

"Who waved good-bye to whom after what?" Weston wanted to know when he got back to the helicopter.

"The Nazis in the submarine waved to the kids in Saleau Cove after showing them around the sub," Lori summarized.

"Oh, that old story." Weston put his hand on the helicopter's shiny orange metal, over the *G* in "Gideon Air." "So—can we get a move on?"

"What do you think about that?" Lori persisted after Gideon had gone to the other side of the helicopter.

Weston fiddled with his life jacket.

"It's possible, of course, but a story like that is virtually impossible to prove."

"So you actually think it's possible?"

"Clearly. Why not? I don't think those kids made it all up. Not all Germans were monsters, and I assume lots of soldiers missed their kids." He looked Lori in the eye. "The past isn't always black-and-white, trust me. An archaeologist learns that very quickly. Here—get in."

Lori didn't have to be told twice. She was happy to be done with this subject. How had it possibly come up again? What did German submarines have to do with her? She recalled that Volker, during his stay in Canada, always responded patiently when confronted with the issue of the Third Reich. Lori was the one who finally couldn't take it anymore.

"You weren't in the war, Volker, and you aren't a Nazi, and you don't give a damn about Hitler, and you'd never hurt a fly," she'd said after one of those conversations. "Why do you have a guilty conscience about things you haven't done and would never do? Aren't you sick of it?"

Volker stared at her, half in amazement, half in irritation.

"It's not a question, Lori, of whether I'm sick of it or not. I must take a position on it today because it happened in my country. I don't feel like a victim or a perpetrator, but I do feel responsible for not letting it be forgotten so it won't ever happen again."

And then he reminded her that it took decades for the Canadian government to apologize for the churches' compulsory residential schools where Indian children were abused, and for simply taking the children away from their parents—and the parents from their children.

Back then, Lori was still in denial about the fact that Volker was right to handle the subject in a mature way, unlike herself. When he pointed out that Canada took in a lot of Nazis after World War II but refused entry to many Jews, she wasn't about to back down.

"So we're back to believing in original sin, are we?" she retorted, whereupon Volker walked out of the room. It took her two days to be generous enough to apologize. At the time, she couldn't admit to herself that the invisible rift between them had widened just a tiny bit more.

The roar of the rotors broke her train of thought. She put on her headset. Gideon's voice came out of nowhere.

"Camera all set?"

Lori nodded. The helicopter wound its way up into the air. Her side of the helicopter had no door, just a net stretched across the opening. Lori watched the landscape below as it got smaller and broader at the same time. Countless inlets ate their way into the rocky coast. Where the land flattened out, gravel beaches arced their way around forested bays. From that height, Lori could see where generations of men had cut down trees for firewood, leaving sparse bushes clinging to the stony ground. Sloughs and small lakes glinted in the washed-out tundra like signal lights.

Lori wasn't sure why, but she forgot everything around her at times like these. The landscape was enchanting, with its breathtaking beauty: black rocks, water, more and more water, the cliffs towering over the ocean, the brown underbrush interspersed with green, and then the shimmering bog of the tundra and the low banks of gnarled bush. She felt as if her soul had separated from her body, been liberated from all mundane things to hover above the earth. She had an all-encompassing feeling that she couldn't pin down, but it was like . . . like a feeling of security. Of belonging. She felt curiously safe in this rough, inhospitable environment.

"Caribou!" Weston, sitting behind her, pointed them out.

Lori shook off her trance and started shooting. She eased out into the net, the yawning void beneath her. The camera was all that mattered right now.

A herd of perhaps ten caribou flew away over the plain. The helicopter made a loop, and the half-moon of a long beach appeared far below, giving way to stony terrain rampant with thick bushes like unkempt tufts of hair.

"Do you see it?" That was Weston.

She scanned the terrain.

"Where?" She'd scarcely asked the question when she saw what he meant. An anomalous form rising from the bedrock like a wart. A foreign body that didn't fit in with the landscape. Gideon circled many times to give Lori the best camera angles. Then he landed on a flat spot several hundred yards away from the burial mound. The helicopter's downdraft flattened the vegetation and created clouds of dust all around.

She stooped down as she quickly scurried away to a spot where she could photograph the two men removing the cargo.

Then the machine lifted off and disappeared over the horizon, the roar growing softer until it died out. Cool air came in off the ocean. Lori looked at the jumble of equipment and cartons on the ground.

"I thought the camp was over a mile away?"

"It is, but we couldn't land there. We've got to lug this stuff over, the tools and everything we need for excavating. Not everything, actually, more's coming."

Weston picked up her tripod and also shouldered her backpack.

She tried to orient herself.

"I've got to look at the burial mound first. Where is it, anyway?"

"Over that way. You can't see it from here because of that rise in the land. No wonder the mound wasn't discovered for so long, even though a lot of boats must have landed here."

They started off. Lori could feel the stony bedrock through the soles of her hiking boots.

"Who did you say discovered it?"

"Who it was, I don't know. A hunter in a pub first told me about it seven years ago. He told me later that, if he hadn't been drunk, he wouldn't have spilled the beans. But other people must have discovered the mound before then; they just didn't think anything of it."

"Did people around here know about it?"

"I don't think most of them did. It reminds me of the Viking settlement in L'Anse aux Meadows at the northern tip of Newfoundland. You know it, of course."

"Yes. That's where the first Vikings landed on the continent a thousand years ago, right?"

"Exactly. The Norwegian, husband-and-wife archaeology team of Helge and Anne-Stine Ingstad once asked some villagers if there were any striking rises or depressions near the coast"—he stopped to free his pant leg from a thorn bush—"and the locals showed them the remains of a nearby ancient settlement."

"Did the people in L'Anse aux Meadows know that the settlement remains were Viking?"

"No, they thought Indians had lived there many centuries before."

"So how did the archaeologists figure out that it was the Vikings?" Lori planted her feet carefully between stones and bushes as she spoke.

"They dug up a typical Viking brooch—the ultimate proof."

One little brooch, Lori thought to herself. Sometimes a very small thing is all it takes to clear up a mystery.

She suddenly noticed she still had her life jacket on. A tiny, blaring yellow dot in the vast tundra. Andrew would die laughing if he could see her. She stopped and looked down at herself with a grin. Weston turned around, and she handed him the camera.

"Here, take a historic picture. I most definitely am the first person to run around the Barrens in a life jacket."

Weston grunted his amusement.

"I thought you were just crazy about bright colors."

He took a few steps back and clicked the camera.

"Think you could find your way back to Stormy Cove from here?"

She shook her head.

"You?"

"More or less. But I'd probably fall into a bog on the way. It can happen to anyone. It happened to George H. W. Bush in Labrador."

"The US president?"

"Yes. He was salmon fishing up in Labrador and wandered onto boggy ground and got stuck up to his hips. A secret service agent and a Mountie had to pull him out. The Americans came within an inch of losing a former president in a bog."

"When was that?"

"I think it was after he'd lost the election to Bill Clinton. Sometime in the nineties."

She rolled her eyes.

"Maybe I'd better leave the life jacket on."

He smiled.

"As you like. That way I can't lose you."

He'd have to have eyes in the back of his head, Lori thought, because Weston was walking three feet ahead of her, a sinewy, slim figure with a seemingly effortless stride, shouldering the tripod and backpack.

She'd loved to have known what he was thinking at that moment. The second "groundbreaking" excavation of his life. Maybe even more significant than the first. If a well-preserved skeleton and a heap of funeral objects were lying beneath the boulders, this dig would make him one of the best-known archaeologists in Canada.

Her curiosity got the best of her.

"Are Beth and Gideon good friends?"

He turned around.

"Beth and Gideon? Why?"

"I just thought—he put his arm around her."

Weston laughed.

"Oh, she's probably trying to keep his spirits up. Gideon's very important to us. He keeps doing us favors when he doesn't have to. But he likes to flirt—at least, when his sister isn't around. She wouldn't put up with that for a second."

He raised his eyes to look across the vast tundra.

"It's very ironic."

An inquiring look on her part.

"It was an incredible fluke that we found the first grave . . . a pure fluke. We simply stumbled over it because our tents were nearby. We didn't have a clue that anything like that was in the vicinity." He shifted the tripod to his other shoulder. "Discovering *this* grave was also pure coincidence."

He shook his head as if he still couldn't believe it.

Lori wrinkled her forehead.

"I thought your crew was living in Gideon's lodge, not tents."

"We did stay there later, during the dig. We had money from the government at that point."

"And from oil companies?"

Weston didn't lose his cool.

"No, universities."

Lori looked back and tried to locate the spot where they had landed.

A thought kept echoing in her mind: finding the ancient Indian grave may have been pure chance, but it was no accident that Jacinta's grave was found. The person who constructed that grave wanted it to be. It took a long time, of course, but the killer knew the new road between Stormy Cove and Cod Cove would go right through there.

And the road workers would eventually find the grave. It was perfectly worked out.

They walked along in silence. Suddenly, Weston changed direction and made a detour that brought them back near the beach that meandered in broad curves around the tundra. He dropped the tripod and put down the backpack beside a depression in the ground.

"Here we are."

Lori could tell he was watching for her reaction.

She walked across the indentation and lowered her camera.

About seventy feet in front of her was a rather long bank rising out of the ground. She could clearly pick out large boulders, though moss and lichens filled up the gaps. She stood stock-still. Transported. It wasn't the exterior of the burial mound itself that thrilled her; it was the thought that people had erected this monument seven thousand years ago, and that she, Lori, on this very day in the third millennium AD, could still behold it.

Like in a dream, she approached a spot where rich green moss and white lichen contrasted with the dark background of the low, scrubby fir trees. And another color caught her eye, the red of rusty sand that circled the rocks. A reddish color that reminded her of the Tartan surface of tennis courts in Vancouver.

She recalled what she'd learned about the first gravesite. That perhaps fifteen people—men and women from several families—had used moose antlers or their bare hands to dig a pit in the ground so deep that they couldn't see over the top, and wide enough for twenty standing people. Then they laid the child's body in it—a ten- or twelve-year-old—on its stomach, made a fire at its feet and beside its head. They laid gifts on the dead child's head and next to its body. And then they did something that particularly baffled the archaeologists: the gravediggers laid a stone slab on the corpse's back. As if its spirit must not escape from the grave under any circumstances.

Finally, they filled the grave up to the top with sand and carried large rocks to it—three hundred of them, each up to twenty-five pounds in weight—and piled them up to form a mound. Like the one before her now.

These people had no idea how long the burial mound would endure, or how long the world would. They might have known a few other clans along the coast, known the animals that would save them from starvation—caribou, sea lions, seals, fish, and a few birds. Their universe was a small section of the shore and the hinterland, with its bears and game. But something motivated them to bury a child, to perform a ritual, to imbue the child's death with a meaning in their world that would allow their life to go on.

Lori looked down to the beach and over the ocean to the cliffs on the horizon. It must have looked exactly like this back then; what she was now seeing was exactly what the people at that time saw when their brief subarctic summer began. Everything was about survival. Surviving hunger, forest fires, the icy winter, bears, and the dark forces whose messages their shamans conveyed.

Lori's gaze fell on Weston, who still stood where he'd dropped her equipment. *He hasn't breathed a word,* she thought. *Because he knows the effect these places have.*

Their eyes met, and he slowly came toward her. He waited for her to say something.

"And you're certain there's a skeleton in that mound?"

"Pretty sure. We found two empty graves in Quebec, but that's because acid soil had dissolved the bones. That's not the case here."

"So graves like these are rare?"

"Seems so or else we'd have found more of them. I think these people couldn't have managed to build many graves like these."

"Why?"

"Because they'd probably have to work on one for almost a week. That's a precious amount of time in a short summer. Within a few weeks, they had to hunt enough animals to make it through the whole winter. There was no time to waste."

"And still they went to the trouble to do it."

She shook red sand off her shoes. Love's labor's lost—she saw that immediately. Sand was stuck fast to the spots where she hadn't been able to scrub off the slime from yesterday's fish. It sort of resembled German measles.

Weston seemed to be deep in thought. Was he thinking about the archaeological treasures under the ground? What if he only found shards or colored dust? He cleared his throat.

"What amazes us the most is that this occurred so early in the history of civilization. Two thousand years before the pyramids. And considering that the people here were truly under the constant threat of death. Wild animals, starvation—it was bitter cold and sometimes there was no ice in the spring, which meant no seal meat. Or there were forest fires and the caribou herd went somewhere else."

"Did they believe in any gods?"

"Not in gods, but probably in forces more powerful than themselves that they had to submit to."

Lori didn't look at him when she asked, "Could it be another human sacrifice?"

He hesitated before answering.

"If it's a child or teenager, I'm not excluding it."

"Why should a child be sacrificed? Is it meant to atone for something?"

He waited longer this time.

"If I only knew." He folded his arms across his chest and rocked on his feet. "If I only knew."

There was a tinge of resigned despair in his voice.

Lori shuddered.

CHAPTER 31

Beth Ontara was obviously angry when she arrived at the burial mound an hour later. Lori was taking detailed shots of the white and orange network of lichens on the rocks.

"Those damn reporters stick their nose into everything," Beth said to Weston. "She turned up when we'd just finished loading."

"What? On the runway?"

"Yes. All of a sudden, her car came speeding toward us, then she braked and hopped out. She was desperate to go with us. No way, I told her. Get lost. Then she worked on Gideon, who just laughed and kept quiet. What a perpetual pain in the ass!"

"Is she still back there?"

"No idea. Maybe she's flitting about the tundra in her jalopy. I hope she falls into a bog. That's the last thing we needed, somebody snooping around."

Beth stamped around the bushes in a rage. Lori could empathize. She felt better now that she wasn't the only one mad at Reanna Sholler. Not a nice trait, Lori realized, but Beth had to defend the secret location of the mound. And *she* had to protect her book project.

"She won't find us," Weston said. "And she hasn't got the dough for a chopper."

He winked at Lori. But Beth was ready with a plan.

"From now on, we need to have somebody stationed here at all times. Day and night. We've got the tents, and I'll organize the guards."

Weston shrugged.

"If you can find volunteers, I won't stop you."

Lori had the impression that Beth wouldn't be stopped with or without his permission. After all, it was Beth who'd saved the artifacts from the fire twenty years ago. She'd guard this site with her life too, and defend it against any and all intruders. She mentally texted Reanna: *You versus Beth? No contest.*

"I'll help Gideon unload," Weston told her, and said to Lori, "Beth will take you back as soon as you're finished."

Lori nodded.

"I'm almost done. Just need a few more close-ups. And a picture with you in it. For scale."

"Put Beth in it. That'll look just as good."

He smiled, and Lori admired the way he rarely drew attention to himself. Was it out of gratitude toward a longtime colleague who was loyal and discreet in almost every situation?

She photographed Beth in front of the burial mound, an athletic figure bending over the monument as if speculating about what was hidden there.

Then she put down her camera to relieve Beth from the unnatural poses that would nevertheless look quite natural in the pictures. She packed up her equipment and, on an impulse, asked Beth for a moment of silence. She needed some kind of ritual before leaving the place. Surprising herself, Lori promised the spirit, whose presence she believed she sensed, to honor the dead person's dignity with her photographs.

When she turned around, she saw Beth eyeing her with some curiosity. To break the spell, Lori struck up a conversation on the way back.

"Do you think you might find projectiles in this grave that look like arrowheads?"

Beth shrugged.

"Dunno. Why do you ask?"

"Because a projectile like that was found in Jacinta's grave."

She was startled by her own boldness. What had gotten into her?

Beth turned around sharply.

"Where did you get that bullshit from?"

"From somewhere—I think it was in a law journal."

"I haven't read anything like that," Beth declared, "and I'd have certainly known if that was the case. It's definitely misinformation."

It was obvious that the archaeologist didn't believe her. That encouraged her to keep poking. Without looking up, Lori said, "You're probably right. Lots of rumors about that case are making the rounds. I heard a few days ago that Jacinta saw Robine Whalen kissing a woman, someone working on the dig, just before she disappeared. How absurd is that! I almost burst out laughing."

Beth was now visibly upset.

"People in this place should be careful about the rumors they spread. This time we know how to guard against lies. This time they won't drag our reputation through the mud. We—"

She didn't end the sentence. It was as if she'd been instructed not to talk about such things publicly. And that's how Lori understood it.

Beth strode ahead energetically, and Lori followed her in silence.

Suspicion took shape in her head.

Beth and Robine.

On the flight back, Lori half-listened to Gideon Moore describing the confusion surrounding the first dig.

The young people they'd hired hadn't a clue about what meticulous work archaeology was, he said. They'd treated it as a fun gig for the summer—young, flighty girls and lazy boys—too many people romping around the site. Everything needed to be better organized, with more supervision, in his opinion.

And there was much coming and going in and out of his lodge, he added, people who had no business being there, but he couldn't keep track of everybody. So a few things went missing. Una Gould, for instance, had stolen Beth's green jeweled bracelet, but what could he, Gideon, do if people left their valuables lying around?

Lori's curiosity was piqued. Would she find more extraordinary things in Una and Cletus's old home?

"Did Beth call Una on it?" she inquired.

"Naw, that Una business came out later, after Beth was long gone. And everybody had lost interest."

"So nobody was watching the lodge the night it burned down?"

Gideon went on the defensive.

"I'd been invited to Lloyd's birthday party and couldn't say no. My brother was in Saleau Cove and my sister with our sick mother."

Very interesting, Lori thought to herself. *Maybe Una also stole the arrowhead?* Without suspecting that a photographer from Vancouver would find it behind the washing machine twenty years later.

But what was with the arrowhead under the seat of Noah's snowmobile?

Lori was back home early that afternoon. From the living room window, she watched Weston's SUV disappearing around the far end of the cove. He wanted her to go back up north as soon as they began excavating. Lori had a piece of toast with Patience's homemade bakeapple jam and the Vancouver sheep cheese. She really had to call her mother that evening to thank her for it.

She took a half-hour nap on the sofa and then diligently started to evaluate the morning's photographs. Her first fear was that the strong sunlight might have robbed the locale of its secrecy, of its unfathomable, mythic nature. But the sunlight in the north was different from

Vancouver sunlight, as she'd already noticed. Here, the sun was subordinate to the landscape, making it more transparent, more massive, often ghostly because of the dark shadows the sun threw.

Lori grew more enthusiastic with each successful photo. She was so immersed that she didn't realize how fast the time was passing. She didn't even hear a car drive up and footsteps on the gravel. Which is why she gave a start when somebody opened the side door.

A man's voice called out, "Hello!"

Noah!

She quickly plucked the colorful barrettes out of her hair and tried to comb it with her fingers. Then she dashed into the kitchen.

Noah was on the landing, holding a plastic bag toward her.

"Thought you ought to have some fresh fish."

"Oh, that's sweet of you, Noah. Yes, I'd like that very much." She could hear herself talking way too fast. "Come in and sit down, and I'll make some tea—or coffee, if you'd like."

He came into the kitchen. "No white wine?"

They both laughed.

"Beer would be great," he said.

She opened the fridge.

"You're back on shore pretty early today."

"Yes," he said, rubbing his cheek. "Had to come in. Sudden strong northeast wind in the afternoon."

Lori looked out the window, and it was indeed windy. How quickly the weather could change here! And other situations too.

"What have you got there?" she said, peeking into the bag. The fish was already filleted.

"Cod, naturally."

He still hadn't sat down but leaned against the china cupboard somewhat awkwardly, beer can in hand.

Lori brushed her hair back, but some recalcitrant strands fell into her face.

"Would you like to stay for supper?"

"So you want me to show you how to fry fish, eh?" He smiled mischievously.

"We catch fish on the West Coast too, mister. I'm no amateur."

"We? How many have *you* caught?"

She laughed as she set the bag on the counter.

"Wait, I'll wash it again," Noah intervened.

They stood beside each other at the sink, and Lori watched his strong hands carefully hold the fillets under the tap, dry them with paper towels, and salt and roll them in flour while she peeled potatoes. There was something strangely intimate in sharing tasks, a naturalness that made her both calm and nervous at the same time.

It felt like her body was electrically charged when she was near him. She only had to shift an inch or two and their hips would have touched.

She peeled in slow motion, to make the magic last. *Maybe it'll never be like this again,* she thought.

He fried the fish while she made a salad—which he refused, calling it rabbit food.

"What was it like on the Barrens?" he asked when they were at the table.

Lori ate her fish ravenously; it was superb. Noah looked on with evident satisfaction.

She briefly described her excursion but wondered if she should mention the rumors about Robine, or her exchange with Beth. He sensed she was holding something back and looked at her expectantly.

So she simply unpacked it all; she wanted to involve him in everything that affected her.

At first he said nothing. Then he placed his fork on his plate.

"Why did you tell her that?"

"Because . . . probably because I wanted to see how'd she react. I mean . . . I don't have to beat around the bush." She crumpled up the napkin beside her plate. "If Jacinta actually did witness Robine and another woman neck—kissing—and gabbed about it and a few days later she disappears without a trace . . ."

"You think that . . . if that's true, Beth Ontara was the other woman?"

"I don't know. Her reaction was rather strong, don't you think?"

He started to eat again without answering. Lori looked straight at him.

"Did you hear those kinds of rumors at the time?"

He put down his fork once more.

Leave him alone, Lori. You're spoiling the lovely mood.

"Yes, of course. Rumors spread like wildfire here."

He drank some more beer and put the can down slowly.

"And anything coming from the Parsons family was mostly mischief. Or even worse."

Noah stared out the kitchen window, as if collecting himself.

"Jacinta's father, Scott Parsons, is . . . he's often up to no good. My dad fished with him for years. Had no choice. Lost his boat in a storm, no insurance, couldn't afford it. All he had was his fishing license. Parsons had a boat but no license. So the two paired up."

"Like a partnership?"

"Yes, more or less."

Lori saw his face growing tense.

"Father didn't find Scott easy to work with. Some mornings he was late and kept him waiting. And Scott always wanted to take the wheel, so father had to work the fish out of the nets and gut them. Much harder than being a helmsman. What Scott really wanted was the fishing license. Often tried to buy it off Father—for peanuts, of course. But Father always refused."

Noah drained his beer, and Lori got another out of the fridge.

"Father was knocked into the water when he was hit by the metal rake for catching scallops."

He sketched the mechanism on the table with his hands.

"The rake hangs from a framework of two poles forming an *A*. Weighs about half a ton. Scott was at the wheel and made a sudden, violent swerve and the rake swung like a super heavy pendulum sideways and . . . and it knocked father overboard. My brother Coburn was on the boat and yelled at Scott to cut the engine and put it hard astern. He could see father surface, and he had the gaff ready for him to grab onto. But either Scott didn't understand Coburn or . . . or he didn't want to. He did everything wrong until Coburn couldn't see him anymore."

Lori felt a tightness in her chest.

"Didn't he have a life jacket?"

"No. Water was bitter cold. Death always comes real fast."

He cleared his throat. "But he still could have been pulled out. Coburn could have pulled him out if Scott hadn't been such an idiot."

"Scott did it on purpose?"

"Nobody on earth could act as stupid as he did. In any case, he got Father's fishing license because they held the boat and everything in common. Didn't bring him any luck."

"How so?"

"Because we all suspected he had let father die. But he blamed my family for the vicious gossip about him that went around everywhere."

"So your families have hated each other's guts ever since," Lori concluded. And after a slight hesitation, she added, "And Glowena became your girlfriend?"

"Big mistake," he admitted. "But you make them when you're young. I think I was just rebelling against my family."

And Glowena was apparently very pretty, Lori thought to herself, *and what a challenge to win her heart against Scott Parsons's will.*

"Back to your question," Noah said, suddenly looking tired. "We didn't believe a word Jacinta said. She was easily manipulated and gossiped about everything. On top of that, she was always hanging around with Una, and Una had a loose tongue."

"But now, looking back . . . could there have been some truth in it?"

Noah shrugged. "So what would that mean? That one of the women archaeologists killed Jacinta and buried her in a strange grave because she was a gossip? You really think that?"

Lori laid her hands in her lap. Now that Noah had said it out loud, her little theory sounded crazy. Absurd.

"Did the police ever follow up on it?"

"They probably followed the wrong clues, or they'd have caught the killer."

Lori thought it was time to drop it. She wanted to enjoy the rest of the meal at least. But Noah asked, "What was the thing they found in Jacinta's grave like?"

"It looked like a fish or a bird, depending on how you looked at it. It was in the first burial mound, but it's really a projectile, an arrowhead. Somebody put it in Jacinta's grave."

She mashed a potato before going on.

"I also found a duplicate of it in this house, between the washing machine and the dryer. And another one under the seat of your snowmobile."

He gave a start, then seemed to remember. He blinked, and his eyes looked off into the distance in search of an answer.

"I bought that snowmobile from Selina Gould. She wanted to get rid of it after Cletus died. Found some small tools in it."

They both reflected on that as they finished their food. Lori cleared the plates.

"I'm sorry, I didn't mean to bring up that business," she said. "It was supposed to be a fun evening, and instead I've upset you."

Now Noah got up as well, took the plates out of her hand, and put them on the counter.

"Don't give it another thought. It's important for me that we can talk about these things. I want you to tell me everything. Any chocolate ice cream in the fridge?"

"It's vanilla, but with chocolate chips. I . . ."

Noah put his hand on her arm and gave her an imploring look. She responded without moving, and he pulled her toward him. She felt his arms around her back, pressing her against him. She let it happen, didn't resist when he laid his rough cheek on her neck, his face very near hers. She melted in the warmth of their two bodies. This was the point of no return, she thought.

They stayed like that for a while, without speaking, overcome by their emotions.

She heard her name called from far away. But it wasn't Noah. They separated, flustered.

Molly's voice reached them as if from another world.

She stood on the landing, holding up a seashell.

"I painted it for you," she shouted.

Lori saw it was a conch, pink, speckled with white.

From outside, Patience called for Molly, who turned around in a snit but wasn't about to leave.

"Thank you, Molly! I'll find a perfect place for it," Lori said. "But your mom's calling, you ought to . . ."

Patience appeared in the doorway, her face all red.

"I told her she should wait, but she just ran off."

She took Molly's hand firmly and smiled apologetically.

"I saw you've got visitors, so I didn't want to bother you . . ."

"No problem, Patience. By the way, Molly said a woman came here to see me the other day. Do you know who it was?"

"A woman?" She thought for a minute. "Must have been Selina Gould. I saw her go by."

"Oh! I have to pay the rent. Totally forgot."

Molly tugged at her mother's hand.

"I smell good, Lori. Want a sniff?"

"Later, Molly. I'll come over soon. Thanks for the pretty shell."

Patience shoved her daughter out the door.

The phone rang. Noah was at the kitchen window. He turned toward her with a grin.

She sighed and shook her head. "A little more privacy wouldn't hurt."

"People here can smell when something's up, and they don't want to be left out. Don't you want to pick it up?"

Before she could think of a rejoinder, the answering machine clicked on.

"Hi, Mom, Andrew here. Give me a call. I've got something to tell you."

Her mood changed instantly. She looked at the time. Midnight in Germany. Andrew had never called her here; it was always she who reached for the receiver first. He texted if he wanted something.

"It's my son. He's with his dad in Germany. I wonder why he called." She knew she looked worried.

Noah understood immediately.

He shyly reached out his big, worn-out fingers for her hands.

"I'd better leave. Got to go to the boat anyway, a few things to take care of. Coming fishing tomorrow? Just you this time."

Once again, that mischievous look she liked so much.

"Sure, love to, when?"

"Six o'clock. We can phone about the weather."

"Fine."

He hugged her, and she felt his surprisingly soft lips on her neck for a second.

Her eyes were glued to him as he walked across the kitchen with that firm fisherman's step and disappeared from sight. She didn't snap out of her daze until she heard his truck's motor.

Then she called Andrew's cell phone. He sounded wide awake despite the late hour.

"Hi, Mom, how's it goin'?"

"Andrew, did something happen?"

"Nope, why?"

"Because you called me at midnight, my dearest boy."

"Midnight? . . . Oh, I didn't realize it was that late. We don't have school tomorrow—some holiday, whatever. Can finally sleep in!"

"How did you do on your last exams? I haven't heard a thing. No news is good news?"

"Oh, yeah. They were OK. Near the top of the class in math. Though I'm not that into it. I like biology better—dissecting mice and all that."

"What? You dissect mice? Isn't that cruelty to animals?"

"Mom, they're dead when we cut them up. And when dead dolphins wash up on shore, they get dissected too. How else you gonna know what killed them?"

He was right, of course, but she had to get used to imagining her son at a dissecting table.

"How's it goin' out there in the sticks?"

"Did you see the pictures of the whales and the tortoise? And the shark?"

"Yeah, cool. The shark especially. Can you take a shark jaw back home for me?"

Back home! So Andrew was thinking about coming back to Vancouver, but she knew better than to press him on it.

"I'll try—assuming it's even legal. I'll ask one of the fishermen."

"You don't have to kill one to get it. They probably got something like it stored in a shed."

"So nice you're for protecting sharks, sweetie. They're having a rough time of it these days."

"Some people came here the other day," Andrew suddenly changed the subject. "Wanted to know where you were."

"Who were they?"

"Dunno. I thought maybe people who knew Rosemarie and Franz. A man and a woman."

"Does Volker know them?"

"Dad wasn't home. But they asked me . . . I didn't have a clue, but they just kept asking stuff. I was outside with Rainer on my skateboard, and they were talking to us and wanted to know about Canada. Like where I lived, in the East or West—they were just asking, so I said Newfoundland in the East and Vancouver in the West, and they asked if you could go whale watching in Vancouver, and I said yeah, in the East too, and my mom's in Newfoundland right now and there's twenty species of whales there."

Right after this torrent of words, the line went quiet.

"Mom, you still there?"

"Yes, I'm here . . . I'm just trying to make sense of it. Were they young or old?"

"Hmm, older. Rainer just *had* to blab about it at supper. He can't keep his trap shut. Dad wanted to know what they asked about and said if I'd told complete strangers what town you're in, then I had to let you know right away. I told him I'd said Stormy Cove. No clue why they kept asking dumb questions. I forgot about it for a few days until Dad reminded me to call you and tell you about it."

"What else did they say to you?"

"That some friends were traveling in Newfoundland and might come by to see you."

"Did Franz or Rosemarie say . . . Did you ask them who the people might be?"

"Dad asked, but they didn't know."

"Is Dad still up?"

"Nope, why? Can he call you?"

She heard the hope in his voice that he could wiggle off the hook and out of an obviously embarrassing position.

"Maybe I'll call him tomorrow. Andrew, sweetie, don't worry about it. How could you know what they were after? But I've told you before not to give any personal information to strangers . . ."

"Yeah, on the Internet, but this wasn't the Internet."

"I know, but you'll be more careful from now on, right?"

"Mom, why's Dad making such a big deal about this?"

"Because . . . because he probably wants to teach you a lesson. But you've learned now, right? I don't even tell my old friends personal things about you either."

"Sorry, Mom, it won't happen again."

Do you miss me? she wanted to ask.

"I miss you, my dearest boy. And I'm proud that you're getting so good at German."

"Yeah, German's real cool. I'll blow away the guys in Vancouver."

She laughed in delight. *He said Vancouver!*

"I'll look into the shark jaw situation—that's a promise. Sleep well, *Andreas.*"

"Mom, you can forget about *Andreas.* It's all English names over here, Kevin and Brian and . . . like, Patrick. They think it's awesome."

"Here the popular names are biblical things like Noah and Ezz, for Ezekiel, and Nimrod."

"Nimrod—whoa! Hot! I've got to tell the guys about that one. Talk to you later, Mom."

Lori thought about the phone call while doing the dishes. Well, that and Noah. She was filled with an intoxicating feeling somewhere between ecstasy and fear.

She recalled every gesture, every glance, and replayed their conversation sentence by sentence.

We've got to be able to talk about everything, he'd declared.

Why in the world had she mistrusted him for so long?

Falling asleep, she suddenly realized who had stolen the arrowhead from her home.

CHAPTER 32

Later, when events came thick and fast, a shadow fell on that day when she'd gone out to sea with Noah. But she made a solemn vow to preserve forever the beauty and magic of everything from those hours—to enshrine them. She printed out the photographs and stuck them in an album; the happiness in those pictures suppressed the memory, bit by bit, of the dark hours that were to follow.

The smell of the ocean was thrilling that morning—fresh and slightly fishy. She heard the gulls screaming and the waves gurgling against the waiting boats; saw the houses on the cove in the clear morning light, and felt the promise of a new day that would be utterly unlike any other. Noah—he stopped puttering around and watched her walking down to the wharf. She could read the pride and desire in his eyes, and relief too, that she hadn't changed her mind.

He simply smiled at her without revealing anything to the other fishermen who were busily loading colored plastic crates on board.

"Sleep well?" was his light-hearted greeting, while not taking his eyes off her. His curiosity trumped his shyness.

"I was a little keyed up, kept waking up," she confessed, flashing him a knowing smile.

He grinned in return.

"Ocean makes you nervous?"

"Not the ocean." Her smile broadened.

Ah, but the ocean exerted its pull on her with all its might as Nate steered for open water. The waves glittered like a kaleidoscope, silver and green and white and blue. She let her hair blow in the wind and tried to imagine the marine animals that dwelt in the depths of the sea. She'd grown up by the Pacific, but she'd never experienced the ocean the way she did in Stormy Cove. Here it seemed more majestic and mysterious.

She watched Noah free the massive cods from the netting, cutting off heads and cleaning guts out from bellies amid the cries of the gulls.

He moved with lithe assurance, almost with dignity, and enjoyed feeling her eyes upon him.

He sometimes raised his head, and the longing that shone in his dark eyes made Lori's blood course hot through her body.

You must never let this man down, she promised herself.

They leaned against the rail together as they wolfed down their sandwiches. The engine puttered softly.

He asked, with his mouth full, "Gosh, what's a beautiful woman like you doing with two stinking old fishermen on a boat?"

"Eating a sandwich," she shot back. And a minute later, "I'm sure I smell like fish now."

"Because you're a mermaid."

She pointed to her windbreaker.

"Look. Scales everywhere."

He laughed.

"Look good on you."

"Do you know the fairy tale about the fisherman and his wife?"

"Fairy tale?"

"A German one. We grew up with it, but maybe nobody here knows it."

She looked out on the water over to the shore while she tried to recollect the details.

"It goes something like this: A fisherman catches a turbot or a halibut but in reality it's an enchanted prince who asks the fisherman to let him go. The fisherman takes pity on him and sets him free. He tells his wife what happened, and she says he should have asked for something in return. So he goes back and calls for the fish to reappear, and so he does, and the fisherman asks him for a house more beautiful than the old hut they were living in."

Nate, listening from the open wheelhouse, interrupted her.

"Yeah, wives always want a prettier house and prettier furniture and a new TV."

"And you buy Emma everything," Noah commented.

"The wife actually does get a nicer house, but then she wants a castle, and the fisherman has to again ask the turbot for one, and she gets it. And then she wants—"

"A trip to Hawaii," Nate shouted.

"No she wants to be a queen, and then the pope, and then God."

"Always knew God's a woman," Noah joked. "So nice at first, then comes the punishment."

"Maybe God is a woman, but not the fisherman's wife," Lori corrected him, "because the enchanted prince sends her back to her old hut."

"Hey, we fellows don't live in old cottages," Noah said.

"It's only a fairy tale, my dear, and a German one to boot."

Nate emitted a grunt of amusement.

"I'd have grabbed the turbot and not let it go. It would have brought in a heap of money."

"No, no, the fairy tale's got it wrong!" Noah shouted. "The fisherman is the enchanted prince, not the turbot. That's obvious!"

Lori laughed. "So the wife can ask him for anything?"

He looked at her sideways. "Well, what does she wish for?"

She was spared having to answer because a loud swooshing sound made all three of them whip around.

They could just make out a round dance of black and white plunging into the waves.

"Orcas!"

Lori aimed her camera at the spot where the whales had vanished. "I didn't know there were killer whales in Newfoundland!"

"We ordered them specially for you, my dear. They know we got a photographer on board."

Again Lori couldn't answer because the whales breached a second time, but now she was ready. She even managed to keep her balance, though the boat was rocking hard in their wake. They breached twice more, entrancingly elegant despite their weight, until they disappeared into the infinite ocean vastness.

"Fantastic!" Lori yelled. "How fantastic was that!"

Noah raised his eyebrows in amusement.

"So, am I an enchanted prince or not?"

"Then you gotta take her dancing tonight," Nate butted in. "The Glorious Jiggers are on."

"Can't dance," Noah muttered as he went back to pulling in the nets.

"Gotta see the Glorious Jiggers," Nate shouted to Lori. "They're really good, and all of Stormy Cove will be at the Hardy Sailor."

He disappeared into the wheelhouse, and the boat's engine drowned out Noah's mumbled protests.

The Glorious Jiggers' loudspeakers beat the most thunderous boat engine by a country mile. In Vancouver, Lori always brought earplugs to rock concerts, but now she was hopelessly at the mercy of the cacophony. But that wasn't the only irritation that spoiled her listening pleasure; she couldn't find Noah in the mob of people. He'd promised to meet her in the pub as soon as he was back from the fish plant in Saleau Cove, where he was delivering the cod that evening. She'd gone for a quick walk with Rusty around the bay before washing and drying her hair and putting on her tightest pants and the only sparkly blouse she'd brought from Vancouver. She felt so pretty that she took a selfie. It might turn out to be her author photo for the book.

But no matter how she combed through the crowd in the Hardy Sailor, she found no trace of Noah. Maybe he'd chickened out about dancing in front of so many people, introvert that he was. Or was he afraid everybody would see that he was courting Lori? She felt a thousand eyes on her, but maybe it was just her camera attracting attention as always.

She didn't rule out the possibility that Noah *was* there, and she simply couldn't find him. It was like the Tokyo subway in the bar. There were certainly more bodies present than in all of Stormy Cove; as Nate had predicted, they came from the surrounding villages as well. The Glorious Jiggers were touted as the cultural highlight of the year.

Then it occurred to her she hadn't seen Nate anywhere either. Same for Archie and Ezz and whatever all those Whalens' names were.

But she did spot Noah's sister Greta, who had poured herself into a red T-shirt with gold sequins. Lori waved madly in her direction, but Greta didn't respond. Lori had no choice but to push through the wall of people, targeting the place where she hoped Greta was. All of a sudden, she was face-to-face with the T-shirt.

"Let's talk outside!" Lori bellowed as loudly as she could.

Greta indicated the way with a nod and cleared a path faster than Lori could have.

The humidity and heat of the room dissipated immediately in the cool evening air. Lori could breathe again.

"Wow, that feels good!" Greta exclaimed, flapping the hem of her top and setting the sequins dancing.

"Have you seen Noah anywhere in there?" Lori asked. "We were supposed to meet."

"He's not here," Greta answered drily.

"Are you sure? Hard to find anybody in there."

"Yes, guaranteed. Noah's out on his boat with the others looking for somebody."

"Looking for somebody? In the water?"

"Nope, on Frenchman's Hill."

"Why? Who is it?"

"You haven't heard?"

"Heard what?"

Greta was really stingy with her information.

"The reporter."

"Who?" Lori asked, knowing the answer full well.

"Reanna Sholler. She didn't show up for work today, and nobody can find her."

Greta lit a cigarette. Lori had never seen her smoking until now.

"Why—why are they going out there?"

Greta blew smoke to the side to spare Lori. She took her time responding.

"Because Noah took her."

"He took Reanna out there?"

"Yes."

The cool air suddenly hit her like an icy wave, and Lori felt like a person drowning.

"But when? I—I was with Noah today and . . . and yesterday evening. He was at my place yesterday evening."

"Until what time? Days are longer now. He must've taken her on his boat after he left yesterday. She wanted to go real bad, so she begged him to take her when he was finished working on his boat. She wanted to look at the cemetery on Frenchman's Hill, take pictures of a couple of tombstones in the evening light. She told Noah that John Glaskey would pick her up. But John says he's never heard of her, they never set anything up."

"So Noah came back all by himself? He simply left her behind in the cove near Frenchman's Hill?"

Greta took a stiff drag that rapidly shortened her cigarette.

"Well, it isn't dangerous over there. Just a cemetery and a flock of sheep. John Glaskey's sheep. It's the end of June, so she won't freeze. And it's light out till ten."

"I didn't know about the cemetery."

"Folks wanted to keep their dead as far away as possible, apparently."

Lori folded her arms. She was shivering. But beads of sweat appeared on Greta's forehead.

"Who said Reanna was missing?"

"Will. Will Spence. She didn't come to the office this morning, and he couldn't find her at her place. She'd been out all night, evidently. She has a room in Effie Spence's house—Will's mother. Nobody knew where she was."

"How . . . how did people know that . . . Noah . . ."

"They were seen together. Don't you know? People see everything around here."

Greta trod on her cigarette butt.

Lori stood there as if paralyzed.

Noah and Reanna were seen going away, then he was seen coming back alone.

"I told him he'd better keep his hands off."

"Off what?" Lori knew she didn't want to hear the reply.

"Reanna looks like Glowena. Glowena Parsons. Spittin' image."

She took a few short steps to the entrance and adjusted her neckline.

"Let's go. We don't want to miss the whole concert. No use mucking around in the past. That'll get you nowhere."

Carl Pelley, 54, detective, from Corner Brook

Of course crimes are committed here. Happens here, there, and everywhere. Why should people living here be superior? Just because they're in small, isolated communities? When I read in the papers that this place is supposed to be safe, I feel like tossing the paper on the fire. Yes, I know, people here leave their homes unlocked. But only in rural areas. Definitely not in St. John's anymore. Where there's money, you'll find crooks. And where there's poverty, too.

I've always been convinced that the Jacinta Parsons case can be solved even after twenty years.

People in Stormy Cove hoard their secrets, of course. They don't go to the police if they know something. Unless they're the injured party. And sometimes not even then. They want nothing to do with cops. Their motto: I won't hurt you, and you won't hurt me. But a lot goes on under cover of darkness, that's for sure. Fishermen steal one another's tools or gasoline. Or the fish out of their nets. I've seen it all. I remember when some sheep disappeared in Stormy Cove, a long time ago. The owner didn't have the least idea who did it. Until some years later when a guy got plastered and bragged about it. And do you know what? The thieves didn't live far away. So-called friends. They stole the sheep from a family with a dozen kids. But I swear, if that family's house had burned down, those same people—those thieves—would have built them a new house with their bare hands. They're like that around here. Nothing's black-and-white.

I'll tell you something: you just wait long enough, and somebody's going to talk. They think nothing's going to happen to them after twenty years. They think time fixes everything. But it ain't so, uh-uh, that's not the way it is.

We've never given up on Jacinta. Who do you mean? The fisherman's wife, the one who wanted to leave her husband and then disappeared? Yes, OK, so we do have some unsolved cases. But what do you expect—anybody here can easily disappear, and sometimes it's quite natural. In a blizzard. Or falling out of a boat. Or a hunting accident that's hushed up. God knows I've gone through enough of that in my time.

Sure we had suspects. But no evidence. And no witnesses. Just rumors aplenty. And you can't build a case on rumors. Whenever you're starting to get serious—omertà, as the Italian Mafia says. Silence. Just a wall of silence.

And then, suddenly, something gets the ball rolling. Something nobody saw coming. Then skeletons crawl out of the closet, and tongues start wagging. And if the guilty parties don't talk, others do it for them.

CHAPTER 33

"Every stone, every grain of sand speaks to us," Lloyd Weston pronounced.

He stood with legs wide apart beside the burial mound as Beth Ontara and two students cataloged every single stone and its precise location. The monument was to be reconstructed exactly as it had been found.

Lori photographed each step of the procedure but had difficulty concentrating. Noah and the search party had combed every corner of Frenchman's Hill until dark but didn't find a trace of Reanna.

Will Spence had alerted the police. Reanna Sholler was now officially a missing person.

When Lori came home the previous night from the Hardy Sailor, she found Noah's message on the answering machine, saying he couldn't come to the pub because he was helping look for a missing person.

She tried to reach him the next morning, but by then it was six o'clock and his boat had probably just set out.

Weston phoned her an hour later. She first thought it was a good idea to fly with the archaeologists to the Barrens. That would get her mind off her dark thoughts and hidden fears about Noah. She was determined to find out the exact circumstances of his trip to Frenchman's Hill with Reanna—and his intentions.

But it turned out she was just hanging around without much to do most of the time while the others painstakingly brushed off the top layer of the burial mound. She watched Beth lugging a boulder that weighed at least twenty-five pounds. Although Beth was strong, it must have been backbreaking work.

A drizzle set in later, and the site was covered up with plastic tarps. Gideon flew her back, along with a representative from NORPUNT visiting the site, while the excavation crew crawled into their tents.

So Lori found herself back home much earlier than expected. Her plans to call her mother for advice were derailed when she saw she had a visitor.

She didn't immediately recognize the classy, well-dressed lady emerging from a white rental car. But Molly's words popped into her head. Maybe it hadn't been Selina Gould asking for her? The stranger came up to the house and knocked on the door.

"Hello! I hope I'm not disturbing you," the lady said with a pronounced accent. Lori now recognized her: the German baron's wife. She hurried downstairs.

"Please come in," she replied before bringing her visitor up to the kitchen, then deciding on the living room.

"So you do recognize me," declared the lady, who hadn't removed her shoes.

"Yes, but your name . . ."

"Ruth, Ruth von Kammerstein. But please call me Ruth—everybody uses given names here."

Ruth turned down Lori's offer of a coffee.

"Might you have some water? Bottled spring water?"

Lori didn't, but went to get some orange juice, which Ruth thinned with tap water. Lori poured herself some juice—undiluted—as well, and sat down. The baroness took off her green loden jacket with embroidered sleeves—Lori had seen ones like it in Germany—and laid it beside her on the sofa. Lori estimated that she was in her late forties, a soignée, slim lady with a broad face but surprisingly small hands and expressive eyes. Her dark blond hair was straight and pulled back with a red band.

"You're probably wondering why I'm here," her visitor began as she smoothed down her casual dark blue pleated skirt. It occurred to Lori that Ruth von Kammerstein might well be the only woman ever seen in Stormy Cove wearing a pleated skirt.

"I came by last week, but you weren't in. I . . . I'm here in fact for a friend of mine, Waltraud; she's the mother of the young woman who used to live in the therapeutic community at Lindenhold. You lived there once, didn't you?"

The baroness immediately recognized her faux pas. "No, not in the *community*, of course, but in the *house*, am I right?"

The palms of Lori's hands felt damp. This was about Katja's death. It had to happen. Eventually the past always catches up.

"I know it must be very difficult for you to recall your time there; it's hard for all of us, but particularly for Waltraud and her husband. Waltraud implored me to talk to you, since we were already in Newfoundland. Do you remember Katja?"

Ruth von Kammerstein's voice was firm but not unfriendly. If Lori hadn't lived with Germans before, she'd have probably regarded her visitor's presence as slightly pushy.

It suddenly dawned on Lori who it was that had quizzed Andrew: Katja's parents.

She sat bolt upright in her armchair, "Did your friends speak to my son in Lindenhold recently?"

"Yes, exactly," the baroness said in delight, as if Lori had uttered a password. "Your son told them you were here in Newfoundland—isn't that a crazy coincidence! Although"—she leaned forward as if sharing a secret—"we would even have flown to Vancouver. You see, we'd go to any length for poor Waltraud."

Lori turned cold. "What's so urgent that you would have come to Vancouver to find me?"

"You see, Waltraud always wanted to tell you something, but somehow didn't have the courage to—she suffered so much because of Katja. Her daughter's death aged her twenty years, believe me."

Lori was speechless, her head spinning. Ruth couldn't know anything about her confrontation with Katja in the kitchen, nor could Waltraud. Unless Katja told them? But did Katja have the time for that before her . . . terrible end?

The baroness sipped her juice, holding the glass in both hands as if she had to cling to something solid. Which didn't offer Lori any comfort as she waited, mesmerized, for whatever Ruth was about to disclose. Reproaches. Accusations. Or even worse: the threat of revenge.

But things took a different turn.

"You photographed Katja once, I believe," Ruth said in that familiar German accent. "That gorgeous picture where she looks so happy. That's what I told Waltraud. Katja looks happy. And completely . . . healthy. So fresh and healthy. Full of dreams. You know the picture I mean, don't you?"

Lori was so taken by surprise that she nodded mechanically.

"You should know that Katja gave it to her parents as a present. And said that's the woman she wanted to be. The one in the photograph. That's who she wanted to be. She said she knew now that it was possible because she had some evidence. That very picture, you understand?"

"I think—"

"Do you know what Katja told her mother? 'Lori sees the beauty in me. Not sickness and weakness—the beauty.' Aren't those wonderful words?"

Lori felt uncomfortable. Luckily, the baroness didn't wait for a response.

"You gave Katja hope, and you know, hope was the best thing anyone could give her. And you gave Waltraud and Erhardt hope as well. And Waltraud wishes to thank you for that."

Lori looked at her visitor blankly.

"But Katja . . . she, I mean, this hope, in the end she didn't . . ."

". . . make it a reality, is that what you mean? True, but Katja ultimately chose the path she did, and we'll never know why. There's something we all had to learn: to let go. We had to let Katja go. A few days before she died, she tried to get more money from her parents. We all knew what that meant. She wanted it for drugs. But Waltraud and Erhardt had to turn her down. Somebody eventually did slip her some. She begged from just about everybody. You, too? Did she ask you for money too?"

Lori shook her head. The baroness folded her arms across her chest and leaned back.

"We tried our hardest. But we could not save Katja. She was the only one who could save herself. But she decided differently."

The conversation was too much for Lori. She wished the woman would disappear, just dissipate.

But Ruth kept on talking.

"Waltraud and Erhardt still have your photograph. That's how they wanted to remember Katja. It's a great consolation for them both, that picture. And I'm happy to be able to finally tell you that."

Lori tried to respond but couldn't utter a sound.

Ruth looked at her with empathy.

"I know it was terribly hard for people in Lindenhold back then. Franz and Rosemarie did so much for Katja. But sometimes you're just powerless. That's the way it is. Powerless. But I've kept you long enough. I have one more question. Shall I give Waltraud and Erhardt a message from you?"

Lori stared at the baroness as if she were asking for a handout.

She racked her brains feverishly to try to extricate herself from the situation. Her thoughts turned to Katja's mother, to the loss and suffering and pain she'd gone through. Emotions her own experience had taught her all too well.

She cleared her throat.

"Please tell her . . . tell her it's nice to know that . . . we sometimes do more good than we are ever aware of."

The baroness's face lit up at once.

"Yes, that's true, so very true. And that's why I needed to pass this on, and it was of great concern for Waltraud and Erhardt too."

She stood up.

"It's very nice indeed that we met this way. Opportunities like this don't come along very often. It is too bad my husband could not be here; he was tied up with his affairs."

She put on her loden jacket, and Lori escorted her to the door. Before going down the stairs, the baroness turned around.

"You know, Katja simply got into bad company. One should not associate with certain people. You have to steer clear of them, or they'll be the death of you."

Ruth von Kammerstein lifted her chin so high that her lips formed a line. Then her features relaxed, and she expressed some words of farewell that Lori, under different circumstances, would have found moving.

Lori made her way back to the living room and collapsed into the armchair, stunned. She was unable to think straight. She didn't know how much time had passed when the telephone snapped her out of her brooding.

"Hello, my dearest. So what kind of a day are you having?"

Lisa Finning's words triggered an emotional tsunami. Lori burst into tears, and her pitiful attempts to respond to her mother's alarmed questions were drowned in loud sobs.

"Lori! What's the matter? What happened?"

"It wasn't . . . it maybe wasn't . . . my fault at all," she finally choked out.

"What isn't your fault?"

"Katja . . . the Katja thing."

"What are you talking about?"

"Katja, she was in Lindenhold."

A pause. Then her mother's voice.

"The girl who overdosed?"

Lori sobbed again, but Lisa Finning, with well-practiced patience, wheedled out answers to her questions.

Lori told her everything: the scene in the kitchen, Lori's anger at Katja, the knife in Katja's hand, her panic and fear because of Andrew, Katja's flight.

She threw in the baroness's visit and the message from Katja's mother.

"And you've thought all this time that you were to blame for Katja's death?"

It was less of a question than a summarizing conclusion to Lori's story.

"Oh, my dear child, why didn't you tell me?"

"I thought . . . thought the fewer people who knew, the better. You always say that."

"Yes, but Lori, that doesn't apply in every situation, just to my work." Her mother sighed. "You simply made assumptions . . . in the state you were in at the time. You couldn't see clearly. It might have been—and it's pure supposition, don't misunderstand me—it might have been that Katja actually got the knife out to help you. And it wouldn't surprise me if she . . . if she suddenly realized what a dreary life that was. A woman preparing beans in the kitchen for fifteen people while they're outside taking in the sunshine."

"What are you trying to say? That I . . . that this . . . my life was so demoralizing that Katja killed—"

"No, for God's sake! I just meant you do not have the foggiest notion what was going on in Katja's head during those few seconds, and that there is no causal connection between you losing your temper for a minute in the kitchen and what followed. The chain of events had begun much earlier, and you couldn't have done a thing to break it."

Lori heard a lawyer's voice now and not her mother's. Moments like these used to intimidate her, but now the factual tone of voice was reassuring.

"And something else, Lori. This should really stay between us. Her parents needn't know what went on. We don't know the truth and never will, and it would be no consolation for her parents. It would only open up old wounds—and for what purpose? We still wouldn't be able to clear anything up."

"So still keep it a secret?"

"It's an act of love toward the parents, who obviously have found some kind of peace. They could decide they themselves were to blame for not giving Katja money. But that wouldn't have helped their daughter either—just the opposite. And now dry your tears, my dear girl."

"Mom, have you sometimes cried . . . after Dad and Clifford's accident?"

"Yes, of course, but never in front of you. In bed, occasionally. There are . . . certain things over which we have no influence, Lori. And things we can't prevent. To come to this realization you often need . . . I'd call it a certain humility toward life."

"Thank you, Mom, for everything. And for the beautiful care package. I was thrilled."

"You see? It's the little things that count. I must be off, meeting to get to, but I wanted to give you a quick call—you're very important to me."

"You're important to me, too, Mom, really important."

Lori rarely expressed her feelings to her mother. Lisa Finning didn't seem to need her to. But this time, Lori could hear the speechless surprise at the other end.

A brief pause, and then a slightly shaky voice said, "I'm lucky to have a daughter like you." After her confession, Lisa Finning hung up quickly.

Lori wandered through the house like a sleepwalker, from the living room to the kitchen, down to the basement, upstairs again to her office. Then she settled into a seat by the large window. Fog lay on the hills behind the cove. The street was shiny and wet, and a light breeze blew the smoke from the chimneys to the northwest. She hadn't mentioned Reanna's disappearance or the bind Noah was in to her mother, and certainly hadn't said a word about her own misgivings.

Maybe it was better; her mother would have warned her to keep her nose out of things, but it was already too late.

Lori got out her diary and filled several pages.

She finally conceded she was hungry; she'd eaten nothing since breakfast.

It was getting on toward evening when she was in the laundry room and heard a car drive up fast. Then somebody at the side door.

She hurried to the stairs and found Noah standing there. She was startled by the exhausted look on his face. He simply stared at her, saying not a word. She went over and took his calloused, freezing cold hand.

"Come in," she said.

She filled the kettle, but Noah waved her off.

"I've got to get back right away. We're going out again to keep up the search."

She turned around.

"Noah, what *exactly* happened? I've got to know."

He rubbed his forehead as if to collect his thoughts.

"She came to the landing stage while I was cleaning up. Asked if I could take her over to Frenchman's Hill. Wanted to see the cemetery for a story."

"And what time was that?"

"Seven or half past. She said John Glaskey would bring her back. John sometimes checks on his sheep on the island. So I dropped her off there and came back. Then I heard the next day that Will Spence was looking for her. And for me, too, because somebody saw me in the boat with her. Told him to go ask John Glaskey, that he picked her up. But John said she never asked him. He'd never talked to her."

She watched Noah as calmly as she could.

"Would John have lied?"

Noah shook his head.

"John's an honest man. Known him a long time. No, I really don't think so."

"Why did Reanna ask you? I mean, of all the fishermen?"

He looked at her in bewilderment.

"I . . . I was the only one down there. Nobody else."

"And why did you agree so fast? Why did you go along with it?"

Noah frowned. He avoided her gaze, looked out the window.

Lori suspected it was his way of keeping his emotions in check.

"It's not what you think. That . . . no . . . it's not that." He stopped, groping for the right words. "But there *is* something . . . I had a suspicion. You should know that Reanna . . . she's a dead ringer for Glowena."

"Glowena Parsons."

"Yes." He still stared out the window.

She didn't recognize her own voice when she asked, "And that's why you want to be with Reanna?"

"I thought . . . I wanted to find out if she was my daughter."

His words exploded in the quiet room.

"Your daughter? You and Glowena had a daughter?"

Noah's face puckered up, as if a branding iron had been planted on his skin.

"When Glowena left, there . . . it was rumored she was pregnant."

"By you?"

"Yes."

"And? Did she ever come back to see you about it?"

No . . . and I never heard anything about her for the longest time. It's possible that . . . her parents would have done everything in their power to see that we'd never get in touch. Six years ago she came back for her great-aunt's funeral, and we talked just for a bit."

Lori stared at him. Then she laid her hand on his arm.

"Noah, I think that if she had a child by you, the Parsons would have come to see you. They'd have made you pay child support. They wouldn't have let you get away with it. Do you understand what I'm saying?"

He muttered some incomprehensible words while gazing at the floor. He seemed overwhelmed by the events washing over him.

She increased the pressure on his arm.

"Noah, Reanna is not your daughter. She's not Glowena's either. I know that for a fact."

"What . . . why do you think . . ."

She took her hand away and stepped back a little.

"Somebody made some inquiries about her. It . . . I thought it very peculiar that she knew all kinds of personal things about me, and that she showed up here and challenged me about them. I wondered why she was so weirdly interested in me and my family."

She folded her arms.

"A friend of mine knows everybody who's anybody in the media, and she found out that Reanna Sholler was a gossip reporter for a Vancouver tabloid. But she got caught using other people's work—plagiarizing. She was kicked off the paper, but her father had connections with the publisher of the *Cape Lone Courier* in Halifax and got her the job here."

Noah looked at her with raised eyebrows.

"Her *biological* father," Lori emphasized, "and her biological mother is an interior decorator with wealthy clients on the North Shore in Vancouver. Reanna was born in Montreal. Her real name's Annabelle."

"She's not from Ontario?"

"No, and not from Timmins and not from Trifton. Reanna most certainly didn't want anybody here to find out who she was and why she'd lost her job in Vancouver."

Noah shook his head in disbelief.

"But she's a dead ringer for Glowena."

"But not you," Lori remarked drily. "You should see my mom—no resemblance whatsoever. At least not outwardly."

She withheld the fact that her friend Danielle had also tracked Glowena Parsons to Alberta and sent Lori a photograph of her. Noah's ex might have been pretty as a picture once, but the woman in that photo looked haggard. Lori felt sorry for her. Maybe Glowena had given up somehow, after her younger sister's death.

Lori had something else on the tip of her tongue.

"Noah, was Reanna wearing a life jacket when she was with you?"

He pondered for a moment.

"Yes."

"What color?"

"Yellow. All ours are yellow. Why?"

"Noah, it would be smart if you went to the police and told them that right now. Don't wait for them to come to you."

His face shut down immediately, and Lori saw she was up against a brick wall.

"I haven't done anything. Why should I talk to them? If they want something from me, they can come and get it."

"The police need your help. Every detail's important."

Noah clammed up.

He can be so damn stubborn, she thought. *That must have got him into trouble the last time.*

"Gotta go. The guys are waiting," he said abruptly, making for the stairs. Then he turned around.

"She didn't give it back to me, the life jacket. I didn't even notice."

When the door shut, Lori was too exhausted to feel anything.

She ran a bath and let the tension flow away in the hot water.

Soap bubbles ran through her fingers.

But the baroness's voice echoed in her mind as she toweled off and wrapped herself in her bright blue bathrobe later.

One should not associate with certain people.

Why did Reanna have to pick Noah for whatever she wanted to do? As if there weren't other fishermen she could have asked.

Lori was about to turn off the lamp on her nightstand when an image rose in her mind. An image of Reanna. She was with someone, but it wasn't Noah. Where had she seen that image before?

Tomorrow. She'd figure it out tomorrow, Lori resolved, and fell asleep immediately.

CHAPTER 34

Selina Gould stood in her doorway, knitting in one hand, the money Lori gave her in the other. The old woman was incapable of dealing with checks, so she wanted the rent in cash.

"Now they're looking for a neon-pink jacket," she said, weighing which to put down first, the wool socks she'd started on or the money. She decided on the money.

Lori followed her into the parlor and sat down.

"A neon-pink jacket? Who'd you hear that from?"

"Mavis. The police want us to be on the lookout for anything pink. The poor girl. They won't find her. They didn't find Una."

"I thought Una ran away."

"Why should she? Cletus always treated her well. She had a house, and Cletus bought her a car: a Corvette. The sporty model. She had it good." Selina sounded resentful.

"What happened to the car?"

"I sold it to one of Fred Charn's sons in Saleau Cove."

"You sold Cletus's snowmobile too, didn't you?"

"Yes, to Noah. He had more use for it. I couldn't steer the thing— far too heavy for me."

"Selina, I've been wanting to ask you something. I found something in the laundry room. It looks like the arrowhead they found in that ancient Indian grave. During the excavations, you know?"

Selina put the bills on her little parlor table loaded with porcelain figurines.

"What did they find?"

Lori explained it in more detail.

"I put that arrowhead on my kitchen table. In Cletus's house. It wasn't there afterward. Is it possible you took it? I mean, because you thought it belonged to Cletus?"

Lori wouldn't have been surprised if Selina had taken offense, but the old woman still seemed not to comprehend what she was trying to say.

"An arrowhead from the excavations? No, Cletus certainly didn't have anything like that. He never worked there. They didn't want him. They gave everybody a job except Cletus. And do you know why? Because he wasn't in the program."

"Program?"

"The government make-work program. He never tried to get in. But they could have given him a job nevertheless. Why should some people profit from it when others don't, eh? It's just not fair."

"Was Cletus unemployed? Didn't he fish?"

"But he didn't have a license. He'd work on other boats sometimes, but there wasn't always work to be had. But, you know, he always brought me fish. He was always watching out in case anybody saw him. He also brought me meat. You just have to keep a sharp eye out."

A poacher, Lori thought to herself, *with a preference for hard-core pornography.*

"So if he didn't work that summer," Lori said, "what did he do all day?"

"I don't really know now. Probably hung around with his girlfriend."

"And who was that?"

"You don't know? Greta Whalen. But that fell apart the same summer."

She didn't seem comfortable talking about it, because she came back to Reanna.

"They'll never find that reporter, I know it. Or they'd have found Una too."

Selina Gould was wrong.

They found Reanna Sholler that same day.

A speck of color caught Gideon Moore's eye as he was flying over the edge of the Barrens where the ocean peters out into a sheltered bay.

He brought the helicopter down and reported to the police that he'd found a neon-pink jacket. Just a jacket.

About thirty volunteers—almost all of them coming by boat—and four policemen arriving by helicopter scoured the area. Noah joined them. Barely an hour later, John Glaskey's party stumbled across Reanna's body. She was naked from the waist down.

The police found an object on the corpse that they immediately sealed in a plastic bag.

It didn't take long for it to circulate all over Stormy Cove that the reporter had been strangled with her own panties.

Noah Whalen and John Glaskey were taken to the police station in Saleau Cove for questioning. Lori heard from Patience that the police were starting to pay close attention to the villagers. She figured it was only a matter of time before they'd show up at her place, so she took Rusty out early. But the police didn't come that day. She found out from Nate's wife, Emma, that Noah and John were still being detained in Saleau Cove.

She drove to the store and parked on the shoulder because all the spaces in front of the supermarket were taken. When she opened the door, the conversation died, and all eyes were riveted on her.

She recognized Rusty's owner, Vera Quinton, and her husband, Tom; right behind them was Ginette Hearne, her face radiating schadenfreude; beside her was Selina Gould; even old Elsie Smith was there with her sons and some people whose names she couldn't recall. She wished Aurelia or one of her nice friends were there for support, but she had to handle the situation all by herself.

She said hello in the direction of the counter and went to get a chicken out of the freezer. Armed with the bird, she walked to the cash register, and the group soundlessly made way for her. The chicken slipped out of her hand and banged on the counter.

Mavis typed in the amount without saying a word, the frills on her raspberry-colored blouse rustling. She cast significant glances at those standing around.

But Ginette couldn't contain herself.

"Is Noah back from Saleau Cove yet?" she asked.

Lori knew all ears had pricked up expectantly.

"I don't know," she muttered, digging a twenty-dollar bill out of her pocket. Then she threw politeness to the wind and whirled around.

"You can think what you want, but Noah is innocent. If I were in your shoes I'd be prepared, because one thing's for sure—the murderer is among us. But you can bet your life it's not Noah."

She picked up the ice-cold chicken and ignored the plastic bag Mavis held out for her. Before closing the door, and just as Ginette opened her mouth to speak, she shouted, "If everybody spoke the truth around here, then not one innocent person would be under suspicion."

At that moment, she recognized a cousin of Noah's in the group, staring at Lori as if she were a zombie.

Not even his relatives will go to bat for him, she thought as she ran down the wooden stairs to her car.

When the police came to her home, she was ready for them.

There were two of them: an older man and the young policeman who'd warned her at the Birch Tree Lodge about polar bears. *As if that was all people had to look out for here.*

It was one of those days when the sunshine made everything sparkle, even weathered house facades and the colorful bellies of rotting wooden boats. A steady wind would often stream across the bay on those days. Lori and Rusty had gone to explore new paths along the coast, and gusts threatened to blow them over the cliffs. Grass from the previous year was withered and exhausted, forming a soft blanket over the bright green blades that protruded upward, hard and straight, like spear tips.

When she got back home, Lori lay down, tired from the brisk walk and from a night of worried thoughts that kept her awake. She heard the house groaning and shuddering with the blasts of wind. Noah couldn't have gone out to fish in such strong winds anyway; that must have provided some small consolation, given the nightmare he was living.

A loud knocking made her jump.

She went to the kitchen window on tiptoe and peeked out. The media had already reported briefly on the dead reporter on the Barrens, and soon Lori would have to hide from reporters coming to Stormy Cove.

The police car said it all. She let the two men in and took them up to the kitchen. They all sat down at the table, where nobody from outside the house could see them. The older officer had a longish face topped by a thin wreath of wavy gray hair, with two vertical creases in his forehead that gave him a slightly troubled look. He identified himself as Detective Carl Pelley and offered her his card. He'd evidently been briefed by his younger partner.

"You're a photographer, then," he began. "What's your book about?"

"About life in a Newfoundland fishing village."

The young policeman, whose name she'd forgotten, wrote in his notebook. She couldn't read anything because he was too far away.

"And why Stormy Cove?"

"I saw a picture of it once. It's beautifully situated, with the bay and the harbor . . . and there aren't many fishing villages left in Newfoundland with people who actually still fish."

"And you think that'll be of interest to folks in Vancouver?"

"Yes, it's an unknown world, and maybe it won't be around for very long."

The words had become like a mantra.

"Did you know Reanna Sholler?"

"I met her a few times: on the beach, on the wharf. We went out to see the icebergs with Noah Whalen. She took pictures too. But otherwise, I really don't know her."

"And why did you go with him?"

She looked the detective straight in the eye.

"Because he offered to take me. I depend on fishermen to help me in my work."

"What's your relationship with Noah Whalen?"

The young policeman squirmed on his chair.

"I'm a friend of his; he's helped me several times. For instance, he invited me to a family gathering where I could take photos. He's a nice, obliging person."

"How close is your friendship?"

She was astonished at how she kept her cool.

"We do *not* have an intimate relationship, if that's what you mean. Even if people here might say something different."

The detective appeared to accept this.

"And how is . . . how *was* the relationship between Reanna Sholler and Noah Whalen?"

She thought for a second before replying.

"I think she'd noticed how helpful he was and used him for her work."

"And for Noah Whalen? What was Reanna to him?"

"You'll have to ask him yourself."

Pelley scratched his—poorly shaven—throat.

"I'd like to know what *you* think about it."

"I think the locals are curious about every outsider who comes to town. There's not much going on around here. Reanna Sholler was sure to attract attention because she's . . . from another province and—and she was interested in what was happening in the village. That was probably flattering for Noah, and for everybody else."

"And for you?"

Why does he keep coming back to me?

"It sounds . . . horribly petty now that something so awful has happened to her. But since you asked . . . it was a bit of a bother at times when she got in the way of my work."

"How's that?"

"If she walked in front of my camera or . . . wanted to photograph the same things."

"For instance?"

"She wanted to photograph the excavations—you probably know about the burial mound on the Barrens. She desperately wanted to go up there, but Lloyd Weston hired me exclusively. He's the lead archaeologist."

"Yes, I know him."

The two men exchanged glances. A sudden realization struck Lori, a logical, terrifying thought that she didn't dare articulate.

Pelley reached into his coat pocket and laid something on the table.

A small object in a plastic bag.

The arrowhead.

The detective leaned so far over that his bald spot was easy to see.

"Does this object say anything to you?"

"May I?"

She brought the plastic bag closer.

"I found something like this . . . an arrowhead . . . I found one in this house, between the washing machine and the dryer. I told Lloyd Weston about it because I thought it might have something to do with his first dig, but he never did anything about it."

"Where is it now?"

"I left it on this table, and the other day, when I got home, it was gone. I thought . . ." She stopped in midsentence, and for the first time, she did not feel in control of the situation. She'd said too much.

"Yes? What did you think?"

The detective was no greenhorn or hick cop—that was clear. He wouldn't be fooled easily. *Better stick to the truth.*

"I thought Selina Gould might have taken it because she was apparently in this house when I was out. She still thinks of it as her house—or her son's, which I can understand in a certain way."

"Did you ask her?"

The man wasn't letting go. Like a bulldog.

"Yes, but she said she didn't know anything."

The detective cleared his throat.

"We found the object lying on Reanna Sholler's body."

Lori was so shocked that she gawked at Pelley, dumbstruck.

He observed her closely.

"That surprises you?"

Lori nodded.

"Why?"

The younger policeman fidgeted on his chair again.

"Because . . . because of the simple way you put it. Normally the police withhold information that only the perpetrator would know."

Pelley smiled, allowing his young partner to smile as well.

"Do you watch a lot of mysteries on TV?"

Lori leaned back. She understood his smile. Surely the search party that'd found Reanna must have seen the arrowhead on her body. It wasn't a secret now, but she was the only one who hadn't known. She got out of it with the lamest of excuses.

"My mother's a defense lawyer."

No follow-up from Pelley. The cop smiled.

"So we have the possibility that somebody took the item from your house. Who might it have been, apart from Selina Gould?"

Lori felt a chill. *Don't trust that smile.*

"Reanna. She was waiting in front of my house last week when I got home."

"You think she'd gone inside and stolen the arrowhead?"

"Maybe she thought it was pretty."

It was a weak argument—she could tell by the investigator's eyes. But his voice remained invariably patient.

"Who else could have made off with the arrowhead?"

"I leave the door unlocked, like everybody here. It could have been anyone."

Silence. The detective kept his eyes lowered. His companion was writing assiduously.

"Did Noah Whalen know about the arrowhead?"

She leapt up.

"Mr. Pelley, it was not Noah. Noah's not the murderer. Whoever killed Reanna would not have let himself be seen in a boat with her that evening, which is what Noah did. He wasn't the only one she had dealings with."

The officer sat up and took notice.

"No? Who else did you see Reanna with?"

"May I get my laptop from the office?"

She went and got it without waiting for an answer and set it down in front of the men.

Then she called up a specific picture.

"Here, I'll zoom in. I happened to snap this when I was taking Rusty for a walk. Rusty is Tom and Vera Quinton's husky. I recognize Reanna on the ATV, but who's the driver?"

The younger officer spoke up.

"I think I know whose ATV that is."

Lori waited for a name, but the policemen said nothing. The detective clearly knew as well.

At last, Pelley said, "May I have that picture?"

Lori nodded.

"I'll print it out."

From her office, she could hear the two of them conferring in low tones, but the noisy printer drowned out their words.

The detective pocketed the picture, and when he reached the landing, he turned to her.

"Is there anything else you'd like to tell us?"

Good tactic, I must admit.

She hesitated for a moment and then told him, "I asked Noah if Reanna wore a life jacket on board."

"Did she?"

"Yes, it was yellow. And she didn't give it back."

The detective was lost in thought as he ran his hand along the grain of the wainscoting. Then he turned around to go downstairs.

"A photographer really has an eagle eye," he said.

Lori said spontaneously, "Sometimes I think in colors."

It sounded awkward, but some things just can't be said any better.

She would recall those words later and how she was able to put it all in a nutshell.

The red streaks said something to her. They were from the frozen partridgeberries Aurelia had picked the previous September and given to her as a gift. Lori wanted to try to make a partridgeberry pie to get her mind off it all. The berry juice turned her fingers red.

No blood around Reanna's body. The killer had strangled her. No knife. No bashed-in skull. Just marks from strangulation, that's what she'd heard. The murderer hadn't taken out his rage on her, it seemed, but he'd wanted to keep her from talking. Or he wanted to make his own statement, over and above the murder. With the arrowhead.

She thought now that Reanna hadn't stolen it. Maybe one of the searchers left it on her body.

Poor Reanna, Lori thought. *She's dead and can't talk, and here we are, speculating about her.* A murder victim and now a victim again—of rumors. A hundredfold insult to a person killed so violently. And she, Lori, had constantly done wrong by the kid. Reanna was an inexperienced young reporter who was attempting to recover from a setback. So what if she was gauche? So she exploited her charms. So what?

She'd probably been pleased with her good luck at finding a professional colleague in what must have seemed a desolate dump to a young city gal. And Lori had rejected her advances. Did she die quickly? Did she know what was happening to her? How long did she shake with fear in the face of death? Or did she feel angry at her tormenter, angry at being helpless and at his mercy?

Reanna had been murdered, and life in the village just seemed to go on. It's probably how people in Stormy Cove had coped with injustice and misfortune forever. But this was no accident; it was murder. The second one in twenty years. At least.

And here she was, baking her partridgeberry pie as if nothing had happened.

She got the sugar bowl out of the cupboard and found she'd forgotten to buy more. She had no choice: she had to run the gantlet at the store again.

As she drove past the church, she looked at the sign out front. The old quotation had been replaced with "God Holds His Protecting Hand over You Wherever You Are."

"Not in Stormy Cove," she said aloud. "Not here."

She slowed down at the fork leading to the harbor. Somebody was walking along the street ahead of her. It was Patience; she'd never seen her neighbor in the village without a car.

Lori rolled down the window, and Patience leaned in, her hair fluttering in the wind.

"Where's your car?"

"Ches has it. His truck's in the garage."

"Where are you going? Can I give you a lift?"

"I was just going to the store. I'm out of aspirin."

"Get in, I'll take you there."

Lori waited in the car in front of the store. Patience had kindly offered to buy sugar for her, and she'd accepted. She had no desire to meet any staring eyes.

"Are you in pain?" Lori inquired on the way back.

"Headache. Comes and goes."

Lori looked at her sideways. Patience seemed pale and shrunken.

"I have a bottle of water in my handbag."

"Thanks." Even her voice sounded different somehow.

Lori wanted to play for time in order to talk to her some more.

"If it's all right with you, I'd like to pop over to the other side of the cove. I want to get a shot from there; everything's so twinkly and nice. Or should I take you home right now?"

"No, no, a bit of fresh air will do me good."

"Where's Molly?"

"At Granny's."

When they reached the end of the bay, they stayed in the car.

"Is Noah back yet?" Patience asked.

Lori shook her head. "I don't know why they're holding him this long."

"He's sure to come back today. I'm sure Noah's done nothing, but he's a key witness."

Lori took a deep breath. "The police were at my place today. At yours too?"

"No. What would they want with me? I don't have anything to do with it."

Lori thought Patience seemed nervous. *Yes, what would the police want with her?*

"I think it's just routine. They're asking around. I think that . . . that this time they want to solve the murder quickly, not have it drag out the way it did with Jacinta."

Patience said nothing. Lori took a risk and startled her with a question.

"They found an arrowhead on the body, like the one I found in my house. It looks like a bird carved out of bone, or like a fish. Did you ever happen to see Una with something like that? Or was anything like that lying around her house when you were there?"

Patience pressed her fingers against her temples.

"I was almost never in her house."

"Wait, weren't you friends?"

Patience hesitated a minute and replied, "Una was definitely not my kind of friend. She was deceitful as a snake."

Lori looked at Patience in astonishment. She'd never heard her gentle neighbor talk like that. And there was more to come.

"Una was after Ches. She'd come to see him when I was out at births. She left him suggestive notes. And she always wanted to dance with him in the Hardy Sailor."

"What? How did Ches take it?"

"He said he didn't have any interest in Una. He said to me she flirted with everyone."

"Did you confront her?"

"No. I told Archie."

"Archie? Why?"

"Because everybody respects him. Archie has a lot of influence. She wouldn't have dared to . . ."

"Yes?"

"There's no messing with Archie. He'd have torn such a strip off her back that she'd never have tried anything with Ches ever again."

"And what happened?"

"I don't know."

"But did Archie go after her?"

"I suppose."

"Did Una . . . Did she ever say anything to you?"

"Yes, she was furious with me. Said I was crazy to think her and Ches had something going. She said Ches was of no interest to her whatsoever. And that Archie had no say in this and should mind his own damn business and be thankful that some people don't tell what they know about him."

"What did she mean?"

"Dunno."

Lori thought this was very odd.

"So how did it all turn out?"

"What do you mean?"

"I mean, what happened after that?"

"Una ran off three days later."

No sound in the car except the biting wind. The two of them stared at the houses of Stormy Cove, the clear light bathing them in a vulnerable innocence.

This is what people will see in my picture, Lori thought. A cluster of small, modest houses on the shore of a mighty ocean—the simple dwellings of people living a hard life. People would see the truth of it and come to the wrong conclusion at the same time.

She turned to Patience. "Ginette said that Una would never have run away by herself, only with a man, but with somebody who could pay the bills."

"Fair enough, but certainly not with my husband. You can see that now."

"Patience, I have to ask: What do you think happened to Una?"

Patience still wouldn't look at her.

"I think Archie told her his opinion and she couldn't take it and skipped town."

"But nobody used her credit card after she disappeared. And she left her cell phone behind."

"She wasn't stupid. They could have used those to track her down."

Lori saw the point. But she had an odd feeling.

"Have you ever talked to Archie about this?"

"No."

"So you don't know what he said to Una?"

"No. Can you take your picture so we can go back? My head is pounding."

"Yes, of course, I'll take you home right now and come back for my shot after."

A few minutes later, as Patience was opening her front door, she stopped for a moment.

"I don't wish anything bad on Una, but my life has improved an awful lot since she left. She made problems for everybody."

She attempted a tiny smile.

"Thanks for the ride. I'll feel better tomorrow. And Noah will definitely be back by then."

Patience was dead-on. That evening, Lori saw his pickup in front of his house. Patience called a little later. Somebody had seen Noah on the wharf. But he didn't come to Lori's and didn't call.

She dialed his number. No answer.

Maybe he needed some time. Maybe he was busy with his boat. After all, he had to catch up on the work he'd missed the past three days.

But not even a phone call.

Had she misjudged? Maybe she wasn't as important to him as she thought.

We should be able to talk about everything. He *did* say that.

She barely slept that night.

She was struck by the stillness of the next morning. No wind. Exhausted, she lurched over to the large living room window. The water was so smooth that it reflected the houses and cliffs.

Though she didn't feel like it, she walked down to the boats with her camera. The sight of Noah's pickup was like a stab to the heart. His boat was gone, of course. Nobody had asked her if she wanted to go out fishing on such a glorious day.

Lloyd Weston didn't call either. Patience didn't drop in. The telephone didn't make a peep. It was as if they all had abandoned her.

But her in-box was abuzz. Her mother, Danielle, Mona Blackwood, and some Vancouver friends bombarded her with questions about Reanna Sholler's murder. They'd all heard about it on the news. No requests from reporters, though—almost a miracle. It paid off that she'd told none of her professional colleagues about her project. And Danielle had kept mum.

Lori put the e-mails off until later; she couldn't bring herself to answer them. When the phone rang in the afternoon, she had to hold back from answering it on the first ring.

It took several seconds before she recognized Aurelia, the librarian. She sounded like a messenger from another world.

"I found another book about Marguerite," Aurelia announced. "Marguerite de Roberval."

Several seconds later, Lori caught up.

"The French princess who was marooned?"

"*Princess* is a bit much. She was nobility. You said you were interested in her. I had the book sent from St. John's. Shall I hold it for you?"

It was an invitation to come to the library. Lori's heart felt tight.

"I'll be there right away."

"We're closed today, but how's tomorrow after one?"

"Yes, that should work. Unless I'm off with the archaeologists."

"Oh, they've stopped digging for the time being . . . because of the murder, you know."

"Oh, really? I didn't hear that. Thanks for telling me."

"It's about the safety of the female students, eh? They've got to catch the killer first."

The students—strangers, just like Reanna. And herself. Surely they weren't thinking the way they did last time, that the killer was an outsider? That it had nothing to do with themselves?

"But the women in the village, maybe they aren't safe either," she said. "Do you feel safe, Aurelia?"

A brief pause.

"It *is* scary, for sure, but what can you do? My husband says it might have been a wild animal."

"But you can't believe that! Reanna was strangled."

"I don't know what to think. But last night I locked the doors. My husband gave me hell, naturally."

"I've locked my doors too, ever since—"

She intended to say, "since the arrowhead disappeared," but she bit her tongue.

"Hopefully the murder will be solved soon," she heard Aurelia say. "Or else there'll be bad blood again."

Lori wanted to ask what she meant by that, but across the way, she saw Noah getting out of his pickup.

She quickly said good-bye and ran to her Toyota.

Now she didn't care how many people saw her going to Noah's house.

She didn't find him in the kitchen. Just as she shouted his name, she heard water running. The shower.

What the hell. She could wait. Right there, in the kitchen. That was certainly against Stormy Cove rules, but she was upset enough to break the rules.

The noise stopped. She called his name again. A door opened.

"Hello?"

"It's me, Lori."

A few seconds of silence, then his voice.

"Be right there."

He appeared a few minutes later, which seemed like an eternity to her. Her heart was in her throat when she saw him, his clean T-shirt stuck into his tight jeans, his damp black hair shiny. He fixed his dark inquiring eyes on her as they sat down across from each other at the table.

"You look tired," he said.

She nodded.

"You too. Hard to sleep recently."

He slowly curved his hand over his freshly shaved chin.

"Yeah."

Nothing more than that.

"I was concerned because I didn't hear from you."

He looked at his hands.

"I'm sorry, but I was pretty much up to my ears in it, as you can imagine."

Lori said slowly, "Yes, I can imagine, but—"

"Did you tell the police about that life jacket?"

"Yes. Why?"

"What exactly did you say?"

"That she didn't give it back to you. Why?"

He frowned.

"They searched for it."

"Well, sure, I'd do the same thing if I were the police."

"They found it."

"Where?"

"In Jack's father's garage. They searched the whole house."

"I don't get it . . . how did it—what does Jack's father have to do with it?"

"Nothing, of course. But they took Jack in."

The words hung in the room like a black cloud.

Jack. The seventeen-year-old hunter.

Noah raised his head.

"It's a disaster."

"Maybe he's an important witness."

"His father says Jack hasn't got an alibi."

"His father's stupid. He shouldn't go around talking crap like that. It really won't help his son."

Then something crossed her mind.

The photo. Reanna sitting on the ATV's rear seat. Someone up front. Jack.

"Lori, Jack's father is my cousin."

She really wanted to take his hand but didn't know how. Noah seemed so distant.

"Don't worry, Noah, they must have found traces of DNA on the body—that'll clear it up fast."

Now she saw the horror in his face. She wanted for all the world to slap herself in the mouth.

He shoved his chair back and got up. She sat there, frozen.

Silence in the kitchen.

He leaned over the dish rack, head down, hands clutching the edge.

"Noah, oh my God, is it possible that . . ."

He shook his head vigorously.

"Jack's family will never survive this. I know that. Never survive."

Lori's thoughts were racing. Was it possible that this seventeen-year-old . . . a kid who slept with women like Ginette. Who probably hoped to have sex with Reanna . . . He probably promised to take her to the burial mound so he could lure her to Frenchman's Hill. He went in his own boat and entered the bay from the other side so he wouldn't be seen with Reanna. Jack, the hunter, who was always mucking around on the tundra. A kid who was already killing animals at his age. And when he met any resistance, he resorted to force . . . Reanna didn't stand a chance. And the arrowhead? Did Jack steal it from Lori's house? Maybe he was looking for something else, money or valuables. Good that she'd locked her office.

She walked over to Noah. Her voice was a whisper.

"Only one person hasn't survived this tragedy. Reanna is dead. She was killed, whoever did it. *She* didn't survive."

He straightened up, his face ashen.

"I know, I know. But Jack's just a dumb kid, a hotshot. He's not a killer."

"Nobody said he was. We don't know the facts; it's all just speculation."

He fell silent. He was breathing far too rapidly.

Her stomach was in knots.

"Noah, are you angry with me? Do you blame me for telling the police about the life jacket?"

He didn't look back at her as he said, "Let the police do their own work. No need to interfere. Better that way."

Not interfere. Say nothing. Sweep everything under the rug.

"Oh, sure, so the murder still won't be solved even after twenty years? So that the murderer gets off scot-free? All because it might be one of your people?"

The tension, her pent-up rage, her exhaustion—all of it fueled her emotional outburst.

"What if it had been *your* daughter, Noah? What if Reanna had actually been your daughter? Should people keep their mouths shut then? She's not your daughter, but she is somebody's daughter, Noah!"

He stood there, a stone statue. She knew her words tormented him, but she couldn't do it any other way.

"I've heard stories about Jack's father. That he forced his daughter to sleep with him. I'm sure the whole village knows it—including you. It's not a cozy, safe little world here, and Jack's a product of it."

He said nothing, which just egged her on.

"I wanted to help you, Noah, because I know you're innocent. They were wrong to suspect you of being involved in what happened with Jacinta for the past twenty years. Enough! It's an offense that smells rank to heaven. I know what my priorities are. I know where my loyalties lie. But I realize now that your loyalty will always be to something else. To people like you, no matter what they may have done or may do. At least some good's come out of this conversation."

He didn't move a muscle. Not even when she said, "I'd better leave."

She slipped on her shoes without tying them and shut the door behind her.

CHAPTER 35

"Sweetie, didn't you shoot off your mouth just a tad?"

Danielle's cell phone headset slightly distorted her voice. She was driving her babies all around Vancouver because the sound of the car's motor transmuted an hours-long crying jag into peaceful slumber.

"Worth inventing the automobile just for this," she joked.

It didn't take long for Danielle to figure out that the humming motor wouldn't lull her desperate friend in Stormy Cove to sleep. She tried objective analysis.

"I mean, what *are* your priorities anyway? What's your loyalty to?" she asked, after Lori's detailed replay of her quarrel with Noah.

"That's easy: I don't want Noah to be under suspicion," Lori explained, intuiting where Danielle was taking this.

"Is that everything?"

"Yes . . . wait . . . what do you mean by *everything?*"

"Put yourself in Noah's shoes. All he's got is family. It's his be-all and end-all. Everything he has is that village. If they turn against him, his world goes to pieces."

"But that's how they're acting now, Danielle, they're turning against him! Nobody's coming to his defense!"

"Not even his family?"

"Not the way we would, not in so many words, and . . . and . . ."

"With libel suits and lawyers, you mean?"

Lori hunted for the words.

"They simply don't talk about it; they behave as if nothing's happened. But it will never go away because the suspicion is always there, like a ghost."

"And you're the white knight who's going to slay this dragon for him?"

Lori sighed. She could hear the skepticism in Danielle's voice.

"What are you trying to tell me, dearest friend of mine?"

"That Noah doesn't have to be loyal or anything else to you because—excuse me for being blunt—he gets nothing from you."

"And what else?" Lori waited before answering. She knew her friend was holding something back.

"Maybe you should step away from the whole business for a while. Come to Vancouver for two, three weeks. The story about that reporter is all over the national news. You don't want to see your face on the screen after the TV gangs show up."

Lori heard the side door open. She was seized by a frantic hope that it was Noah.

"I'll think about it," she said without much conviction. "My nerves are shot."

"It's nothing compared to two tiny babies who don't stop screaming, believe me. Hopefully we'll see you soon."

"You're worth your weight in gold, Danielle. I'll call soon. Bye."

She still had the phone in her hand when she arrived at the kitchen stairway.

Where she stopped, rooted to the spot.

The woman on the landing held her shoes in her hands.

"Can we talk for a minute, if I'm not disturbing you?"

"No, no, I'm just a bit surprised, I—"

"I tried calling," Beth Ontara said, "but the line was always busy. And since I was in the area . . ."

"Tea?" Lori asked, offering the archaeologist a seat.

Beth ran her fingers nervously through her short hair. Lori had never seen Beth so restless.

"I'd love it."

Beth looked around, less out of curiosity, it seemed to Lori, than to choose her words before speaking.

"I'm taking a bit of a risk by coming here, and for that reason—can you treat our conversation with discretion?"

Lori sat down slowly.

"Basically, yes, but I have no idea what it's about."

"Nothing you have to worry about. It concerns stolen artifacts."

Lori braced herself.

"I don't understand."

"I've learned that a so-called arrowhead was found around Reanna Sholler's body. And somebody told me it was in this house before then. Is that true?"

The kettle was already boiling, and Lori took the opportunity to stand up.

"Whoever told you that?"

"It makes no difference."

"It makes a difference to me because there's a murder investigation, and too many people are spreading stuff around."

Beth took the tea and piled sugar into it. She didn't take the condensed milk.

"OK, I heard it from Lloyd. Where he got it from, I don't know."

Lori took a moment to think.

"Probably from me. I told him about the arrowhead last time I was up at the Birch Tree Lodge. He did say it might be a projectile tip, like an arrowhead. But I told him maybe I'd been wrong about what I found and he never mentioned it again."

Now it was Beth's turn to be astonished.

"What? Lloyd's known about it for that long? That's awesome!" She quickly composed herself. "I guess I need to tell you the back-story here. The dig at the first burial mound should have been led by Carl Wizhop, but he got very sick. Lloyd was his assistant and fairly young at the time, but he was considered capable of leading the dig. Wizhop wanted to give him remote support, so to speak, as best he could. Lloyd . . . don't get me wrong, he's a brilliant archaeologist . . . but practical organization is not his thing. I was forever reminding him that the crew must always be supervised, but he didn't buy it. Particularly the volunteers."

Beth looked to Lori, who nodded to show she followed.

"It's not like I think all workers are thieves, but on the other hand, they don't understand how valuable the things that we dig up are."

"Are volunteers even allowed to dig? Isn't that what archaeologists are there for?"

"Yes, you'd think so. However, conditions back then were sometimes chaotic. I did my best, but ultimately—well, I couldn't be everywhere at once. Early on I suspected that artifacts were disappearing. I went to Lloyd about it but he refused to believe me. No wonder: It would have damaged his reputation. And he was at the beginning of his career."

"Is that why he didn't seem bothered when I mentioned what I found?"

"I assume so. Especially not now, when expectations are so high about the second dig. He's a guy who thinks that problems go away if you ignore them long enough."

"But his professional curiosity must be bigger than—"

"Than his fear of a possible scandal?"

Beth shook her head and put her tea cup to her mouth, and a loud slurp followed.

"Nobody wants a scandal, including me. That hurts everybody: us, the locals, the university—it would be a huge catastrophe. It would drive Aurelia up the wall."

"Aurelia? What's she got to do with anything?"

"She's Gideon Moore's sister. Didn't you know?"

Lori shook her head. Everybody really was related to everybody else here. Aurelia must have assumed that Lori knew. But the next question was on the tip of her tongue.

"Were those thefts the reason why you had the artifacts from Gideon's lodge moved to a guarded container?"

"Yes, exactly, somebody had to step in."

"But some personal effects were stolen as well, right?"

"Who says so?"

"Gideon. He told me Una stole a valuable bracelet of yours."

She gawked at Lori for a moment.

"He said that? There's no way he could have known."

"He said it was a bracelet with green gems."

"How could he know? I never reported the theft."

"You didn't tell anybody? Forgive me, but I find that hard to understand."

"No, not the cops or anybody. Just imagine the feeling that would have been created at the dig if everybody thought I suspected them of robbery. I'd warned them again and again to lock up all their valuables."

"Beth, what brings you here?" Lori asked.

Beth leaned forward.

"I'm dying to know: Did you find any more artifacts in this house?"

Lori waited a beat before telling the truth.

"No." *Not in the house.*

Beth lowered her head and looked at her with knitted eyebrows.

"If you find or hear anything, please let me know immediately."

Lori nodded.

"I assume Cletus Gould must have stolen the arrowhead. Why hadn't you given him a job at the dig?"

"Oh, he worked a few days for us. But he came and went when it suited him. And he messed with Gideon. They couldn't stand each other. Gideon was more important to us, as you can imagine."

Lori said nothing in the hope that Beth would leave. And she did, but not without making one last remark.

"It's better if this little talk stays between us. It could affect you too, y'know."

"Me? Why?"

"If Lloyd loses his job, then you can kiss your exclusive photographs good-bye."

Lori watched Beth putting on her gym shoes. She wanted to burst out laughing but controlled herself.

"I'm not interested in the least if Lloyd or anybody else loses their job," Beth said with deliberate slowness. "But maybe other people are sawing off the limb he's sitting on."

Lori waved good-bye and turned around. She heard the door slam when she was in her office. Her heart was beating wildly. What a strange visit! Lori couldn't read it one way or another. Beth Ontara was playing an inscrutable game.

Beth mustn't find out anything about the arrowhead under the seat of Noah's snowmobile. Not before Jacinta's killer was found.

⊰✦⊱

Richard Smallwood, 56, Anglican minister

I don't have much time; it'll have to be a quick interview. I have four parishes that are far apart; maybe you cannot conceive of what that means, seeing where you come from. I'm almost continually on the move. Yes,

Stormy Cove needs my encouragement—and God's help, of course—after all that's occurred. It's a tragedy, or several rolled into one. These are wounds that take a long time to heal. People are insecure and upset—that's only natural—but they must not lose their trust in God's loving-kindness; I remind them of this time and again.

The Whalens? They rarely go to church, just for weddings and funerals. And many of the younger generation never come at all. You're right, neither does Noah Whalen. It's not a secret. Not since his father passed away.

Yes, I did meet the photographer from Vancouver. She came to see me because she wanted to take photographs of an interment. I wasn't sure at first, but death is a part of life, and the Johnstons had no objection—it was Joseph Johnston's burial. He fell from the deck into the fish hole. He was only forty-six. The Johnstons didn't mind her coming; they thought it was an honor for Joseph not to be forgotten so quickly. The Johnstons knew the photographer; she'd been in Stormy Cove about three months and got along well with people. She had such a . . . friendly manner, but was reserved too, you know.

Not until she sided with Noah did she . . . rub some people the wrong way, if I may put it thusly. But not everybody.

To be brief: I gave my approval. But under the condition that I could view the pictures beforehand, before they were published. I have a certain responsibility there. Lori was very discreet at the burial. Nobody actually took notice that a photographer was present.

Yes, she did indeed show me the photographs. I understand nothing about photography, of course, but the pictures—you should have seen them. So much dignity there. A sublimity, I might venture to say. How she captured the family's mourning. And how people could sometimes . . . be lost. So vulnerable in this rigorous life. But she gave them dignity. And the graveyard and the surroundings—she caught it well. It had an almost biblical effect. I hope one of the pictures will appear in the book. She had a heart for the people here. In spite of everything. Of that I am certain.

Just one thing before I really must go—I have a christening in Isle View. There was a figure in one photo—I can't say which; as a minister I cannot— a figure standing somewhat apart. Everyone's eyes were on the coffin. Just this one person was looking at the camera. Properly distrustful, that gaze. Everyone else there had forgotten the camera. But not that person. Even at the time I found it unusual.

When I think back on it, I get the shivers.

A prophetic picture, as I often think today. Prophetic.

CHAPTER 36

In the middle of the night, Lori was woken up by a racket outside. She stumbled out to the kitchen to see what was going on.

A car door slammed next door, and she heard Ches's truck roaring and his tires squealing. She peeked out the window to catch his rear lights as they vanished into the dark. Then she saw the glow from a fire in the direction of the harbor. She stared in apprehension at the flames flickering before a black background.

She threw on a jacket and ran next door, where the lights were all on. Patience was at the window.

"A boat's on fire!" she shouted to Lori.

"Whose?" Lori sounded hoarse.

"I don't know. Ches just drove down."

Lori gave voice to a terrible suspicion.

"Isn't Noah's boat on that side of the harbor?"

"I'm not sure," Patience replied, but a glance at her face said it all.

"I've got to get over there," she said, running like a hunted deer back to her house, where she hurriedly threw on some clothes.

She was at the moorings a few minutes later, where about two dozen people were assembled.

Her camera was set to go in her car, but she couldn't bring herself to take it out. She joined the crowd that was so transfixed by the fire that they didn't notice her arrival.

Suddenly, somebody grabbed her arm.

"Don't," Greta Whalen urged. "You'll have that sight before your eyes for the rest of your life."

"It's Noah's boat, isn't it?"

"Come and give me a ride home. Then we can talk."

Lori was too shaken to argue.

Arriving at Greta's modest home, Lori realized she should have gone over there long ago.

Rubber boots in the entranceway, blue overalls on a hook on the wall.

"Is your husband back?" Lori inquired.

"No, he's still in Alberta. He works for six weeks and then gets three weeks off. He'll be back next week."

"How can you stand it here by herself?"

Greta shrugged.

"We need something to live on, and there's big bucks working on the tar sands."

That explained her new kitchen: dark imitation wood and a green-speckled countertop with every imaginable appliance on it, like a display of trophies.

Lori dropped into a chair.

"It's arson, isn't it?"

"Yes, some bastard set fire to the boat, sure as shooting."

"Where's Noah? Was he at the wharf?"

"He and Archie and a couple of men tried to put the fire out. But with all the oil and grease on the boat it's hopeless."

"Did you talk to him? How is he?"

"Didn't say much, but it's a disaster. The boat's not insured."

"What? He's got no insurance?" It was worse than she'd thought.

"No, way too expensive. What fisherman can afford it nowadays?"

Lori buried her face in her hands.

"It's all my fault," she said, on the verge of tears.

"Why the hell is it your fault? You didn't set the boat on fire."

Greta put a bottle of rum and two glasses on the table.

"Here, drink this. Want some Coke in it?"

Lori shook her head. She didn't need rum or Coke—she just wanted to wake up from her nightmare.

"I told the police Reanna was wearing a yellow life jacket, and they found it in Jack's parents' garage. And they arrested Jack."

"So what?"

Greta poured two fingers of rum and mixed it with Coke. Lori pushed some strands of hair away from her face.

"Now everybody thinks Noah ratted on Jack."

Greta uttered a note of disapproval.

"They don't arrest a person because of one life jacket—anybody could have worn it. I guarantee they already had a suspect in mind."

Lori thought it best to keep quiet about her picture with Jack's ATV and Reanna.

"But why would anybody burn down Noah's boat?" she asked.

"Because somebody or other wanted to settle a score with him, or maybe not with him, maybe with Archie or Nate or another one of my brothers."

"Why is it always Noah? It started way back with Jacinta. And there were plenty of suspects then. Cletus Gould, for instance."

She looked into Greta's eyes, pleading with her.

"You were Cletus's girlfriend back then. You must have gotten wind of something."

Greta stared at her, shocked at the turn the conversation was taking.

"Cletus would never kill anybody."

"I found an arrowhead in his house. The same kind of arrowhead that was found in Jacinta's grave. How do you explain that?"

"What? Who'd you hear that from?"

"I can't tell you. But the police will put two and two together."

"They were already here. I told them everything I knew. Cletus never killed anybody."

"But he stole an arrowhead."

"What for? What would he do with a thing like that?"

"Maybe out of revenge, because the archaeologists fired him?"

Greta stopped talking and averted her gaze. She seemed to be in another place, far away.

"Greta, why did you leave Cletus that summer?"

"It was in the fall."

"Whenever. Why?"

"Our relationship had been more or less on the rocks for a while. It didn't come out of the blue."

Greta looked at Lori's glass.

"Sure you don't want any rum?"

"No, I don't feel like drinking."

Lori suddenly felt dead tired.

"I'm going home."

She got to her feet.

"You don't have to blame yourself for anything," Greta said as she saw Lori out. "Jack will be home soon."

Lori had those words on her mind until her eyelids finally shut sometime in the early hours of the morning.

She didn't wake up until eleven o'clock. She went straight to work on her laptop to keep from going to the window to look down at the harbor. It was high time to get in touch with Mona Blackwood.

But she didn't get very far. The first thing she saw was a headline: "Suspect in Sholler Murder Confesses." It took Lori's breath away. She had no idea the Royal Canadian Mounted Police would get Jack to talk so fast. She feverishly scanned the article.

> *Jack Day, 17, of Stormy Cove, confessed to the murder of the 23-year-old journalist Reanna Sholler, according to Corner Brook police. The police will make a statement on the sequence of events at a Friday press conference. Sources close to the police say that Day strangled the young woman. They say Sholler arranged to meet Day on the north shore of the bay near Frenchman's Hill to follow him to the burial mound on the Barrens where excavations are currently underway. The mound's location has not been made public until now. Day has report- edly been charged with rape. Unofficial sources say he confessed after assurances that he would be tried in juvenile court and not as an adult, which would significantly reduce a possible sentence. Jack Day's fam- ily has no comment at this time. Day has no criminal record and recently completed high school.*

Lori sent Mona a link to the article and suggested a phone call.

She made breakfast in a mental fog, surprised she had any appetite at all. But she gobbled down two pieces of toast, a fried egg, and a banana. Her survival instinct had kicked in.

Lisa Finning was the first to call.

"Come home for a while, my dearest," was her gambit.

"I can't."

"Is it the book?"

"Yes, that too."

"So it's the man?"

Lori didn't answer.

"Are the police leaving you alone?"

"They were here. Questioned me about Reanna Sholler."

Lori didn't mention some other disquieting news that she had heard: A woman reporter who said she was Reanna's aunt was making the rounds in Stormy Cove. Reportedly, she had already talked to half a dozen people. She said she worked for *Smart Woman*, a reputable magazine.

This made Lori nervous. It was worrisome enough that Lisa Finning knew about the police.

"I thought they would. No cause for alarm, or is there? There's been a confession."

"Yes. But Jacinta's death is still unaccounted for."

"You won't want to hear this, my darling, but a lot of cases never do get solved. I grapple with them every day—that's the reality of it."

"But innocent people are suspects."

"Don't let it eat you up. Save your energy for the job."

"Somebody set fire to Noah's boat."

"What? Who's Noah?"

"The man."

"Ah." Silence. And then, "Arson cases involving boats rarely make it very far because the evidence burns so fast."

"His boat wasn't insured."

"Oh! That's awful. That . . . in that case, somebody's really being vicious. Let me know right away if there's anything I can do."

"You don't have to bail me out this time, Mom."

"I know, Lori, that's all behind us. But it doesn't hurt to ask people for help. I do it too, you know."

Lori regretted her remark.

"I didn't mean it like that. It's just that so many terrible things are happening."

"You know, sometimes it's necessary to physically get away from a stressful situation."

"I simply can't leave here now."

"I mean the man."

"Noah? He'd never leave this village. He just can't. He's never been anywhere else."

"Maybe he can get out now. Maybe it's his big chance."

Is she thinking that if he comes to live in my world, then the magic will be gone for me? Her mother didn't have a clue about life in Stormy Cove. But she couldn't blame her. You've got to experience some things firsthand to understand them. She was relieved when her mother had to take another call.

Lori's brain was screaming for fresh air. She hung her camera around her neck and went to pick up Rusty. The dampness on her skin predicted rain, but she could still see a few bands of blue in the overcast sky. There wasn't a boat on the bay. A pleasantly warm wind massaged the ruffled water. Lori couldn't get the houses behind her fast enough. She climbed up to the high plateau. There she took several deep breaths and gazed in all directions. The ocean surface trembled like the flank of a tense animal. Rusty rooted around for mice in the tufts of grass.

She'd never be able to describe to her friends how this rocky, austere, forbidding landscape, the sparse vegetation, moved her so. Perhaps it was the combination of the fragile and vulnerable with tough, muscular resistance. One was unthinkable without the other. She loved the lichens, rocks, and grasses and ponds, and now the fine little bright blossoms in delicate white, pink, violet, buttery yellow that would soon become berries. Her photographs would capture all that beauty, the beauty she'd discovered during those reverent moments.

She hopped from stone to stone, balanced on unsteady grass hillocks while Rusty relished wading in the mud. She let him pull her through low bushes, and as he picked up the scent of a moose track, she closed her eyes so she could see everything anew on opening them.

When she got back late in the afternoon, the answering machine light was blinking.

"Please call me as soon as possible." The urgency in Lloyd Weston's voice was disquieting.

She couldn't reach his cell phone so she left a message.

He called her seconds later.

"What's up, Lloyd?"

"Have you heard? They arrested Beth."

"What? Why?"

"Don't know exactly. I'm still trying to get her a lawyer."

"That's . . . I can hardly believe it. What's she charged with?"

"That's what I'd like to know. Nobody will tell me anything. It's a disaster."

"Did you try the police?"

"Yes, and not only me, but they stonewall and stonewall. It's enough to drive you insane."

"But they can't arrest her without charges. What's going to happen to the dig?"

"No idea. Everything's up in the air. Goddamn it! First Sholler's murdered. And now Beth's been arrested."

"They're two separate things, Lloyd. They must be!" Her voice was starting to crack too.

"I'm going to go crazy! It's just like back then!"

Apart from Beth, none of the team was directly involved back then. But Lori didn't bring it up, saying instead, "Beth came by yesterday."

"Oh? What did she want?"

"She asked me if I'd found any more arrowheads or other artifacts in the house. You apparently told her about the arrowhead."

"What did I say? What arrowhead?"

"The one that looks like a fish or a bird. I mentioned it to you in the Birch Tree—"

"Yes, yes, I remember. But I didn't say a thing about it to Beth. No way she heard that from me."

Things were getting more and more tangled. Lori felt some tension at her temples heralding a headache.

Lloyd's voice sounded like an echo.

"Do the police know about it?"

"About what?"

"Beth dropping in?"

"Nobody's asked me about it yet."

"Maybe it's got something to do with them."

"With what?"

"With the arrowheads."

Lori wanted some clarification, but Weston wriggled his way out of the conversation with a hasty apology for needing to hang up.

She plopped down on the sofa and sat there for a while, stunned.

She didn't want to hear anything, think anything, feel anything.

Fog was creeping over the hill, its edges transparent like a fine web, dark and menacing on the horizon. It made the world of Stormy Cove smaller and tighter than it already was.

She twitched when the phone rang but didn't move an inch. It was her passive rebellion against the events steamrolling over her.

But she couldn't escape them. The answering machine kicked in.

"Lori, it's Emma. You can pick up the bakeapple jelly Winnie promised you. Drop by her place anytime."

Two things registered with Lori. Noah's mother had never promised her bakeapple jelly. And she hadn't called herself but commissioned her daughter-in-law to do it. *Winnie is summoning me.*

She should deal with Winnie right away. Perhaps she'd learn something about Noah, whose truck wasn't at his place, as a glance out the window told her.

Winnie Whalen was not alone; Nate was with her in the living room. The TV was on, and Lori recognized *The Price Is Right*, where contestants guessed the price of certain products. She didn't find the program quite so ridiculous since Nate admitted that thanks to it, he'd found an ointment for the itchy eczema he'd picked up from the constant moisture while out fishing.

Winnie was sitting in front of the TV, beside an aquarium with a single goldfish. Lori couldn't understand a word she said until Nate turned down the TV.

The old lady repeated her question, "How's your day been?"

Lori knew that she should say "Fine," but she balked.

"Sad. I still can't believe . . . it's a nightmare."

"That reporter should not have gone out with Jack, and at night, she—"

"Mother," Nate interrupted her.

But she didn't leave it alone.

"Jack's always caused problems, even as a little kid. My ducks had chicks, and he crushed them with his boots. Isn't that so, Nate?"

"Yeah, sure, but things are bad enough. We don't have to dredge that up now."

"He always gets everything from his parents. He's driven three snowmobiles into the ground. And then they buy him an ATV for twelve thousand dollars. Somebody like that must think he's entitled to everything."

Nate kept quiet, but his face had an agonized look.

"And now Jack's parents say it was an accident. That they were just romping around. Who believes such a thing? He always grabbed our girls."

"Mother, Lori doesn't want to hear this."

Winnie looked out the window, but her words were addressed to Lori.

"What you said in the store was right. Noah is not a murderer."

In the store. Lori coming to Noah's defense. Of course Winnie Whalen had heard about it. This was her way of thanking Lori.

Her eyes wandered back to her visitor.

"But you won't put it in your book, will you?"

"Put what?"

"This business about Jack."

As if it were only about Jack.

She folded her hands.

"I'm making a coffee table book. But I think that there'll be other people who will write about Reanna."

"Yes. Vera said a woman's already going from house to house and talking to people. She's supposed to be a relative of the reporter. But she's got no business being here."

Nate cleared his throat.

"I've got to go, Mother. Are you going to give Lori her jelly?"

"It's in the fridge."

Nate saw Lori out.

Tiny drops of mist hung in the air.

"I'm going to my cabin in the woods," Nate said. "Noah's there. He's repairing our wood stove." Nate looked at his shoes. "It's very beautiful there. Maybe you'd like to take a few pictures."

Lori zipped up her windbreaker.

"Maybe Noah would like to be alone."

"I think . . . it'd be better if he had somebody with him. I can't stay. Got to take my boys to Saleau Cove for their basketball game."

She could tell by Nate's embarrassed look how much this request cost him.

"OK," she said, "I'll get my camera out of the car."

She arrived in an enchanted setting. A clearing opened up before them, surrounded by low trees that only half blocked the view of a little lake. Not a trace of coastal fog. Diffuse soft sunlight flooded the green oasis. Lori got out of the truck and looked around. Noah's pickup was parked in front of a rough-hewn cabin. Moose antlers above the red-painted door, three blue plastic chairs, and clutter all over a narrow wood patio. The customary lace curtains in the windows, bright pink this time, and to top it all off, a hanging mobile with Snow White and the dwarves.

Noah came through the doorway, his flannel shirt half-unbuttoned. He tried to conceal his surprise, but Lori could see he was pleased.

"I thought you were bringing tools and spare parts," he shouted to Nate, who was dragging a pipe along.

"Sure, what do you think this is?" Nate retorted, pointing to a drill. "Make the lady some coffee."

Noah bounced up and down on his toes.

"Oh, I don't think she came here for that."

CHAPTER 37

After taking off her shoes and socks, Lori rolled up her pant legs and waded into the lake. She could only take the cold water if she ran back to the narrow strip of beach every now and then to thaw out.

"C'mon in!" she shouted to Noah, who was sitting on a rock, watching in amusement.

He shook his head.

"I only look at water from above."

She felt smooth stones underfoot and sluggish seaweed tickling her ankles. A weight seemed to lift from her shoulders.

Noah took the camera and clicked the shutter again and again. She spread out her arms as if trying to embrace everything. Everything and him.

On the shore, she dried her feet with her socks and climbed up on Noah's rock. They sat there in silence for a while, listening to the soft rustling of the wind and the water lapping at the shore.

"It's beautiful," she said softly. "I'm so thankful that this much beauty still exists."

Noah looked over quietly and then put an arm around her. She pressed her head to his shoulder. Nothing mattered more than the nearness of his body, the longing for his touch, the warmth of his lips when he kissed her, gently and then with the full force of his desire.

Hand in hand they walked down the worn path to the cabin.

Now and then they embraced and kissed. He stroked his strong fingers over her cheeks and lips. She felt his repressed emotion. Her hands meandered over his back. He drew her to him with both arms, carefully and powerfully. He felt even better than she'd dreamed of during those lonely nights.

They embraced on the steps of the patio and smiled coyly at each other while Noah tried to repair the stove, because "otherwise our toes will freeze tonight, and you'll only remember the cold," as he explained.

A wave of tenderness flooded over her.

"Freeze, tonight? Far from it."

She kissed the back of his neck and stroked him until he abandoned his project and carried her to the old bed with its colorful quilt.

"You're the most wonderful woman I've ever met," he murmured as he leaned over her. "I'm so happy you're turning my life upside down."

She took his face in her hands and drew him down toward her.

Noah needn't have had any fear. The cold couldn't hurt her as long as she lay in his arms. She carefully wrapped herself in the blankets afterward. By the light of kerosene lamps, they drank Iceberg Beer and ate the poached salmon Noah had brought from home—cold, with Miracle Whip. Her eyes devoured him, and he was as delighted by it as a little kid.

Their conversations were intimate and probing, but they completely avoided discussing the events in Stormy Cove, as if protecting their precious hours together from whatever was to come.

The next morning, they stayed under the covers, talking and laughing, and, when words weren't enough, seeking out each other's bodies all over again.

Only when a strong wind came up and the cabin walls creaked and trembled did they surface from their warm cocoon and take note of where they were. Lori stayed in bed and watched Noah work on the stove, drinking in the concentration on his face, his purposeful, deft gestures, the sway of his hips. He looked up, met her gaze, and gave her a smile, half-embarrassed, half-flattered.

"Like what you see?"

"I certainly do."

She pulled the blankets around her more tightly.

"Where did you learn all that?"

"You mean my artful lovemaking or this here?"

They both laughed.

"I do *not* need to hear any particulars about the first bit. Where did you learn how to fix a wood stove?"

"Dunno, probably by watching. Always fun to watch. I wanted to be an engineer, took the entry course in Saleau Cove, but my parents didn't have the money for me to keep studying. So I took up fishing."

"Did you already have . . ." she was about to add "a boat" but caught herself in time. "Did you already have a fishing license?"

"No, not then. I fished with a jigger, a fishhook. You had to swish your hands back and forth in the water to get them to bite. Sometimes I was out on the water for sixteen hours; my hands hurt like crazy at night."

"All alone out there for sixteen hours at a stretch?"

"Yep, had no choice. Had to earn money somehow. Sometimes came back at night with two hundred cod."

She looked out the window and saw the bushes swaying in the wind. Sixteen hours at sea by yourself, day after day after day. How little she knew about him!

Noah stood up with a grin.

"So you see, I can wait patiently until I catch something."

"I'm not a something," she protested.

"But you'll admit I caught you?"

"First tell me if we're ever going to be able to make coffee on that thing."

By way of an answer, he dove onto the bed and buried her underneath him.

An hour later, a fire was burning in the stove, and Noah made coffee for them to drink in bed while he read her Newfoundland stories. His own library, he confessed, mainly consisted of shipwrecks, sailor's yarns, true murder cases, and Newfoundland titles like *Grandpa, Tell Us a Story*, *We're Still Fishin'*, and *Survival on the Raging Sea*.

Lori snuggled up next to him.

"I'm getting a new book about Marguerite de Roberval. Aurelia had it sent specially from the library in St. John's."

He smiled.

"That story really has its claws in you, eh?"

"I definitely want to go there again," she said. "I've got to take a couple of pictures of the Isle of Demons."

"Didn't the howling scare you off?"

"I admit it was the creepiest thing I've ever experienced. I don't know what I'd do if I heard it again. But I'm fascinated. There must be a natural explanation for it."

"If there is, nobody's found it yet. Nobody around here believes there is."

"Will you come with me again?"

He didn't reply. It took a few seconds until it occurred to her that it was impossible—he didn't have a boat anymore. How could she be so stupid!

She immediately proposed a walk through the woods around the cabin. The wind that had shaken the walls a half hour before had finally relented.

They wandered over to a nearby abandoned lodge that once belonged to a Newfoundlander who'd made a pile of money in Alberta, had grand plans for a new life in his native province but went bankrupt, leaving the half-finished lodge to fall to ruins.

On the way back, they almost got lost on the moose paths through the bush, but they heard cars close by that helped them locate the gravel road. When they saw the cabin again, a white Chevrolet Tahoe was sitting beside it. They turned a corner. Noah still held Lori's hand.

Greta was in one of the blue plastic chairs, smoking.

"Pretty nice love nest you've got here," she said, not sounding very cheerful.

Lori detected circles under her eyes and hard lines around her mouth. One look at that face and she knew that their carefree hours were over.

Greta gave no reason for her unannounced arrival; that wasn't on the Stormy Cove list of rules.

Noah opened the door,

"Like to join us for lunch?"

Greta released the smoke from her lungs.

"No, but you got a beer?"

During their picnic of bread, cheddar, ham, and canned peaches, they talked about Nate's cabin and other people's and how Nate had to install running water because otherwise Emma would never go there.

Noah mentioned the decrepit lodge, and at that moment, Greta lit another cigarette and said, "I know how Jacinta died."

She looked straight out through the trees at the shimmering lake and spoke rapidly, as if afraid she might be interrupted.

"Cletus and me were together in the woods behind where Gideon's lodge had been, not too close to it—would have been too conspicuous—and not near Aurelia and Gideon's mother's house. Not that we expected anybody to go strolling through the woods and catch us at it. Aurelia's mother was never one to go walking much, with those bad legs of hers, but we didn't want to take any risks. We used to do it mostly in the car, but you can't always find a private place to park, especially during the day, and we just felt like doing it outdoors one nice sunny day. So we were down by the pond where the snowmobile path goes past—What's it called, Noah?"

"Black Duck Pond." He sounded hoarse. Lori shot him a glance, but he didn't look back.

Scared. He's scared.

"That's it, but I think it's called Darrell's Pond now since Darrell Arnold fell in on his snowmobile. Anyway, we didn't hear anything at first, I mean, we were pretty loud ourselves, if you get my meaning. But when we were finished, Cletus said, 'What's that?' I heard it too, a shout somewhere; we got dressed and ran as fast as we could to help. We came out of the woods right where the bog begins, and then we heard the voice again. But we didn't see anything, and Cletus said somebody must be stuck. We went around the bog to the east. Cletus thought he could see a head and part of a body. I've got bad eyes, and I was quite a ways away, but the voice . . . 'Is that Jacinta?' I asked him. He wasn't sure. He wanted to go right into the bog. I didn't want to let him, much too dangerous, but he said he had to. I grabbed his arm. 'Let somebody else do it,' I yelled at him. 'It'll be too late," he said. He shook me off. I'll never forget it. First he jumped over the wet spots, then crawled on his stomach like an animal. I heard him shout: 'Don't move! Don't move!' But she was probably struggling the whole time and sinking all the faster. I didn't hear her voice again. He told me afterward that when he got to her, all he could see was the top of her head."

Greta took a drag on her cigarette and blew the smoke out her nose. Noah braced his elbows on his thighs and grabbed his temples.

"He left his orange hunting cap on the spot and crawled all the way back. 'She's a goner.' That's all he said."

Greta put the beer can to her lips and made loud glugging noises. Nobody uttered a word. Lori wanted to run from the scene. But it was too late for that; Greta had made her a confidante.

"If we'd told the Parsonses, if they'd have found out we were there when Jacinta died, they'd have made life hell for us. Noah, you know that. They would have blamed us for her death. They'd have said we chased her into the bog. Or hadn't helped her. Isn't that right, eh? Aren't I right!"

Noah didn't move for several long seconds.

"She was probably following us," he said.

"What? Following who?" Greta seemed to return from another world.

"Glowena and me."

He stared at the empty plate in front of him.

"Jacinta was always spying on us. Glowena said their father made her do it and then he'd question Jacinta about us."

"Why? Were you two at Black Duck Pond too?"

Noah writhed around on his chair.

"No, not that day. Glowena was working at the dig, and I was fishing with Abe and Seb. But we met there a lot. Every other day, for a spell."

Again Lori felt the urge to flee, but she couldn't move her limbs, like in a bad dream.

Greta nodded vigorously. "Can well imagine that Scott Parsons was hard on Glowena. Jacinta always used to cuddle up to her father and give him the gossip about people."

It's not about the Parsonses, it's about you two, Lori thought.

As if Greta had read her mind, she said, "I asked Cletus what we should do. He said he'd take care of it. We promised to keep silent as the grave. We were extra careful not to be seen sneaking back home—we were used to that, naturally. We never spoke about it again, not a word. But I knew he went back because he had to fetch his cap. I didn't put two and two together until . . . until they found Jacinta's grave."

She crushed her cigarette butt on the empty beer can.

"Christ, I thought it served them right! *We* had to live with the knowledge that Scott Parsons let father die a lousy, stinking death," she blurted out as if in response to Lori's reproachful thoughts. "And Scott just walked away from it. Is that fair? Cletus tried to save Jacinta. He risked his life. He could have sunk into the bog too. But the Parsonses would have used it against us and hung us out to dry. They were that pissed that we wanted Father's fishing license back. They were just waiting for an excuse. So it's Scott Parsons who's the killer. He's the murderer."

Lori lifted her head up. Above her, islands of clouds drifted through the sky like hot-air balloons; delicate blue gaps peeked out and closed up. Greta went into the cabin. She had on knee-length shorts and a white tracksuit top with a kangaroo pocket. Lori had to remind herself that twenty years had gone by since Cletus and Greta's rendezvous in the woods.

Lori suddenly felt Noah's fingers interlocking with hers. She looked into his eyes for a moment, then turned away when Greta came out of the cabin.

"Why did you tell us this?" Lori asked. She was surprised at how steady her voice sounded.

Greta leaned against the patio railing, her thin pants flopping around her knees.

"Because—you said at my place, no, you said it in the store, that the truth would turn out to be very different from what a lot of people think. And that people would be surprised when the truth came out, because innocent people finally wouldn't be under suspicion. Now, there it is; that's the truth. Is it what you imagined? Are *you* surprised now?"

Lori opened her mouth to protest that she'd been talking about Reanna, but then she grasped the deeper meaning behind Greta's questions, even if Greta wasn't fully aware of it herself.

What did the truth look like anyway? Was it Greta's truth? Or was it a truth that sank in the bog with Jacinta twenty years ago?

Not even her mother was concerned with some objective idea of truth when she defended people in court. For her, the point was to do her best for her clients under the given circumstances.

Do your best under the given circumstances.

She untangled her fingers from Noah's so she could concentrate on her reply.

"I can only answer that question if I'm sure I really do know the truth. For the moment, I only know what you're telling me, Greta. You think you saw a head, recognized a voice, but you were far away. You only know what Cletus told you. From what I've heard, Cletus wasn't a person that could be trusted in every respect. He was a poacher and very likely stole things."

"What? What did he do?" Greta wanted to know, but Lori brushed the question aside.

"Look, you have no idea what really happened to Jacinta. Whether she was actually in the bog, whether it was Cletus who buried her body in that grave or somebody else. You two never talked about it again, and there's nobody who can corroborate your account or refute it. The way I see it, it's all speculation, and if this story gets onto the grapevine, it would bring people even more grief without offering them definitive closure. Greta, I know how people can take guilt upon themselves without wanting to."

Greta glared at her.

"You don't believe me?"

Lori pushed some wisps of hair out of her face.

"I'm a lawyer's daughter. I see no evidence, no witnesses, nothing; only what someone thinks she saw but can't verify."

Greta pounded the beer can on the wooden railing, more out of helplessness than aggression. She looked around like a wild animal seeking a way to escape.

"So what am I supposed to do?"

Lori said nothing. She'd gone as far as she could.

For a while, the quiet scene was punctuated by Greta's beer can banging hollowly on the wood.

Then Noah leaned forward, his brow furrowed, his heavy hands pressed together.

"What should you do? I'll tell you what to do. Stop telling tales that could send innocent people to their graves from the heartache."

CHAPTER 38

Lloyd Weston fought to find out anything about Beth Ontara's arrest, and failed. But the *Cape Lone Courier* could. It reported that the archaeologist had been selling prehistoric artifacts on the black market. A tip from the world of art dealers and an undercover operation were reported to have led to her arrest. The paper did not specify what sort of artifacts she'd sold, but did publish a full-page obituary of their murdered colleague, Reanna Sholler. Lori still couldn't believe the young woman was really dead. A life in bloom—simply stamped out.

The next bit of information came from a source Lori would never have expected.

The day after her conversation with Greta, Lori went to the library to pick up the book Aurelia had ordered for her.

She leafed through the slim volume in search of hard facts about the historic Marguerite de Roberval. It wasn't just a legend; it turned out she actually existed and—as Lori read in the introduction—was supposed to have been the first European woman to survive the Newfoundland winter.

Lori snapped the book shut.

"This is exactly what I need! I'm going to the Isle of Demons tomorrow."

"Oh, really? Who's taking you?"

Aurelia knew it couldn't be Noah. His demolished ship was the talk of the town.

"Archie. He wants to be sure the demons don't kidnap me."

"Noah going too?"

"Yes, he and Archie want to see if fishermen from long ago left any useful tools around."

"Archie's grandfather used to have a summer fishing cottage there."

"He did? Archie never mentioned that."

"No surprise. His wife doesn't want him to go there. I'm amazed she's letting him take you." She laughed, but then her face grew serious. "Did you hear about the archaeologist who was arrested?"

Lori nodded. "I can't imagine her trying to sell archaeological objects. It doesn't seem at all like her. She did everything to protect the artifacts. It doesn't add up."

"No, it doesn't, but I really must tell you what I heard from Elsie Smith. You know her, eh? Weren't you at her place for Sunday dinner once? Elsie told me the archaeologist paid her a visit during the first dig all those years ago."

"Yeah, twenty years," Lori said, helping her out.

"Gosh, twenty years! How time flies. So this Beth came to visit Elsie and asked to see the old Eskimo things that Joseph—Elsie's great-uncle—had brought back from Witless Island. Beth said that they weren't Eskimo but Indian and thousands of years old. Beth bought them off Elsie. Isn't that illegal? I mean, maybe it wasn't even Jack at all."

Lori had no desire to argue about Jack's innocence, especially since the police had DNA evidence. Nor did she want to get into how an arrowhead had found its way from Beth Ontara to the reporter's dead body. Lori was convinced Cletus Gould had stolen it—along with the bracelet he then gave Una—from Beth's room in Gideon Moore's lodge because he was angry about being fired. But Beth had never reported the theft in order to prevent bad press from hurting the dig. And now she herself was at the center of a scandal.

Lori apologized for having to leave so soon.

"I absolutely must go read this book before going to the island. And I've still got to take Rusty for his walk."

"When you get back, do come see me. I want to know how it went."

Lori promised.

On the way home from the library, the white Chevy Tahoe came toward her. Lori waved, but Greta didn't stop.

They had all driven back after that conversation yesterday, Greta in front and Noah's pickup following. He wanted to keep an eye on Greta, not only because of the beer. He knew his sister was deeply upset and losing her grip on things. He dropped Lori at her house and then went to Greta's. She didn't ask him what he and his sister had talked about. She and Noah were already bound by a secret that she wanted to keep forever.

After returning from the cabin, Lori had gotten caught up in matters of her own. Andrew had been trying frantically to reach her via text, e-mail, phone . . . He'd heard about a murdered journalist on the Northern Peninsula of Newfoundland and feared the worst. He was audibly relieved to hear her voice, but tried to hide his emotions under a flood of words about sports and events at school. He even told her about a girl in his class who wanted to see Vancouver. When their long conversation ended, Lori's heart was light and heavy at the same time.

And Bobbie Wall from Deer Lake had left an astounding message. Before she could even digest it, a call came in from Mona Blackwood.

Instead of saying hello, Mona pronounced, "Everything's happening so fast there."

Lori found her client's directness soothing.

"You can say that again. I don't exactly know what it all means for our book."

"Why?"

"People here aren't as trusting as they were before."

"Just do what you can. I've looked at the material you sent and I'm impressed. Different from what I'd imagined, but it fits together very nicely: strong images that don't prettify."

Lori chose her words carefully. "Of course, you're interested in more than the pictures."

"I see what I want to. Things will happen as they must; I'm sure about that. Keep your ears and eyes open."

"I'm going to the Isle of Demons tomorrow. That's where the fishermen hear spooky noises."

"What's it called again?"

"Isle of Demons. It's where a French noblewoman was marooned and survived two winters."

"Well, then watch out they don't maroon you there. Break a leg!"

Lori wanted to say that she, unlike so many in Stormy Cove, had no fear of demons.

Noah couldn't come in the end because he needed to check out a secondhand boat in Saleau Cove. Her first reaction was disappointment, but it was her project, after all, not his. She was grateful to him for persuading Archie to take her out at all.

It was a warm summer day when they put out to sea.

"Good we're not fishing for cod today," Archie roared. "We've hit our quota for the week!"

"What's your quota?" Lori shouted back.

"Three thousand pounds per boat per week."

Lori saw Noah's tall figure on the jetty shrinking and shrinking. He'd said good-bye with his hands safely in his jeans pockets—the inquisitive eyes around them prevented a kiss. He'd just whispered furtively in her ear, "Come back soon."

To Lori, his behavior seemed normal; no indication he suspected any of the bystanders might be the arsonist. Maybe he'd convinced himself that a faulty cable or an overheated stove had set the fire. Maybe lies like that were how folks could keep on living in the village without going insane.

Archie had a little motorboat in tow. Lori was on the lookout for more whale spouts, but only whitecaps flashed on the waves.

She looked over at Archie at the helm. The boat's engine was banging so loud they could only exchange a few words. So Lori let her mind wander.

She'd gone to visit Patience the day before. Her neighbor already knew that Lori and Noah had been together at the cabin. And she'd found out that Beth Ontara had come to see Lori before her arrest. After sending Ches and Molly out for ice cream, Patience led off by asking about Beth.

"What did she tell you?"

Lori summarized their conversation and included what she'd learned from Aurelia. "But I'm convinced that Cletus swiped the arrowhead."

Patience sighed. "Now I don't have to feel so bad."

"What? Why?"

"Oh, I wanted to tell you before but . . . I'm really ashamed of myself."

Lori played the waiting game. Patience lowered her eyes. The kitchen smelled of freshly baked cake.

"Una stole from Beth. From Gideon's lodge. Jewelry and money and a Walkman—they were new at the time. We had to stand guard, Jacinta and me. Una gave us a little money to do it. We secretly bought ice cream with the money."

"Did Beth know?"

"No, I don't think so."

Patience still wouldn't look at her.

"Nobody ever caught us. Or nobody said anything, at least. Not even Beth. But I couldn't sleep at night."

"Still, you never ratted on Una. And neither did Jacinta?"

"No, never. I feel terrible about it. I hope Molly will never lie like that."

Watching him work on the boat, Lori doubted that Archie, the man Patience had gone to with her marital worries, knew about this sin of her youth.

She was roused from her thoughts by Archie conferring on the radio with some ships. The Isle of Demons was very close now.

"We're mooring on the other side," he shouted.

On this side, high cliffs rose up before them. Archie had told her some names of the coves on the island, things like Wreck Cove or Misery Point.

Not very heartening. Farther to the north, rocky shores sloped down to the water and mooring was possible. Lori could make out some dilapidated cabins on a hilltop.

Archie dropped anchor in a little bay and checked the chain. They climbed into the motorboat and landed between some rocks, where Archie tied up.

Lori shouldered her camera bag and tripod. Archie wasn't as gallant as Lloyd Weston and didn't help with her things. They had to climb a steep, stony hill to get to the shacks. If there'd been a path once, it was nowhere to be seen now.

From close up, the shacks were in even worse shape than Lori had thought: primitive, rotten rooms made of wood. But she couldn't resist the romance of decay. She lifted her camera.

"Did fisherman really live in these things?"

Archie nodded.

"It was good enough for the summer. You just needed a roof over your head and a wood stove."

Around the back of the hill, Lori discovered a larger structure.

"What's that?"

"That belonged to Philo Pilgrim, a fish merchant who came here to buy. Thought he was too good to sleep in a tarred house."

"When did he stop coming?"

Archie scratched his head.

"Hmm, maybe forty years ago."

The fish merchant's house was still standing: gray board walls, rooms like a square box with gaping holes for windows, bits of white door frames still visible—but no doors. Lori peeked inside.

The floors had collapsed in several places, but the hallway between the rooms looked passable. She looked at Archie. He shook his head.

"Place is ready to fall in, but don't let me stop you."

She eased her way inside. A demolished stairway led to an upper story. The room on the right side looked like it'd been hit by a storm. Broken china was strewn on the floor, rusty tin lay under some scratched-up enamel, and there were broken chairs, wet rags, and scraps of leather.

And one more thing. A rather new-looking beer bottle.

On the other side of the hall, a mass of rotten something or other had gushed out of a lump that once might have been a sofa or a mattress.

Lori got to work. Archie kept an eye on her through the holes in the walls.

Very soon, beads of sweat dripped from her forehead. Why did today of all days have to be this hot in a place that was always cold?

She went outside to get a bottle of water from her backpack.

"I'd like to see the other side of the island," she said.

Archie was wiping sweat off his forehead as well. "There aren't any shacks over there."

But maybe there's evidence pointing to Marguerite de Roberval.

"Oh, that's fine," Lori chirped. "I'm just so grateful to be here and I want to see as much as possible."

"OK, but first I need to get a beer from the boat. Don't go far, I'm not very good on my hind legs."

Lori figured Archie would be gone awhile, so she wandered away from the shacks, determined to find the stone grotto she'd read about. The cave couldn't be down near water level, but it also needed to be someplace protected from the wind, which ruled out the exposed heights above the cliffs. In Lori's estimation, the cave couldn't be very far from the little bay where they'd moored.

She went around a deep ravine and climbed a hill to get a better view. The book had informed her that the island was eight miles long and three wide, much too big to be thoroughly explored.

For better or worse, she'd have to ask for help from Archie. She took a shortcut to get back to the fish merchant's house and stopped in a conveniently dense thicket to relieve herself. As she was finishing up, her eyes focused on a depression. A large hole overgrown with leaves opened before her—she'd been squatting just a few steps away! She pushed some branches aside, trying to see how deep the hole was. She pulled a flashlight from her backpack, but its beam didn't reach the bottom.

Then she had an idea. She tied her spare bootlaces to the flashlight and lowered it down into the dark.

In the shaking light, Lori saw something white, gleaming faintly. Her heart beat wildly. She waited for the flashlight to stop swinging. Bones.

She slowly moved the light back and forth. There was no doubt about it: a human skeleton lay there.

It must have been Damienne, Marguerite's servant. Or maybe Marguerite's lover!

Lori hauled up the flashlight and left the thicket. Dropping her backpack and tripod, she shouted for Archie.

She couldn't find him anywhere. When she reached the fish merchant's house, Lori spotted Archie coming toward her from the spot where they'd separated.

She motioned to him to follow her. He hesitated at first, but she yelled, "A skeleton! I found a skeleton!"

That got him moving. He reached the shaft, breathing heavily, and kneeled down.

His eyes followed her flashlight beam, but he didn't say a word.

Lori couldn't contain her impatience. "Who could that be? Is it a grave?"

"No, it's a root cellar."

"A what?"

"A deep pit in the earth for storing carrots and turnips and potatoes, sometimes berries and jam, because it's cool down there in summer. And in winter nothing would freeze. You build a sod roof over it."

"How did people get down there?"

"By ladder."

She looked at him in some puzzlement.

"But then why is there a body?"

He shrugged. His sweat-slicked face clouded over.

Lori moved around to the other side of the cellar. Something green winked at her from the depths. "What's that?"

She squinted down the shaft. Now she could see clearly. Green beads.

She froze. Green gems. A stolen bracelet.

Lori slowly drew herself up, fighting against an invisible weight threatening to hurl her downward.

"I think I know who it is."

Archie looked at her and then down into the pit.

"That's Una's body."

"Bullshit!" Archie exclaimed.

"Una stole a bracelet of green gems from Beth Ontara. There are green gems down there. It's Una."

Archie fell silent. But his wrinkled face was working hard. He had to know she was right. He probably had seen Una wearing the flashy bracelet. Or perhaps Patience had told Archie about the theft in her anger over Una chasing Ches.

"Oh my God!" Lori screamed as a terrible certainty seized her. "Oh my God!"

Archie struggled to his feet. "I'm going back to the boat to radio a few people."

Lori picked up her backpack. "I'm coming too."

"No, it's better if I go so you don't have to drag all that stuff all over. I'll be right back."

She didn't argue, though she suspected there was something Archie wasn't saying, and sat down in the shade. Her thoughts started whirling.

Una was murdered. What else could it be? Either she was killed here or somebody had carried her corpse over to throw it into the root cellar.

Lori took a swig from her water bottle and wondered if she should take some photographs.

But this was a crime scene. And it was Una's grave.

Was her death somehow connected to Jacinta's? Lori didn't buy Greta's story. It didn't add up. How could Cletus possibly haul out a body from a bog on his own—and without sinking into it himself?

But why would Greta lie? To protect somebody? But who could it be?

Did Una know how Jacinta died? Is that why she was killed?

Lori wished Noah were there so she could talk it over with him. He must have had doubts about Greta's story too. Lori had wanted to ask him about it, but she was afraid. Afraid where the conversation might lead.

She heard a sudden, muffled drone. She scanned the horizon but saw nothing.

The droning sound came closer. Could it be the police so soon? Impossible. Archie was probably just getting to his boat now. So who could it be? She spotted something in the air over the ocean. A helicopter. An orange speck. Gideon Moore. Probably just passing by. He flew around the area all the time for oil companies.

Did Archie see Gideon too? She was annoyed he'd left her alone in this terrible place. Who was he going to call anyway? His brothers? The police? The Coast Guard?

A disquieting feeling crept over her. Her instincts told her to run to a nearby rock and climb up it, the camera around her neck. From there, she could see Archie's boat and the little speedboat as well.

She rotated her zoom lens to get a closer view.

Some movement on board caught her eye. Archie came out of the wheelhouse carrying a rifle. What the hell? Did he think Una's killer was prowling the island?

That was absurd.

She watched him lower the gun down into the speedboat to bring it ashore. What was he thinking?

Lori followed him through the telephoto lens. Her uneasy feeling grew stronger.

Archie hadn't seemed upset about Una's dead body. More like worried. Worried about what?

She remembered Patience saying she'd complained to Archie about Una. Una had screamed at Patience that she knew Archie had a skeleton in the closet. What did she mean by that? Was she threatening Archie? Blackmailing him? But for what?

Was this the insurance fraud she'd heard whispered about? Had Archie burned down his buddy Gideon's lodge? The way he once burned Gideon's boat, and they'd split the insurance money?

The helicopter circled toward the island. She began to wave her arms frantically. The helicopter lost altitude and disappeared behind a hilltop.

Lori dashed back to the bushes, grabbed her things, and ran toward the spot where the copter had come down. The racket of its rotors could still be heard. Gideon couldn't be far away.

She stumbled and struggled over rough terrain, and kept thinking she'd reach the helicopter any minute. But she was frustrated time and again. Her mouth was dry, and even the light breeze didn't cool her off. She started to climb up a hill to orient herself. Stopping to catch her breath, Lori looked up and saw movement. She looked closer and froze.

On top of the hill was the silhouette of a slim figure. But it surely wasn't . . . but it couldn't be . . .

She blinked to sharpen her vision. It must be a mirage, a hallucination.

But the figure moved, waved to her, shouted something.

As if pulled by magic threads, Lori dragged herself uphill, step by step. The climb seemed interminable. Why did she have this stupid, heavy tripod on her back?

Again that voice calling above her, but she was breathing too hard to answer.

Twenty feet to go, ten, five, one. Then Lori slid to the ground, only able to get two words out: "You? Here?"

"I had to come," Aurelia answered.

"Why?"

Aurelia sat down beside her. "Gideon said it was much too dangerous for you to be wandering around this place. The buildings are ready to collapse. And there are gorges everywhere."

"Archie—" Lori started to say.

"Archie only thinks about himself. He hasn't the slightest interest in watching after people who don't know the place. How *could* he leave you on your own? You could trip and get hurt. Where is he, anyway?"

"He went back to his boat to get a gun."

"See! All he thinks about is duck hunting."

Duck hunting. Of course! Exhausted, Lori closed her eyes. Was she losing her mind? Had the past days and weeks taken more of a toll than she'd realized? The awful events had come one after another, blow after blow, and she'd no real time to absorb them.

She was suddenly struck by the silence. The noise of the helicopter's motor had stopped. Lori looked around.

"Where's Gideon?"

"He'll be here in a minute. We saw you waving. Gideon sent me after you as soon as we landed."

Beth Ontara's remark popped into Lori's head. Aurelia, Gideon's sister who keeps a tight rein on her younger brother. Aurelia, who helped him out at his office.

"Where'd he land?"

"On a helipad down there."

"There's a helipad?"

"Yes, didn't you know? Because of the lighthouse on the north end of the island. But it's unmanned now, all automated."

She turned her head. "Here he comes."

Gideon was obviously more used to flying aircraft than to hiking. Particularly on hot days. His T-shirt was dripping with sweat.

"Well, we've found one stranded passenger," he called, huffing and puffing. "Where's Archie?"

"He's went to get his gun from the boat," Aurelia replied.

Gideon was startled. "His gun? Where's he now?"

"I don't know. I lost sight of him," Lori said.

Gideon and Aurelia exchanged glances.

"Didn't he want to look for old tools in the shacks? Did he find anything?"

"I don't think so, but we—"

"You'd better go look for Archie," Aurelia broke in. "We don't want him to mistake us for ducks."

It was meant to be funny, but nobody laughed.

Gideon wavered. "So you were up at the shacks?"

"Yes, but I wanted to get some pictures of the landscape and then saw your helicopter."

Something held Lori back from telling them about her blood-chilling find. She couldn't absorb any more emotional stress at that moment. Her nerves were shot. She just wanted to get back to Stormy Cove and the safety of her own home. Let other people deal with Una's grave.

It had nothing to do with her. She'd had enough traumas dumped on her. She'd pried into too many deep dark secrets. Now she drew the line. Enough.

It wasn't her village. Not her business. Not her responsibility. Not her fault.

But her resolution came too late.

"He can't be far," Gideon said. "You two stay here. I don't want to have to go looking for you too."

Lori was relieved not to have to help find Archie, but she wished they could wait for the two men in the shade.

She offered Aurelia some water, who turned it down. She didn't seem bothered by the sun.

"Did you find any clues about Marguerite de Roberval?" she asked.

"No."

"You know, there must be bodies buried around somewhere, three of them."

Lori didn't say anything.

"Her lover, her child, and her maid."

Lori still didn't respond.

"But they'll probably never be found. What do you think?"

"No idea."

"The soil isn't very acidic here, so bones don't dissolve—Did you know that?"

"Yes, I learned that at the dig on the Barrens."

Lori put the bottle to her lips and took a drink.

They both fell silent.

Lori began to feel that anxiety again.

"If Archie were duck hunting, shouldn't we hear shots?" she inquired.

Aurelia looked at her sideways.

"Yes. Why?"

"Gideon shouldn't have gone off without a gun. I should have warned him."

"About what? About Archie?"

"Yes, he . . . he was giving me the creeps."

"Archie? How's that?"

"We found something."

"Oh." Aurelia's expression froze. "What?"

"A skeleton in a pit. Aurelia, I think it's Una. She had a bracelet with green gems, right?"

Now it was Aurelia's turn to be silent. She wrung her hands painfully, making Lori more and more agitated. She crunched caribou moss between her fingers.

"That's why I'm worried about the gun. What did Archie need it for? He didn't say anything about ducks. Am I being paranoid or what?"

"Gideon got all worked up when I told him that you were coming here to look for Marguerite's cave. He said Archie never should have brought you out."

"Why? Did he . . . did Gideon suspect something? Was he worried about my safety?"

But Aurelia didn't seem to be listening. She was staring hard at the ocean.

"Una was after Gideon. Even though she was married. She was after our money. I told her if she didn't stop bugging Gideon I'd tell Cletus. But she didn't listen."

Lori studied Aurelia closely, attempting to understand what she was saying.

"Gideon and Una . . . Are you trying to say that they had an affair?"

"For Gideon it was all in the past. He only had eyes now for Bella, his present wife. But Una just wouldn't let it go. I confronted her about it. She said I shouldn't get involved or else . . ."

"Or else what?" Lori asked, increasingly distraught.

"She saw me."

"Aurelia, I'm following you less and less."

"She saw me before the lodge burned down. She said she had a witness too."

"A witness? To what?"

Lori still didn't quite get it, but she felt a sinister hunch taking shape.

"That I was there, in the lodge." Aurelia's voice sounded impatient, as if Lori were a dim-witted child.

"Before the fire?"

"Yes."

"Did you have anything to do with the fire? You couldn't have—"

"We needed the insurance money. Gideon wanted to start a new business. We didn't have the money for anything like that. The lodge wasn't making enough."

An invisible hand wrapped itself around Lori's throat.

"And Gideon knew that Una threatened to expose you?"

"Yes, I told him."

Lori waited a second before saying, "And after that, Una disappeared."

Aurelia said nothing.

"Una would never have given you away, Aurelia, because she'd already committed a crime by not telling the police what she knew. And because she went into the lodge to steal something."

"But I didn't know . . . I'd never have dreamed . . ." Her voice broke off.

"That Gideon would kill her?" Lori said.

Aurelia covered her face with her hands. "I don't know how to save you, I don't know how to save you . . ."

Lori's brain was working overtime.

"We've got to hide, Aurelia, we've got to get away from here before he gets back."

She jumped up, but Aurelia didn't budge.

"Now you know everything about me. And about Gideon. What are you going to do?"

Look for Archie. He's got a gun. He went back for it when he heard the helicopter. Because he'd figured out who the killer was. He knows who brought Una here by helicopter, dead or alive. He heard the helicopter and knew he had to defend himself. Both of us.

But Lori had abandoned the protective cover where Archie had left her.

Spurred on by the courage of despair, she started talking a blue streak.

"Aurelia, I won't tell anyone. You've done nothing wrong. Nobody got hurt. You can't turn me over to Gideon!"

The librarian looked up at her, squinting in the sun. "But what about Gideon?"

It dawned on Lori that Aurelia would defend her brother no matter what. She'd never let him down. Family ties were stronger than murder here.

Lori fled, leaving her backpack and tripod behind.

She staggered through thick undergrowth that slowed her down but provided visual cover. Gideon couldn't possibly search the entire island, and if she and Archie didn't get back to Stormy Cove before dark, then Noah would start moving heaven and earth.

She frantically scanned her surroundings and decided to risk crossing a rocky plateau with sparse vegetation and little pools of water. She heard a shot, a second shortly after it, then a third.

They seemed to come from the direction of the boat. Then silence. Her heart raced.

Archie's gun.

She tore ahead. Twigs left bloody scratches all over her bare arms. Several times she had to pull her shoes out of the muck. Jacinta crossed her mind, but she kept pushing farther, farther, farther.

Suddenly, she saw the shacks—she hadn't realized she was heading back that way. But she couldn't hide there—that would be the first place he'd look.

She caught sight of two huge boulders several hundred feet away. She could reach them in a straight line, but that was over open terrain and she might be seen. So she decided to go through the bushes and approach the rocks from the back. But the bushes crackled and rustled, making far more noise than she liked.

She was on the point of changing direction when she heard a voice, loud and clear. An unholy fear swept through her.

"Stop!"

Then, "Turn around!"

She turned in the direction of the voice.

Gideon Moore was pointing a gun at her.

It must be Archie's gun. *He's killed Archie!*

Gideon lowered his weapon.

"Why didn't you stay with Aurelia?"

A kernel of hope sprung up in Lori. She wasn't dead yet. Maybe there was room to maneuver.

"She sent me to find you. She was afraid of Archie. We didn't hear any shots. Archie wasn't duck hunting."

"No, Archie's not duck hunting. Where's Aurelia?"

"I don't know."

"Then we'll find her together. Walk ahead of me, but don't run or I'll shoot."

She did as she was ordered.

Why doesn't he shoot me?

She looked for paths to escape, but the sparse vegetation eliminated any hope. It held her prisoner.

She didn't know how long he drove her ahead like a beast. It seemed like half an eternity.

Finally, a hill came into sight that looked familiar.

But she didn't see Aurelia.

"Where is she? What did you two talk about?" Gideon barked.

He's jumpy. Why? Doesn't he trust her?

And where was Aurelia? Lori got an answer a split second later.

A figure emerged from beneath some fir trees. No, two figures.

A woman. Aurelia.

And a man with a gun. Archie.

He had a tight grip on Aurelia, using her as a shield.

"Drop the gun, Gideon, for your sister's sake."

In answer, Gideon grabbed Lori and tightened an arm around her throat.

"This girl isn't going to live!" he shouted.

Archie's voice was cold. "Whatever. She's not my family. It's over, Gideon."

"You shouldn't have been snooping on me, Archie. Then we wouldn't have this problem!"

"Only an idiot would throw a body in a root cellar. And hide a gun on the island to boot."

"I had to get rid of Una, man. She saw Aurelia at the lodge and was going to tell the cops. She'd have squealed on you too about the boat. I did you a favor. Come on, Archie! We'll get rid of this foreigner and forget everything. Nobody has to know a goddamn thing. It's best for all of us."

Lori's heart skipped a beat.

Then Archie spoke up. "Drop the gun, Gideon. Then we can talk."

The pressure on her neck lessened a bit. Gideon seemed to be weighing the situation. Her eyes fastened on something. Her backpack on the ground. The tripod beside it.

"Let Aurelia go first."

"Not if you're still holding Lori."

"What do you want? Nobody can pin anything on me, nobody!"

"Don't kid yourself. You flew out here when Una disappeared. Nobody else was on the island, just you. And that flight's recorded in the Coast Guard logbook. And here we all thought you were helping search for Una."

"So what? I was here. Doesn't prove anything."

"You're not going to get away with this, Gideon. Una wasn't the only one who saw Aurelia that night at the lodge. And that person is not dead."

Patience's face flashed through Lori's mind. *He must mean Patience.*

"Don't be an ass—" Gideon's words were drowned out by a terrifying sound.

A long, dreadful keening, penetrating and shrill.

The demons.

Followed by a scream, unbearably loud and very near.

Aurelia shrieked, overcome with fear, teeth bared.

She screamed and screamed and screamed.

Gideon's chokehold slackened, and in a flash, Lori ducked sideways. She grabbed the tripod with both hands and swung it with all her might at the body beside her.

Gideon stumbled. Lori slammed him with the tripod wherever she could, again and again until he fell over, and she would have kept on beating him if Archie hadn't pulled her back.

"Stop! Stop!" he shouted. "I've got him under control!"

She took everything in as if through a haze: Archie picking up Gideon's gun, Gideon covered in blood on the ground, Aurelia fleeing, Archie shouting, "Give me your bootlaces."

He stooped down to bind Gideon's hands and feet with them.

Just as he finished, the ghastly howling stopped.

Later, she heard the men in uniform talking as they accompanied her to the boat. One of them said, "They found the body. She jumped off the cliff."

Lori knew they meant Aurelia.

Later, Archie brought his boat in a long way from the harbor to avoid the nosy crowds.

Noah was waiting there beside his pickup; she could see him from a distance. When the boat docked, he came running, his face creased and worried, and his mouth twitched when he saw blood on her T-shirt.

She laid her head on his chest and held him tight.

"She fought for her life," Archie reported. "Gutsy as a bull moose."

Noah put an arm around her shoulders.

"Come on, we're going home."

CHAPTER 39

Their bags were packed, the gas tank was full, and Noah double-checked the oil and washer fluid.

Lori leaned under the open hood and rubbed his bare back under his shirt.

"I'm going to say good-bye to Rusty."

She walked down the hill for the last time, without so much as a glance at the faces behind the windowpanes, then turned right and ignored the passing cars.

She'd made sure that Tom Quinton would be at work and that she could see his wife alone. Vera registered surprise when her visitor came into the kitchen as she was loading the dishwasher.

"You can't be here to walk Rusty."

Lori shook her head.

"No, we're leaving right now. But there's something I wanted to talk to you about. About a little get-together at a B and B in Deer Lake."

"Deer Lake? What sort of get-together?" Vera smiled nervously.

"I don't want to go into details, but it took place last April. In Bobbie Wall's B and B."

"I don't know what you're talking about." The smile vanished.

"Oh, yes you do. A secret get-together of three—let's say . . . acquaintances. I happened to be in the next room that night."

Vera's face collapsed like a chilled soufflé. Lori saw to her satisfaction that she'd hit the bull's-eye.

"As I said, it was secret, wasn't it? Of course you don't want your husband to find out about it. Or the whole village. And it can still be kept secret provided that . . . provided we can come to an agreement."

Vera didn't utter a word, but her dilated pupils spoke volumes.

"Rusty loves his walks, as you know, and he needs one every day without fail. Wouldn't that be a nice thing for you to do? As long as Rusty's happy, I won't breathe a word about this. Does that sound like a good deal?"

Vera slammed the dishwasher door shut and straightened up, red in the face.

She arranged the dishtowels on their hooks and put the detergent tabs in the cupboard. She picked up the broom and paused.

"Fanny and Rosy started walking their dogs. They're in pretty good shape now, you know. Fresh air and exercise would probably do me good."

"You bet!" Lori replied. "Best to start right away—today."

She was on her way to the door when Vera asked, "Noah's going to Vancouver with you?"

Lori nodded.

"For how long?"

"I don't know."

"I wish I could get away from here too."

Lori met Vera's gaze of resignation.

"I really believe you."

Then she closed the door.

CHAPTER 40

The gate to Mona Blackwood's fortresslike estate slid open as if by a phantom hand. The mansion came into view after the taxi drove around a park, where a fountain composed a perpetually changing symphony of water plumes. It took Lori's breath away. Mona's home on the outskirts of Calgary was a monument of futurist architecture, with massive horizontals and imposing glass walls. A multifaceted element rose at an angle out of the structure, so loosely integrated with it that it was as if a fantastic spaceship had come down from the sky and landed on the building. Lori would have expected to find this sort of cutting-edge experimental design in Vancouver, not in nouveau riche, oil-moneyed Calgary—"Cowboy Town," as Lori secretly called it. She scolded herself for her prejudice, which her boss shared.

Lori interpreted it as a good sign that Mona had invited her over.

A young man—the same one from Mona's office in Calgary?—guided her through a vestibule decorated with artwork and into a room with a ceiling so high that every visitor was compelled to emit a one-syllable word of amazement.

"Wow!" Lori exclaimed.

The two-story living room framed a breathtaking view of the deep valley and meandering river below, with an endless chain of hills in the background. The young man reacted to her rapture with a smile, as if taking credit for it all. He left her in front of the wall of glass.

Lori was still standing there, immobile, entranced, when a voice came from behind her.

"Wouldn't that be a lovely shot? I think I have the most beautiful view in Calgary."

"It wouldn't surprise me," Lori replied.

She'd remembered Mona as being more severe and serious, less pretty too. This time, she wore a close-fitting white blouse over patterned beige capris and a bright, cheerful hair band.

It didn't take long, though, for the businesswoman in her to come straight to the point, once they were sitting on a sofa that Lori recognized as a Charles Eames.

"We're delighted with your pictures, and we think there's already enough for a beautiful book." Mona smiled with satisfaction. "I don't want to delay publication any further. Now is the ideal time for it, don't you think?"

Lori agreed, knowing her client had already made up her mind.

"There are no changes regarding the financial arrangements and . . ." Mona turned her head because an elegant woman around Lori's age had come into the room, bearing a tray of drinks.

"You will, of course, have a say in the design. By the way, I'd like you to meet my partner, Robine."

A silvery voice exclaimed, "Let me set this down first, Mona, or there'll be an accident!"

Lori stared in disbelief at the woman who slid the tray across a coffee table hewn from a massive tree trunk. That dark hair, those deep-set, expressive eyes, that strong mouth, and most of all, the way her smile changed her face . . .

"Robine Whalen?"

The elegant woman brushed back her thick hair.

"That's right. I look like Noah, don't I? That's what everybody always said. But he's got bigger hands."

She laughed. "Coffee?"

Mona stood up.

"Not for me. I've got to make a quick phone call. Excuse me," she said, turning to Lori. "Robine's dying to hear everything about Stormy Cove."

"It's been so long since I left," Robine sighed, her eyes following Mona as she strode out of the room. "Fifteen years, sixteen . . . I couldn't stand it anymore, as you can probably understand."

"I'm not the right person to judge the place," Lori said cautiously. "I didn't grow up there."

Her eyes were riveted on Noah's sister.

"Oh, you are very much the right person, after everything that's happened."

Robine rolled her skillfully made-up eyes.

"But the folks in Stormy Cove will love you for this book. You've presented them with a memorial. And after all you've been through."

"Was that basically your intention, I mean . . . to memorialize them?"

Robine stirred her coffee with a little silver spoon. Then she burst into laughter.

"I'd love to see their faces in Stormy Cove when they discover I'm the publisher!"

Lori raised her eyebrows.

"Is that the reason you sent me to Stormy Cove?"

"There were . . . many different reasons. Beth Ontara was one. Maybe the most important one."

Lori waited. She hadn't forgotten the rumors about Robine and Beth.

Robine leaned back on the sofa and crossed her slim legs, her deep blue dress shimmering. She could have passed for a lady from Calgary's wealthy elite. Maybe she'd become one already.

"Beth was my first great love. And you never forget your first love, do you? Beth encouraged me when I still had . . . inhibitions about admitting who I was. I was in seventh heaven. And a new world opened up to me. I suddenly knew where I belonged. As a woman to women."

Robine gestured with her manicured hands—and their dazzling rings—to emphasize her words.

"But then Beth dropped me like a hot potato."

Lori followed her, spellbound. She could not picture this stunning, confident woman in Stormy Cove. Not as Winnie Whalen's daughter. Not on the wharf and not in Mavis's store.

"You were fifteen, right?" Lori interjected. "Beth wouldn't have wanted to cause a scandal."

Robine twisted her red lips a little.

"It wasn't that. She had her eye on Jacinta. I always thought Beth was behind Jacinta's disappearance. Jacinta would definitely have blabbed about it at home if Beth had kissed her. That wouldn't have helped Beth any."

Robine looked straight at Lori.

"And the grave. Beth was strong enough to construct one like that. Beth's as strong as a man."

Lori said nothing. *First love, first heartbreak—the anger never goes away.*

Robine's smile reappeared.

"But they caught her. So much for her dreams of fame and honor. And now I hear they've found another prehistoric grave on the Barrens. Even older than the first—an archaeological sensation. And it's Lloyd Weston who's getting all the applause. That must stab Beth right in the heart."

Lori didn't know why, but somehow she felt the need to defend the archaeologist.

"I think Beth must have smuggled and sold those artifacts because she wanted to finance the dig. I can't think of any other explanation. She was so anxious about the findings from the first grave."

Robine's voice remained gracious, but her words shot across the room like arrows.

"Shows how wrong you can be about people. Beth was always out for herself. She couldn't care less about anything else. Lori, you believe in the goodness in people—I can see it in your photographs."

Lori screwed up her courage.

"Why did you and Mona really send me to Stormy Cove? Did you hope I could find Jacinta's killer? And now you're disappointed?"

"Oh, no. No, no. Don't think that!"

Robine picked up her coffee cup.

"But tell me about Noah. How's he liking it in Vancouver?"

Lori knew why Robine had changed the subject. But she went along with it. She was *not* going to get answers to all her questions so fast. Maybe never.

"He's doing fine, under the circumstances. I think he's enjoying the fact that nobody knows him there. He feels . . . freer. Nobody's watching him. But he misses fishing."

"Can't he fish in Vancouver?"

"Sort of. He found a part-time job. He's been hired on a ship that goes out for six weeks for black cod near the Queen Charlotte Islands. It's new to him, but it pays well, and he wants to earn enough for a new boat."

"Does he ever talk about me?"

Lori hesitated. Before she could answer, Robine went on.

"I know him well enough to know the answer's 'no.' He can't figure me out—it's all foreign to him, maybe even threatening. I'm amazed that he went away with you. He must love you very much."

Lori concentrated on not spilling her coffee.

"His greatest love is most certainly fishing," she said at last, "and his village."

"See! I call that stupidity!" Robine exclaimed. "They treated him like dirt there, and he still clings to them. Did you know that Glowena was pregnant by Cletus when she left Stormy Cove?"

Lori nearly dropped her cup.

Robine leaned toward her and laid a delicate hand on Lori's arm for a second. Her expensive perfume hung in the air.

"I can't reveal how I know that, but it's true. Glowena ought to tell everybody the truth, at long last."

In the taxi, Lori could still feel Robine's hand on her arm. Robine's emotional voice couldn't disguise one fact: she knew the seed she'd planted.

Lori called Danielle from the taxi.

"I'm in Calgary and on the way to the airport. I don't have much time, but remember how you tracked down Glowena Parsons in Edmonton? Can you give me her address and phone number, please?"

Glowena Parsons Colmane, 37, social worker

I'm sure you're glad I've reconsidered. I'm the last piece in your puzzle, eh? Well, now that I've told the police everything, I can tell you too. Then your report will at least get it right. I really like reading your magazine, actually.

So Reanna Sholler was your niece? She must have admired you. I mean, Reanna became a reporter just like you.

I'm very sorry for you—and for Reanna. Whatever you think about me, I think it's terrible when a woman dies so young. And in such a horrible way. I never got over Jacinta's death, even if . . . Look at me; I look much older than I am. I hate myself, I . . .

You mean why didn't I go to the police all those years? The truth would have killed my mother. She was devastated when Jacinta disappeared. I couldn't drive yet another dagger into her heart. But it killed her just the same, only more slowly . . . Excuse me, I don't usually cry so easily, but Mother died six months ago . . .

What was your question? It's like you said, there were deep dark secrets in our family, things you never talk about. Yes, the death of Noah's father was one of them. I know my father let Abram Whalen drown on purpose.

Why did I go out with Noah back then? Revenge on my father. I always rebelled against him. I was wild, I admit. It's not by chance that I chose this profession. I know how easily young people can get sidetracked.

I got along well with Mother. But Jacinta was Daddy's little darling girl. He sicced her on me. She was always spying on me. I really couldn't do anything about it; father was to blame. Of course, I didn't realize it at the time. She was just a pain. And then she found out about me and Cletus. I've come to think that Cletus must've tipped her off. Why? Probably to get at Noah. He never liked Noah. But it was my fault too. I should never have gotten mixed up with Cletus. But, like I told you already, I was a mess. I drank a lot. You do things and then later you wish you hadn't. I got knocked up. I knew right away it was Cletus's. I just knew. And Fred, my oldest, is the spitting image of Cletus. But Cletus didn't want to let Greta go. I went looking for the two of them in the woods. Jacinta followed me as usual. I tried to shake her. I ran as fast as I could. She yelled that if I didn't wait for her, she'd tell father about Cletus and me.

I took a shortcut through the bog because I thought she wouldn't dare follow. I knew a safe path. But she didn't. I couldn't shake her off. I mean, not right away.

I heard her shout but just ignored it. I was so furious at her. I ran through the woods on the other side of the bog. But then I heard Cletus shouting. I went back to the edge of the woods and saw Cletus crawling on his stomach across the bog. Then I saw Jacinta's head. It all happened so fast.

No, I didn't move a muscle. I just watched Cletus. I knew Dad would kill me if he found out.

Greta? Never saw her at all. When Cletus crawled back, I hid so he wouldn't see me. I ran back to the dig and worked for a couple of hours like nothing had happened. What was I supposed to do? It was too late for Jacinta.

Then I sneaked away. I found Cletus in the shed behind his mother's house. Selina was working in the fish plant at the time and wasn't home.

I told him the whole story. Sure, he was surprised, but not shocked. Cletus wasn't easily shocked. He was always so angry at everybody. Always believed they were doing him wrong.

"I don't want to leave her in there," I told Cletus. "She needs a proper grave."

We laid down boards so we could walk on the bog and pulled Jacinta out with ropes. That is, Cletus pulled her out and I helped; he was strong as a bear.

What about the dirt on my clothes? I wore old clothes at the dig because you always get dirty there. I used to carry clean clothes with me. We didn't have much time. It was going on six and I had to get home.

"I'll finish up," Cletus said. "I'll make her a grave, but not here—it'll be discovered too fast."

How could I ever suspect what he had in mind? A grave similar to that prehistoric grave. He wanted to throw suspicion on the archaeologists. Because they fired him. He'd never forgiven them. But everyone suspected Noah.

My family moved away. That was OK by me. I went to Edmonton, for work and because of the baby. I brought Fred into the world. Then I got married.

No, he never got in touch with me. Cletus never knew about his child. Noah either. What was I supposed to say to him?

But his sister Robine called me a few months ago. She knew about Cletus's child. My ex-husband must have broadcast it. He was so angry about the divorce.

And a woman from Vancouver tracked me down. No, not the photographer—she just called recently. I didn't want to see her. No, she was friendly. She said she knew what it was like to live with a ghost from the past.

I was in no way prepared to talk about it, so I hung up. But I knew that things wouldn't be the same for long.

That it was all going to catch up with me.

At long last.

AUTHOR'S ACKNOWLEDGMENTS

I would first like to thank the Canadian fishermen on the Great Northern Peninsula in Newfoundland who were the inspiration for this novel. They fearlessly go out in their little boats onto the wild North Atlantic and risk their lives to feed their families. Their courage, their modesty, and their resilience have made a profound impression on me. Like my heroine, Lori Finning, I borrowed their rubber boots and life jackets. These men would give you the shirt off their backs.

The coastal fishermen took me out on their boats and taught me about their hard work. I strove for accuracy and attention to detail in this book. If nevertheless some errors have slipped in, they are all attributable to me.

I know from my own experience what life is like in a Newfoundland fishing village, a so-called outport. I lived for months in such a community and met many friendly and helpful people. The village of Stormy Cove is a product of my imagination, as are the people inhabiting it.

The history of the Canadian province of Newfoundland and Labrador is fascinating. Some historical events and facts have found their way into this novel. Anybody wishing to read more about its history will find a wealth of information in the books listed under "Works Consulted." The Canadian archaeologist Robert McGhee patiently gave me information about prehistoric burial mounds. The prehistoric grave in the present novel is, to be sure, not identical with the site in L'Anse Amour in Labrador. The excavations there were carefully organized by knowledgeable professionals. The excavation in the present book is very different. Here I gave free rein to my imagination.

What would an author be without sample readers?

Peter and Rosa Stenberg, Susanna Niederer, Erika Imhof, Klaus Uhr, Gisela Dalvit, and Susanne Keller—you have rendered an invaluable service with your criticisms, suggestions, and enthusiasm. I am deeply in your debt with gratitude.

The editor Anna Rosenwong polished my translated manuscript with admirable knowledge and care.

I am also impressed by the commitment and competence of the AmazonCrossing team: Gabriella Page-Fort, who ferreted out and acquired my books for the North American market; the marketing team, whose skills saw to it that my novels continue to find a growing market. And last but not least: my wonderful and prolific translator, Gerald Chapple, who repeated the miracle of recreating my story in English—a process that leaves me awestruck. His wife, Nina Chapple, a highly attentive reader, knows how to put the proverbial dot on the *i*. To all of you, my warmest thanks!

TRANSLATOR'S ACKNOWLEDGMENTS

I would like to acknowledge with much gratitude the indispensable help of the following people in making this translation possible. Gabriella Page-Fort of AmazonCrossing, who again expertly navigated a manuscript through the acquisition and publishing processes with steady support and unfailing good humor. Anna Rosenwong did an outstandingly thorough job of editing; Brittany Dowdle did excellent "arm's-length" copyediting; and the translator's wife and patient first reader, Nina, gave as always a fledgling manuscript an insightful scrubbing. Special tribute is due the novel's author, Bernadette Calonego, the sine qua non, for giving the translation of the novel she created several scrupulous examinations and providing a host of improvements and corrections. Any residual errors or infelicities remain the responsibility of the translator.

WORKS CONSULTED

Beckel, Annemarie. *Silence of Stone: A Novel of Marguerite de Roberval.* St. John's: Breakwater Books, 2008.

McGhee, Robert. *The Burial at L'Anse-Amour.* Ottawa: National Museum of Man, 1976.

Tuck, James A., and Robert J. McGhee. "An Archaic Indian Burial Mound in Labrador," *Scientific American* 235, no. 5 (November 1976), 122–29.

ABOUT THE AUTHOR

Photo © Rae Ellingham

Bernadette Calonego was born in Switzerland and grew up on the shores of Lake Lucerne. She was just eleven years old when she published her first story, in a Swiss newspaper. She went on to earn a teaching degree from the University of Fribourg, which she put to good use in England and Switzerland before switching gears to become a journalist. After several years working with the Reuters news agency and a series of German-language newspapers, she moved to Canada and began writing fiction. *Stormy Cove* is her fourth novel. As a foreign correspondent, she has published stories in *Vogue*, *GEO*, and *SZ Magazin*. She splits her time between Vancouver, British Columbia, and Newfoundland.

For more information, visit www.bernadettecalonego.com.